THE STORY OF
AN AFRICAN FARM

THE STORY OF
AN AFRICAN FARM

BY

OLIVE SCHREINER

(mrs. S. C. Cronwright Schreiner)

WITH AN INTRODUCTION BY

S. C. CRONWRIGHT-SCHREINER

BOSTON

LITTLE, BROWN, AND COMPANY

1925

To

MY FRIEND

MRS. JOHN BROWN

OF BURNLEY

THIS LITTLE FIRSTLING OF MY PEN

IS LOVINGLY INSCRIBED

South Kensington, London,
June, 1883.

AUTHOR'S PREFACE TO SECOND EDITION

I HAVE to thank cordially the public and my critics for the reception they have given this little book.

Dealing with a subject that is far removed from the round of English daily life, it of necessity lacks the charm that hangs about the ideal representation of familiar things, and its reception has therefore been the more kindly.

A word of explanation is necessary. Two strangers appear on the scene, and some have fancied that in the second they have again the first, who returns in a new guise. Why this should be we cannot tell; unless there is a feeling that a man should not appear upon the scene, and then disappear, leaving behind him no more substantial trace than a mere book; that he should return later on as husband or lover, to fill some more important part than that of the mere stimulator of thought.

Human life may be painted according to two methods. There is the stage method. According to

that each character is duly marshalled at first, and
ticketed; we know with an immutable certainty that
at the right crises each one will reappear and act his
part, and, when the curtain falls, all will stand before it bowing. There is a sense of satisfaction in
this, and of completeness. But there is another
method — the method of the life we all lead. Here
nothing can be prophesied. There is a strange coming and going of feet. Men appear, act and react
upon each other, and pass away. When the crisis
comes, the man who would fit it does not return.
When the curtain falls, no one is ready. When the
footlights are brightest, they are blown out; and what
the name of the play is no one knows. If there sits
a spectator who knows, he sits so high that the players
in the gaslight cannot hear his breathing. Life may
be painted according to either method; but the
methods are different. The canons of criticism that
bear upon the one cut cruelly upon the other.

It has been suggested by a kind critic that he
would better have liked the little book if it had been
a history of wild adventure; of cattle driven into
inaccessible "kranzes" by Bushmen; "of encounters
with ravening lions, and hair-breadth escapes." This
could not be. Such works are best written in Picca-
dilly or in the Strand; there the gifts of the creative
imagination, untrammelled by contact with any fact,
may spread their wings.

But, should one sit down to paint the scenes among which he has grown, he will find that the facts creep in upon him. Those brilliant phases and shapes which the imagination sees in far-off lands are not for him to portray. Sadly he must squeeze the color from his brush, and dip it into the gray pigments around him. He must paint what lies before him.

JUNE, 1888.

GLOSSARY.

Since several Dutch and Colonial words occur in this work, the subjoined Glossary is given, explaining the principal ones.

Benaauwdheit	Indigestion.
Brakje	A little cur of low degree.
Bultong	Dried meat.
In-span	To harness.
Kappje	A sun-bonnet.
Karroo	The wide sandy plains in some parts of South Africa.
Karroo-bushes	The bushes that take the place of grass on these plains.
Kartel	The wooden bed fastened in an ox-wagon.
Kopje	A small hillock, or " little head."
Kraal	The space surrounded by a stone wall or hedged with thorn branches, into which sheep or cattle are driven at night.
Mealies	Indian corn.
Meerkat	A small weasel-like animal.
Meiboss	Preserved and dried apricots.
Nachtmaal	The Lord's Supper.
Out-span	To unharness, or a place in the field where one unharnesses.
Predikant	Parson.
Reim	Leather rope.
Schlecht	Bad.
Sloot	A dry watercourse.
Spook	A ghost.
Stamp-block	A wooden block hollowed out, in which mealies are placed to be pounded before being cooked.
Upsitting	In Boer courtship the man and girl are supposed to sit up together the whole night.
Velschoen	Shoes of undressed leather.

WE must see the first images which the external world casts upon the dark mirror of the mind; or must hear the first words which awaken the sleeping powers of thought, and stand by his earliest efforts, if we would understand the prejudices, the habits, and the passions that will rule his life. The entire man is, so to speak, to be found in the cradle of the child.

ALEXIS DE TOCQUEVILLE.

CONTENTS.

PART I.

CHAPTER I.

CHAPTER IX.

PART II.

CHAPTER I.

INTRODUCTION

In March, 1875, Olive Schreiner, aged twenty, went, at a salary of £30 a year, as governess in the family of Mr. Stoffel Fouché, an Afrikander farmer (a Boer), on the farm Klein Ganna Hoek in the mountain veld of the Karoo of the Cape Colony. This farm lies west of the railway, about twenty-five miles almost south of the village of Cradock. There was then no railway within 200 miles of the farm and the journey to Cradock took four hours by cart. The house was isolated, many things were primitive, and on the wild veld game was plentiful. Olive's only room was her bedroom, with a simple bedstead, a box to hold her clothes and nothing else except the books she was reading. This room was part of a flat-roofed lean-to set up against the northern wall of the house next to the kitchen and under the same roof; it was mud-floored and the roof leaked, so that when heavy rain fell she used to cover herself with an umbrella and lead the water away by a little furrow in the floor. Until she secured a basin she used to wash in the little stream in the kloof or ravine which ran up the mountain almost from her door. Such was the room in which she wrote at least a considerable part of what was to be *The Story of an African Farm*. She left this situation at the end

of April, 1876, after the eldest daughter, a powerful
girl, had struck her because she had been awarded
less marks than a younger pupil.

Her next situation, again as governess and at the
same salary, was at Ratel Hoek, a farm between
Cradock and Tarkastad, belonging to Mr. Martin,
another Afrikander. At Klein Ganna Hoek the
household language was solely Afrikaans ("The
Taal"), and probably it was there that Olive first
had to speak the "Dutch" language; but the
Martins were bi-lingual. The owner of Ratel Hoek
was in affluent circumstances and had a large,
well-furnished house; Olive had excellent rooms,
was kindly treated and was happy. But she was
a bad asthmatic and the situation of the house was
so unsuited to her chest that she eventually had to
leave. At Ratel Hoek, in addition to doing an
incredible amount of other writing and reading,
she continued working at a novel then called *Thorn
Kloof*, but which was eventually to be known as
The Story of an African Farm. She always said
she had written this novel at Klein Ganna Hoek,
and, although there is no mention of it in her 1875–
1876 journal, she must have written a considerable
amount of it there, as is proved by several entries
in her Ratel Hoek journal. For instance (in addition to the fact that it is certain she wrote the
first draft of "The Watch" in 1873), only three
months after she left Klein Ganna Hoek, she writes
that she has decided to finish *Thorn Kloof* before
revising an earlier novel (*Undine*) which she had

finished while at Fouché's; in March, 1877, there
are references to "A Boer Wedding," and in the beginning of December 1878 she was writing "Waldo's
Letter." It is thus clear that, by the end of 1878,
she had practically finished the novel. Later
events seem to indicate she may even then have
been revising it.

In March, 1879, she left Ratel Hoek and, at the
beginning of August, was re-installed as governess
with the Fouchés, at a higher salary, at Lelie Kloof,
a farm high up in the mountain range about five
hours by cart south-east of Cradock. Here she
was free from asthma and was strong and well and
so remained until she left; and it was here that she
finished *Thorn Kloof* late in 1879 or early in 1880,
for in the latter year she sent the manuscript to
Mrs. John Brown at Burnley, England, asking her
to find a publisher.

Mrs. Brown (who still lives) does not remember
whether the novel had a name, but says "the
description of Lyndall was a word-picture of Olive
herself, of her own form and face," as she knew her
in 1873. At the request of Dr. and Mrs. Brown, a
friend and relative in Edinburgh consulted a publisher of standing, who, while eulogising the novel,
thought it needed some cutting down. Mrs. Brown
returned the manuscript to Olive at Lelie Kloof
with this opinion and recommendation, and Olive
did what, in her discretion, she thought might be
necessary. As far as my knowledge goes, she received no other advice, nor do I know what she cut

out or condensed except that (as she told me) the most important and longest condensation was a dream of Tant' Sannie's, given originally in full, now represented by the paragraph that occurs early in the first chapter, beginning: "She had gone to bed, as she always did, in her clothes." There is an interesting entry in her Lelie Kloof journal in which she refers to the novel, previously referred to as *Thorn Kloof* or "the new work," by another name: "I have begun to revise *Lyndall*. Must leave out much, feel a little sore." Lyndall was her mother's maiden name. I do not know when Olive decided to abandon the name *Lyndall* and to adopt the title of *The Story of An African Farm*. She told Havelock Ellis that at one time she thought of calling the book *Mirage*, with the sub-title "A Series of Abortions," but decided against it because she found a book had already been published under that name and because she feared also it might be open to misconstruction.

Olive left Lelie Kloof in February, 1881, taking the novel with her, and arrived in England (which she had never seen before) at the end of March. As soon as she was settled down, she began her attempts to get *The Story of an African Farm* published, but it was rejected by one publisher after another. She was almost in despair when Chapman and Hall accepted it, acting on the advice of their "reader," George Meredith. The story that Meredith, who was a stranger to her, assisted her in any way whatever, is wholly untrue. The first edition, a small one in two volumes, was published late in January, 1883, and was soon sold out. The author's name was given simply as "Ralph Iron," and there was no dedication or preface. This edition brought Olive £18 2s. 11d. In July, 1883 a second edition was published. This was in one volume and contained a short preface as well as the dedication to Mrs. John Brown and the author's name in brackets beneath the original pen-name "Ralph Iron." Olive used to tell with amusement how surprised Mr. Chapman was when, having asked "Ralph Iron, Esq." to call, a small, shy, girlish-looking, young woman was ushered in, instead of the big, powerful man expected. Many subsequent editions have of course been issued. By far the largest sales have been in America, where unfortunately the book was not copyrighted.

Much of the book is clearly autobiographical, in its subjective states especially; for instance, there can be no doubt that the incidents of "The Watch" and "The Sacrifice" in the first chapter are actually her own childish experiences; "Times and Seasons" (as she stated in a letter to me, given in the *Life*) are in part at least a relation of the actual workings of her own mind as a child at Healdtown (from the age of six to the age of eleven). Readers interested in the chapter "Waldo's Stranger" may like to know who "The Stranger" was, and how and when and where Olive met him. In June, 1871, Olive, aged sixteen, was on a visit to her aunt, Mrs. Rolland at Hermon, a Native Mission Station in Basutoland, to which the Rev. Mr. Rolland had been appointed, and their daughter was there also. These three women were alone in the Mission House, which, Olive said, was about fifty miles from the nearest white residence. One wet, cold, dark night there was a knock. The lonely women were alarmed, but Olive opened the door and a white man entered, a member of the Cape Civil Service, who, on behalf of the Native Affairs Department, was making a tour of inspection of the Native Territories. This was "Waldo's Stranger." His name was Bertram, and he was about thirty years old. Like Waldo's Stranger he was on horseback and actually carried in his saddlebag Herbert Spencer's *First Principles* (which is the book the "Stranger" is supposed to give Waldo). Bertram lent Olive *First Principles* and, before he rode away next morning, had a talk with her on Art. She says he was "exactly like" Waldo's Stranger, and, indeed, the resemblance, mentally and physically, is close. The allegory is, of course, her own, nor can it be open to doubt that, whatever Bertram said to her on Art, has been elaborated and transmuted. Bertram was to return in three days, which was thus the length of time this sixteen-year-old country girl had in which to read Herbert Spencer's great book. She had never had schooling worth anything to her: all that she knew was from intercourse with her cultured mother and from her own insatiable thirst for knowledge and reading, worked upon by her precocious and penetrating intellect.

Of the characters in the novel, Lyndall and Waldo are in large part two sides of Olive herself and are so meant to be, though there were more than two sides to her complex personality; Waldo, however ("as far as he is not myself," Olive used to say), had an original, a man I knew; and it is remarkable how accurately Olive (who was only seventeen when she met him) has shown a comprehension of the deeps of his nature, discernible to but few others. Lyndall is a more evident side of Olive than Waldo is; the likeness is both mental and physical. Old Otto, the German overseer, is Olive's own father, acknowledged by the family to be a true and beautiful delineation of the old man. Some of Tant' Sannie's characteristics are founded upon a not uncommon South African type, of which the good housewife at Klein Ganna Hoek was, in some respects, an example; the study is, however, objective and humorous, and is not meant wholly to portray Mrs. Fouché, for whom Olive had an affectionate and humorous admiration, and who was much offended and wrote Olive a violent letter when some mischievous person told her she was Tant' Sannie. Gregory Rose is founded on an original, too (whom I knew), an admirable man whom Olive thought highly of and whose gentle side she drew lovingly and sympathetically. Strange to relate Bonaparte Blenkins (whose son I knew) also had an original, an irresponsible Irishman, though of course Bonaparte is drawn objectively and is a caricature. "Lyndall's Stranger" (who was not Waldo's

Stranger) and Em represent no one in particular, and the main incidents of the story are imaginary.

I conclude with a few opinions on *The Story of an African Farm* by some eminent persons. Lecky, the historian, held it to be among the best novels in the English language. Sir Charles Dilke, a man of unusual intellect and literary taste and of wide culture, said it was the greatest novel in the English language, greater than *The Pilgrim's Progress*. Gladstone was "deeply impressed" by it, and "much struck with its power and force, more than he had been with any book for a long time"; meeting her in 1889, in consequence of his admiration for the book, he got into "deep talk" with her and "would not let her go." Cecil Rhodes said it "enraptured him"; he was "unable to account for its spendour"; again and again he referred to the concluding chapters as "masterpieces," and to the book itself as a work of "profound genius," pointing out that it had been written "amid desert surroundings, with which alone, practically speaking, she had been acquainted." Edward Carpenter, Havelock Ellis, Arthur Symons and many others have borne testimony from personal knowledge to their conviction that the book was the intimate revelation of the writer's emotional and intellectual life.

S. C. CRONWRIGHT-SCHREINER.

ROME,
  January, 1924.

THE STORY OF
AN AFRICAN FARM

THE STORY OF AN AFRICAN FARM.

PART I.

CHAPTER I.

SHADOWS FROM CHILD-LIFE.

The Watch.

THE full African moon poured down its light from
the blue sky into the wide, lonely plain. The dry,
sandy earth with its coating of stunted "karroo"
bushes a few inches high, the low hills that skirted
the plain, the milk-bushes with their long finger-like
leaves, all were touched by a weird and an almost op-
pressive beauty as they lay in the white light.

In one spot only was the solemn monotony of
the plain broken. Near the centre a small solitary
"kopje" rose. Alone it lay there, a heap of round
ironstones piled one upon another, as over some giant's
grave. Here and there a few tufts of grass or small
succulent plants had sprung up among its stones, and
on the very summit a clump of prickly pears lifted
their thorny arms, and reflected, as from mirrors, the
moonlight on their broad fleshy leaves. At the foot
of the "kopje" lay the homestead. First, the stone-
walled sheep kraals and Kaffir huts; beyond them
the dwelling-house, — a square red brick building

2

with thatched roof. Even on its bare red walls, and the wooden ladder that led up to the loft, the moonlight cast a kind of dreamy beauty, and quite etherealized the low brick wall that ran before the house, and which enclosed a bare patch of sand and two straggling sunflowers. On the zinc roof of the great open wagon-house, on the roofs of the outbuildings that jutted from its side, the moonlight glinted with a quite peculiar brightness, till it seemed that every rib in the metal was of burnished silver.

Sleep ruled everywhere, and the homestead was not less quiet than the solitary plain.

In the farm-house, on her great wooden bedstead, Tant' Sannie, the Boer-woman, rolled heavily in her sleep.

She had gone to bed, as she always did, in her clothes, and the night was warm, and the room close, and she dreamed bad dreams, — not of the ghosts and devils that so haunted her waking thoughts; not of her second husband, the consumptive Englishman, whose grave lay away beyond the ostrich-camps, nor of her first, the young Boer, but only of the sheep's trotters she had eaten for supper that night. She dreamed that one stuck fast in her throat, and she rolled her huge form from side to side, and snorted horribly.

In the next room, where the maid had forgotten to close the shutter, the white moonlight fell in in a flood, and made it light as day. There were two small beds against the wall. In one lay a yellow-haired child, with a low forehead and a freckled face; but the loving moonlight hid defects here as elsewhere, and showed only the innocent face of a child in its first sweet sleep.

The figure in the companion bed belonged of right
to the moonlight, for it was of quite elfin-like beauty.
The child had dropped her cover on the floor, and the
moonlight looked in at the naked little limbs. Presently she opened her eyes, and looked at the moonlight
that was bathing her.

"Em!" she called to the sleeper in the other bed,
but received no answer. Then she drew the cover
from the floor, turned her pillow, and pulling the
sheet over her head, went to sleep again.

Only in one of the outbuildings that jutted from
the wagon-house, there was some one who was not
asleep. The room was dark; door and shutter were
closed; not a ray of light entered anywhere. The
German overseer, to whom the room belonged, lay
sleeping soundly on his bed in the corner, his great
arms folded, and his bushy gray and black beard rising
and falling on his breast. But one in the room was
not asleep. Two large eyes looked about in the darkness, and two small hands were smoothing the patchwork quilt. The boy, who slept on a box under the
window, had just awakened from his first sleep. He
drew the quilt up to his chin, so that little peered
above it but a great head of silky black curls, and the
two black eyes. He stared about in the darkness.
Nothing was visible, not even the outline of one
worm-eaten rafter, nor of the deal table, on which lay
the Bible from which his father had read before they
went to bed. No one could tell where the tool-box was,
and where the fire-place. There was something very
impressive to the child in the complete darkness.

At the head of his father's bed hung a great silver
hunting-watch. It ticked loudly. The boy listened
to it, and began mechanically to count. Tick — tick

— tick! one, two, three, four! He lost count presently, and only listened. Tick — tick — tick — tick!

It never waited; it went on inexorably; and every time it ticked, *a man died!* He raised himself a little on his elbow and listened. He wished it would leave off.

How many times had it ticked since he came to lie down? A thousand times, a million times, perhaps.

He tried to count again, and sat up to listen better.

"Dying, dying, dying!" said the watch; "dying, dying, dying!"

He heard it distinctly. Where were they going to, all those people?

He lay down quickly, and pulled the cover up over his head; but presently the silky curls reappeared.

"Dying, dying, dying!" said the watch; "dying, dying, dying!"

He thought of the words his father had read that evening — "*For, wide is the gate and broad is the way, that leadeth to destruction, and many there be which go in thereat.*"

"Many, many, many!" said the watch.

"*Because strait is the gate, and narrow is the way that leadeth unto life, and few there be that find it.*"

"Few, few, few!" said the watch.

The boy lay with his eyes wide open. He saw before him a long stream of people, a great dark multitude, that moved in one direction; then they came to the dark edge of the world, and went over. He saw them passing on before him, and there was nothing that could stop them. He thought of how that stream had rolled on through all the long ages of the past — how the old Greeks and Romans had gone over; the countless millions of China and India, they

were going over now.   Since he had come to bed, how
many had gone !

And the watch said, "Eternity, eternity, eternity !"
"Stop them ! stop them !" cried the child.

And all the while the watch kept ticking on ; just
like God's will, that never changes or alters, you may
do what you please.

Great beads of perspiration stood on the boy's forehead. He climbed out of bed, and lay with his face
turned to the mud floor.

"O God, God ! save them !" he cried in agony.
"Only some; only a few ! Only, for each moment I
am praying here, one !" He folded his little hands
upon his head. "God ! God ! save them !"

He grovelled on the floor.

Oh, the long, long ages of the past, in which they
had gone over ! Oh, the long, long future, in which
they would pass away ! O, God ! the long, long,
long eternity, which has no end !

The child wept, and crept closer to the ground.

The Sacrifice.

The farm by daylight was not as the farm by
moonlight. The plain was a weary flat of loose red
sand, sparsely covered by dry karroo bushes, that
cracked beneath the tread like tinder, and showed
the red earth everywhere. Here and there a milk-
bush lifted its pale-colored rods, and in every direction the ants and beetles ran about in the blazing
sand. The red walls of the farm-house, the zinc roofs
of the outbuildings, the stone walls of the kraals,
all reflected the fierce sunlight, till the eye ached and
blenched. No tree or shrub was to be seen far or

near. The two sunflowers that stood before the door,
out-stared by the sun, drooped their brazen faces to
the sand; and the little cicada-like insects cried aloud
among the stones of the "kopje."

The Boer-woman, seen by daylight, was even less
lovely than when, in bed, she rolled and dreamed.
She sat on a chair in the great front room, with her
feet on a wooden stove, and wiped her flat face with
the corner of her apron, and drank coffee, and in Cape
Dutch swore that the beloved weather was damned.
Less lovely, too, by daylight was the dead Englishman's child, her little step-daughter, upon whose
freckles and low wrinkled forehead the sunlight had
no mercy.

"Lyndall," the child said to her little orphan cousin,
who sat with her on the floor threading beads, "how
is it your beads never fall off your needle?"

"I try," said the little one, gravely, moistening her
tiny finger. "That is why."

The overseer, seen by daylight, was a huge German,
wearing a shabby suit, and with a childish habit of
rubbing his hands and nodding his head prodigiously
when pleased at anything. He stood out at the
kraals, in the blazing sun, explaining to two Kaffir
boys the approaching end of the world. The boys, as
they cut the cakes of dung, winked at each other,
and worked as slowly as they possibly could; but the
German never saw it.

Away beyond the "kopje," Waldo, his son, herded
the ewes and lambs, — a small and dusty herd, —
powdered all over from head to foot with red sand,
wearing a ragged coat, and shoes of undressed leather,
through whose holes the toes looked out. His hat
was too large, and had sunk down to his eyes, con-

cealing completely the silky black curls. It was a
curious small figure. His flock gave him little trouble.
It was too hot for them to move far; they gathered
round every little milk-bush as though they hoped to
find shade, and stood there motionless in clumps. He
himself crept under a shelving rock that lay at the
foot of the "kopje," stretched himself on his stomach,
and waved his dilapidated little shoes in the air.

Soon, from the blue bag where he kept his dinner,
he produced a fragment of slate, an arithmetic, and a
pencil. Proceeding to put down a sum with solemn
and earnest demeanor, he began to add it up aloud:
"Six and two is eight, and four is twelve, and two
is fourteen, and four is eighteen." Here he paused.
"And four is eighteen — and — four — is — eighteen."
The last was very much drawled. Slowly the pencil
slipped from his fingers, and the slate followed it into
the sand. For a while he lay motionless, then began
muttering to himself, folded his little arms, laid his
head down upon them, and might have been asleep,
but for a muttering sound that from time to time proceeded from him. A curious old ewe came to sniff
at him; but it was long before he raised his head.
When he did, he looked at the far-off hills with his
heavy eyes.

"Ye shall receive, ye shall receive, — *shall, shall,
shall,*" he muttered.

He sat up then. Slowly the dulness and heaviness
melted from his face; it became radiant. Mid-day
had come now, and the sun's rays were poured down
vertically; the earth throbbed before the eye.

The boy stood up quickly, and cleared a small space
from the bushes which covered it. Looking carefully,
he found twelve small stones of somewhat the same

size; kneeling down, he arranged them carefully on the cleared space in a square pile, in shape like an altar. Then he walked to the bag where his dinner was kept; in it was a mutton chop and a large slice of brown bread. The boy took them out, and turned the bread over in his hand, deeply considering it. Finally he threw it away, and walked to the altar with the meat, and laid it down on the stones. Close by, in the red sand, he knelt down. Sure, never since the beginning of the world was there so ragged and so small a priest. He took off his great hat, and placed it solemnly on the ground, then closed his eyes and folded his hands. He prayed aloud, —

"O God, my Father, I have made Thee a sacrifice. I have only twopence, so I cannot buy a lamb. If the lambs were mine I would give Thee one; but now I have only this meat; it is my dinner-meat. Please, my Father, send fire down from heaven to burn it. Thou hast said, Whosoever shall say unto this mountain, Be thou cast into the sea, nothing doubting, it shall be done. I ask for the sake of Jesus Christ. Amen."

He knelt down with his face upon the ground, and he folded his hands upon his curls. The fierce sun poured down its heat upon his head and upon his altar. When he looked up he knew what he should see — the glory of God! For fear his very heart stood still, his breath came heavily; he was half suffocated. He dared not look up. Then at last he raised himself. Above him was the quiet blue sky, about him the red earth; there were the clumps of silent ewes and his altar — that was all.

He looked up — nothing broke the intense stillness of the blue overhead. He looked round in astonish-

ment, then he bowed again, and this time longer than
before.

When he raised himself the second time, all was
unaltered. Only the sun had melted the fat of the
little mutton-chop, and it ran down upon the stones.

Then the third time he bowed himself. When at
last he looked up, some ants had come to the meat on
the altar. He stood up, and drove them away. Then
he put his hat on his hot curls, and sat in the shade.
He clasped his hands about his knees. He sat to
watch what would come to pass. The glory of the
Lord God Almighty! He knew he should see it.

"My dear God is trying me," he said; and he sat
there through the fierce heat of the afternoon. Still
he watched and waited when the sun began to slope;
and when it neared the horizon and the sheep began
to cast long shadows across the karroo, he still sat
there. He hoped when the first rays touched the hills,
till the sun dipped behind them and was gone. Then
he called his ewes together, and broke down the altar,
and threw the meat far, far away into the field.

He walked home behind his flock. His heart was
heavy. He reasoned so: "God cannot lie. I had
faith. No fire came. I am like Cain — I am not His.
He will not hear my prayer. God hates me."

The boy's heart was heavy. When he reached the
kraal gate the two girls met him.

"Come," said the yellow-haired Em, "let us play
'coop.' There is still time before it gets quite dark.
You, Waldo, go and hide on the 'kopje'; Lyndall and
I will shut eyes here, and we will not look."

The girls hid their faces in the stone wall of the
sheep kraal, and the boy clambered half way up the
"kopje." He crouched down between two stones, and

gave the call. Just then the milk-herd came walking out of the cow kraal with two pails. He was an ill-looking Kaffir.

"Ah!" thought the boy, "perhaps he will die to-night, and go to hell! I must pray for him, I must pray!"

Then he thought, "Where am *I* going to?" and he prayed desperately.

"Ah! this is not right at all," little Em said, peeping between the stones, and finding him in a very curious posture. "What *are* you doing, Waldo? It is not the play, you know. You should run out when we come to the white stone. Ah, you do not play nicely."

"I — I will play nicely now," said the boy, coming out, and standing sheepishly before them; "I — I only forgot; I will play now."

"He has been to sleep," said freckled Em.

"No," said beautiful little Lyndall, looking curiously at him; "he has been crying."

She never made a mistake.

The Confession.

One night, two years after, the boy sat alone on the "kopje." He had crept softly from his father's room, and come there. He often did, because, when he prayed or cried aloud, his father might awake and hear him; and none knew his great sorrow, and none knew his grief but he himself, and he buried them deep in his heart.

He turned up the brim of his great hat, and looked at the moon, but most at the leaves of the prickly pear that grew just before him. They glinted, and glinted, and glinted, just like his own heart — cold, so hard, and very wicked. His physical heart had pain also; it seemed full of little bits of glass that hurt. He had sat there for half an hour, and he dared not go back to the close house.

He felt horribly lonely. There was not one thing so wicked as he in all the world, and he knew it. He folded his arms and began to cry — not aloud; he sobbed without making any sound, and his tears left scorched marks where they fell. He could not pray; he had prayed night and day for so many months; and to-night he could not pray. When he left off crying, he held his aching head with his brown hands. If one might have gone up to him and touched him kindly — poor, ugly little thing ! Perhaps his heart was almost broken.

With his swollen eyes he sat there on a flat stone at the very top of the "kopje"; and the tree, with every one of its wicked leaves, blinked, and blinked, and blinked at him. Presently he began to cry again, and then stopped his crying to look at it. He was quiet for a long while, then he knelt slowly and bent forward. There was a secret he had carried in his heart for a year. He had not dared to look at it; he had not whispered it to himself; but for a year he had carried it. "I hate God !" he said. The wind took the words and ran away with them, among the stones, and through the leaves of the prickly pear. He thought it died away half down the "kopje." He had told it now.

"I love Jesus Christ, but I hate God."

The wind carried away that sound as it had done the first. Then he got up, and buttoned his old coat about him. He knew he was certainly lost now; he did not care. If half the world were to be lost, why not he too ? He would not pray for mercy any more. Better so — better to know certainly. It was ended now. Better so.

He began scrambling down the sides of the "kopje" to go home.

Better so, — but oh, the loneliness, the agonized pain, for that night, and for nights on nights to come! The anguish that sleeps all day on the heart like a heavy worm, and wakes up at night to feed!

There are some of us who in after years say to Fate, "Now deal us your hardest blow, give us what you will; but let us never again suffer as we suffered when we were children."

The barb in the arrow of childhood's suffering is this: its intense loneliness, its intense ignorance.

CHAPTER II.

At last came the year of the great drought, the year of 1862. From end to end of the land the earth cried for water. Man and beast turned their eyes to the pitiless sky, that like the roof of some brazen oven arched overhead. On the farm, day after day, month after month, the water in the dams fell lower and lower; the sheep died in the fields; the cattle, scarcely able to crawl, tottered as they moved from spot to spot in search of food. Week after week, month after month, the sun looked down from the cloudless sky, till the karroo bushes were leafless sticks, broken into the earth, and the earth itself was naked and bare; and only the milk-bushes, like old hags, pointed their shrivelled fingers heavenwards, praying for the rain that never came.

. . . . .

It was on an afternoon of a long day in that thirsty summer, that on the side of the "kopje" farthest from the homestead the two girls sat. They were somewhat grown since the days when they played hide-and-seek there, but they were mere children still.

Their dress was of dark coarse stuff; their common blue pinafores reached to their ankles, and on their feet they wore home-made "vel-schoen."

They sat under a shelving rock, on the surface of which were still visible some old Bushman-paintings, their red and black pigments having been preserved through long years from wind and rain by the over-hanging ledge, — grotesque oxen, elephants, rhinoceroses, and a one-horned beast, such as no man ever has seen or ever shall see.

The girls sat with their backs to the paintings. In their laps were a few fern and ice-plant leaves, which by dint of much searching they had gathered under the rocks.

Em took off her big brown "kappje" and began vigorously to fan her red face with it; but her companion bent low over the leaves in her lap, and at last took up an ice-plant leaf, and fastened it to the front of her blue pinafore with a pin.

"Diamonds must look as these drops do," she said, carefully bending over the leaf, and crushing one crystal drop with her delicate little nail. "When I am grown up," she said, "I shall wear real diamonds, exactly like these in my hair."

Her companion opened her eyes, and wrinkled her low forehead.

"Where will you find them, Lyndall? The stones are only crystals that we picked up yesterday. Old Otto says so."

"And you think that I am going to stay *here* always?"

The lip trembled scornfully.

"Ah, no!" said her companion. "I suppose some day we shall go somewhere; but now we are only twelve, and we cannot marry till we are seventeen. Four years, five — that is a long time to wait. And we might not have diamonds if we did marry."

"And you think that I am going to stay here till then?"

"Well, where *are* you going?" asked her companion.

The girl crushed an ice-plant leaf between her fingers.

"Tant' Sannie is a miserable old woman," she said. "Your father married her when he was dying, because he thought she would take better care of the farm, and of us, than an Englishwoman. He said we should be taught, and sent to school. Now she saves every farthing for herself, buys us not even one old book. She does not ill-use us — why? Because she is afraid of your father's ghost. Only this morning she told her Hottentot that she would have beaten you for breaking the plate, but that three nights ago she heard a rustling and a grunting behind the pantry door, and knew it was your father coming to 'spook' her. She is a miserable old woman," said the girl, throwing the leaf from her; "but I intend to go to school."

"And if she won't let you?"

"I shall make her."

"How?"

The child took not the slightest notice of the last question, and folded her small arms across her knees.

"But why do you want to go, Lyndall?"

"There is nothing helps in this world," said the child, slowly, "but to be very wise, and to know everything, — to be clever."

"But I should not like to go to school!" persisted the small freckled face.

"And you do not need to. When you are seventeen this Boer-woman will go. You will have this farm and everything that is upon it for your own;

but I," said Lyndall, "will have nothing. I must learn."

"Oh, Lyndall, *I* will give you some of my sheep!" said Em, with a sudden burst of pitying generosity.

"I do not want your sheep," said the girl, slowly; "I want things of my own. When I am grown up," she added, the flush on her delicate features deepening at every word, "there will be nothing that I do not know. I shall be rich, very rich; and I shall wear, not only for best, but every day, a pure white silk, and little rosebuds, like the lady in Tant' Sannie's bed-room, and my petticoats will be embroidered, not only at the bottom, but all through."

The lady in Tant' Sannie's bed-room was a gorgeous creature from a fashion-sheet, which the Boerwoman, somewhere obtaining, had pasted up at the foot of her bed, to be profoundly admired by the children.

"It would be very nice!" said Em; but it seemed a dream of quite too transcendent a glory ever to be realized.

At this instant there appeared at the foot of the "kopje" two figures, — the one, a dog, white and sleek, one yellow ear hanging down over his left eye; the other, his master, a lad of fourteen, and no other than the boy Waldo, grown into a heavy slouching youth. The dog mounted the "kopje" quickly; his master followed slowly. He wore an aged jacket much too large for him, and rolled up at the wrists, and, as of old, a pair of dilapidated "vel-schoen" and a felt hat. He stood before the two girls at last.

"What have you been doing to-day?" asked Lyndall, lifting her eyes to his face.

"Looking after ewes and lambs below the dam. Here," he said, holding out his hand awkwardly, "I brought them for you!"

There were a few green blades of tender grass.

"Where did you find them?"

"On the dam wall."

She fastened them beside the leaf on her blue pinafore.

"They look nice there!" said the boy, awkwardly rubbing his great hands and watching her.

"Yes; but the pinafore spoils it all. It is not pretty."

He looked at it closely.

"Yes, the squares are ugly; but it looks nice upon you, — beautiful!"

He now stood silent before them, his great hands hanging loosely at either side.

"Some one has come to-day," he mumbled out, suddenly, when the idea struck him.

"Who?" asked both girls.

"An Englishman on foot."

"What does he look like?" asked Em.

"I did not notice; but he has a very large nose," said the boy, slowly. "He asked the way to the house."

"Did n't he tell you his name?"

"Yes; Bonaparte Blenkins."

"Bonaparte!" said Em, "why, that is like the reel Hottentot Hans plays on the violin, —

"'Bonaparte, Bonaparte, my wife is sick;
    In the middle of the week, but Sundays not,
I give her rice and beans for soup' —

It is a funny name!"

"There was a living man called Bonaparte once," said she of the great eyes.

"Ah, yes, I know," said Em, — "the poor prophet whom the lions ate. I am always so sorry for him."

Her companion cast a quiet glance upon her.

"He was the greatest man who ever lived," she said, "the man I like best."

"And what did he do?" asked Em, conscious that she had made a mistake, and that her prophet was not the man.

"He was one man, only one," said her little companion slowly, "yet all the people in the world feared him. He was not born great, he was common as we are; yet he was master of the world at last. Once he was only a little child, then he was a lieutenant, then he was a general, then he was an emperor. When he said a thing to himself, he never forgot it. He waited, and waited, and waited, and it came at last."

"He must have been very happy," said Em.

"I do not know," said Lyndall; "but he had what he said he would have, and that is better than being happy. He was their master, and all the people were white with fear of him. They joined together to fight him. He was one, and they were many, and they got him down at last. They were like the wild cats when their teeth are fast in a great dog, like cowardly wild cats," said the child, "they would not let him go. They were many; he was only *one*. They sent him to an island in the sea, a lonely island, and kept him there fast. He was one man, and they were many, and they were terrified at him. It was glorious!" said the child.

"And what then?" said Em.

"Then he was alone there in that island with men to watch him always," said her companion, slowly and quietly, "and in the long lonely nights he used to lie awake and think of the things he had done in the old days, and the things he would do if they let him go again. In the day when he walked near the shore it seemed to him that the sea all around him was a cold chain about his body, pressing him to death."

"And then?" said Em, much interested.

"He died there in that island; he never got away."

"It is rather a nice story," said Em; "but the end is sad."

"It is a terrible, hateful ending," said the little teller of the story, leaning forward on her folded arms; "and the worst is, it is true. I have noticed," added the child very deliberately, "that it is only the made-up stories that end nicely; the true ones all end so."

As she spoke the boy's dark, heavy eyes rested on her face.

"You have read it, have you not?"

He nodded. "Yes; but the brown history tells only what he did, not what he thought."

"It was in the brown history that I read of him," said the girl; "but I *know* what he thought. Books do not tell everything."

"No," said the boy, slowly drawing nearer to her and sitting down at her feet. "What you want to know they never tell."

Then the children fell into silence, till Doss, the dog, growing uneasy at its long continuance, sniffed at one and the other, and his master broke forth suddenly —

"If *they* could talk, if *they* could tell us now,"

he said, moving his hand out over the surrounding objects — "then we would know something. This 'kopje,' if it could tell us how it came here! The 'Physical Geography' says," he went on most rapidly and confusedly, "that what are dry lands now were once lakes; and what I think is this—these low hills were once the shores of a lake; this 'kopje' is some of the stones that were at the bottom, rolled together by the water. But there is this — how did the water come to make one heap here alone, in the centre of the plain?" It was a ponderous question; no one volunteered an answer. "When I was little," said the boy, "I always looked at it and wondered, and I thought a great giant was buried under it. Now I know the water must have done it; but how? It is very wonderful. Did one little stone come first, and stop the others as they rolled?" said the boy with earnestness, in a low voice, more as speaking to himself than to them.

"Oh, Waldo, God put the little 'kopje' here," said Em with solemnity.

"But how did He put it here?"

"By wanting."

"But how did the wanting bring it here?"

"Because it did."

The last words were uttered with the air of one who produces a clinching argument. What effect it had on the questioner was not evident, for he made no reply, and turned away from her.

Drawing closer to Lyndall's feet, he said after a while in a low voice, —

"Lyndall, has it never seemed to you that the stones *were* talking with you? Sometimes," he added in a yet lower tone, "I lie under there with my sheep, and it seems that the stones are really speaking — speaking of the old things, of the time when the strange fishes and animals lived that are turned into stone now, and the lakes were here ; and then of the time when the little Bushmen lived here, so small and so ugly, and used to sleep in the wild-dog holes, and in the 'sloots,' and eat snakes, and shoot the bucks with their poisoned arrows. It was one of them, one of these old wild Bushmen, that painted those," said the boy, nodding towards the pictures — " one who was different from the rest. He did not know why, but he wanted to make something beautiful — he wanted to make something, so he made these. He worked hard, very hard, to find the juice to make the paint ; and then he found this place where the rocks hang over, and he painted them. To us they are only strange things, that make us laugh ; but to him they were very beautiful."

The children had turned round, and looked at the pictures.

" He used to kneel here naked, painting, painting, painting ; and he wondered at the things he made himself," said the boy, rising and moving his hand in deep excitement. " Now the Boers have shot them all, so that we never see a little yellow face peeping out among the stones." He paused, a dreamy look coming over his face. "And the wild bucks have gone, and those days, and we are here. But we will be gone soon, and only the stones will lie on here, looking at everything like they look now. I know that it is I who am thinking," the fellow added slowly, "but it seems as though it were they who are talking. Has it never seemed so to you, Lyndall ? "

" No, it never seems so to me," she answered.

The sun had dipped now below the hills, and the boy, suddenly remembering the ewes and lambs, started to his feet.

"Let us also go to the house and see who has come," said Em, as the boy shuffled away to rejoin his flock, while Doss ran at his heels, snapping at the ends of the torn trousers as they fluttered in the wind.

CHAPTER III.

As the two girls rounded the side of the "kopje," an unusual scene presented itself. A large group was gathered at the back door of the homestead.

On the doorstep stood the Boer-woman, a hand on each hip, her face red and fiery, her head nodding fiercely. At her feet sat the yellow Hottentot maid, her satellite, and around stood the black Kaffir maids, with blankets twisted round their half-naked figures. Two, who stamped "mealies" in a wooden block, held the great stampers in their hands, and stared stupidly at the object of attraction. It certainly was not to look at the old German overseer, who stood in the centre of the group, that they had all gathered together. His salt-and-pepper suit, grizzly black beard, and gray eyes, were as familiar to every one on the farm as the red gables of the homestead itself; but beside him stood the stranger, and on him all eyes were fixed. Ever and anon the new-comer cast a glance over his pendulous red nose to the spot where the Boer-woman stood, and smiled faintly.

"I'm not a child," cried the Boer-woman, in low Cape Dutch, "and I wasn't born yesterday. No, by the Lord, no! You can't take *me* in! My mother didn't wean me on Monday. One wink of my eye and I see the whole thing. I'll have no tramps sleeping on my farm," cried Tant' Sannie blowing. "No, by the devil, no! not though he had sixty-times-six red noses."

There the German overseer mildly interposed that the man was not a tramp, but a highly respectable individual, whose horse had died by an accident three days before.

"Don't tell me," cried the Boer-woman; "the man is n't born that can take *me* in. If he'd had money, would n't he have bought a horse? Men who walk are thieves, liars, murderers, Rome's priests, seducers! I see the devil in his nose!" cried Tant' Sannie, shaking her fist at him; "and to come walking into the house of this Boer's child, and shaking hands as though he came on horseback! Oh, no, no!"

The stranger took off his hat, a tall battered chimney-pot, and disclosed a bald head, at the back of which was a little fringe of curled white hair; and he bowed to Tant' Sannie.

"What does she remark, my friend?" he inquired, turning his crosswise-looking eyes on the old German.

The German rubbed his old hands, and hesitated.

"Ah — well — ah — the — Dutch — you know — do not like people who walk — in this country — ah!"

"My dear friend," said the stranger, laying his hand on the German's arm, "I should have bought myself another horse, but crossing, five days ago, a full river, I lost my purse — a purse with five hundred pounds in it. I spent five days on the bank of the river trying to find it — could n't. Paid a Kaffir nine pounds to go in and look for it at the risk of his life — could n't find it."

The German would have translated this information, but the Boer-woman gave no ear.

"No, no; he goes to-night. See how he looks at me — a poor, unprotected female! If he wrongs me, who is to do me right?" cried Tant' Sannie.

"I think," said the German in an undertone, "if you did n't look at her quite so much it might be advisable. She — ah — she — might — imagine that you liked her too well, — in fact — ah —"

"Certainly, my dear friend, certainly," said the stranger, "I shall not look at her."

Saying this he turned his nose full upon a small Kaffir of two years old. That small naked son of Ham became instantly so terrified that he fled to his mother's blanket for protection, howling horribly.

Upon this the new-comer fixed his eyes pensively on the stamp-block, folding his hands on the head of his cane. His boots were broken, but he still had the cane of a gentleman.

"You vaggabonds se Engelschman!" said Tant' Sannie, looking straight at him.

This was a near approach to plain English; but the man contemplated the block abstractedly, wholly unconscious that any antagonism was being displayed toward him.

"You might not be a Scotchman or anything of that kind, might you?" suggested the German. "It is the English that she hates."

"My dear friend," said the stranger, "I am Irish, every inch of me — father Irish, mother Irish. I 've not a drop of English blood in my veins."

"And you might not be married, might you?" persisted the German. "If you had a wife and children, now? Dutch people do not like those who are not married."

"Ah," said the stranger, looking tenderly at the

block, "I have a dear wife and three sweet little children — two lovely girls and a noble boy."

This information having been conveyed to the Boer-woman, she, after some further conversation, appeared slightly mollified; but remained firm to her conviction that the man's designs were evil.

"For dear Lord!" she cried, "all Englishmen are ugly; but was there ever such a red-rag-nosed thing with broken boots and crooked eyes before? Take him to your room," she cried to the German; "but all the sin he does I lay at your door."

The German having told him how matters were arranged, the stranger made a profound bow to Tant' Sannie, and followed his host, who led the way to his own little room.

"I thought she would come to her better self soon," the German said joyously. "Tant' Sannie is not wholly bad, far from it, far." Then seeing his companion cast a furtive glance at him, which he mistook for one of surprise, he added quickly, "Ah, yes, yes, we are all a primitive people here — not very lofty. We deal not in titles. Every one is Tanta and Oom — aunt and uncle. This may be my room," he said, opening the door. "It is rough, the room is rough; not a palace — not quite. But it may be better than the fields, a little better!" he said, glancing round at his companion. "Come in, come in. There is something to eat — a mouthful: not the fare of emperors or kings; but we do not starve, not yet," he said, rubbing his hands together, and looking round with a pleased, half-nervous smile on his old face.

"My friend, my dear friend," said the stranger, seizing him by the hand, "may the Lord bless you, the Lord bless and reward you — the God of the fatherless

and the stranger.   But for you I would this night
have slept in the fields, with the dews of heaven upon
my head."

Late that evening Lyndall came down to the cabin
with the German's rations.   Through the tiny square
window the light streamed forth, and without knocking she raised the latch and entered.   There was a fire
burning on the hearth, and it cast its ruddy glow over
the little dingy room, with its worm-eaten rafters and
mud floor, and broken white-washed walls.   A curious
little place, filled with all manner of articles.   Next
to the fire was a great tool-box; beyond that the little
bookshelf with its well-worn books; beyond that, in
the corner, a heap of filled and empty grain-bags.
From the rafters hung down straps, "reims," old boots,
bits of harness, and a string of onions.   The bed was
in another corner, covered by a patchwork quilt of
faded red lions, and divided from the rest of the room
by a blue curtain, now drawn back.   On the mantel-
shelf was an endless assortment of little bags and
stones; and on the wall hung a map of South Germany, with a red line drawn through it to show where
the German had wandered.   This place was the one
home the girls had known for many a year.   The house
where Tant' Sannie lived and ruled was a place to sleep
in, to eat in, not to be happy in.   It was in vain she
told them they were grown too old to go there; every
morning and evening found them there.   Were there
not too many golden memories hanging about the old
place for them to leave it?

Long winter nights, when they had sat round the
fire, and roasted potatoes, and asked riddles, and the
old man had told of the little German village, where,
fifty years before, a little German boy had played at

snowballs, and had carried home the knitted stockings of a little girl who afterwards became Waldo's
mother; did they not seem to see the German peasant
girls walking about with their wooden shoes and yellow braided hair, and the little children eating their
suppers out of little wooden bowls when the good
mothers called them in to have their milk and
potatoes ?

And were there not yet better times than these ?
Moonlight nights, when they romped about the door,
with the old man, yet more a child than any of them,
and laughed till the old roof of the wagon-house
rang ?

Or, best of all, were there not warm, dark, starlight
nights, when they sat together on the doorstep, holding each other's hands, singing German hymns, their
voices rising clear in the still night air, — till the
German would draw away his hand suddenly to wipe
quickly a tear the children must not see ? Would
they not sit looking up at the stars and talking of
them, — of the dear Southern Cross, red, fiery Mars,
Orion, with his belt, and the Seven Mysterious Sisters, — and fall to speculating over them ? How old
are they ? Who dwells in them ? And the old German would say that perhaps the souls we loved lived
in them; *there* in that little twinkling point was perhaps the little girl whose stockings he had carried
home; and the children would look up at it lovingly,
and call it "Uncle Otto's star." Then they would
fall to deeper speculations, — of the times and seasons wherein the heavens shall be rolled together as
a scroll, and the stars shall fall as a fig-tree casteth
her untimely figs, and there shall be time no longer;
"when the Son of man shall come in His glory, and

all His holy angels with Him." In lower and lower tones they would talk, till at last they fell into whispers; then they would wish good-night softly, and walk home hushed and quiet.

To-night, when Lyndall looked in, Waldo sat before the fire, watching a pot which simmered there, with his slate and pencil in his hand; his father sat at the table, buried in the columns of a three-weeks-old newspaper; and the stranger lay stretched on the bed in the corner, fast asleep, his mouth open, his great limbs stretched out loosely, betokening much weariness. The girl put the rations down upon the table, snuffed the candle, and stood looking at the figure on the bed.

"Uncle Otto," she said presently, laying her hand down on the newspaper, and causing the old German to look up over his glasses, "how long did that man say he had been walking?"

"Since this morning, poor fellow! A gentleman — not accustomed to walking — horse died — poor fellow!" said the German, pushing out his lip, and glancing commiseratingly over his spectacles in the direction of the bed where the stranger lay, with his flabby double chin, and broken boots, through which the flesh shone.

"And do you believe him, Uncle Otto?"

"Believe him? why of course I do. He himself told me the story three times *distinctly*."

"If," said the girl, slowly, "he had walked for only one day, his boots would not have looked so; and if —"

"*If!*" said the German, starting up in his chair, irritated that any one should doubt such irrefragable evidence, — "*if!* Why, he told me *himself!* Look

how he lies there!" added the German, pathetically;
"worn out, poor fellow! We have something for him
though," pointing with his forefinger over his shoulder to the saucepan that stood on the fire. "We are
not cooks, — not French cooks, not quite; but it's
drinkable, drinkable, I think; better than nothing, I
think," he added, nodding his head in a jocund manner, that evinced his high estimation of the contents
of the saucepan and his profound satisfaction therein.
"Bish! bish! my chicken," he said, as Lyndall tapped
her little foot up and down upon the floor. "Bish!
bish! my chicken, you will wake him!"

He moved the candle so that his own head might
intervene between it and the sleeper's face; and,
smoothing his newspaper, he adjusted his spectacles
to read.

The child's gray-black eyes rested on the figure on
the bed, then turned to the German, then rested on
the figure again.

"*I* think he is a liar. Good-night, Uncle Otto,"
she said slowly, turning to the door.

Long after she had gone, the German folded his
paper up methodically, and put it in his pocket.

The stranger had not awakened to partake of the
soup, and his son had fallen asleep on the ground.
Taking two white sheepskins from the heap of sacks
in the corner, the old man doubled them up, and lifting the boy's head gently from the slate on which it
rested, placed the skins beneath it.

"Poor lambie, poor lambie!" he said, tenderly patting the great rough bear-like head; "tired, is he!"

He threw an overcoat across the boy's feet, and
lifted the saucepan from the fire. There was no place
where the old man could comfortably lie down himself,

so he resumed his seat.   Opening a much-worn Bible,
he began to read, and as he read pleasant thoughts
and visions thronged on him.

"I was a stranger, and ye took me in," he read.

He turned again to the bed where the sleeper
lay.

"I was a stranger."

Very tenderly the old man looked at him.   He saw
not the bloated body nor the evil face of the man ; but
as it were under deep disguise and fleshly conceal-
ment, the form that long years of dreaming had made
very real to him.   "Jesus, lover, and is it given to us,
weak and sinful, frail and erring, to serve *Thee*, to
take *Thee* in!" he said softly, as he rose from his
seat.   Full of joy, he began to pace the little room.
Now and again as he walked he sang the lines of a
German hymn, or muttered broken words of prayer.
The little room was full of light.   It appeared to the
German that Christ was very near him, and that at
almost any moment the thin mist of earthly darkness
that clouded his human eyes might be withdrawn,
and that made manifest of which the friends at Em-
maus, beholding it, said, "It is the Lord."

Again, and yet again, through the long hours of
that night, as the old man walked, he looked up to
the roof of his little room, with its blackened rafters,
and yet saw them not.   His rough bearded face was
illuminated with a radiant gladness ; and the night
was not shorter to the dreaming sleepers than to him
whose waking dreams brought heaven near.

So quickly the night fled, that he looked up with
surprise when at four o'clock the first gray streaks of
summer dawn showed themselves through the little
window.   Then the old man turned to rake together

the few coals that lay under the ashes, and his son,
turning on the sheepskins, muttered sleepily to know
if it were time to rise.

"Lie still, lie still! I would only make a fire," said
the old man.

"Have you been up all night?" asked the boy.

"Yes; but it has been short, very short. Sleep
again, my chicken; it is yet early."

And he went out to fetch more fuel.

CHAPTER IV.

BLESSED IS HE THAT BELIEVETH.

BONAPARTE BLENKINS sat on the side of the bed. He had wonderfully revived since the day before, held his head high, talked in a full sonorous voice, and ate greedily of all the viands offered him. At his side was a basin of soup, from which he took a deep draught now and again as he watched the fingers of the German who sat on the mud floor before him mending the bottom of a chair.

Presently he looked out, where, in the afternoon sunshine, a few half-grown ostriches might be seen wandering listlessly about, and then he looked in again at the little white-washed room, and at Lyndall, who sat in the doorway looking at a book. Then he raised his chin, and tried to adjust an imaginary shirt-collar. Finding none, he smoothed the little grey fringe at the back of his head, and began, —

"You are a student of history, I perceive, my friend; from the study of these volumes that lie scattered about this apartment, this fact has been made evident to me."

"Well — a little — perhaps — it may be," said the German, meekly.

"Being a student of history then," said Bonaparte, raising himself loftily, "you will doubtless have heard of my great, of my celebrated kinsman, Napoleon Bonaparte?"

"Yes, yes," said the German, looking up.

4

"I, sir," said Bonaparte, "was born at this hour, on an April afternoon, three-and-fifty years ago. The nurse, sir, — she was the same who attended when the Duke of Sutherland was born, — brought me to my mother. 'There is only one name for this child,' she said, 'he has the nose of his great kinsman;' and so Bonaparte Blenkins became my name — Bonaparte Blenkins. Yes, sir," said Bonaparte, "there is a stream on *my* maternal side that connects me with a stream on *his* maternal side."

The German made a sound of astonishment.

"The connection," said Bonaparte, "is one which could not be easily comprehended by one unaccustomed to the study of aristocratic pedigrees; but the connection is close."

"Is it possible!" said the German, pausing in his work with much interest and astonishment. "Napoleon an Irishman!"

"Yes," said Bonaparte, "on the mother's side, and that is how we are related. There wasn't a man to beat him," said Bonaparte, stretching himself — "not a man except the Duke of Wellington. And it's a strange coincidence," added Bonaparte, bending forward, "but *he* was a connection of mine. His nephew, the Duke of Wellington's nephew, married a cousin of mine. *She* was a woman! See her at one of the court balls — amber satin — daisies in her hair! Worth going a hundred miles to look at her! Often seen her there myself, sir!"

The German moved the leather thongs in and out, and thought of the strange vicissitudes of human life, which might bring the kinsman of dukes and emperors to his humble room.

Bonaparte appeared lost among old memories.

"Ah, that Duke of Wellington's nephew!" he broke forth suddenly; "many's the joke I've had with him. Often came to visit me at Bonaparte Hall. Grand place I had then — park, conservatory, servants. He had only one fault, that Duke of Wellington's nephew," said Bonaparte, observing that the German was deeply interested in every word; "he was a coward — what you might call a coward. You've never been in Russia, I suppose?" said Bonaparte fixing his crosswise-looking eyes on the German's face.

"No, no," said the old man, humbly. "France, England, Germany, a little in this country; it is all I have travelled."

"*I*, my friend," said Bonaparte, "have been in every country in the world, and speak every civilized language, excepting only Dutch and German. I wrote a book of my travels — noteworthy incidents. Publisher got it — cheated me out of it. Great rascals those publishers! Upon one occasion the Duke of Wellington's nephew and I were travelling in Russia. All of a sudden one of the horses dropped down dead as a door-nail. There we were — cold night — snow four feet thick — great forest — one horse not being able to move sledge — night coming on — wolves.

"'Spree!' says the Duke of Wellington's nephew.

"'Spree, do you call it?' says I; 'look out.'

"There, sticking out under a bush, was nothing less than the nose of a bear. The Duke of Wellington's nephew was up a tree like a shot; I stood quietly on the ground, as cool as I am at this moment, loaded my gun, and climbed up the tree. There was only one bough.

"'Bon,' said the Duke of Wellington's nephew, 'you'd better sit in front.'

"'All right,' said I; 'but keep your gun ready. There are more coming.' He'd got his face buried in my back.

"'How many are there?' said he.

"'Four,' said I.

"'How many are there now?' said he.

"'Eight,' said I.

"'How many are there now?' said he.

"'Ten,' said I.

"'Ten! ten!' said he; and down goes his gun.

"'Wallie,' I said, 'what have you done? We're dead men now.'

"'Bon, my old fellow,' said he, 'I couldn't help it; my hands trembled so!'

"'Wall,' I said, turning round and seizing his hand, 'Wallie, my dear lad, good-bye. I'm not afraid to die My legs are long — they hang down — the first bear that comes and I don't hit him, off goes my foot. When he takes it, I shall give you my gun and go. You may yet be saved; but tell, oh, tell Mary Ann that I thought of her, that I prayed for her!'

"'Good-bye, old fellow!' said he.

"'God bless you!' said I.

"By this time the bears were sitting in a circle all round the tree. Yes," said Bonaparte impressively, fixing his eyes on the German, "a regular exact circle. The marks of their tails were left in the snow, and I measured it afterwards; a drawing-master couldn't have done it better. It was that saved me. If they'd rushed on me at once, poor old Bon would never have been here to tell this story. But they came on, sir, *systematically*, one by one. All the rest sat on their tails and waited.   The first fellow came up, and I shot him; the second fellow — I shot him; the third — I shot him.   At last the tenth came; he was the biggest of all — the leader you may say.

"'Wall,' I said, 'give me your hand.   My fingers are stiff with the cold; there is only one bullet left; I shall miss him.   While he is eating me, you get down and take your gun; and live, dear friend, live to remember the man who gave his life for you!'   By that time the bear was at me.   I felt his paw on my trousers.

"'Oh, Bonnie! Bonnie!' said the Duke of Wellington's nephew.   But I just took my gun, and put the muzzle to the bear's ear — over he fell — dead!"

Bonaparte Blenkins waited to observe what effect his story had made.   Then he took out a dirty white handkerchief, and stroked his forehead, and more especially his eyes.

"It always affects me to relate that adventure," he remarked, returning the handkerchief to his pocket. "Ingratitude — base, vile ingratitude — is recalled by it!   That man, that man, who but for me would have perished in the pathless wilds of Russia, that man in the hour of my adversity forsook me."   The German looked up.   "Yes," said Bonaparte, "I had money; I had lands; I said to my wife, 'There is Africa, a struggling country; they want capital; they want men of talent; they want men of ability to open up that land.   Let us go.'

"I bought eight thousand pounds worth of machinery, — winnowing, ploughing, reaping machines; I loaded a ship with them.   Next steamer I came out — wife, children, all.   Got to the Cape.   Where is the ship with the things? Lost — gone to the bottom! And the box with the money? Lost — nothing saved!

"My wife wrote to the Duke of Wellington's nephew; I did n't wish her to; she did it without my knowledge.

"What did the man do whose life I saved? Did he send me thirty thousand pounds? say, 'Bonaparte, my brother, here is a crumb?' No; he sent me nothing.

"My wife said, 'Write.' I said, 'Mary Ann, NO. While these hands have power to work, NO. While this frame has power to endure, NO. Never shall it be said that Bonaparte Blenkins asked of any man.'"

The man's noble independence touched the German.

"Your case is hard; yes, that *is* hard," said the German, shaking his head.

Bonaparte took another draught of the soup, leaned back against the pillows, and sighed deeply.

"I think," he said after a while, rousing himself, "I shall now wander in the benign air, and taste the gentle cool of evening. The stiffness hovers over me yet; exercise is beneficial."

So saying he adjusted his hat carefully on the bald crown of his head, and moved to the door. After he had gone the German sighed again over his work, —

"Ah, Lord! So it is! Ah!"

He thought of the ingratitude of the world.

"Uncle Otto," said the child in the doorway, "did you ever hear of ten bears sitting on their tails in a circle?"

"Well, not of ten, exactly; but bears do attack travellers every day. It is nothing unheard of,"

said the German. "A man of such courage too!
Terrible experience, that!"

"And how do we know that the story is true, Uncle
Otto?"

The German's ire was roused.

"That is what I do hate!" he cried. "Know that
is true! How do you know that anything is true?
Because you are told so. If we begin to question
everything, — proof, proof, proof, what will we have
left to believe? How do you know the angel opened
the prison door for Peter, except that Peter said so?
How do you know that God talked to Moses, except
that Moses wrote it? That is what I hate!"

The girl knit her brows. Perhaps her thoughts
made a longer journey than the German dreamed of;
for, mark you, the old little dream how their words
and lives are texts and studies to the generation that
shall succeed them. Not what we are taught, but
what we see, makes us, and the child gathers the
food on which the adult feeds to the end.

When the German looked up next, there was a look
of supreme satisfaction in the little mouth and the
beautiful eyes.

"What dost see, chicken?" he asked.

The child said nothing, and an agonizing shriek was
borne on the afternoon breeze.

"O God! my God! I am killed!" cried the voice
of Bonaparte, as he with wide-open mouth and shaking flesh fell into the room followed by a half-grown
ostrich, who put its head in at the door, opened its
beak at him, and went away.

"Shut the door! shut the door! As you value my
life, shut the door!" cried Bonaparte, sinking into a
chair, his face blue and white, with a greenishness

about the mouth. "Ah, my friend," he said tremu-
lously, "eternity has looked me in the face! My
life's thread hung upon a cord! The valley of the
shadow of death!" said Bonaparte, seizing the German's arm.

"Dear, dear, dear!" said the German, who had
closed the lower half of the door, and stood much
concerned beside the stranger, "you have had a fright.
I never knew so young a bird to chase before; but
they will take dislikes to certain people. I sent a
boy away once, because a bird would chase him. Ah,
dear, dear!"

"When I looked round," said Bonaparte, "the red
and yawning cavity was above me, and the reprehen-
sible paw raised to strike me. My nerves," said Bonaparte, suddenly growing faint, "always delicate —
highly strung — are broken — broken! You could
not give a little wine, a little brandy, my friend?"

The old German hurried away to the bookshelf, and
took from behind the books a small bottle, half of
whose contents he poured into a cup. Bonaparte
drained it eagerly.

"How do you feel now?" asked the German, looking at him with much sympathy.

"A little, *slightly* better."

The German went out to pick up the battered
chimney-pot which had fallen before the door.

"I am sorry you got the fright. The birds are bad
things till you know them," he said sympathetically,
as he put the hat down.

"My friend," said Bonaparte, holding out his hand,
"I forgive you; do not be disturbed. Whatever the
consequences, I forgive you. I know, I believe, it
was with no ill-intent that you allowed me to go

out. Give me your hand. I have no ill-feeling, —
none!"

"You are very kind," said the German, taking the
extended hand, and feeling suddenly convinced that
he was receiving magnanimous forgiveness for some
great injury, "you are very kind."

"Don't mention it," said Bonaparte.

He knocked out the crown of his caved-in old hat,
placed it on the table before him, leaned his elbows
on the table and his face in his hands, and contemplated it.

"Ah, my old friend," he thus apostrophized the hat,
"you have served me long, you have served me faith-
fully, but the last day has come. Never more shall
you be borne upon the head of your master; never
more shall you protect his brow from the burning rays
of summer or the cutting winds of winter. Henceforth bare-headed must your master go. Good-by,
good-by, old hat!"

At the end of this affecting appeal the German rose.
He went to the box at the foot of his bed; out of it
he took a black hat, which had evidently been seldom
worn and carefully preserved.

"It's not exactly what you may have been accustomed to," he said nervously, putting it down beside
the battered chimney-pot, "but it might be of some
use, — a protection to the head, you know."

"My friend," said Bonaparte, "you are not following my advice; you are allowing yourself to be re-
proached on my account. Do not make yourself
unhappy. No; I shall go bare-headed."

"No, no, no!" cried the German, energetically. "I
have no use for the hat, — none at all. It is shut up
in the box."

"Then I will take it, my friend. It is a comfort to one's own mind when you have unintentionally injured any one to make reparation. I know the feeling. The hat may not be of that refined cut of which the old one was, but it will serve, — yes, it will serve. Thank you," said Bonaparte, adjusting it on his head, and then replacing it on the table. "I shall lie down now and take a little repose," he added; "I much fear my appetite for supper will be lost."

"I hope not, I hope not," said the German, reseating himself at his work, and looking much concerned as Bonaparte stretched himself on the bed, and turned the end of the patchwork quilt over his feet.

"You must not think to make your departure, not for many days," said the German, presently. "Tant' Sannie gives her consent, and — "

"My friend," said Bonaparte, closing his eyes sadly, "you are kind; but were it not that to-morrow is the Sabbath, weak and trembling as I lie here, I would proceed on my way. I must seek work; idleness but for a day is painful. *Work, labor,* — that is the secret of all true happiness!"

He doubled the pillow under his head, and watched how the German drew the leather thongs in and out.

After a while Lyndall silently put her book on the shelf, and went home, and the German stood up and began to mix some water and meal for roaster-cakes. As he stirred them with his hands, he said, —

"I make always a double supply on Saturday night; the hands are then free as the thoughts for Sunday."

"The blessed Sabbath!" said Bonaparte.

There was a pause. Bonaparte twisted his eyes without moving his head, to see if supper were already on the fire.

"You must sorely miss the administration of the Lord's word in this desolate spot," added Bonaparte. "Oh, how love I Thine house, and the place where Thine honor dwelleth!"

"Well, we do; yes," said the German; "but we do our best. We meet together, and I — well, I say a few words, and perhaps they are not wholly lost, not quite."

"Strange coincidence," said Bonaparte; "my plan always was the same. Was in the Free State once — solitary farm — one neighbor. Every Sunday I called together friend and neighbor, child and servant, and said, 'Rejoice with me, that we may serve the Lord,' and then I addressed them. Ah, those were blessed times," said Bonaparte; "would they might return!"

The German stirred at the cakes, and stirred, and stirred, and stirred. He could give the stranger his bed, and he could give the stranger his hat, and he could give the stranger his brandy; but his Sunday service!

After a good while he said, —

"I might speak to Tant' Sannie; I might arrange; you might take the service in my place, if it —"

"My friend," said Bonaparte, "it would give me the profoundest felicity, the most unbounded satisfaction; but in these worn-out habiliments, in these deteriorated garments, it would not be possible, it would not be fitting that I should officiate in service of One, whom, for respect, we shall not name. No, my friend, I will remain here; and, while you are assembling yourselves together in the presence of the Lord, I, in my solitude, will think of and pray for you. No; I will remain here!"

It was a touching picture — the solitary man there

praying for them. The German cleared his hands
from the meal, and went to the chest from which he
had taken the black hat. After a little careful feeling
about, he produced a black cloth coat, trousers, and
waistcoat, which he laid on the table, smiling knowingly. They were of new shining cloth, worn twice a
year, when he went to the town to "nachtmaal." He
looked with great pride at the coat as he unfolded it
and held it up.

"It's not the latest fashion, perhaps, not a West
End cut, not exactly; but it might do; it might serve
at a push. Try it on, try it on!" he said, his old gray
eyes twinkling with pride.

Bonaparte stood up, and tried on the coat. It fitted
admirably; the waistcoat could be made to button by
ripping up the back, and the trousers were perfect;
but below were the ragged boots. The German was
not disconcerted. Going to the beam where a pair of
top-boots hung, he took them off, dusted them carefully, and put them down before Bonaparte. The old
eyes now fairly brimmed over with sparkling enjoyment.

"I have only worn them once. They might serve;
they might be endured."

Bonaparte drew them on, and stood upright, his head
almost touching the beams. The German looked at
him with profound admiration. It was wonderful
what a difference feathers made in the bird.

CHAPTER V.

SUNDAY SERVICES.

Service No. 1.

THE boy Waldo kissed the pages of his book and looked up. Far over the flat lay the "kopje," a mere speck; the sheep wandered quietly from bush to bush; the stillness of the early Sunday rested everywhere, and the air was fresh.

He looked down at his book. On its page a black insect crept. He lifted it off with his finger. Then he leaned on his elbow, watching its quivering antennæ and strange movements, smiling.

"Even you," he whispered, "shall not die. Even you He loves. Even you He will fold in His arms when He takes everything and makes it perfect and happy."

When the thing had gone, he smoothed the leaves of his Bible somewhat caressingly. The leaves of that book had dropped blood for him once; they had taken the brightness out of his childhood; from between them had sprung the visions that had clung about him, and made night horrible. Adderlike thoughts had lifted their heads, had shot out forked tongues at him, asking mockingly strange trivial questions that he could not answer, miserable child: —

*Why did the women in Mark see only one angel and
the women in Luke two? Could a story be told in opposite ways and both ways be true? Could it? could
it? Then again: Is there nothing always right, and
nothing always wrong? Could Jael, the wife of Heber
the Kenite, "put her hand to the nail, and her right
hand to the workman's hammer"? and could the Spirit
of the Lord chant pœans over her, loud pœans, high
pœans, set in the book of the Lord, and no voice cry out,
It was a mean and dastardly sin to lie, and kill the
trusting in their sleep? Could the friend of God
marry his own sister and be beloved, and the man who
does it to-day goes to hell, to hell? Was there nothing
always right or always wrong?*

Those leaves had dropped blood for him once; they
had made his heart heavy and cold; they had robbed
his childhood of its gladness; now his fingers moved
over them caressingly.

"My Father God knows, my Father knows," he said.
"We cannot understand; He knows." After a while
he whispered, smiling: "I heard your voice this
morning when my eyes were not yet open; I felt you
near me, my Father. Why do you love me so?"
His face was illuminated. "In the last four months
the old question has gone from me. I know you are
good; I know you love everything; I know, I know,
I know! I could not have borne it any more, — not
any more." He laughed softly. "And all the while
I was so miserable you were looking at me and loving
me, and I never knew it. But I know it now; I feel
it," said the boy, and he laughed low. "I feel it!"
he laughed.

After a while he began partly to sing, partly to
chant, the disconnected verses of hymns — those which

spoke his gladness — many times over. The sheep, with their senseless eyes, turned to look at him as he sang.

At last he lapsed into quiet. Then, as the boy lay there staring at bush and sand, he saw a vision.

He had crossed the river of Death, and walked on the other bank in the Lord's land of Beulah. His feet sank into the dark grass, and he walked alone. Then, far over the fields, he saw a figure coming across the dark green grass. At first he thought it must be one of the angels; but as it came nearer he began to feel what it was. And it came closer, — closer to him; and then the voice said, "Come!" and he knew surely Who it was. He ran to the dear feet and touched them with his hands; yes, he held them fast! He lay down beside them. When he looked up, the face was over him, and the glorious eyes were loving him; and they two were there alone together.

He laughed a deep laugh; then started up like one suddenly awakened from sleep.

"O God!" he cried, "I cannot wait; I cannot wait! I want to die; I want to see Him; I want to touch Him. Let me die!" He folded his hands, trembling. "How can I wait so long — for long, long years perhaps? I want to die — to see Him. I will die any death. Oh, let me come!"

Weeping, he bowed himself, and quivered from head to foot. After a long while he lifted his head.

"Yes; I will wait, I will wait. But not long; do not let it be very long, Jesus King. I want you; oh, I want you, — soon, soon!" He sat still, staring across the plain with his tearful eyes.

Service No. 2.

In the front room of the farm-house sat Tant' Sannie in her elbow-chair. In her hand was her great brass-clasped hymn-book, round her neck was a clean white handkerchief, under her feet was a wooden stove. There too sat Em and Lyndall, in clean pinafores and new shoes. There too was the spruce Hottentot in a starched white kappje, and her husband on the other side of the door, with his wool oiled and very much combed out, and staring at his new leather boots. The Kaffir servants were not there, because Tant' Sannie held they were descended from apes, and needed no salvation. But the rest were gathered for the Sunday service, and waited the officiator.

Meanwhile Bonaparte and the German approached arm in arm — Bonaparte resplendent in the black cloth clothes, a spotless shirt, and a spotless collar; the German in the old salt-and-pepper suit, casting shy glances of admiration at his companion.

At the front door Bonaparte removed his hat with much dignity, raised his shirt collar, and entered. To the centre table he walked, put his hat solemnly down by the big Bible, and bowed his head over it in silent prayer.

The Boer-woman looked at the Hottentot, and the Hottentot looked at the Boer-woman.

There was one thing on earth for which Tant' Sannie had a profound reverence, which exercised a subduing influence over her, which made her for the time a better woman — that thing was new, shining black cloth. It made her think of the "predikant"; it made her think of the elders, who sat in the top pew of the church on Sundays, with the hair so nicely

oiled, so holy and respectable, with their little swallow-tailed coats; it made her think of heaven, where
everything was so holy and respectable, and nobody
wore tan-cord, and the littlest angel had a black tail-
coat. She wished she had n't called him a thief and
a Roman Catholic. She hoped the German had n't
told him. She wondered where those clothes were
when he came in rags to her door. There was no
doubt, he was a very respectable man, a gentleman.

The German began to read a hymn. At the end of
each line Bonaparte groaned, and twice at the end
of every verse.

The Boer-woman had often heard of persons groan-
ing during prayers, to add a certain poignancy and
finish to them; old Jan Vanderlinde, her mother's
brother, always did it after he was converted; and
she would have looked upon it as no especial sign of
grace in any one; but to groan at hymn-time! She
was startled. She wondered if he remembered that
she shook her fist in his face. This was a man of
God. They knelt down to pray. The Boer-woman
weighed two hundred and fifty pounds, and could not
kneel. She sat in her chair, and peeped between her
crossed fingers at the stranger's back. She could not
understand what he said; but he was in earnest. He
shook the chair by the back rail till it made quite a
little dust on the mud floor.

When they rose from their knees, Bonaparte solemnly seated himself in the chair, and opened the
Bible. He blew his nose, pulled up his shirt-collar,
smoothed the leaves, stroked down his capacious
waistcoat, blew his nose again, looked solemnly round
the room, then began, —

" All liars shall have their part in the lake which

5

burneth with fire and brimstone, which is the second death."

Having read this portion of Scripture, Bonaparte paused impressively, and looked all round the room.

"I shall not, my dear friends," he said, "long detain you. Much of our precious time has already fled blissfully from us in the voice of thanksgiving and the tongue of praise. A few, a very few, words are all I shall address to you, and may they be as a rod of iron dividing the bones from the marrow, and the marrow from the bones.

"In the first place, what is a liar?"

The question was put so pointedly, and followed by a pause so profound, that even the Hottentot man left off looking at his boots and opened his eyes, though he understood not a word.

"I repeat," said Bonaparte, "what is a liar?"

The sensation was intense; the attention of the audience was riveted.

"Have you any of you ever seen a liar, my dear friends?" There was a still longer pause. "I hope not; I truly hope not. But I will tell you what a liar is. I knew a liar once, — a little boy who lived in Cape Town, in Short Market Street. His mother and I sat together one day, discoursing about our souls.

"'Here, Sampson,' said his mother, 'go and buy sixpence of "meiboss" from the Malay round the corner.'

"When he came back, she said, 'How much have you got?'

"'Five,' he said.

"He was afraid if he said six and a half she'd ask for some. And, my friends, that was a *lie*. The half of a meiboss stuck in his throat, and he died, and was buried. And where did the soul of that little liar go to, my friends? It went to the lake of fire and brimstone. This brings me to the second point of my discourse.

"What is a lake of fire and brimstone? I will tell you, my friends," said Bonaparte, condescendingly. "The imagination unaided cannot conceive it; but by the help of the Lord I will put it before your mind's eye.

"I was travelling in Italy once on a time; I came to a city called Rome, — a vast city, — and near it is a mountain which spits forth fire. Its name is Etna. Now, there was a man in that city of Rome who had not the fear of God before his eyes, and he loved a woman. The woman died, and he walked up that mountain spitting fire, and when he got to the top he threw himself in at the hole that is there. The next day I went up. I was not afraid; the Lord preserves His servants. And in their hands shall they bear thee up, lest at any time thou fall into a volcano. It was dark night when I got there, but in the fear of the Lord I walked to the edge of the yawning abyss, and looked in. That sight, — that sight, my friends, is impressed upon my most indelible memory. I looked down into the lurid depths upon an incandescent lake, — a melted fire, a seething sea; the billows rolled from side to side, and on their fiery crests tossed the white skeleton of the suicide. The heat had burned the flesh from off the bones; they lay as a light cork upon the melted fiery waves. One skeleton hand was raised upwards, the finger pointing to heaven; the other, with outstretched finger, pointing downwards, as though it would say, 'I go below; but you, Bonaparte, may soar above' I gazed; I stood entranced. At that instant there was a crack in the lurid lake; it swelled, expanded, and the skeleton of the suicide disappeared, to be seen no more by mortal eye."

Here again Bonaparte rested, and then continued, —

"The lake of melted stone rose in the crater, it swelled higher and higher at the side, it streamed forth at the top. I had presence of mind; near me was a rock; I stood upon it. The fiery torrent was vomited out, and streamed on either side of me. And through that long and terrible night I stood there alone upon that rock, the glowing fiery lava on every hand, — a monument of the long-suffering and tender providence of the Lord, who spared me that I might this day testify in your ears of Him.

"Now, my dear friends, let us deduce the lessons that are to be learned from this narrative.

"Firstly: let us never commit suicide. That man is a fool, my friends, that man is insane, my friends, who would leave this earth, my friends. Here are joys innumerable, such as it hath not entered into the heart of man to understand, my friends. Here are clothes, my friends; here are beds, my friends; here is delicious food, my friends. Our precious bodies were given us to love, to cherish. Oh, let us do so! Oh, let us never hurt them; but care for and love them, my friends!"

Every one was impressed, and Bonaparte proceeded.

"Secondly: let us not love too much. If that young man had not loved that young woman, he would not have jumped into Mount Etna. The good men of old never did so. Was Jeremiah ever in love, or Ezekiel, or Hosea, or even any of the minor prophets? No. Then why should we be? Thousands are rolling in that lake at this moment who would say, 'It was love that brought us here.' Oh, let us think always of our own souls first.

> " ' A charge to keep I have,
>   A God to glorify ;
>   A never-dying soul to save,
>   And fit it for the sky.'

"Oh, beloved friends, remember the little boy and the meiboss; remember the young girl and the young man; remember the lake, the fire, and the brimstone; remember the suicide's skeleton on the pitchy billows of Mount Etna; remember the voice of warning that has this day sounded in your ears; and what I say to you I say to all — watch! May the Lord add his blessing!"

Here the Bible closed with a tremendous thud. Tant' Sannie loosened the white handkerchief about her neck and wiped her eyes, and the colored girl, seeing her do so, sniffled. They did not understand the discourse, which made it the more affecting. There hung over it that inscrutable charm which hovers forever for the human intellect over the incomprehensible and shadowy. When the last hymn was sung, the German conducted the officiator to Tant' Sannie, who graciously extended her hand, and offered coffee and a seat on the sofa. Leaving him there, the German hurried away to see how the little plum pudding he had left at home was advancing; and Tant' Sannie remarked that it was a hot day. Bonaparte gathered her meaning as she fanned herself with the end of her apron. He bowed low in acquiescence. A long silence followed. Tant' Sannie spoke again. Bonaparte gave her no ear; his eye was fixed on a small miniature on the opposite wall, which represented Tant' Sannie as she had appeared on the day before her confirmation, fifteen years before, attired in green muslin. Suddenly he started to his feet, walked up to the picture, and took his stand before it. Long and wistfully he gazed into its features; it was easy to see that he was deeply moved. With a sudden movement, as though no longer able to restrain himself, he seized the picture, loosened it from its nail, and held it close to his eyes. At length, turning to the Boer-woman, he said, in a voice of deep emotion, —

"You will, I trust, dear madam, excuse this exhibition of my feelings; but this — this little picture recalls to me my first and best beloved, my dear departed wife, who is now a saint in heaven."

Tant' Sannie could not understand; but the Hottentot maid, who had taken her seat on the floor beside her mistress, translated the English into Dutch as far as she was able.

"Ah, my first, my beloved!" he added, looking tenderly down at the picture. "Oh, the beloved, the beautiful lineaments! My angel wife! This is surely a sister of yours, madam?" he added, fixing his eyes on Tant' Sannie.

The Dutchwoman blushed, shook her head, and pointed to herself.

Carefully, intently, Bonaparte looked from the picture in his hand to Tant' Sannie's features, and from the features back to the picture. Then slowly a light broke over his countenance; he looked up, it became a smile; he looked back at the miniature, his whole countenance was effulgent.

"Ah, yes; I see it now," he cried, turning his delighted gaze on to the Boer-woman; "eyes, mouth, nose, chin, the very expression!" he cried. "How is it possible I did not notice it before?"

"Take another cup of coffee," said Tant' Sannie. "Put some sugar in."

Bonaparte hung the picture tenderly up, and was turning to take the cup from her hand, when the German appeared, to say that the pudding was ready and the meat on the table.

"He's a God-fearing man, and one who knows how to behave himself," said the Boer-woman as he went out at the door. "If he is ugly, did not the Lord make him? And are we to laugh at the Lord's handiwork? It is better to be ugly and good than pretty and bad; though of course it's nice when one is both," said Tant' Sannie, looking complacently at the picture on the wall.

In the afternoon the German and Bonaparte sat before the door of the cabin. Both smoked in complete silence — Bonaparte with a book in his hands and his eyes half closed; the German puffing vigorously, and glancing up now and again at the serene blue sky overhead.

"Supposing — you — you, in fact, made the remark to me," burst forth the German suddenly, "that you were looking for a situation."

Bonaparte opened his mouth wide, and sent a stream of smoke through his lips.

"Now supposing," said the German, — "merely supposing, of course, — that some one, — some one in fact, should make an offer to you, say, to become school-master on their farm and teach two children, two little girls, perhaps, and would give you forty pounds a-year, would you accept it? — just supposing, of course."

"Well, my dear friend," said Bonaparte, "that would depend on circumstances. Money is no consideration with me. For my wife I have made provision for the next year. My health is broken. Could I meet a place where a gentleman would be treated as a gentleman I would accept it, however small the remuneration. With me," said Bonaparte, "money is no consideration."

"Well," said the German, when he had taken a whiff or two more from his pipe, "I think I shall go up and see Tant' Sannie a little. I go up often on Sunday afternoon to have a general conversation, to see her, you know. Nothing — nothing particular, you know."

The old man put his book into his pocket, and walked up to the farm-house with a peculiarly knowing and delighted expression of countenance.

"He doesn't suspect what I'm going to do," soliloquized the German; "has n't the least idea. A nice surprise for him."

The man whom he had left at his doorway winked at the retreating figure with a wink that was not to be described.

CHAPTER VI.

BONAPARTE BLENKINS MAKES HIS NEST.

"Ah, what is the matter?" asked Waldo, stopping at the foot of the ladder, with a load of skins on his back that he was carrying up to the loft. Through the open door in the gable little Em was visible, her feet dangling from the high bench on which she sat. The room, once a storeroom, had been divided by a row of mealie bags into two parts — the back being Bonaparte's bedroom, the front his schoolroom.

"Lyndall made him angry," said the girl tearfully; "and he has given me the fourteenth of John to learn. He says he will teach me to behave myself, when Lyndall troubles him."

"What did she do?" asked the boy.

"You see," said Em, hopelessly turning the leaves, "whenever he talks she looks out at the door, as though she did not hear him. To-day she asked him what the signs of the Zodiac were, and he said he was surprised that she should ask him; it was not a fit and proper thing for little girls to talk about. Then she asked him who Copernicus was; and he said he was one of the Emperors of Rome, who burned the Christians in a golden pig, and the worms ate him up while he was still alive. I don't know why," said Em plaintively, "but she just put her books under her arm and walked out; and she will never come to his school again, she says, and she *always* does what she says.

And now I must sit here every day alone," said Em, the great tears dropping softly.

"Perhaps Tant' Sannie will send him away," said the boy, in his mumbling way, trying to comfort her.

"No," said Em, shaking her head; "no. Last night when the little Hottentot maid was washing her feet, he told her he liked such feet, and that fat women were so nice to him; and she said I must always put him pure cream in his coffee now. No; he'll never go away," said Em, dolorously.

The boy put down his skins, and fumbled in his pocket, and produced a small piece of paper containing something. He stuck it out towards her.

"There, take it for you," he said. This was by way of comfort.

Em opened it, and found a small bit of gum, a commodity prized by the children; but the great tears dropped down slowly upon it.

Waldo was distressed. He had cried so much in his morsel of life that tears in another seemed to burn him.

"If," he said, stepping in awkwardly and standing by the table, "if you will not cry I will tell you something — a secret."

"What is that?" asked Em, instantly becoming decidedly better.

"You will tell it to no human being?"

"No."

He bent nearer to her, and with deep solemnity said, —

"*I have made a machine!*"

Em opened her eyes.

"Yes; a machine for shearing sheep. It is almost

done," said the boy. "There is only one thing that is not right yet; but it will be soon. When you think, and think, and think, all night and all day, it comes at last," he added mysteriously.

"Where is it?"

"Here! I always carry it here," said the boy, putting his hand to his breast, where a bulging-out was visible. "This is a model. When it is done, they will have to make a large one."

"Show it me."

The boy shook his head.

"No, not till it is done. I cannot let any human being see it till then."

"It is a beautiful secret," said Em; and the boy shuffled out to pick up his skins.

That evening father and son sat in the cabin eating their supper. The father sighed deeply sometimes. Perhaps he thought how long a time it was since Bonaparte had visited the cabin; but his son was in that land in which sighs have no part. It is a question whether it were not better to be the shabbiest of fools, and know the way up the little stair of imagination to the land of dreams, than the wisest of men, who see nothing that the eyes do not show, and feel nothing that the hands do not touch. The boy chewed his brown bread, and drank his coffee; but in truth he saw only his machine finished — that last something found out and added. He saw it as it worked with beautiful smoothness; and over and above, as he chewed his bread and drank his coffee, there was that delightful consciousness of something bending over him and loving him. It would not have been better in one of the courts of heaven, where the walls are set with rows of the King of Glory's amethysts and milk-white pearls, than there, eating his supper in that little room.

As they sat in silence there was a knock at the door. When it was opened the small woolly head of a little nigger showed itself. She was a messenger from Tant' Sannie: the German was wanted at once at the homestead. Putting on his hat with both hands, he hurried off. The kitchen was in darkness, but in the pantry beyond Tant' Sannie and her maids were assembled.

A Kaffir girl, who had been grinding pepper between two stones, knelt on the floor, the lean Hottentot stood with a brass candlestick in her hand, and Tant' Sannie, near the shelf, with a hand on each hip, was evidently listening intently, as were her companions.

"What may it be?" cried the old German, in astonishment.

The room beyond the pantry was the store-room. Through the thin wooden partition there arose at that instant, evidently from some creature ensconced there, a prolonged and prodigious howl, followed by a succession of violent blows against the partition wall.

The German seized the churn-stick, and was about to rush round the house, when the Boer-woman impressively laid her hand upon his arm.

"That is his head," said Tant' Sannie, "that is his head."

"But what might it be?" asked the German, looking from one to the other, churn-stick in hand.

A low hollow bellow prevented reply, and the voice of Bonaparte lifted itself on high.

"Mary Ann! my angel! my wife!"

"Isn't it dreadful?" said Tant' Sannie, as the blows were repeated fiercely. "He has got a letter; his wife is dead. You must go and comfort him," said Tant' Sannie at last, "and I will go with you. It would not be the thing for me to go alone — me, who am only thirty-three, and he an unmarried man now," said Tant' Sannie, blushing and smoothing out her apron.

Upon this they all trudged round the house in company, the Hottentot maid carrying the light, Tant' Sannie and the German following, and the Kaffir girl bringing up the rear.

"Oh," said Tant' Sannie, "I see now it was n't wickedness made him do without his wife so long — only necessity."

At the door she motioned to the German to enter, and followed him closely. On the stretcher behind the sacks Bonaparte lay on his face, his head pressed into a pillow, his legs kicking gently. The Boerwoman sat down on a box at the foot of the bed. The German stood with folded hands looking on.

"We must all die," said Tant' Sannie at last; "it is the dear Lord's will."

Hearing her voice, Bonaparte turned himself on his back.

"It's very hard," said Tant' Sannie; "I know, for I've lost two husbands."

Bonaparte looked up into the German's face.

"Oh, what does she say? Speak to me words of comfort!"

The German repeated Tant' Sannie's remark.

"Ah, I — I also! Two dear, dear wives, whom I shall never see any more!" cried Bonaparte, flinging himself back upon the bed.

He howled till the tarantulas, who lived between the rafters and the zinc roof, felt the unusual vibration, and looked out with their wicked bright eyes to see what was going on.

Tant' Sannie sighed, the Hottentot maid sighed, the Kaffir girl, who looked in at the door, put her hand over her mouth and said, "Mow-wah!"

"You must trust in the Lord," said Tant' Sannie. "He can give you more than you have lost."

"I do, I do!" he cried; "but, oh, I have no wife! I have no wife!"

Tant' Sannie was much affected, and came and stood near the bed.

"Ask him if he won't have a little pap, — nice, fine, flour pap. There is some boiling on the kitchen fire."

The German made the proposal, but the widower waved his hand.

"No, nothing shall pass my lips. I should be suffocated. No, no! Speak not of food to me!"

"Pap, and a little brandy in," said Tant' Sannie, coaxingly.

Bonaparte caught the word.

"Perhaps, — perhaps, if I struggled with myself, for the sake of my duties I might imbibe a few drops!" he said, looking with quivering lip up into the German's face. "I must do my duty, must I not?"

Tant' Sannie gave the order, and the girl went for the pap.

"I know how it was when my first husband died. They could do nothing with me," the Boer-woman said, "till I had eaten a sheep's trotter, and honey, and a little roaster-cake. *I* know."

Bonaparte sat up on the bed with his legs stretched out in front of him, and a hand on each knee, blubbering softly.

"Oh, she was a woman! You are very kind to try and comfort me; but she was my wife. For a woman that is my wife I could live; for the woman that is my wife I could die! For a woman that is my wife I could — Ah! that sweet word *wife;* when will it rest upon my lips again?"

When his feelings had subsided a little, he raised the corners of his turned-down mouth, and spoke to the German with flabby lips.

"Do you think she understands me? Oh, tell her every word, that she may know I thank her!"

At that instant the girl reappeared with a basin of steaming gruel and a black bottle.

Tant' Sannie poured some of its contents into the basin, stirred it well, and came to the bed.

"Oh, I can't, I can't! I shall die! I shall die!" said Bonaparte, putting his hands to his side.

"Come, just a little!" said Tant' Sannie, coaxingly; "just a drop!"

"It's too thick! it's too thick! I should choke."

Tant' Sannie added from the contents of the bottle, and held out a spoonful; Bonaparte opened his mouth like a little bird waiting for a worm, and held it open, as she dipped again and again into the pap.

"Ah, this will do your heart good!" said Tant' Sannie, in whose mind the relative functions of heart and stomach were exceedingly ill-defined.

When the basin was emptied the violence of his grief was much assuaged; he looked at Tant' Sannie with gentle tears.

"Tell him," said the Boer-woman, "that I hope he

will sleep well, and that the Lord will comfort him, as the Lord only can."

"Bless you, dear friend, God bless you!" said Bonaparte.

When the door was safely shut on the German, the Hottentot, and the Dutch-woman, he got off the bed, and washed away the soap he had rubbed on his eye-lids.

"Bon," he said, slapping his leg, "you're the 'cutest lad I ever came across. If you don't turn out the old Hymns-and-prayers, and pummel the Ragged-coat, and get your arms round the fat one's waist and a wed-ding-ring on her finger, then you are not Bonaparte. But you *are* Bonaparte. Bon, you're a fine boy!"

Making which pleasing reflection, he pulled off his trousers and got into bed cheerfully.

CHAPTER VII.

HE SETS HIS TRAP.

"MAY I come in? I hope I do not disturb you, my dear friend," said Bonaparte, late one evening, putting his nose in at the cabin door, where the German and his son sat finishing their supper.

It was now two months since he had been installed as schoolmaster in Tant' Sannie's household, and he had grown mighty and more mighty day by day. He visited the cabin no more, sat close to Tant' Sannie drinking coffee all the evening, and walked about loftily with his hands under the coat-tails of the German's black cloth, and failed to see even a nigger who wished him a deferential good morning. It was therefore with no small surprise that the German perceived Bonaparte's red nose at his door.

"Walk in, walk in," he said joyfully. "Boy, boy, see if there is coffee left. Well, none. Make a fire. We have done supper, but — "

"My dear friend," said Bonaparte, taking off his hat, "I came not to sup, not for mere creature comforts, but for an hour of brotherly intercourse with a kindred spirit. The press of business and the weight of thought — but they alone — may sometimes prevent me from sharing the secrets of my bosom with him for whom I have so great a sympathy. You perhaps wonder when I shall return the two pounds —"

"Oh, no, no! Make a fire, make a fire, boy. We

6

will have a pot of hot coffee presently," said the German, rubbing his hands and looking about, not knowing how best to show his pleasure at the unexpected visit.

For three weeks the German's diffident "Good evening" had met with a stately bow, the chin of Bonaparte lifting itself higher daily; and his shadow had not darkened the cabin doorway since he came to borrow the two pounds. The German walked to the head of the bed, and took down a blue bag that hung there. Blue bags were a speciality of the German. He kept above fifty stowed away in different corners of his room — some filled with curious stones, some with seeds that had been in his possession fifteen years, some with rusty nails, buckles, and bits of old harness; in all, a wonderful assortment, but highly prized.

"We have something here not so bad," said the German, smiling knowingly, as he dived his hand into the bag and took out a handful of almonds and raisins; "I buy these for my chickens. They increase in size, but they still think the old man must have something nice for them. And the old man — well, a big boy may have a sweet tooth sometimes, may he not? Ha, ha!" said the German, chuckling at his own joke, as he heaped the plate with almonds. "Here is a stone — two stones to crack them — no late patent improvement — well, Adam's nut-cracker; ha, ha! But I think we shall do. We will not leave them uncracked. We will consume a few without fashionable improvements."

Here the German sat down on one side of the table, Bonaparte on the other; each one with a couple of flat stones before him, and the plate between them.

"Do not be afraid," said the German, "do not be afraid. I do not forget the boy at the fire; I crack for him. The bag is full. Why, this is strange," he said suddenly, cracking open a large nut; "three kernels! I have not observed that before. This must be retained. This is valuable." He wrapped the nut gravely in paper, and put it carefully in his waistcoat pocket. "Valuable, very valuable!" he said, shaking his head.

"Ah, my friend," said Bonaparte, "what joy it is to be once more in your society!"

The German's eye glistened, and Bonaparte seized his hand and squeezed it warmly. They then proceeded to crack and eat. After a while Bonaparte said, stuffing a handful of raisins into his mouth, —

"I was so deeply grieved, my dear friend, that you and Tant' Sannie had some slight unpleasantness this evening."

"Oh, no, no," said the German; "it is all right now. A few sheep missing; but I make it good myself. I give my twelve sheep, and work in the other eight."

"It is rather hard that you should have to make good the lost sheep," said Bonaparte; "it is no fault of yours."

"Well," said the German, "this is the case. Last evening I count the sheep at the kraal — twenty are missing. I ask the herd; he tells me they are with the other flock; he tells me so *distinctly*; how can I think he lies? This afternoon I count the other flock. The sheep are not there. I come back here; the herd is gone; the sheep are gone. But I cannot — no, I will not — believe he stole them," said the German, growing suddenly excited. "Some one else, but not he.

I know that boy; I knew him three years. He is a good boy. I have seen him deeply affected on account of his soul. And she would send the police after him! I say I would rather make the loss good myself. I will not have it; he has fled in fear. I know his heart. It was," said the German, with a little gentle hesitation, "under my words that he first felt his need of a Saviour."

Bonaparte cracked some more almonds, then said, yawning, and more as though he asked for the sake of having something to converse about, than from any interest he felt in the subject —

"And what has become of the herd's wife?"

The German was alight again in a moment.

"Yes; his wife. She has a child six days old, and Tant' Sannie would turn her out into the fields this night. That," said the German, rising, "that is what I call cruelty — diabolical cruelty. My soul abhors that deed. The man that could do such a thing I could run him through with a knife!" said the German, his gray eyes flashing, and his bushy black beard adding to the murderous fury of his aspect. Then suddenly subsiding, he said, — "But all is now well; Tant' Sannie gives her word that the maid shall remain for some days. I go to Oom Muller's to-morrow to learn if the sheep may not be there. If they are not, then I return. They are gone; that is all. I make it good."

"Tant' Sannie is a singular woman," said Bonaparte, taking the tobacco bag the German passed to him.

"Singular! Yes," said the German; "but her heart is on her right side. I have lived long years with her, and I may say I have for her an affection, which she

returns. I may say," added the German with warmth,
— "I may say, that there is not one soul on this farm
for whom I have *not* an affection."

"Ah, my friend," said Bonaparte, " when the grace
of God is in our hearts, is it not so with us all? Do
we not love the very worm we tread upon, and as we
tread upon it ? Do we know distinctions of race, or
of sex, or of color ? *No !*

> "'Love so amazing, so divine,
> It fills my soul, my life, my all.'"

After a time he sank into a less fervent mood, and
remarked, —

"The colored female who waits upon Tant' Sannie
appears to be of a virtuous disposition, an individual
who — "

"Virtuous !" said the German; "I have confi-
dence in her. There is that in her which is pure,
that which is noble. The rich and high that walk
this earth with lofty eyelids might exchange with
her."

The German here got up to bring a coal for Bonaparte's pipe, and they sat together talking for a while.
At length Bonaparte knocked the ashes out of his
pipe.

"It is time that I took my departure, dear friend,"
he said; "but, before I do so, shall we not close this
evening of sweet communion and brotherly intercourse
by a few words of prayer ? Oh, how good and how
pleasant a thing it is for brethren to dwell together in
unity ! It is like the dew upon the mountains of
Hermon; for there the Lord bestowed a blessing, even
life for evermore."

"Stay and drink some coffee," said the German.

"No, thank you, my friend; I have business that must be done to-night," said Bonaparte. "Your dear son appears to have gone to sleep. He is going to take the wagon to the mill to-morrow! What a little *man* he is."

"A fine boy."

But though the boy nodded before the fire, he was not asleep, and they all knelt down to pray.

When they rose from their knees Bonaparte extended his hand to Waldo, and patted him on the head.

"Good-night, my lad," he said. "As you go to the mill to-morrow, we shall not see you for some days. Good-night! Good-by! The Lord bless and guide you; and may He bring you back to us in safety to find us all *as you have left us!*" He laid some emphasis on the last words. "And you, my dear friend," he added, turning with redoubled warmth to the German, "long, long shall I look back to this evening as a time of refreshing from the presence of the Lord, as an hour of blessed intercourse with a brother in Jesus. May such often return! The Lord bless you," he added, with yet deeper fervor, "richly, richly!"

Then he opened the door, and vanished out into the darkness.

"He, he, he!" laughed Bonaparte, as he stumbled over the stones. "If there is n't the rarest lot of fools on this farm that ever God Almighty stuck legs to. He, he, he! When the worms come out, then the blackbirds feed. Ha, ha, ha!" Then he drew himself up; even when alone he liked to pose with a certain dignity, — it was second nature to him.

He looked in at the kitchen-door. The Hottentot maid who acted as interpreter between Tant' Sannie and himself was gone, and Tant' Sannie herself was in bed.

"Never mind, Bon, my boy," he said, as he walked round to his own room, "to-morrow will do. He, he, he!"

CHAPTER VIII.

HE CATCHES THE OLD BIRD.

At four o'clock the next afternoon the German rode
across the plain, returning from his search for the lost
sheep. He rode slowly, for he had been in the saddle
since sunrise and was somewhat weary, and the heat
of the afternoon made his horse sleepy as it picked its
way slowly along the sandy road. Every now and
then a great red spider would start out of the karroo
on one side of the path and run across to the other,
but nothing else broke the still monotony. Presently,
behind one of the highest of the milk-bushes that
dotted the roadside, the German caught sight of a
Kaffir woman, seated there evidently for such shadow
as the milk-bush might afford from the sloping rays
of the sun. The German turned the horse's head out
of the road. It was not his way to pass a living creature without a word of greeting. Coming nearer, he
found it was no other than the wife of the absconding
Kaffir herd. She had a baby tied on her back by a
dirty strip of red blanket; another strip hardly larger
was twisted round her waist; for the rest, her black
body was naked. She was a sullen, ill-looking woman,
with lips hideously protruding.

The German questioned her as to how she came
there. She muttered in broken Dutch that she had
been turned away. Had she done evil? She shook
her head sullenly. Had she had food given her?

She grunted a negative, and fanned the flies from her baby. Telling the woman to remain where she was, he turned his horse's head to the road, and rode off at a furious pace.

"Hard-hearted! cruel! Oh, my God! Is this the way? Is this charity?"

"Yes, yes, yes," ejaculated the old man as he rode on; but presently his anger began to evaporate, his horse's pace slackened, and by the time he had reached his own door he was nodding and smiling.

Dismounting quickly he went to the great chest where his provisions were kept. Here he got out a little meal, a little mealies, and a few roaster-cakes. These he tied up in three blue handkerchiefs, and putting them into a sail-cloth bag, he strung them over his shoulders. Then he looked circumspectly out at the door. It was very bad to be discovered in the act of giving; it made him red up to the roots of his old grizzled hair. No one was about, however, so he rode off again. Beside the milk-bush sat the Kaffir woman still, — like Hagar, he thought, thrust out by her mistress in the wilderness to die. Telling her to loosen the handkerchief from her head, he poured into it the contents of his bag. The woman tied it up in sullen silence.

"You must try to get to the next farm," said the German.

The woman shook her head; she would sleep in the field.

The German reflected. Kaffir women were accustomed to sleep in the open air; but then the child was small, and after so hot a day the night might be chilly. That she would creep back to the huts at the homestead when the darkness favored her, the German's

sagacity did not make evident to him. He took off
the old brown salt-and-pepper coat, and held it out to
her. The woman received it in silence, and laid it
across her knee. "With that they will sleep warmly;
not so bad. Ha, ha!" said the German. And he rode
home, nodding his head in a manner that would have
made any other man dizzy.

"I wish he would not come back to-night," said Em,
her face wet with tears.

"It will be just the same if he comes back to-morrow," said Lyndall.

The two girls sat on the step of the cabin, waiting
for the German's return. Lyndall shaded her eyes
with her hand from the sunset light.

"There he comes," she said, "whistling 'Ach Jerusalem du schöne' so loud I can hear him here."

"Perhaps he has found the sheep."

"Found them!" said Lyndall. "He would whistle
just so if he knew he had to die to-night."

"You look at the sunset, eh, chickens?" the German said, as he came up at a smart canter. "Ah,
yes, that *is* beautiful!" he added, as he dismounted,
pausing for a moment with his hand on the saddle
to look at the evening sky, where the sun shot up
long flaming streaks, between which and the eye thin
yellow clouds floated. "Ei! you weep?" said the
German, as the girls ran up to him.

Before they had time to reply the voice of Tant'
Sannie was heard.

"You child of the child of the child of a Kaffir's
dog, come here!"

The German looked up. He thought the Dutch-
woman, come out to cool herself in the yard, called

to some misbehaving servant. The old man looked round to see who it might be.

"You old vagabond of a praying German, are you deaf?"

Tant' Sannie stood before the steps of the kitchen; upon them sat the lean Hottentot, upon the highest stood Bonaparte Blenkins, both hands folded under the tails of his coat, and his eyes fixed on the sunset sky.

The German dropped the saddle on the ground.

"Bish, bish, bish! what may *this* be?" he said, and walked towards the house. "Very strange!"

The girls followed him, — Em still weeping, Lyndall with her face rather white and her eyes wide open.

"And I have the heart of a devil, did you say? You could run me through with a knife, could you?" cried the Dutch-woman. "I could not drive the Kaffir maid away because I was afraid of *you*, was I? Oh, you miserable rag! I loved you, did I? I would have liked to marry you, would I? *would* I? WOULD I?" cried the Boer-woman; "you cat's tail, you dog's paw! Be near my house to-morrow morning when the sun rises," she gasped, "my Kaffirs will drag you through the sand. They would do it gladly, any of them, for a bit of tobacco, for all your prayings with them."

"I am bewildered, I am bewildered," said the German, standing before her and raising his hand to his forehead; "I — I do not understand."

"Ask him, ask him!" cried Tant' Sannie, pointing to Bonaparte; "he knows. You thought he could not make me understand, but he did, he did, you old fool! I know enough English for that. You be

here," shouted the Dutch-woman, "when the morning
star rises, and I will let my Kaffirs take you out and
drag you, till there is not one bone left in your old
body that is not broken as fine as 'bobootie' meat, you
old beggar! All your rags are not worth that they
should be thrown out on to the ash-heap," cried the
Boer-woman; "but I will have them for my sheep.
Not one rotten hoof of your old mare do you take with
you; I will have her, — all, all for my sheep that you
have lost, you godless thing!"

The Boer-woman wiped the moisture from her mouth
with the palm of her hand.

The German turned to Bonaparte, who still stood
on the step absorbed in the beauty of the sunset.

"Do not address me; do not approach me, lost
man," said Bonaparte, not moving his eye nor lowering
his chin. "There is a crime from which all nature
revolts; there is a crime whose name is loathsome to
the human ear, — that crime is yours; that crime is
ingratitude. This woman has been your benefactress;
on her farm you have lived; after her sheep you have
looked; into her house you have been allowed to enter
and hold divine service, — an honor of which you
were never worthy. And how have you rewarded
her? Basely, basely, basely!"

"But it is all false, — lies and falsehoods. I must,
I will speak," said the German, suddenly looking
round bewildered. "Do I dream? Are you mad?
What may it be?"

"Go, dog!" cried the Dutch-woman; "I would have
been a rich woman this day if it had not been for
your laziness. Praying with the Kaffirs behind the
kraal walls! Go, you Kaffir's dog!"

"But what then is the matter? What may have

happened since I left ? " said the German turning to the Hottentot woman who sat upon the step.

She was his friend; she would tell him kindly the truth. The woman answered by a loud, ringing laugh.

" Give it him, old missis !   Give it him !"

It was so nice to see the white man who had been master hunted down.   The colored woman laughed, and threw a dozen mealie grains into her mouth to chew.

All anger and excitement faded from the old man's face.   He turned slowly away, and walked down the little path to his cabin, with his shoulders bent; it was all dark before him.   He stumbled over the threshold of his own well-known door.

Em, sobbing bitterly, would have followed him ; but the Boer-woman prevented her by a flood of speech which convulsed the Hottentot, so low were its images.

" Come, Em," said Lyndall, lifting her small, proud head, " let us go in.   We will not stay to hear such language."

She looked into the Boer-woman's eyes.   Tant' Sannie understood the meaning of the look if not the words.   She waddled after them, and caught Em by the arm.   She had struck Lyndall once, years before, and had never done it again, so she took Em.

" So you will defy me, too, will you, you English-man's ugliness !" she cried, as with one hand she forced the child down, and held her head tightly against her knee; with the other she beat her first upon one cheek, and then upon the other.

For one instant Lyndall looked on, then she laid

her small fingers on the Boer-woman's arm. With the exertion of half its strength Tant' Sannie might have flung the girl back upon the stones. It was not the power of the slight fingers, tightly though they clinched her broad wrist — so tightly that at bedtime the marks were still there; but the Boer-woman looked into the clear eyes and at the quivering white lips, and with a half-surprised curse relaxed her hold. The girl drew Em's arm through her own.

"Move!" she said to Bonaparte, who stood in the door; and he, Bonaparte the invincible, in the hour of his triumph, moved to give her place.

The Hottentot ceased to laugh, and an uncomfortable silence fell on all the three in the doorway.

Once in their room, Em sat down on the floor, and wailed bitterly. Lyndall lay on the bed with her arm drawn across her eyes, very white and still.

"Hoo, hoo!" cried Em; "and they won't let him take the gray mare; and Waldo has gone to the mill. Hoo, hoo! And perhaps they won't let us go and say good-by to him. Hoo, hoo, hoo!"

"I wish you would be quiet," said Lyndall, without moving. "Does it give you such felicity to let Bonaparte know he is hurting you? We will ask no one. It will be supper time soon. Listen, — and when you hear the chink of the knives and forks we will go out and see him."

Em suppressed her sobs, and listened intently, kneeling at the door. Suddenly some one came to the window and put the shutter up.

"Who was that?" said Lyndall, starting.

"The girl, I suppose," said Em. "How early she is this evening!"

But Lyndall sprang from the bed, and seized the handle of the door, shaking it fiercely. The door was locked on the outside. She ground her teeth.

"What is the matter?" asked Em.

The room was in perfect darkness now.

"Nothing," said Lyndall quietly; "only they have locked us in."

She turned, and went back to bed again. But ere long Em heard a sound of movement. Lyndall had climbed up into the window, and with her fingers felt the wood-work that surrounded the panes. Slipping down, the girl loosened the iron knob from the foot of the bedstead, and climbing up again she broke with it every pane of glass in the window, beginning at the top and ending at the bottom.

"What are you doing?" asked Em, who heard the falling fragments.

Her companion made her no reply, but leaned on every little cross-bar, which cracked and gave way beneath her. Then she pressed with all her strength against the shutter. She had thought the wooden buttons would give way, but by the clinking sound she knew that the iron bar had been put across. She was quite quiet for a time. Clambering down, she took from the table a small one-bladed pen-knife, with which she began to peck at the hard wood of the shutter.

"What are you doing now?" asked Em, who had ceased crying in her wonder, and had drawn near.

"Trying to make a hole," was the short reply.

"Do you think you will be able to?"

"No; but I am trying."

In an agony of suspense Em waited. For ten minutes Lyndall pecked. The hole was three-eighths of an inch deep; then the blade broke into ten pieces.

"What has happened now?" asked Em, blubbering afresh.

"Nothing," said Lyndall. "Bring me my night-gown, a piece of paper, and the matches."

Wondering, Em fumbled about till she found them.

"What are you going to do with them?" she whispered.

"Burn down the window."

"But won't the whole house take fire, and burn down, too?"

"Yes."

"But will it not be very wicked?"

"Yes, very. And I do not care."

She arranged the night-gown carefully in the corner of the window, with the chips of the frame about it. There was only one match in the box. She drew it carefully along the wall. For a moment it burned up blue, and showed the tiny face with its glistening eyes. She held it carefully to the paper. For an instant it burned up brightly, then flickered and went out. She blew the spark, but it died also. Then she threw the paper on the ground, trod on it, and went to her bed, and began to undress.

Em rushed to the door, knocking against it wildly.

"Oh, Tant' Sannie! Tant' Sannie! Oh, let us out!" she cried. "Oh, Lyndall, what are we to do?"

Lyndall wiped a drop of blood off the lip she had bitten.

"I am going to sleep," she said. "If you like to sit there and howl till the morning, do. Perhaps you will find that it helps; I never heard that howling helped any one."

Long after, when Em herself had gone to bed and was almost asleep, Lyndall came, and stood at her bedside.

"Here," she said, slipping a little pot of powder into her hand; "rub some on to your face. Does it not burn where she struck you?"

Then she crept back to her own bed. Long, long after, when Em was really asleep, she lay still awake, and folded her hands on her little breast, muttering, "When that day comes, and I am strong, I will hate everything that has power, and help everything that is weak." And she bit her lip again.

The German looked out at the cabin door for the last time that night. Then he paced the room slowly, and sighed. Then he drew out pen and paper, and sat down to write, rubbing his old gray eyes with his knuckles before he began : —

My Chickens, — You did not come to say good-by to the old man. Might you? Ah, well, there is a land where they part no more, where saints immortal reign.

I sit here alone, and I think of you. Will you forget the old man? When you wake to-morrow, he will be far away. The old horse is lazy, but he has his stick to help him; that is three legs. He comes back one day with gold and diamonds. Will you welcome him? Well, we shall see. I go to meet Waldo. He comes back with the wagon; then he follows me. Poor boy! God knows! There is a land where all things are made right, but that land is not here.

7

My little children, serve the Saviour; give your hearts to Him while you are yet young. Life is short.

Nothing is mine; otherwise I would say, Lyndall, take my books, Em my stones. Now I say nothing. The things are mine; it is not righteous, God knows! But I am silent. Let it be. But I feel it, I must say I feel it.

Do not cry too much for the old man. He goes out to seek his fortune, and comes back with it in a bag, it may be.

I love my children. Do they think of me? I am old Otto, who goes out to seek his fortune.

O. F.

Having concluded this quaint production, he put it where the children would find it the next morning, and proceeded to prepare his bundle. He never thought of entering a protest against the loss of his goods; like a child he submitted, and wept. He had been there eleven years, and it was hard to go away. He spread open on the bed a blue handkerchief, and on it put one by one the things he thought most necessary and important, — a little bag of curious seeds, which he meant to plant some day, an old German hymn-book, three misshapen stones that he greatly valued, a Bible, a shirt, and two handkerchiefs; then there was room for nothing more. He tied up the bundle tightly, and put it on a chair by his bedside.

"That is not much; they cannot say I take much," he said, looking at it.

He put his knotted stick beside it, his blue tobacco bag and his short pipe, and then inspected his coats. He had two left — a moth-eaten overcoat, and a black alpaca out at the elbows. He decided for the overcoat; it was warm certainly, but then he could carry it over his arm, and only put it on when he met some one along the road. It was more respectable than the black alpaca. He hung the greatcoat over the back of the chair, and stuffed a hard bit of roaster-cake under the knot of the bundle, and then his preparations were completed. The German stood contemplating them with much satisfaction. He had almost forgotten his sorrow at leaving, in his pleasure at preparing. Suddenly he started; an expression of intense pain passed over his face. He drew back his left arm quickly, and then pressed his right hand upon his breast.

"Ah, the sudden pang again!" he said.

His face was white, but it quickly regained its color. Then the old man busied himself in putting everything right.

"I will leave it neat. They shall not say I did not leave it neat," he said. Even the little bags of seeds on the mantel-piece he put in rows and dusted. Then he undressed and got into bed. Under his pillow was a little story-book. He drew it forth. To the old German a story was no story. Its events were as real and as important to himself as the matters of his own life. He could not go away without knowing whether that wicked Earl relented, and whether the Baron married Emilina. So he adjusted his spectacles, and began to read. Occasionally, as his feelings became too strongly moved, he ejaculated, "Ah, I thought so! — That was a rogue! — I saw it before! I knew it from the beginning!" More than half an hour had passed, when he looked up to the silver watch at the top of his bed.

"The march is long to-morrow; this will not do," he said, taking off his spectacles, and putting them carefully into the book to mark the place. "This will be good reading as I walk along to-morrow," he added, as he stuffed the book into the pocket of the greatcoat; "very good reading." He nodded his head, and lay down. He thought a little of his own troubles, a good deal of the two little girls he was leaving, of the Earl, of Emilina, of the Baron; but he was soon asleep — sleeping as peacefully as a little child, upon whose innocent soul sorrow and care cannot rest.

It was very quiet in the room. The coals in the fire-place threw a dull red light across the floor, upon the red lions on the quilt. Eleven o'clock came, and the room was very still. One o'clock came. The glimmer had died out, though the ashes were still warm, and the room was very dark. The gray mouse, who had its hole under the tool-box, came out and sat on the sacks in the corner; then, growing bolder, the room was so dark, it climbed the chair at the bedside, nibbled at the roaster-cake, took one bite quickly at the candle, and then sat on his haunches, listening. It heard the even breathing of the old man, and the steps of the hungry Kaffir dog going his last round in search of a bone or a skin that had been forgotten; and it heard the white hen call out as the wild cat ran away with one of her brood, and it heard the chicken cry. Then the gray mouse went back to its hole under the tool-box, and the room was quiet. And two o'clock came. By that time the night was grown dull and cloudy. The wild cat had gone to its home on the "kopje;" the Kaffir dog had found a bone, and lay gnawing it.

An intense quiet reigned everywhere. Only in her room the Boer-woman tossed her great arms in her sleep; for she dreamed that a dark shadow with outstretched wings fled slowly over her house, and she moaned, and shivered. And the night was very still.

But, quiet as all places were, there was a quite peculiar quiet in the German's room. Though you strained your ear most carefully, you caught no sound of breathing.

He was not gone, for the old coat still hung on the chair — the coat that was to be put on when he met any one; and the bundle and stick were ready for to-morrow's long march. The old German himself lay there, his wavy black hair just touched with gray thrown back upon the pillow. The old face was lying there alone in the dark, smiling like a little child's — oh, so peacefully. There is a stranger whose coming, they say, is worse than all the ills of life, from whose presence we flee away trembling; but he comes very tenderly sometimes. And it seemed almost as though Death had known and loved the old man, so gently it touched him. And how could it deal hardly with him — the loving, simple, childlike old man?

So it smoothed out the wrinkles that were in the old forehead, and fixed the passing smile, and sealed the eyes that they might not weep again; and then the short sleep of time was melted into the long, long sleep of eternity.

"How has he grown so young in this one night?" they said when they found him in the morning.

Yes, dear old man; to such as you time brings no age. You die with the purity and innocence of your childhood upon you, though you die in your gray hairs.

CHAPTER IX.

BONAPARTE stood on the ash-heap. He espied across the plain a moving speck, and he chucked his coat-tails up and down in expectancy of a scene.

The wagon came on slowly. Waldo lay curled among the sacks at the back of the wagon, the hand in his breast resting on the sheep-shearing machine. It was finished now. The right thought had struck him the day before as he sat, half asleep, watching the water go over the mill-wheel. He muttered to himself with half-closed eyes, —

"To-morrow smooth the cogs — tighten the screws a little — show it to them." Then after a pause — "Over the whole world — the whole world — mine, that I have made!" He pressed the little wheels and pulleys in his pocket till they cracked. Presently his muttering became louder — "And fifty pounds — a black hat for my dadda — for Lyndall a blue silk, very light; and one purple like the earth-bells, and white shoes." He muttered on — "A box full, full of books. They shall tell me all, all, all," he added, moving his fingers desiringly; "why the crystals grow in such beautiful shapes, why lightning runs to the iron, why black people are black, why the sunlight makes things warm. I shall read, read, read," he muttered slowly. Then came over him suddenly what he called "The presence of God"; a sense of a good, strong something folding him round. He smiled through his half-shut eyes. "Ah, Father, my own Father, it is so sweet to feel you, like the warm sunshine. The Bibles and books cannot tell of you, and all I feel you. They are mixed with men's words; but you — "

His muttering sank into inaudible confusion, till, opening his eyes wide, it struck him that the brown plain he looked at was the old home farm. For half an hour they had been riding in it, and he had not known it. He roused the leader, who sat nodding on the front of the wagon in the early morning sunlight. They were within half a mile of the homestead. It seemed to him that he had been gone from them all a year. He fancied he could see Lyndall standing on the brick wall to watch for him, his father, passing from one house to the other, stopping to look.

He called aloud to the oxen. For each one at home he had brought something. For his father a piece of tobacco, bought at the shop by the mill; for Em a thimble; for Lyndall a beautiful flower dug out by the roots, at a place where they had "out-spanned"; for Tant' Sannie a handkerchief. When they drew near the house, he threw the whip to the Kaffir leader, and sprang from the side of the wagon to run on. Bonaparte stopped him as he ran past the ash-heap.

"Good morning, my dear boy. Where are you running to so fast, with your rosy cheeks?"

The boy looked up at him, glad even to see Bonaparte.

"I am going to the cabin," he said, out of breath.

"You won't find them in just now — not your good old father," said Bonaparte.

"Where is he?" asked the lad.

"There, beyond the camps," said Bonaparte, waving

his hand oratorically towards the stone-walled ostrich-camps.

"What is he doing there?" asked the boy.

Bonaparte patted him on the cheek, kindly.

"We could not keep him any more, it was too hot. We've buried him, my boy," said Bonaparte, touching with his finger the boy's cheek. "We couldn't keep him any more. He, he, he!" laughed Bonaparte, as the boy fled away along the low stone wall, almost furtively, as one in fear.

.   .   .   .   .   .

At five o'clock Bonaparte knelt before a box in the German's room. He was busily unpacking it.

It had been agreed upon between Tant' Sannie and himself, that now the German was gone he, Bonaparte, was to be no longer schoolmaster, but overseer of the farm. In return for his past scholastic labors he had expressed himself willing to take possession of the dead man's goods and room. Tant' Sannie hardly liked the arrangement. She had a great deal more respect for the German dead than the German living, and would rather his goods had been allowed to descend peacefully to his son. For she was a firm believer in the chinks in the world above, where not only ears, but eyes might be applied to see how things went on in this world below. She never felt sure how far the spirit-world might overlap this world of sense, and, as a rule, prudently abstained from doing anything which might offend unseen auditors. For this reason she abstained from ill-using the dead English-man's daughter and niece, and for this reason she would rather the boy had had his father's goods. But it was hard to refuse Bonaparte anything when she and he sat so happily together in the evening drinking coffee, Bonaparte telling her in the broken Dutch he was fast learning, how he adored fat women, and what a splendid farmer he was.

So at five o'clock on this afternoon Bonaparte knelt in the German's room.

"Somewhere here it is," he said, as he packed the old clothes carefully out of the box, and finding nothing packed them in again. "Somewhere in this room it is; and if it's here Bonaparte finds it," he repeated. "You didn't stay here all these years without making a little pile somewhere, my lamb. You weren't such a fool as you looked. Oh, no!" said Bonaparte.

He now walked about the room, diving his fingers in everywhere, sticking them into the great crevices in the wall and frightening out the spiders, rapping them against the old plaster till it cracked and fell in pieces, peering up the chimney, till the soot dropped on his bald head and blackened it. He felt in little blue bags; he tried to raise the hearthstone; he shook each book, till the old leaves fell down in showers on the floor.

It was getting dark, and Bonaparte stood with his finger on his nose, reflecting. Finally he walked to the door, behind which hung the trousers and waistcoat the dead man had last worn. He had felt in them, but hurriedly, just after the funeral the day before; he would examine them again. Sticking his fingers into the waistcoat pockets, he found in one corner a hole. Pressing his hand through it, between the lining and the cloth, he presently came into contact with something. Bonaparte drew it forth — a small, square parcel, sewed up in sail-cloth. He gazed at it, squeezed it; it cracked, as though full of bank notes. He put it quickly into his own waistcoat pocket, and peeped over the half-door to see if there was any one coming. There was nothing to be seen but the last rays of yellow sunset light, painting the karroo bushes in the plain, and shining on the ash-heap, where the fowls were pecking. He turned and sat down on the nearest chair, and taking out his pen-knife ripped the parcel open. The first thing that fell was a shower of yellow faded papers. Bonaparte opened them carefully one by one, and smoothed them out on his knee. There was something very valuable to be hidden so carefully, though the German charac-ters he could not decipher. When he came to the last one, he felt something hard in it.

"You've got it, Bon, my boy! you've got it!" he cried, slapping his leg hard. Edging nearer to the door, for the light was fading, he opened the paper carefully. There was nothing inside but a plain gold wedding-ring.

"Better than nothing!" said Bonaparte, trying to put it on his little finger, which, however, proved too fat.

He took it off, and set it down on the table before him, and looked at it with his crosswise eyes.

"When that auspicious hour shall have arrived, Sannie," he said, "when, panting, I shall lead thee, lighted by Hymen's torch, to the connubial altar, then upon thy fair amaranthine finger, my joyous bride, shall this ring repose.

> "Thy fair body, O my girl,
>   Shall Bonaparte possess;
>   His fingers in thy money-bags,
>   He therein, too, shall mess."

Having given utterance to this flood of poesy, he sat lost in joyous reflection.

" ' He therein, too, *shall* mess,' " he repeated medita-
tively.

At this instant, as Bonaparte swore, and swore truly
to the end of his life, a slow and distinct rap was
given on the crown of his bald head.

Bonaparte started, and looked up. No reim, or
strap, hung down from the rafters above, and not
a human creature was near the door. It was growing dark; he did not like it. He began to fold
up the papers expeditiously. He stretched out his
hand for the ring. The ring was gone! Gone, although no human creature had entered the room;
gone, although no form had crossed the doorway!
Gone!

He would not sleep there, that was certain.

He stuffed the papers into his pocket. As he did so,
three slow and distinct taps were given on the crown
of his head. Bonaparte's jaw fell; each separate joint
lost its power; he could not move; he dared not rise;
his tongue lay loose in his mouth.

"Take all, take all!" he gurgled in his throat. "I
— I do not want them. Take —"

Here a resolute tug at the gray curls at the back of
his head caused him to leap up, yelling wildly. Was
he to sit still paralyzed, to be dragged away *bodily* to
the devil ? With terrific shrieks he fled, casting no
glance behind.

.   .   .   .   .

When the dew was falling, and the evening was
dark, a small figure moved towards the gate of the
farthest ostrich-camp, driving a bird before it. When
the gate was opened and the bird driven in and the
gate fastened, it turned away, but then suddenly
paused near the stone wall.

"Is that you, Waldo?" said Lyndall, hearing a sound.

The boy was sitting on the damp ground with his back to the wall. He gave her no answer.

"Come," she said, bending over him, "I have been looking for you all day."

He mumbled something.

"You have had nothing to eat. I have put some supper in your room. You must come home with me, Waldo."

She took his hand, and the boy rose slowly.

She made him take her arm, and twisted her small fingers among his.

"You must forget," she whispered. "Since it happened I walk, I talk, I never sit still. If we remember, we cannot bring back the dead." She knit her little fingers closer among his. "Forgetting is the best thing. He did not watch it coming," she whispered presently. "That is the dreadful thing, to *see* it coming!" She shuddered. "I want it to come so to me too. Why do you think I was driving that bird?" she added quickly. "That was Hans, the bird that hates Bonaparte. I let him out this afternoon; I thought he would chase him, and perhaps kill him."

The boy showed no sign of interest.

"He did not catch him; but he put his head over the half-door of your cabin, and frightened him horribly. He was there, busy stealing your things. Perhaps he will leave them alone now; but I wish the bird had trodden on him."

They said no more till they reached the door of the cabin.

"There is a candle and supper on the table. You

must eat," she said authoritatively. "I cannot stay with you now, lest they find out about the bird."

He grasped her arm, and brought his mouth close to her ear.

"There is no God!" he almost hissed; "no God; not anywhere!"

She started.

"*Not anywhere!*"

He ground it out between his teeth, and she felt his hot breath on her cheek.

"Waldo, you are mad!" she said, drawing herself from him instinctively.

He loosened his grasp, and turned away from her also.

In truth, is it not life's way? We fight our little battles alone; you yours, I mine. We must not help or find help.

When your life is most real, to me you are mad; when your agony is blackest, I look at you and wonder. Friendship is good, — a strong stick; but when the hour comes to lean hard it gives. In the day of their bitterest need all souls are alone.

Lyndall stood by him in the dark, pityingly, wonderingly. As he walked to the door, she came after him.

"Eat your supper; it will do you good," she said.

She rubbed her cheek against his shoulder, and then ran away.

In the front room the little woolly Kaffir girl was washing Tant' Sannie's feet in a small tub, and Bonaparte, who sat on the wooden sofa, was pulling off his shoes and stockings that his own feet might be washed also. There were three candles burning in the room, and he and Tant' Sannie sat close together, with the lean Hottentot not far off; for when ghosts are about, much light is needed, there is great strength in numbers. Bonaparte had completely recovered from the effects of his fright in the afternoon, and the numerous doses of brandy that it had been necessary to administer to him to effect his restoration had put him into a singularly pleasant and amiable mood.

"That boy Waldo," said Bonaparte, rubbing his toes, "took himself off coolly this morning as soon as the wagon came, and has not done a stiver of work all day. *I'll* not have that kind of thing now I'm master of this farm."

The Hottentot maid translated.

"Ah, I expect he's sorry that his father's dead!" said Tant' Sannie. "It's nature, you know. I cried the whole morning when my father died. One can always get another husband, but one can't get another father," said Tant' Sannie, casting a sidelong glance at Bonaparte.

Bonaparte expressed a wish to give Waldo his orders for the next day's work, and, accordingly, the little woolly-headed Kaffir was sent to call him. After a considerable time the boy appeared, and stood in the doorway.

If they had dressed him in one of the swallow-tailed coats, and oiled his hair till the drops fell from it, and it lay as smooth as an elder's on sacrament Sunday, there would still have been something unanointed in the aspect of the fellow. As it was, standing there in his strange old costume, his head presenting much the appearance of having been deeply rolled in sand, his eyelids swollen, the hair hanging over his forehead, and a dogged sullenness on his features, he presented most the appearance of an ill-conditioned young buffalo.

"Beloved Lord!" cried Tant' Sannie, "how he looks! Come in, boy. Could n't you come and say good-day to me? Don't you want some supper?"

He said he wanted nothing, and turned his heavy eyes away from her.

"There's a ghost been seen in your father's room," said Tant' Sannie. "If you're afraid, you can sleep in the kitchen."

"I will sleep in our room," said the boy, slowly.

"Well, you can go now," she said; "but be up early to take the sheep. The herd — "

"Yes, be up early, my boy," interrupted Bonaparte, smiling. "I am to be master of this farm now; and we shall be good friends, I trust, very good friends, if you try to do your duty, my dear boy."

Waldo turned to go, and Bonaparte, looking benignly at the candle, stretched out one unstockinged foot, over which Waldo, looking at nothing in particular, fell with a heavy thud upon the floor.

"Dear me, I hope you are not hurt, my boy!" said Bonaparte. "You'll have many a harder thing than that though, before you've gone through life," he added consolingly, as Waldo picked himself up.

The lean Hottentot laughed till the room rang again, and Tant' Sannie tittered till her sides ached.

When he had gone, the little maid began to wash Bonaparte's feet.

"Oh, Lord, beloved Lord, how he did fall! I can't think of it," cried Tant' Sannie, and she laughed again. "I always did know he was not right; but this evening any one could see it," she added, wiping the tears of mirth from her face. "His eyes are as wild as if the devil was in them. He never *was* like other children. The dear Lord knows, if he does n't walk alone for hours talking to himself. If you sit in the room with him you can see his lips moving the whole time; and if you talk to him twenty times, he does n't hear you. Daft-eyes; he's as mad as mad can be."

The repetition of the word "mad" conveyed meaning to Bonaparte's mind. He left off paddling his toes in the water.

"Mad, mad? *I* know that kind of mad," said Bonaparte, "and I know the thing to give for it. The front end of a little horsewhip, the tip! Nice thing; takes it out," said Bonaparte.

The Hottentot laughed, and translated.

"No more walking about and talking to themselves on this farm now," said Bonaparte; "no more minding of sheep and reading of books at the same time. The point of a horsewhip is a little thing, but I think he 'll have a taste of it before long." Bonaparte rubbed his hands and looked pleasantly across his nose; and then the three laughed together grimly.

And Waldo in his cabin crouched in the dark in a corner, with his knees drawn up to his chin.

CHAPTER X.

Doss sat among the karroo bushes, one yellow ear drawn over his wicked little eye, ready to flap away any adventurous fly that might settle on his nose. Around him in the morning sunlight fed the sheep; behind him lay his master polishing his machine. He found much comfort in handling it that morning. A dozen philosophical essays, or angelically attuned songs for the consolation of the bereaved, could never have been to him what that little sheep-shearing machine was that day.

After struggling to see the unseeable, growing drunk with the endeavor to span the infinite, and writhing before the inscrutable mystery, it is a renovating relief to turn to some simple, feelable, weighable substance ; to something which has a smell and a color, which may be handled and turned over this way and that. Whether there be or be not a hereafter, whether there be any use in calling aloud to the Unseen Power, whether there be an Unseen Power to call to, whatever be the true nature of the *I* who call and of the objects around me, whatever be our meaning, our internal essence, our cause (and in a certain order of minds death and the agony of loss inevitably awaken the wild desire, at other times smothered, to look into these things), whatever be the nature of that which lies beyond the unbroken wall which the

8

limits of the human intellect build up on every hand, this thing is certain — a knife will cut wood, and one cogged wheel will turn another. This is sure.

Waldo found an immeasurable satisfaction in the handling of his machine; but Doss winked and blinked, and thought it all frightfully monotonous out there on the flat, and presently dropped asleep, sitting bolt upright. Suddenly his eyes opened wide; something was coming from the direction of the homestead. Winking his eyes and looking intently, he perceived it was the gray mare. Now Doss had wondered much of late what had become of her master. Seeing she carried some one on her back, he now came to his own conclusion, and began to move his tail violently up and down. Presently he pricked up one ear and let the other hang; his tail became motionless, and the expression of his mouth was one of decided disapproval bordering on scorn. He wrinkled his lips up on each side into little lines.

The sand was soft, and the gray mare came on so noiselessly that the boy heard nothing till Bonaparte dismounted. Then Doss got up and moved back a step. He did not approve of Bonaparte's appearance. His costume, in truth, was of a unique kind. It was a combination of the town and country. The tails of his black cloth coat were pinned up behind to keep them from rubbing; he had on a pair of moleskin trousers and leather gaiters, and in his hand he carried a little whip of rhinoceros hide.

Waldo started and looked up. Had there been a moment's time he would have dug a hole in the sand with his hands and buried his treasure. It was only a toy of wood, but he loved it, as one of necessity loves what has been born of him, whether of the flesh or spirit. When cold eyes have looked at it, the feathers are rubbed off our butterfly's wing forever.

"What have you here, my lad?" said Bonaparte, standing by him, and pointing with the end of his whip to the medley of wheels and hinges.

The boy muttered something inaudible, and half-spread his hand over the thing.

"But this seems to be a very ingenious little machine," said Bonaparte, seating himself on the ant-heap, and bending down over it with deep interest. "What is it for, my lad?"

"Shearing sheep."

"It is a very nice little machine," said Bonaparte. "How does it work, now? I have never seen anything so ingenious!"

There was never a parent who heard deception in the voice that praised his child — his first-born. Here was one who liked the thing that had been created in him. He forgot everything. He showed how the shears would work with a little guidance, how the sheep would be held, and the wool fall into the trough. A flush burst over his face as he spoke.

"I tell you what, my lad," said Bonaparte emphatically, when the explanation was finished, "we must get you a patent. Your fortune is made. In three years' time there 'll not be a farm in this colony where it is n't working. You 're a genius, that 's what *you* are!" said Bonaparte, rising.

"If it were made larger," said the boy, raising his eyes, "it would work more smoothly. Do you think there would be any one in this colony who would be able to make it?"

"I 'm sure they could," said Bonaparte; "and if

not, why I'll do my best for you. I'll send it to
England. It must be done somehow. How long
have you worked at it?"

"Nine months," said the boy.

"Oh, it is such a nice little machine," said Bonaparte, "one can't help feeling an interest in it.
There is only *one* little improvement, one very little
improvement, I should like to make."

Bonaparte put his foot on the machine, and crushed
it into the sand. The boy looked up into his face.

"Looks better now," said Bonaparte, "does n't it?
If we can't have it made in England, we'll send it
to America. Good-by; ta-ta," he added. "You're a
great genius, a born genius, my dear boy; there's no
doubt about it."

He mounted the gray mare and rode off. The dog
watched his retreat with cynical satisfaction; but his
master lay on the ground with his head on his arms,
in the sand, and the little wheels and chips of wood
lay on the ground around him. The dog jumped on
to his back, and snapped at the black curls, till, finding that no notice was taken, he walked off to play
with a black beetle. The beetle was hard at work
trying to roll home a great ball of dung it had been
collecting all the morning; but Doss broke the ball,
and ate the beetle's hind legs, and then bit off its
head. And it was all play, and no one could tell
what it had lived and worked for. A striving, and
a striving, and an ending in nothing.

CHAPTER XI.

HE SNAPS.

" I HAVE found something in the loft," said Em to Waldo, who was listlessly piling cakes of fuel on the kraal wall, a week after. " It is a box of books that belonged to my father. We thought Tant' Sannie had burned them."

The boy put down the cake he was raising, and looked at her.

" I don't think they are very nice, — not stories," she added, " but you can go and take any you like."

So saying, she took up the plate in which she had brought his breakfast, and walked off to the house.

After that the boy worked quickly. The pile of fuel Bonaparte had ordered him to pack was on the wall in half an hour. He then went to throw salt on the skins laid out to dry. Finding the pot empty, he went to the loft to refill it.

Bonaparte Blenkins, whose door opened at the foot of the ladder, saw the boy go up, and stood in the doorway waiting for his return. He wanted his boots blacked. Doss, finding he could not follow his master up the round bars, sat patiently at the foot of the ladder. Presently he looked up longingly, but no one appeared. Then Bonaparte looked up also, and began to call; but there was no answer. What could the boy be doing? The loft was an unknown land to Bonaparte. He had often wondered what was up there; he liked to know what was in all locked-up places and out-of-the-way corners, but he was afraid to climb the ladder. So Bonaparte looked up, and in the name of all that was tantalizing questioned what the boy did up there. The loft was used only as a lumber-room. What could the fellow find up there to keep him so long?

Could the Boer-woman have beheld Waldo at that instant, any lingering doubt which might have remained in her mind as to the boy's insanity would instantly have vanished; for, having filled the salt-pot, he proceeded to look for the box of books among the rubbish that filled the loft. Under a pile of sacks he found it, — a rough packing-case, nailed up, but with one loose plank. He lifted that, and saw the even backs of a row of books. He knelt down before the box, and ran his hand along its rough edges, as if to assure himself of its existence. He stuck his hand in among the books, and pulled out two. He felt them, thrust his fingers in among the leaves, and crumpled them a little, as a lover feels the hair of his mistress. The fellow gloated over his treasure. He had had a dozen books in the course of his life; now here was a mine of them open at his feet. After a while he began to read the titles, and now and again opened a book and read a sentence; but he was too excited to catch the meanings distinctly. At last he came to a dull, brown volume. He read the name, opened it in the centre, and where he opened began to read. 'T was a chapter on property that he fell upon, — Communism, Fourierism, St. Simonism, — in a work on Political Economy. He read down one page, and turned over to the next; he read down that without changing his posture by an inch; he read the next, and the next, kneeling

all the while with the book in his hand, and his lips
parted.

All he read he did not fully understand; the
thoughts were new to him; but this was the fellow's
startled joy in the book, — the thoughts were his;
they belonged to him; he had never thought them
before, but they were his.

He laughed silently and internally, with the still
intensity of triumphant joy.

So, then, all thinking creatures did not send up the
one cry, "As Thou, dear Lord, hast created things in
the beginning, so are they now, so ought they to be,
so will they be, world without end; and it does n't
concern us what they are. Amen." There were men
to whom not only "kopjes" and stones were calling out
imperatively, "What are we, and how came we here?
Understand us, and know us," but to whom even the
old, old relations between man and man, and the customs of the ages called, and could not be made still
and forgotten.

The boy's heavy body quivered with excitement.
So he was not alone, not alone. He could not quite
have told any one why he was so glad, and this
warmth had come to him. His cheeks were burning.
No wonder that Bonaparte called in vain, and Doss
put his paws on the ladder, and whined till three-
quarters of an hour had passed. At last the boy put
the book in his breast, and buttoned it tightly to him.
He took up the salt-pot, and went to the top of the
ladder. Bonaparte, with his hands folded under his
coat-tails, looked up when he appeared, and accosted
him.

"You've been rather a long time up there, my lad,"
he said, as the boy descended with a tremulous haste,

most unlike his ordinary slow movements. "You
did n't hear me calling, I suppose?"

Bonaparte whisked the tails of his coat up and
down as he looked at him. He, Bonaparte Blenkins,
had eyes which were very far-seeing. He looked at
the pot. It was rather a small pot to have taken
three-quarters of an hour in the filling. He looked at
the face. It was flushed. And yet, Tant' Sannie
kept no wine, — he had not been drinking; his eyes
were wide open and bright, — he had not been sleeping; there was no girl up there, — he had not been
making love. Bonaparte looked at him sagaciously.
What would account for the marvellous change in the
boy coming down the ladder from the boy going up the
ladder? *One* thing there was : did not Tant' Sannie
keep in the loft "bultongs," and nice smoked sausages?
There must be something nice to *eat* up there! Aha!
that was it!

Bonaparte was so interested in carrying out this
chain of inductive reasoning that he quite forgot to
have his boots blacked.

He watched the boy shuffle off with the salt-pot
under his arm; then he stood in his doorway and
raised his eyes to the quiet blue sky, and audibly pro-
pounded this riddle to himself.

"What is the connection between the naked back
of a certain boy with a greatcoat on and a salt-pot
under his arm, and the tip of a horsewhip? Answer:
No connection at present, but there will be soon."

Bonaparte was so pleased with this sally of his wit that
he chuckled a little, and went to lie down on his bed.

There was bread-baking that afternoon, and there
was a fire lighted in the brick oven behind the house,
and Tant' Sannie had left the great wooden-elbowed

chair in which she passed her life, and waddled out
to look at it. Not far off was Waldo, who, having
thrown a pail of food into the pigsty, now leaned
over the sod-wall looking at the pigs. Half of the
sty was dry, but the lower half was a pool of mud,
on the edge of which the mother sow lay with closed
eyes, her ten little ones sucking; the father pig,
knee-deep in the mud, stood running his snout into a
rotten pumpkin and wriggling his curled tail.

Waldo wondered dreamily as he stared why they
were pleasant to look at. Taken singly they were
not beautiful; taken together they were. Was it not
because there was a certain harmony about them?
The old sow was suited to the little pigs, and the
'ittle pigs to their mother, the old boar to the rotten
pumpkin, and all to the mud. They suggested the
thought of nothing that should be added, of nothing
that should be taken away. And, he wondered on
vaguely, was not *that* the secret of all beauty, that
you who look on — So he stood dreaming, and
leaned farther and farther over the sod-wall, and
looked at the pigs.

All this time Bonaparte Blenkins was sloping down
from the house in an aimless sort of way; but he
kept one eye fixed on the pigsty, and each gyration
brought him nearer to it. Waldo stood like a thing
asleep when Bonaparte came close up to him.

In old days, when a small boy, playing in an Irish
street-gutter, he, Bonaparte, had been familiarly
known among his comrades under the title of Tripping Ben; this, from the rare ease and dexterity
with which, by merely projecting his foot, he could
precipitate any unfortunate companion on to the
crown of his head. Years had elapsed, and Tripping

Ben had become Bonaparte; but the old gift was in him still. He came close to the pigsty. All the defunct memories of his boyhood returned on him in a flood, as with an adroit movement he inserted his leg between Waldo and the wall, and sent him over into the pigsty.

The little pigs were startled at the strange intruder, and ran behind their mother, who sniffed at him. Tant' Sannie smote her hands together and laughed; but Bonaparte was far from joining her. Lost in reverie, he gazed at the distant horizon.

The sudden reversal of head and feet had thrown out the volume that Waldo carried in his breast. Bonaparte picked it up, and began to inspect it, as the boy climbed slowly over the wall. He would have walked off sullenly, but he wanted his book, and waited till it should be given him.

"Ha!" said Bonaparte, raising his eyes from the leaves of the book which he was examining. "I hope your coat has not been injured; it is of an elegant cut. An heirloom, I presume, from your paternal grandfather. It looks nice now."

"Oh, Lord! oh, Lord!" cried Tant' Sannie, laughing and holding her sides; "how the child looks — as though he thought the mud would never wash off. Oh, Lord, I shall die! You, Bonaparte, are the funniest man I ever saw."

Bonaparte Blenkins was now carefully inspecting the volume he had picked up. Among the subjects on which the darkness of his understanding had been enlightened during his youth, Political Economy had not been one. He was not, therefore, very clear as to what the nature of the book might be; and as the name of the writer, J. S. Mill, might, for anything he knew to the contrary, have belonged to a venerable member of the British and Foreign Bible Society, it by no means threw light upon the question. He was not in any way sure that Political Economy had nothing to do with the cheapest way of procuring clothing for the army and navy, which would be certainly both a political and economical subject.

But Bonaparte soon came to a conclusion as to the nature of the book and its contents, by the application of a simple rule now largely acted upon, but which, becoming universal, would save much thought and valuable time. It is of marvellous simplicity, of infinite utility, of universal applicability. It may easily be committed to memory, and runs thus: —

Whenever you come into contact with any book, person, or opinion of which you absolutely comprehend nothing, declare that book, person, or opinion to be immoral. Bespatter it, vituperate against it, strongly insist that any man or woman harboring it is a fool, or a knave, or both. Carefully abstain from studying it. Do all that in you lies to annihilate that book, person, or opinion.

Acting on this rule, so wide in its comprehensiveness, so beautifully simple in its working, Bonaparte approached Tant' Sannie with the book in his hand. Waldo came a step nearer, eying it like a dog whose young has fallen into evil hands.

"This book," said Bonaparte, "is not a fit and proper study for a young and immature mind."

Tant' Sannie did not understand a word, and said, "What ?"

"This book," said Bonaparte, bringing down his finger with energy on the cover, "this book is *sleg, sleg, Davel, Davel!*"

Tant' Sannie perceived from the gravity of his countenance that it was no laughing matter. From the words *sleg* and *Davel* she understood that the book was evil, and had some connection with the prince who pulls the wires of evil over the whole earth.

"Where did you get this book?" she asked, turning her twinkling little eyes on Waldo. "I wish that my legs may be as thin as an Englishman's if it is n't one of your father's. He had more sins than all the Kaffirs in Kaffirland, for all that he pretended to be so good all those years, and to live without a wife because he was thinking of the one that was dead! As though ten dead wives could make up for one fat one with arms and legs!" cried Tant' Sannie, snorting.

"It was not my father's book," said the boy, savagely. "I got it from your loft."

"My loft! my book! How dare you?" cried Tant' Sannie.

"It was Em's father's. She gave it me," he muttered more sullenly.

"Give it here. What is the name of it? What is it about?" she asked, putting her finger upon the title.

Bonaparte understood.

"Political Economy," he said slowly.

"Dear Lord!" said Tant' Sannie, "cannot one hear from the very sound what an ungodly book it is! One can hardly say the name. Have n't we got curses enough on this farm?" cried Tant' Sannie, eloquently; "my best imported Merino ram dying of nobody knows what, and the short-horn cow casting her two calves, and the sheep eaten up with the scab and the drought? And is *this* a time to bring ungodly

things about the place, to call down the vengeance of
Almighty God to punish us more? Did n't the minister tell me, when I was confirmed, not to read any
book except my Bible and hymn-book, that the devil
was in all the rest? And I never have read any
other book," said Tant' Sannie, with virtuous energy,
"and I never will!"

Waldo saw that the fate of his book was sealed,
and turned sullenly on his heel.

"So you will not stay to hear what I say!" cried
Tant' Sannie. "There, take your Polity-gollity-
gominy, your devil's book!" she cried, flinging the
book at his head, with much energy.

It merely touched his forehead on one side, and fell
to the ground.

"Go on," she cried; "I know you are going to talk
to yourself. People who talk to themselves always
talk to the devil. Go and tell him all about it. Go,
go, run!" cried Tant' Sannie.

But the boy neither quickened nor slackened his
pace, and passed sullenly round the back of the
wagon-house.

Books have been thrown at other heads before and
since that summer afternoon by hands more white
and delicate than those of the Boer-woman; but
whether the result of the process has been in any
case wholly satisfactory, may be questioned. We
love that with a peculiar tenderness, we treasure it
with a peculiar care, it has for us quite a fictitious
value, for which we have suffered. If we may not
carry it anywhere else, we will carry it in our hearts,
and always to the end.

Bonaparte Blenkins went to pick up the volume,
now loosened from its cover, while Tant' Sannie

pushed the stumps of wood farther into the oven. Bonaparte came close to her, tapped the book knowingly, nodded, and looked at the fire. Tant' Sannie comprehended, and taking the volume from his hand threw it into the back of the oven. It lay upon the heap of coals, smoked, flared, and blazed, and the "Political Economy" was no more, — gone out of existence, like many another poor heretic of flesh and blood.

Bonaparte grinned; and to watch the process brought his face so near the oven door that the white hair on his eyebrows got singed. He then inquired if there were any more in the loft.

Learning that there were, he made signs indicative of taking up armfuls and flinging them into the fire. But Tant' Sannie was dubious. The deceased Englishman had left all his personal effects specially to his child. It was all very well for Bonaparte to talk of burning the books. He had had his hair spiritually pulled, and she had no wish to repeat his experience.

She shook her head. Bonaparte was displeased. But then a happy thought occurred to him. He suggested that the key of the loft should henceforth be put into his own safe care and keeping, — no one gaining possession of it without his permission. To this Tant' Sannie readily assented, and the two walked lovingly to the house to look for it.

CHAPTER XII.

BONAPARTE BLENKINS was riding home on the gray mare. He had ridden out that afternoon, partly for the benefit of his health, partly to maintain his character as overseer of the farm. As he rode on slowly, he thoughtfully touched the ears of the gray mare with his whip.

"No, Bon, my boy," he addressed himself, "don't propose! You can't marry for four years on account of the will; then why propose? Weedle her, tweedle her, teedle her, but *don't* let her make sure of you. When a woman," said Bonaparte, sagely resting his finger against the side of his nose, — "when a woman is sure of you she does what she likes with you; but when she is n't, you do what you like with her. And I —," said Bonaparte.

Here he drew the horse up suddenly and looked. He was now close to the house; and leaning over the pigsty wall, in company with Em, who was showing her the pigs, was a strange female figure. It was the first visitor that had appeared on the farm since his arrival, and he looked at her with interest. She was a tall pudgy girl of fifteen, weighing a hundred and fifty pounds, with baggy, pendulous cheeks, and up-turned nose. She strikingly resembled Tant' Sannie in form and feature; but her sleepy good eyes lacked the twinkle that dwelt in the Boer-woman's small

orbs. She was attired in a bright green print, wore
brass rings in her ears, and glass beads round her
neck, and was sucking the tip of her large finger as
she looked at the pigs.

"Who is it that has come ?" asked Bonaparte, when
he stood drinking his coffee in the front room.

" Why, my niece, to be sure," said Tant' Sannie, the
Hottentot maid translating. "She's the only daughter of my only brother Paul, and she's come to visit
me. She'll be a nice mouthful to the man that can
get her," added Tant' Sannie. "Her father's got
two thousand pounds in the green wagon box under
his bed, and a farm, and five thousand sheep, and God
Almighty knows how many goats and horses. They
milk ten cows in mid-winter, and the young men are
after her like flies about a bowl of milk. She says
she means to get married in four months, but she
does n't yet know to whom. It was so with me when
I was young," said Tant' Sannie; "I've sat up with
the young men four and five nights a week. And
they will come riding again as soon as ever they
know that the time's up that the Englishman made
me agree not to marry in."

The Boer-woman smirked complacently.

"Where are you going to ?" asked Tant' Sannie,
presently, seeing that Bonaparte rose.

"Ha! I'm just going to the kraals; I'll be in to
supper," said Bonaparte.

Nevertheless, when he reached his own door he
stopped, and turned in there. Soon after he stood before the little glass, arrayed in his best white shirt
with the little tucks, and shaving himself. He had
on his very best trousers, and had heavily oiled the
little fringe at the back of his head, which, however,

refused to become darker. But what distressed him most was his nose; it was very red. He rubbed his finger and thumb on the wall, and put a little white-wash on it; but finding it rather made matters worse he rubbed it off again. Then he looked carefully into his own eyes. They certainly were a little pulled down at the outer corners, which gave them the appearance of looking crosswise; but then they were a nice blue. So he put on his best coat, took up his stick, and went out to supper, feeling on the whole well satisfied.

"Aunt," said Trana to Tant' Sannie when that night they lay together in the great wooden bed, "why does the Englishman sigh so when he looks at me?"

"Ha!" said Tant' Sannie, who was half asleep, but suddenly started, wide awake. "It's because he thinks you look like me. I tell you, Trana," said Tant' Sannie, "the man is mad with love of me. I told him the other night I could n't marry till Em was sixteen, or I'd lose all the sheep her father left me. And he talked about Jacob working seven years and seven years again for his wife. And of course he meant me," said Tant' Sannie, pompously. "But he won't get me so easily as he thinks; he'll have to ask more than once."

"Oh!" said Trana, who was a lumpish girl, and not much given to talking; but presently she added, "Aunt, why does the Englishman always knock against a person when he passes them?"

"That's because you are always in the way," said Tant' Sannie.

"But, Aunt," said Trana, presently, "I think he is very ugly."

9

"Phugh!" said Tant' Sannie. "It's only because we're not accustomed to such noses in this country. In his country he says all the people have such noses, and the redder your nose is the higher you are. He's of the family of the Queen Victoria, you know," said Tant' Sannie, wakening up with her subject; "and he does n't think anything of governors and church elders and such people; they are nothing to him. When his aunt with the dropsy dies, he 'll have money enough to buy all the farms in this district."

"Oh!" said Trana. That certainly made a difference.

"Yes," said Tant' Sannie; "and he's only forty-one, though you 'd take him to be sixty. And he told me last night the real reason of his baldness."

Tant' Sannie then proceeded to relate how, at eighteen years of age, Bonaparte had courted a fair young lady; how a deadly rival, jealous of his verdant looks, his golden flowing hair, had, with a damnable and insinuating deception, made him a present of a pot of pomatum; how, applying it in the evening, on rising in the morning he found his pillow strewn with the golden locks, and looking into the glass beheld the shining and smooth expanse which henceforth he must bear. The few remaining hairs were turned to a silvery whiteness, and the young lady married his rival.

"And," said Tant' Sannie solemnly, "if it had not been for the grace of God, and reading of the Psalms, he says he would have killed himself. He says he could kill himself quite easily if he wants to marry a woman and she won't."

"A le wereld," said Trana; and then they went to sleep.

Every one was lost in sleep soon; but from the window of the cabin the light streamed forth. It came from a dung fire over which Waldo sat brooding. Hour after hour he sat there, now and again throwing a fresh lump of fuel on to the fire, which burned up bravely, and then sank into a great bed of red coals, which reflected themselves in the boy's eyes as he sat there brooding, brooding, brooding. At last, when the fire was blazing at its brightest, he rose suddenly and walked slowly to a beam from which an ox reim hung. Loosening it, he ran a noose in one end and then doubled it round his arm.

"Mine, mine! I have a right," he muttered; and then, something louder, "if I fall and am killed, so much the better!"

He opened the door, and went out into the starlight.

He walked with his eyes bent upon the ground, but overhead it was one of those brilliant southern nights when every space so small that your hand might cover it shows fifty cold white points, and the Milky-Way is a belt of sharp frosted silver. He passed the door where Bonaparte lay dreaming of Trana and her wealth, and he mounted the ladder steps. From those he clambered with some difficulty on to the roof of the house. It was of old rotten thatch with a ridge of white plaster, and it crumbled away under his feet at every step. He trod as heavily as he could. So much the better if he fell.

He knelt down when he got to the far gable, and began to fasten his reim to the crumbling bricks. Below was the little window of the loft. With one end of the reim tied round the gable, the other end round his waist, how easy to slide down to it, and to open it, through one of the broken panes, and to go in, and to fill his arms with books, and to clamber up again! They had burned one book — he would have twenty. Every man's hand was against his — his should be against every man's. No one would help him — he would help himself.

He lifted the black damp hair from his knit forehead, and looked round to cool his hot face. Then he saw what a regal night it was. He knelt silently, and looked up. A thousand eyes were looking down at him, bright and so cold. There was a laughing irony in them.

"So hot, so bitter, so angry? Poor little mortal!"

He was ashamed. He folded his arms, and sat on the ridge of the roof looking up at them.

"*So* hot, *so* bitter, *so* angry?"

It was as though a cold hand had been laid upon his throbbing forehead, and slowly they began to fade and grow dim. Tant' Sannie and the burnt book, Bonaparte and the broken machine, the box in the loft, he himself sitting there, — how small they all became, even the grave over yonder! Those stars that shone on up above so quietly, they had seen a thousand such little existences,— a thousand such little existences fight just so fiercely, flare up just so brightly, and go out; and they, the old, old stars, shone on forever.

"So hot, so angry, poor little soul?" they said.

The reim slipped from his fingers; he sat with his arms folded, looking up.

"We," said the stars, "have seen the earth when it was young. We have seen small things creep out upon its surface — small things that prayed, and loved, and cried very loudly, and then crept under it again.

But we," said the stars, "are as old as the Unknown."

He leaned his chin against the palm of his hand, and looked up at them. So long he sat there that bright stars set and new ones rose, and yet he sat on.

Then at last he stood up, and began to loosen the reim from the gable.

What did it matter about the books? The lust and the desire for them had died out. If they pleased to keep them from him they might. What matter? it was a very little thing. Why hate, and struggle, and fight? Let it be as it would.

He twisted the reim round his arm, and walked back along the ridge of the house.

By this time Bonaparte Blenkins had finished his dream of Trana, and as he turned himself round for a fresh doze he heard the steps descending the ladder. His first impulse was to draw the blanket over his head and his legs under him, and to shout; but recollecting that the door was locked and the window carefully bolted, he allowed his head slowly to crop out among the blankets, and listened intently. Whosoever it might be, there was no danger of their getting at *him*; so he clambered out of bed, and going on tiptoe to the door, applied his eye to the keyhole. There was nothing to be seen; so walking to the window, he brought his face as close to the glass as his nose would allow. There was a figure just discernible. The lad was not trying to walk softly, and the heavy shuffling of the well-known velschoen could be clearly heard through the closed window as they crossed the stones in the yard. Bonaparte listened till they had died away round the corner of the wagon-house; and, feeling that his bare legs were getting cold, he jumped back into bed again.

. . . . . .

"What do you keep up in your loft?" inquired Bonaparte of the Boer-woman the next evening, pointing upwards and elucidating his meaning by the addition of such Dutch words as he knew, for the lean Hottentot was gone home.

"Dried skins," said the Boer-woman, "and empty bottles, and boxes, and sacks, and soap."

"You don't keep any of your provisions there, — sugar, now?" said Bonaparte, pointing to the sugar-basin and then up at the loft.

Tant' Sannie shook her head.

"Only salt, and dried peaches."

"Dried peaches! Eh?" said Bonaparte. "Shut the door, my dear child, shut it tight," he called out to Em, who stood in the dining-room. Then he leaned over the elbow of the sofa, and brought his face as close as possible to the Boer-woman's, and made signs of eating. Then he said something she did not comprehend; then said, "Waldo, Waldo, Waldo," pointed up to the loft, and made signs of eating again.

Now an inkling of his meaning dawned on the Boer-woman's mind. To make it clearer, he moved his legs after the manner of one going up a ladder, appeared to be opening a door, masticated vigorously, said, "Peaches, peaches, peaches," and appeared to be coming down the ladder.

It was now evident to Tant' Sannie that Waldo had been in her loft, and eaten her peaches.

To exemplify his own share in the proceedings, Bonaparte lay down on the sofa, and shutting his eyes tightly, said, "Night, night, night!" Then he sat up wildly, appearing to be intently listening, mimicked with his feet the coming down a ladder, and looked at Tant' Sannie. This clearly showed how, roused in the night, he had discovered the theft.

"He must have been a great fool to eat my peaches," said Tant' Sannie. "They are full of mites as a sheep-skin, and as hard as stones."

Bonaparte, fumbling in his pocket, did not even hear her remark, and took out from his coat-tail a little horsewhip, nicely rolled up. Bonaparte winked at the little rhinoceros horsewhip, at the Boer-woman, and then at the door.

"Shall we call him — Waldo, Waldo?" he said.

Tant' Sannie nodded, and giggled. There was something so exceedingly humorous in the idea that he was going to beat the boy, though for her own part she did not see that the peaches were worth it. When the Kaffir maid came with the wash-tub, she was sent to summon Waldo; and Bonaparte doubled up the little whip, and put it in his pocket. Then he drew himself up, and prepared to act his important part with becoming gravity. Soon Waldo stood in the door, and took off his hat.

"Come in, come in, my lad," said Bonaparte, "and shut the door behind."

The boy came in, and stood before them.

"You need not be so afraid, child," said Tant' Sannie. "I was a child myself once. It's no great harm if you have taken a few."

Bonaparte perceived that her remark was not in keeping with the nature of the proceedings, and of the little drama he intended to act. Pursing out his lips, and waving his hand, he solemnly addressed the boy.

"Waldo, it grieves me beyond expression to have to summon you for so painful a purpose; but it is at the imperative call of duty, which I dare not evade. I do not state that frank and unreserved confession will obviate the necessity of chastisement, which if requisite shall be fully administered; but the nature of that chastisement may be mitigated by free and humble confession. Waldo, answer me as you would your own father, in whose place I now stand to you: have you, or have you not, did you, or did you not, eat of the peaches in the loft?"

"Say you took them, boy, say you took them, then he won't beat you much," said the Dutch-woman, good-naturedly, getting a little sorry for him.

The boy raised his eyes slowly, and fixed them vacantly upon her, then suddenly his face grew dark with blood.

"*So*, you have n't got anything to say to us, my lad?" said Bonaparte, momentarily forgetting his dignity, and bending forward with a little snarl. "But what I mean is just this, my lad — when it takes a boy three-quarters of an hour to fill a salt-pot, and when at three o'clock in the morning he goes knocking about the doors of a loft, it 's natural to suppose there 's mischief in it. It 's certain there *is* mischief in it; and where there's mischief *in*, it must be taken *out*," said Bonaparte, grinning into the boy's face. Then, feeling that he had fallen from that high gravity which was as spice to the pudding, and the flavor of the whole little tragedy, he drew himself up.

"Waldo," he said, "confess to me instantly and without reserve that you ate the peaches."

The boy's face was white now. His eyes were on the ground, his hands doggedly clasped before him.

"What, you do not intend to answer?"

The boy looked up at them once from under his bent eyebrows, and then looked down again.

"The creature looks as if all the devils in hell were in it," cried Tant' Sannie. "Say you took them, boy. Young things will be young things; I was older than you when I used to eat bultong in my mother's loft, and get the little niggers whipped for it. Say you took them."

But the boy said nothing.

"I think a little solitary confinement might perhaps be beneficial," said Bonaparte. "It will enable you, Waldo, to reflect on the enormity of the sin you have committed against our Father in heaven. And you may also think of the submission you owe to those who are older and wiser than you are, and whose duty it is to check and correct you."

Saying this Bonaparte stood up and took down the key of the fuel-house, which hung on a nail against the wall.

"Walk on, my boy," said Bonaparte, pointing to the door; and as he followed him out he drew his mouth expressively on one side, and made the lash of the little horsewhip stick out of his pocket, and shake up and down.

Tant' Sannie felt half sorry for the lad; but she could not help laughing, it was always so funny when one was going to have a whipping, and it would do him good. Anyhow he would forget all about it when the places were healed. Had not she been beaten many times, and been all the better for it?

Bonaparte took up a lighted candle that had been

left burning on the kitchen table, and told the boy to
walk before him. They went to the fuel-house. It
was a little stone erection that jutted out from the
side of the wagon-house. It was low, and without a
window; and the dried dung was piled in one corner,
and the coffee-mill stood in another, fastened on the
top of a short post about three feet high. Bonaparte
took the padlock off the rough door.

"Walk in, my lad," he said.

Waldo obeyed sullenly; one place to him was much
the same as another. He had no objection to being
locked up.

Bonaparte followed him in, and closed the door
carefully. He put the light down on the heap of dung
in the corner, and quietly introduced his hand under
his coat-tails, and drew slowly from his pocket the end
of a rope, which he concealed behind him.

"I'm very sorry, exceedingly sorry, Waldo, my lad,
that you should have acted in this manner. It grieves
me," said Bonaparte.

He moved round towards the boy's back. He hardly
liked the look in the fellow's eyes, though he stood
there motionless. If he should spring on him!

So he drew the rope out very carefully, and shifted
round to the wooden post. There was a slip-knot in
one end of the rope, and a sudden movement drew the
boy's hands to his back and passed it round them. It
was an instant's work to drag it twice round the
wooden post: then Bonaparte was safe.

For a moment the boy struggled to free himself;
then he knew that he was powerless, and stood still.

"Horses that kick must have their legs tied," said
Bonaparte, as he passed the other end of the rope
round the boy's knees. "And now, my dear Waldo,"

taking the whip out of his pocket, "I am going to beat you."

He paused for a moment. It was perfectly quiet; they could hear each other's breath.

"'Chasten thy son while there is hope,'" said Bonaparte, "'and let not thy soul spare for his crying.' Those are God's words. I shall act as a father to you, Waldo. I think we had better have your naked back."

He took out his penknife, and slit the shirt down from the shoulder to the waist.

"Now," said Bonaparte, "I hope the Lord will bless and sanctify to you what I am going to do to you."

The first cut ran from the shoulder across the middle of the back; the second fell exactly in the same place. A shudder passed through the boy's frame.

"Nice, eh?" said Bonaparte, peeping round into his face, speaking with a lisp, as though to a very little child. "*Nith, eh?*"

But the eyes were black and lustreless, and seemed not to see him. When he had given sixteen, Bonaparte paused in his work to wipe a little drop of blood from his whip.

"Cold, eh? What makes you shiver so? Perhaps you would like to pull up your shirt? But I've not quite done yet."

When he had finished he wiped the whip again, and put it back in his pocket. He cut the rope through with his penknife, and then took up the light.

"You don't seem to have found your tongue yet. Forgotten how to cry?" said Bonaparte, patting him on the cheek.

The boy looked up at him — not sullenly, not angrily. There was a wild, fitful terror in the eyes

Bonaparte made haste to go out and shut the door, and leave him alone in the darkness. He himself was afraid of that look.

. . . . . .

It was almost morning. Waldo lay with his face upon the ground at the foot of the fuel-heap. There was a round hole near the top of the door, where a knot of wood had fallen out, and a stream of gray light came in through it.

Ah, it was going to end at last! Nothing lasts forever, not even the night. How was it he had never thought of that before? For in all that long dark night he had been very strong, had never been tired, never felt pain, had run on and on, up and down, up and down; he had not dared to stand still, and he had not known it would end. He had been so strong, that when he struck his head with all his force upon the stone wall it did not stun him nor pain him — only made him laugh. That was a dreadful night. When he clasped his hands frantically and prayed, "O God, my beautiful God, my sweet God, once, only once, let me feel you near me to-night!" he could not feel Him. He prayed aloud, very loud, and he got no answer; when he listened it was all quite quiet — as when the priests of Baal cried aloud to their god — "O Baal, hear us! O Baal, hear us!" but Baal was gone a-hunting.

That was a long wild night, and wild thoughts came and went in it, but they left their marks behind them forever; for, as years cannot pass without leaving their traces behind them, neither can nights into which are forced the thoughts and sufferings of years. And now the dawn was coming, and at last he was very tired. He shivered, and tried to draw the shirt up over his shoulders. They were getting stiff. He had never known they were cut in the night. He looked up at the white light that came in through the hole at the top of the door and shuddered. Then he turned his face back to the ground, and slept again.

Some hours later Bonaparte came towards the fuel-house with a lump of bread in his hand. He opened the door, and peered in; then entered, and touched the fellow with his boot. Seeing that he breathed heavily, though he did not rouse, Bonaparte threw the bread down on the ground. He was alive, that was one thing. He bent over him, and carefully scratched open one of the cuts with the nail of his forefinger, examining with much interest his last night's work. He would have to count his sheep himself that day; the boy was literally cut up. He locked the door, and went away again.

"Oh, Lyndall," said Em, entering the dining-room, and bathed in tears, that afternoon, "I have been begging Bonaparte to let him out, and he won't."

"The more you beg the more he will not," said Lyndall.

She was cutting out aprons on the table.

"Oh, but it's late, and I think they want to kill him," said Em, weeping bitterly; and finding that no more consolation was to be gained from her cousin, she went off blubbering, "I wonder you can cut out aprons when Waldo is shut up like that."

For ten minutes after she was gone Lyndall worked on quietly; then she folded up her stuff, rolled it tightly together, and stood before the closed door of the sitting-room with her hands closely clasped. A flush rose to her face; she opened the door quickly, and walked in, went to the nail on which the key of the fuel-room hung. Bonaparte and Tant' Sannie sat there, and saw her.

"What do you want?" they asked together.

"This key," she said, holding it up, and looking at them.

"Do you mean her to have it?" said Tant' Sannie, in Dutch.

"Why don't you stop her?" asked Bonaparte, in English.

"Why don't you take it from her?" said Tant' Sannie.

So they looked at each other, talking, while Lyndall walked to the fuel-house with the key, her underlip bitten in.

"Waldo," she said, as she helped him to stand up, and twisted his arm about her waist to support him, "we will not be children always; we shall have the power too, some day." She kissed his naked shoulder with her soft little mouth. It was all the comfort her young soul could give him.

CHAPTER XIII.

HE MAKES LOVE.

"Here," said Tant' Sannie to her Hottentot maid, "I have been in this house four years, and never been up in the loft. Fatter women than I go up ladders; I will go up to-day, and see what it is like, and put it to rights up there. You bring the little ladder, and stand at the bottom."

"There's one would be sorry if you were to fall," said the Hottentot maid, leering at Bonaparte's pipe, that lay on the table.

"Hold your tongue, jade," said her mistress, trying to conceal a pleased smile, "and go and fetch the ladder."

There was a never-used trap-door at one end of the sitting-room; this the Hottentot maid pushed open, and setting the ladder against it, the Boer-woman with some danger and difficulty climbed into the loft. Then the Hottentot maid took the ladder away, as her husband was mending the wagon-house, and needed it; but the trap-door was left open.

For a little while Tant' Sannie poked about among the empty bottles and skins, and looked at the bag of peaches that Waldo was supposed to have liked so; then she sat down near the trap-door, beside a barrel of salt mutton. She found that the pieces of meat were much too large, and took out her clasp-knife to divide them.

That was always the way when one left things to servants, she grumbled to herself; but when once she was married to her husband Bonaparte, it would not matter whether a sheep spoiled or no — when once his rich aunt with the dropsy was dead. She smiled as she dived her hand into the pickle-water.

At that instant her niece entered the room below, closely followed by Bonaparte, with his head on one side, smiling mawkishly. Had Tant' Sannie spoken at that moment, the life of Bonaparte Blenkins would have run a wholly different course; as it was, she remained silent, and neither noticed the open trap-door above their heads.

"Sit there, my love," said Bonaparte, motioning Trana into her aunt's elbow-chair, and drawing another close up in front of it, in which he seated himself. "There, put your feet upon the stove, too. Your aunt has gone out somewhere. Long have I waited for this auspicious event!"

Trana, who understood not one word of English, sat down in the chair, and wondered if this was one of the strange customs of other lands, that an old gentleman may bring his chair up to yours, and sit with his knees touching you. She had been five days in Bonaparte's company, and feared the old man, and disliked his nose.

"How long have I desired this moment!" said Bonaparte. "But that aged relative of thine is always casting her unhallowed shadow upon us. Look into my eyes, Trana."

Bonaparte knew that she comprehended not a syllable; but he understood that it is the eye, the tone, the action, and not at all the rational word, that touches the love-chords. He saw she changed color.

"All night," said Bonaparte, "I lie awake; I see
nought but thy angelic countenance. I open my arms
to receive thee — where art thou, where? Thou art
not there!" said Bonaparte, suiting the action to the
words, and spreading out his arms, and drawing them
to his breast.

"Oh, please, I don't understand," said Trana, "I
want to go away."

"Yes, yes," said Bonaparte, leaning back in his
chair, to her great relief, and pressing his hands
on his heart, "since first thy amethystine countenance was impressed *here* — what have I not suffered,
what have I not felt? Oh the pangs unspoken,
burning as an ardent coal in a fiery and uncon-
taminated bosom!" said Bonaparte, bending forward
again.

"Dear Lord!" said Trana to herself, "how foolish
I have been! The old man has a pain in his stomach,
and now, as my aunt is out, he has come to me to
help him."

She smiled kindly at Bonaparte, and pushing past
him, went to the bedroom, quickly returning with a
bottle of red drops in her hand.

"They are very good for 'benaawdheit;' my mother
always drinks them," she said, holding the bottle out.

The face in the trap-door was a fiery red. Like a
tiger-cat ready to spring, Tant' Sannie crouched, with
the shoulder of mutton in her hand. Exactly beneath
her stood Bonaparte. She rose and clasped with both
arms the barrel of salt meat.

"What, rose of the desert, nightingale of the colony, that with thine amorous lay whilest the lonesome
night!" cried Bonaparte, seizing the hand that held
the "vonlicsense." "Nay, struggle not! Fly as a

10

stricken fawn into the arms that would embrace thee, thou — "

Here a stream of cold pickle-water, heavy with ribs and shoulders, descending on his head, abruptly terminated his speech. Half-blinded, Bonaparte looked up through the drops that hung from his eyelids, and saw the red face that looked down at him. With one wild cry he fled. As he passed out at the front door, a shoulder of mutton, well-directed, struck the black coat in the small of the back.

"Bring the ladder! bring the ladder! I will go after him!" cried the Boer-woman, as Bonaparte Blenkins wildly fled into the fields.

.   .   .   .

Late in the evening of the same day, Waldo knelt on the floor of his cabin. He bathed the foot of his dog which had been pierced by a thorn. The bruises on his own back had had five days to heal in, and, except a little stiffness in his movements, there was nothing remarkable about the boy.

The troubles of the young are soon over; they leave no external mark. If you wound the tree in its youth, the bark will quickly cover the gash; but when the tree is very old, peeling the bark off, and looking carefully, you will see the scar there still. All that is buried is not dead.

Waldo poured the warm milk over the little swollen foot; Doss lay very quiet, with tears in his eyes. Then there was a tap at the door. In an instant Doss looked wide awake, and winked the tears out from between his little lids.

"Come in," said Waldo, intent on his work; and slowly and cautiously the door opened.

"Good evening, Waldo, my boy," said Bonaparte

Blenkins in a mild voice, not venturing more than his nose within the door. "How are you this evening?"

Doss growled, and showed his little teeth, and tried to rise, but his paw hurt him so he whined.

"I'm very tired, Waldo, my boy," said Bonaparte, plaintively.

Doss showed his little white teeth again. His master went on with his work without looking round. There are some people at whose hands it is best not to look. At last he said,

"Come in."

Bonaparte stepped cautiously a little way into the room, and left the door open behind him. He looked at the boy's supper on the table.

"Waldo, I've had nothing to eat all day — I'm very hungry," he said.

"Eat!" said Waldo after a moment, bending lower over his dog.

"You won't go and tell her that I am here, will you, Waldo?" said Bonaparte, most uneasily. "You've heard how she used me, Waldo? I've been *badly* treated; you'll know yourself what it is, some day, when you can't carry on a little conversation with a lady, without having salt meat and pickle-water thrown at you. Waldo, look at me; do I look as a gentleman should?"

But the boy neither looked up nor answered, and Bonaparte grew more uneasy.

"You wouldn't go and tell her that I am here, would you?" said Bonaparte, whiningly. "There's no knowing what she would do to me. I've such trust in you, Waldo; I've always thought you such a promising lad, though you mayn't have known it, Waldo."

"Eat," said the boy, "I shall say nothing."

Bonaparte, who knew the truth when another spoke it, closed the door, carefully putting on the button. Then he looked to see that the curtain of the window was closely pulled down, and seated himself at the table. He was soon munching the cold meat and bread. Waldo knelt on the floor, bathing the foot with hands which the dog licked lovingly. Once only he glanced at the table, and turned away quickly.

"Ah, yes! I don't wonder that you can't look at me, Waldo," said Bonaparte; "my condition would touch any heart. You see, the water was fatty, and that has made all the sand stick to me; and my hair," said Bonaparte, tenderly touching the little fringe at the back of his head, "is all caked over like a little plank: you wouldn't think it was hair at all," said Bonaparte, plaintively. "I had to creep all along the stone walls for fear she'd see me, and with nothing on my head but a red handkerchief tied under my chin, Waldo; and to hide in a sloot the whole day, with not a mouthful of food, Waldo. And she gave me such a blow, just here," said Bonaparte.

He had cleared the plate of the last morsel, when Waldo rose and walked to the door.

"O Waldo, my dear boy, you are not going to call her," said Bonaparte, rising anxiously.

"I am going to sleep in the wagon," said the boy, opening the door.

"Oh, we can both sleep in this bed; there's plenty of room. Do stay, my boy, please."

But Waldo stepped out.

"It was such a little whip, Waldo," said Bonaparte, following him deprecatingly. "I didn't think it would hurt you so much. It was such a *little* whip.

I'm *sure* you did n't take the peaches. You are n't going to call her, Waldo, are you?"

But the boy walked off.

Bonaparte waited till his figure had passed round the front of the wagon-house, and then slipped out. He hid himself round the corner, but kept peeping out to see who was coming. He felt sure the boy was gone to call Tant' Sannie. His teeth chattered with inward cold as he looked round into the darkness, and thought of the snakes that might bite him, and the dreadful things that might attack him, and the dead that might arise out of their graves if he slept out in the field all night. But more than an hour passed, and no footstep approached.

Then Bonaparte made his way back to the cabin. He buttoned the door, and put the table against it, and, giving the dog a kick to silence his whining when the foot throbbed, he climbed into bed. He did not put out the light for fear of the ghost, but, worn out with the sorrows of the day, was soon asleep himself.

About four o'clock, Waldo, lying between the seats of the horse-wagon, was awakened by a gentle touch on his head.

Sitting up he espied Bonaparte looking through one of the windows with a lighted candle in his hand.

"I'm about to depart, my dear boy, before my enemies arise; and I could not leave without coming to bid you farewell," said Bonaparte.

Waldo looked at him.

"I shall always think of you with affection," said Bonaparte. "And there's that old hat of yours, if you could let me have it for a keepsake —"

"Take it," said Waldo.

"I thought you would say so, so I brought it with me," said Bonaparte, putting it on. "The Lord bless you, my dear boy. You have n't a few shillings, — just a trifle you don't need, — have you ?"

"Take the two shillings that are in the broken vase."

"May the blessing of my God rest upon you, my dear child," said Bonaparte; "may He guide and bless you. Give me your hand."

Waldo folded his arms closely, and lay down.

"Farewell, adieu!" said Bonaparte. "May the blessing of my God and my father's God rest on you, now and evermore."

With these words the head and nose withdrew themselves, and the light vanished from the window.

After a few moments the boy, lying in the wagon, heard stealthy footsteps as they passed the wagon-house and made their way down the road. He listened as they grew fainter and fainter, and at last died away altogether! and from that night the footstep of Bonaparte Blenkins was heard no more at the old farm.

PART II.

"And it was all play, and no one could tell what it had lived and worked for. A striving, and a striving, and an ending in nothing."

CHAPTER I.

TIMES AND SEASONS.

WALDO lay on his stomach on the sand. Since he prayed and howled to his God in the fuel-house, three years had passed.

They say that in the world to come, time is not measured out by months and years. Neither is it here. The soul's life has seasons of its own; periods not found in any calendar, times that years and months will not scan, but which are as deftly and sharply cut off from one another as the smoothly-arranged years which the earth's motion yields us.

To stranger eyes these divisions are not evident; but each, looking back at the little track his consciousness illuminates, sees it cut into distinct portions, whose boundaries are the termination of mental states.

As man differs from man, so differ these souls' years. The most material life is not devoid of them; the story of the most spiritual is told in them. And

it may chance that some, looking back, see the past
cut out after this fashion : —

I.

The year of infancy, where from the shadowy background of forgetfulness start out pictures of startling
clearness, disconnected, but brightly colored, and in-
delibly printed in the mind. Much that follows fades,
but the colors of those baby-pictures are permanent.

There rises, perhaps, a warm summer's evening; we
are seated on the doorstep; we have yet the taste of
the bread and milk in our mouth, and the red sunset
is reflected in our basin.

Then there is a dark night, where, waking with a
fear that there is some great being in the room, we
run from our own bed to another, creep close to some
large figure, and are comforted.

Then there is remembrance of the pride when, on
some one's shoulder, with our arms around his head,
we ride to see the little pigs, the new little pigs with
their curled tails and tiny snouts, — where do they
come from ?

Remembrance of delight in the feel and smell of the
first orange we ever see; of sorrow which makes us
put up our lip, and cry hard, when one morning we run
out to try and catch the dew-drops, and they melt and
wet our little fingers; of almighty and despairing
sorrow when we are lost behind the kraals, and cannot
see the house anywhere.

And then one picture starts out more vividly than
any.

There has been a thunder-storm; the ground, as far
as the eye can reach, is covered with white hail; the

clouds are gone, and overhead a deep blue sky is showing; far off a great rainbow rests on the white earth.
We, standing in a window to look, feel the cool, un-
speakably sweet wind blowing in on us, and a feeling
of longing comes over us, — unutterable longing, we
cannot tell for what. We are so small, our head only
reaches as high as the first three panes. We look at
the white earth, and the rainbow, and the blue sky;
and oh, we want it, we want, — we do not know what.
We cry as though our heart was broken. When one
lifts our little body from the window we cannot tell
what ails us. We run away to play.

So looks the first year.

II.

Now the pictures become continuous and connected.
Material things still rule, but the spiritual and intellectual take their places.

In the dark night when we are afraid, we pray
and shut our eyes. We press our fingers very hard
upon the lids, and see dark spots moving round
and round, and we know they are heads and wings
of angels sent to take care of us, seen dimly in
the dark as they move round our bed. It is very
consoling.

In the day we learn our letters, and are troubled
because we cannot see why k-n-o-w should be know,
and p-s-a-l-m psalm. They tell us it is so because it *is*
so. We are not satisfied; we hate to learn; we like
better to build little stone houses. We can build them
as we please, and know the reason for them.

Other joys too we have, incomparably greater than
even the building of stone houses.

We are run through with a shudder of delight when
in the red sand we come on one of those white wax
flowers that lie between their two green leaves flat on
the sand. We hardly dare pick them, but we feel
compelled to do so; and we smell and smell till the
delight becomes almost pain. Afterwards we pull the
green leaves softly into pieces to see the silk threads
run across.

Beyond the "kopje" grow some pale-green, hairy-
leaved bushes. We are so small, they meet over our
head; and we sit among them, and kiss them, and they
love us back; it seems as though they were alive.

One day we sit there and look up at the blue sky,
and down at our fat little knees; and suddenly it
strikes us, Who are we? This *I*, what is it? We try
to look in upon ourself, and ourself beats back upon
ourself. Then we get up in great fear, and run home
as hard as we can. We can't tell any one what frightened us. We never quite lose that feeling of *self*
again.

III.

And then a new time rises. We are seven years
old. We can read now — read the Bible. Best of all
we like the story of Elijah in his cave at Horeb, and
the still small voice.

One day, — a notable one, — we read on the "kopje,"
and discover the fifth chapter of Matthew, and read it
all through. It is a new gold mine. Then we tuck
the Bible under our arm, and rush home. They did n't
know it was wicked to take your things again if some
one took them, wicked to go to law, wicked to — !
We are quite breathless when we get to the house;

we tell them we have discovered a chapter they never heard of; we tell them what it says. The old wise people tell us they knew all about it. Our discovery is a mare's-nest to them; but to us it is very real. The Ten Commandments and the old "Thou shalt" we have heard about long enough, and don't care about it; but this new law sets us on fire. We will deny ourself. Our little wagon that we have made, we give to the little Kaffirs. We keep quiet when they throw sand at us, — feeling, oh, so happy! We conscientiously put the cracked teacup for ourselves at breakfast, and take the burnt roaster-cake. We save our money and buy three pence of tobacco for the Hottentot maid who calls us names. We are exotically virtuous. At night we are profoundly religious; even the ticking watch says, "Eternity, eternity! hell, hell, hell!" and the silence talks of God, and the things that shall be.

Occasionally, also, unpleasantly shrewd questions begin to be asked by some one, we know not who, who sits somewhere behind our shoulder. We get to know him better afterwards. Now we carry the questions to the grown-up people, and they give us answers. We are more or less satisfied for the time. The grown-up people are very wise, and they say it was kind of God to make hell, and very loving of Him to send men there; and besides, He couldn't help Himself; and they are very wise, we think, so we believe them — more or less.

IV.

Then a new time comes, of which the leading feature is that the shrewd questions are asked louder.

We carry them to the grown-up people ; they answer us, and we are *not* satisfied.

And now between us and the dear old world of the senses the spirit-world begins to peep in, and wholly clouds it over. What are the flowers to us ? They are fuel waiting for the great burning. We look at the walls of the farm-house and the matter-of-fact sheep kraals, with the merry sunshine playing over all, and do not see it. But we see a great white throne, and Him that sits on it. Around Him stand a great multitude that no man can number, harpers harping with their harps, a thousand times ten thousand, and thousands of thousands. How white are their robes, washed in the blood of the Lamb! And the music rises higher, and rends the vault of heaven with its unutterable sweetness. And we, as we listen, ever and anon, as it sinks on the sweetest lowest note, hear a groan of the damned from below. We shudder in the sunlight.

"The torment," says Jeremy Taylor, whose sermons our father reads aloud in the evening, "comprises as many torments as the body of man has joints, sinews, arteries, etc., being caused by that penetrating and real fire of which this temporal fire is but a painted fire. What comparison will there be between burning for a hundred years' space and to be burning without intermission as long as God is God!"

We remember the sermon there in the sunlight. One comes and asks why we sit there, nodding so moodily ? Ah, they do not see what we see!

> " A moment's time, a narrow space,
>   Divides me from that heavenly place,
>   Or shuts me up in hell."

So says Wesley's hymn, which we sing evening by evening. What matter sunshine and walls, men and sheep?

"The things which are seen are temporal, but the things which are not seen are eternal." They are real.

The Bible we bear always in our breast; its pages are our food; we learn to repeat it. We weep much, for in sunshine and in shade, in the early morning or the late evening, in the field or in the house, the devil walks with us. He comes to us a real person, — copper-colored face, head a little on one side, forehead knit, — asking questions. Believe me, it were better to be followed by three deadly diseases than by him. He is never silenced; without mercy. Though the drops of blood stand out on your heart, he will put his question. Softly he comes up (we are only a wee bit child): "Is it good of God to make hell? Was it kind of Him to let no one be forgiven unless Jesus Christ died?"

Then he goes off, and leaves us writhing. Presently he comes back.

"Do you love Him?" — waits a little. "Do you love Him? You will be lost if you don't."

We say we try to.

"But do you?" Then he goes off.

It is nothing to him if we go quite mad with fear at our own wickedness. He asks on, the questioning devil; he cares nothing what he says. We long to tell some one, that he may share our pain. We do not yet know that the cup of affliction is made with such a narrow mouth that only one lip can drink at a time, and that each man's cup is made to match his lip.

One day we try to tell some one. Then a grave head is shaken solemnly at us. We are wicked, very wicked, it says; we ought not to have such thoughts. God is good, very good. We are wicked, very wicked. That is the comfort we get. Wicked! Oh, Lord! do we not know it? Is it not the sense of our own exceeding wickedness that is drying up our young heart, filling it with sand, making all life a dust-bin for us?

Wicked? We know it! Too vile to live, too vile to die, too vile to creep over this, God's earth, and move among His believing men. Hell is the one place for him who hates his master, and there we do not want to go. This is the comfort we get from the old.

And once again we try to seek for comfort. This time great eyes look at us wondering, and lovely little lips say, —

"If it makes you so unhappy to think of these things, why do you not think of something else, and forget?"

Forget! We turn away, and shrink into ourself. Forget, and think of other things! Oh, God! do they not understand that the material world is but a film, through every pore of which God's awful spirit-world is shining through on us? We keep as far from others as we can.

One night — a rare, clear, moonlight night — we kneel in the window; every one else is asleep, but we kneel, reading by the moonlight. It is a chapter in the prophets telling how the chosen people of God shall be carried on the Gentiles' shoulders. Surely the devil might leave us alone; there is not much handle for him there. But presently he comes.

"Is it right there should be a chosen people?
To Him, who is father to all, should not all be
dear?"

How can we answer him? We were feeling so
good till he came! We put our head down on the
Bible and blister it with tears; then we fold our hands
over our head, and pray till our teeth grind together.
Oh, that from that spirit-world, so real and yet so
silent, that surrounds us, one word would come to
guide us! We are left alone with this devil; and God
does not whisper to us. Suddenly we seize the Bible,
turning it round and round, and say hurriedly, —

"It will be God's voice speaking to us, — His voice
as though we heard it."

We yearn for a token from the inexorably Silent
One.

We turn the book, put our finger down on a page,
and bend to read by the moonlight. It is God's answer. We tremble.

"Then fourteen years after I went up again to
Jerusalem with Barnabas, and took Titus with me
also."

For an instant our imagination seizes it; we are
twisting, twirling, trying to make an allegory. The
fourteen years are fourteen months; we are Paul, and
the devil is Barnabas; Titus is— Then suddenly a
loathing comes to us; we are liars and hypocrites;
we are trying to deceive ourselves. What is Paul to
us? and Jerusalem? who are Barnabas and Titus?
We know not the men. Before we know we seize the
book, swing it round our head, and fling it with all
our might to the farther end of the room. We put
down our head again and weep. Youth and ignorance,
— is there anything else that can weep so? It is as

though the tears were drops of blood congealed beneath the eyelids; nothing else is like those tears.
After a long time we are weak with crying, and lie
silent, and by chance we knock against the wood that
stops the broken pane. It falls. Upon our hot, stiff
face a sweet breath of wind blows. We raise our
head, and with our swollen eyes look out at the beautiful still world, and the sweet night-wind blows in upon
us, holy and gentle, like a loving breath from the lips
of God. Over us a deep peace comes, — a calm, still
joy. The tears now flow readily and softly. Oh, the unutterable gladness! At last, at last we have found it!
"The peace with God." "The sense of sins forgiven."
All doubt vanished, God's voice in the soul, the Holy
Spirit filling us! We feel Him! we feel Him! Oh,
Jesus Christ! through you, through you, this joy! We
press our hands upon our breast, and look upward
with adoring gladness. Soft waves of bliss break
through us. "The peace with God." "The sense of
sins forgiven." Methodists and Revivalists say the
words, and the mocking world shoots out its lip, and
walks by smiling — "Hypocrite!"

There are more fools, and fewer hypocrites than the
wise world dreams of. The hypocrite is rare as ice-
bergs in the tropics; the fool common as buttercups
beside a water-furrow: whether you go this way or
that, you tread on him; you dare not look at your
own reflection in the water but you see one. There is
no cant phrase, rotten with age, but it was the dress
of a living body; none but at heart it signifies a real
bodily or mental condition which some have passed
through.

After hours and nights of frenzied fear of the
supernatural desire to appease the Power above, a

fierce quivering excitement in every inch of nerve and blood-vessel, there comes a time when nature cannot endure longer, and the spring long bent recoils. We sink down emasculated. Up creeps the deadly delicious calm.

"I have blotted out as a cloud thy sins, and as a thick cloud thy trespasses, and will remember them no more forever." We weep with soft transporting joy.

A few experience this; many imagine they experience it; one here and there lies about it. In the main, "The peace with God; a sense of sins forgiven," stands for a certain mental and physical reaction. Its reality those know who have felt it.

And we, on that moonlight night, put down our head on the window, "Oh, God! we are happy, happy; thy child forever. Oh, thank you, God!" and we drop asleep.

Next morning the Bible we kiss. We are God's forever. We go out to work, and it goes happily all day, happily all night; but hardly so happily, not happily at all, the next day; and the next night the devil asks us, "Where is your Holy Spirit?"

We cannot tell.

So month by month, summer and winter, the old life goes on — reading, praying, weeping, praying. They tell us we become utterly stupid. We know it. Even the multiplication table we learned with so much care we forget. The physical world recedes farther and farther from us. Truly we love not the world, neither the things that are in it. Across the bounds of sleep our grief follows us. When we wake in the night we are sitting up in bed weeping bitterly, or find ourself outside in the moonlight, dressed, and

11

walking up and down, and wringing our hands, and we cannot tell how we came there. So pass two years, as men reckon them.

V.

Then a new time.

Before us there were three courses possible, — to go mad, to die, to sleep.

We take the last course; or Nature takes it for us.

All things take rest in sleep; the beasts, birds, the very flowers close their eyes, and the streams are still in winter; all things take rest; then why not the human reason also? So the questioning devil in us drops asleep, and in that sleep a beautiful dream rises for us. Though you hear all the dreams of men, you will hardly find a prettier one than ours. It ran so:

In the centre of all things is a Mighty Heart, which, having begotten all things, loves them; and, having born them into life, beats with great throbs of love towards them. No death for His dear insects, no hell for His dear men, no burning up for His dear world — His own, own world that he has made. In the end all will be beautiful. Do not ask us how we make our dream tally with facts; the glory of a dream is this, — that it despises facts, and makes its own. Our dream saves us from going mad; that is enough.

Its peculiar point of sweetness lay here. When the Mighty Heart's yearning of love became too great for other expression, it shaped itself into the sweet Rose of Heaven, the beloved Man-god.

Jesus! you Jesus of our dream! how we loved you; no Bible tells of you as we knew you. Your sweet hands held ours fast; your sweet voice said always,

"I am here, my loved one, not far off; put your arms about Me, and hold fast."

We find Him in everything in those days. When the little weary lamb we drive home drags its feet we seize on it, and carry it with its head against our face. His little lamb! We feel we have got Him.

When the drunken Kaffir lies by the road in the sun we draw his blanket over his head, and put green branches of milk-bush on it. His Kaffir; why should the sun hurt him?

In the evening, when the clouds lift themselves like gates, and the red lights shine through them, we cry; for in such glory He will come, and the hands that ache to touch Him will hold Him, and we shall see the beautiful hair and eyes of our God. "Lift up your heads, O ye gates; and be ye lifted up, ye everlasting doors, and the King of glory shall come in!"

The purple flowers, the little purple flowers, are His eyes, looking at us. We kiss them, and kneel alone on the flat, rejoicing over them. And "the wilderness and the solitary place shall be glad for Him, and the desert shall rejoice and blossom as a rose."

If ever in our tearful, joyful ecstasy the poor, sleepy, half-dead devil should raise his head, we laugh at him. It is not his hour now.

"If there should be a hell, after all!" he mutters. "If your God should be cruel! If there should be no God! If you should find out it is all imagination! If —"

We laugh at him. When a man sits in the warm sunshine, do you ask him for proof of it? He feels — that is all. And we feel — that is all. We want no proof of our God. We feel, we feel!

We do not believe in our God because the Bible tells us of Him.   We believe in the Bible because He tells us of it.   We feel Him, we feel Him, we feel — — that is all!   And the poor half-swamped devil mutters, —

"But if the day should come when you do not feel?"

And we laugh, and cry him down.

"It will never come — never," and the poor devil slinks to sleep again, with his tail between his legs. Fierce assertion many times repeated is hard to stand against; only time separates the truth from the lie. So we dream on.

One day we go with our father to town, to church. The townspeople rustle in their silks, and the men in their sleek cloth, and settle themselves in their pews, and the light shines in through the windows on the artificial flowers in the women's bonnets.   We have the same miserable feeling that we have in a shop where all the clerks are very smart.   We wish our father had n't brought us to town, and we were out on the karroo.   Then the man in the pulpit begins to preach.   His text is "He that believeth not shall be damned."

The day before the magistrate's clerk, who was an atheist, has died in the street, struck by lightning.

The man in the pulpit mentions no name; but he talks of "The hand of God made visible among us." He tells us how, when the white stroke fell, quivering and naked, the soul fled, robbed of his earthly filament, and lay at the footstool of God; how over its head has been poured out the wrath of the Mighty One, whose existence it has denied; and, quivering and terrified, it has fled to the everlasting shade.

We, as we listen, half start up; every drop of blood in our body has rushed to our head. He lies! he lies! he lies! That man in the pulpit lies! Will no one stop him? Have none of them heard — do none of them know, that when the poor dark soul shut its eyes on earth it opened them in the still light of heaven, that there is no wrath where God's face is, that if one could once creep to the footstool of God, there is everlasting peace there, like the fresh stillness of the early morning? While the atheist lay wondering and afraid, God bent down and said, "My child, *here* I am — I, whom you have not known; I, whom you have not believed in; I am here. I sent My messenger, the white sheet-lightning, to call you home. I am here."

Then the poor soul turned to the light; its weakness and pain were gone forever.

Have they not known, have they not heard, who it is rules?

"For a little moment have I hidden my face from thee; but with everlasting kindness will I have mercy upon thee, saith the Lord thy Redeemer."

We mutter on to ourself, till some one pulls us violently by the arm to remind us we are in church. We see nothing but our own ideas.

Presently every one turns to pray. There are six hundred souls lifting themselves to the Everlasting Light.

Behind us sit two pretty ladies; one hands her scent-bottle softly to the other, and a mother pulls down her little girl's frock. One lady drops her handkerchief; a gentleman picks it up; she blushes. The women in the choir turn softly the leaves of their tune-books, to be ready when the praying is done. It is as though they thought more of the singing than the Everlasting Father. Oh, would it not be more worship of Him to sit alone in the karroo and kiss one little purple flower that He had made ? Is it not mockery? Then the thought comes, " *What doest thou here, Elijah ?* " We who judge, what are we better than they ? — rather worse. Is it any excuse to say, "I am but a child and must come " ? Does God allow any soul to step in between the spirit he made and himself ? What do we there in that place, where all the words are lies against the All Father ? Filled with horror, we turn and flee out of the place. On the pavement we smite our foot, and swear in our child's soul never again to enter those places where men come to sing and pray. We are questioned afterwards. Why was it we went out of the church?

How can we explain ? — we stand silent. Then we are pressed further, and we try to tell. Then a head is shaken solemnly at us. No one *can* think it wrong to go to the house of the Lord; it is the idle excuse of a wicked boy. When will we think seriously of our souls, and love going to church ? We are wicked, very wicked. And we — we slink away and go alone to cry. Will it be always so ? Whether we hate and doubt, or whether we believe and love, to our dearest, are we to seem always wicked ?

We do not yet know that in the soul's search for truth the bitterness lies here, the striving cannot always hide itself among the thoughts ; sooner or later it will clothe itself in outward action ; then it steps in and divides between the soul and what it loves. All things on earth have their price ; and for truth we pay the dearest. We barter it for love and sympathy. The road to honor is paved with thorns ; but on the path to truth at every step you set your foot down on your own heart.

VI.

Then at last a new time — the time of waking : short, sharp, and not pleasant, as wakings often are.

Sleep and dreams exist on this condition — that no one wake the dreamer.

And now life takes us up between her finger and thumb, shakes us furiously, till our poor nodding head is wellnigh rolled from our shoulders, and she sets us down a little hardly on the bare earth, bruised and sore, but preternaturally wide awake.

We have said in our days of dreaming, " Injustice and wrong are a seeming ; pain is a shadow. Our God, He is real, He who made all things, and He only is Love."

Now life takes us by the neck and shows us a few other things, — new-made graves with the red sand flying about them ; eyes that we love with the worms eating them ; evil men walking, sleek and fat; the whole terrible hurly-burly of the thing called life, — and she says, " What do you think of these ? " We dare not say, " Nothing." We feel them ; they are very real. But we try to lay our hands about and feel that other thing we felt before. In the dark night in the fuel-room we cry to our beautiful dream-god — " Oh, let us come near you, and lay our head against your feet. Now in our hour of need be near us." But He is not there ; He is gone away. The old questioning devil is there.

We must have been awakened sooner or later.

The imagination cannot always triumph over reality, the desire over truth. We must have been awakened. If it was done a little sharply, what matter? it was done thoroughly, and it had to be done.

VII.

And a new life begins for us — a new time, a life as cold as that of a man who sits on the pinnacle of an iceberg and sees the glittering crystals all about him. The old looks indeed like a long hot delirium, peopled with phantasies. The new is cold enough.

Now we have no God. We have had two, — the old God that our fathers handed down to us, that we hated, and never liked; the new one that we made for ourselves, that we loved; but now He has flitted away from us, and we see what He was made of — the shadow of our highest ideal, crowned and throned. Now we have no God.

"The fool hath said in his heart, There is no God." It may be so. Most things said or written have been the work of fools.

This thing is certain — he is a fool who says, "No man hath said in his heart, There is no God."

It has been said many thousand times in hearts with profound bitterness of earnest faith.

We do not cry and weep; we sit down with cold eyes and look at the world. We are not miserable. Why should we be? We eat and drink, and sleep all night; but the dead are not colder.

And, we say it slowly, but without sighing, "Yes, we see it now; there is no God."

And, we add, growing a little colder yet, "There is no justice. The ox dies in the yoke, beneath its

master's whip; it turns its anguish-filled eyes on the
sunlight, but there is no sign of recompense to be
made it. The black man is shot like a dog, and it
goes well with the shooter. The innocent are accused, and the accuser triumphs. If you will take the
trouble to scratch the surface anywhere, you will
see under the skin a sentient being writhing in im-
potent anguish."

And we say further, — and our heart is as the heart
of the dead for coldness, — "There is no order; all
things are driven about by a blind chance."

What a soul drinks in with its mother's milk will
not leave it in a day. From our earliest hour we
have been taught that the thought of the heart, the
shaping of the rain-cloud, the amount of wool that
grows on a sheep's back, the length of a draught, and
the growing of the corn, depend on nothing that
moves immutable, at the heart of all things ; but on
the changeable will of a changeable being, whom our
prayers can alter. To us, from the beginning, Nature
has been but a poor plastic thing, to be toyed with
this way or that, as man happens to please his deity
or not, to go to church or not, to say his prayers
right or not, to travel on a Sunday or not. Was it
possible for us in an instant to see Nature as she is
— the flowing vestment of an unchanging reality ?
When a soul breaks free from the arms of a superstition, bits of the claws and talons break themselves off
in him. It is not the work of a day to squeeze them
out.

And so, for us, the human-like driver and guide
being gone, all existence, as we look out at it with
our chilled, wondering eyes, is an aimless rise and
swell of shifting waters. In all that weltering chaos

we can see no spot so large as a man's hand on which
we may plant our foot.

Whether a man believes in a human-like God or
no is a small thing.   Whether he looks into the mental and physical world and sees no relation between
cause and effect, no order, but a blind chance sport-
ing, this is the mightiest fact that can be recorded in
any spiritual existence.   It were almost a mercy to cut
his throat, if indeed he does not do it for himself.

We, however, do not cut our throats.   To do so
would imply some desire and feeling, and we have
no desire and no feeling ; we are only cold.   We do
not wish to live, and we do not wish to die.   One
day a snake curls itself round the waist of a Kaffir
woman.   We take it in our hand, swing it round and
round, and fling it on the ground — dead.   Every
one looks at us with eyes of admiration.   We almost
laugh.   Is it wonderful to risk that for which we
care nothing ?

In truth, nothing matters.   This dirty little world,
full of confusion, and the blue rag, stretched overhead for a sky, is so low we could touch it with our
hand.

Existence is a great pot, and the old Fate who stirs
it round cares nothing what rises to the top and what
goes down, and laughs when the bubbles burst.   And
we do not care.   Let it boil about.   Why should we
trouble ourselves ?   Nevertheless the physical sensa-
tions are real.   Hunger hurts, and thirst, therefore we
eat and drink ; inaction pains us, therefore we work
like galley-slaves.   No one demands it, but we set ourselves to build a great dam in red sand beyond the
graves.   In the gray dawn, before the sheep are let
out, we work at it.   All day, while the young ostriches

we tend feed about us, we work on through the fiercest
heat. The people wonder what new spirit has seized
us now. They do not know we are working for life.
We bear the greatest stones, and feel a satisfaction
when we stagger under them, and are hurt by a pang
that shoots through our chest. While we eat our dinner we carry on baskets full of earth, as though the
devil drove us. The Kaffir servants have a story
that at night a witch and two white oxen come to
help us. No wall, they say, could grow so quickly
under one man's hands.

At night, alone in our cabin, we sit no more brooding over the fire. What should we think of now ?
All is emptiness. So we take the old arithmetic ;
and the multiplication table, which with so much
pains we learned long ago and forgot directly, we learn
now in a few hours, and never forget again. We take
a strange satisfaction in working arithmetical prob-
lems. We pause in our building to cover the stones
with figures and calculations. We save money for a
Latin Grammar and an Algebra, and carry them about
in our pockets, poring over them as over our Bible of
old. We have thought we were utterly stupid, inca-
pable of remembering anything, of learning anything.
Now we find that all is easy. Has a new soul crept
into this old body, that even our intellectual faculties
are changed ? We marvel ; not perceiving that what
a man expends in prayer and ecstasy he cannot have
over for acquiring knowledge. You never shed a tear,
or create a beautiful image, or quiver with emotion,
but you pay for it at the practical, calculating end of
your nature. You have just so much force ; when the
one channel runs over the other runs dry.

And now we turn to Nature. All these years we

have lived beside her, and we have never seen her; now we open our eyes and look at her.

The rocks have been to us a blur of brown; we bend over them, and the disorganized masses dissolve into a many-colored, many-shaped, carefully-arranged form of existence. Here masses of rainbow-tinted crystals, half-fused together; there bands of smooth gray and red methodically overlying each other. This rock here is covered with a delicate silver tracery, in some mineral, resembling leaves and branches; there on the flat stone, on which we so often have sat to weep and pray, we look down, and see it covered with the fossil footprints of great birds and the beautiful skeleton of a fish. We have often tried to picture in our mind what the fossiled remains of creatures must be like, and all the while we sat on them. We have been so blinded by thinking and feeling that we have never seen the world.

The flat plain has been to us a reach of monotonous red. We look at it, and every handful of sand starts into life. That wonderful people, the ants, we learn to know; see them make war and peace, play and work, and build their huge palaces. And that smaller people we make acquaintance with, who live in the flowers. The "bitto" flower has been for us a mere blur of yellow; we find its heart composed of a hundred perfect flowers, the homes of the tiny black people with red stripes, who move in and out in that little yellow city. Every bluebell has its inhabitant. Every day the karroo shows us a new wonder sleeping in its teeming bosom. On our way to work we pause and stand to see the ground-spider make its trap, bury itself in the sand, and then wait for the falling in of its enemy. Farther on walks a horned beetle, and near him starts open the door of a spider, who peeps out carefully and quickly pulls it down again. On a karroo-bush a green fly is laying her silver eggs. We carry them home, and see the shells pierced, the spotted grub come out, turn into a green fly, and flit away. We are not satisfied with what Nature shows us, and will see something for ourselves. Under the white hen we put a dozen eggs, and break one daily, to see the white spot wax into the chicken. We are not excited or enthusiastic about it; but a man is not to lay his throat open, he must think of something. So we plant seeds in rows on our dam-wall, and pull one up daily to see how it goes with them. Alladeen buried her wonderful stone, and a golden palace sprang up at her feet. We do far more. We put a brown seed in the earth, and a living thing starts out — starts upwards — why, no more than Alladeen can we say — starts upwards, and does not desist till it is higher than our heads, sparkling with dew in the early morning, glittering with yellow blossoms, shaking brown seeds with little embryo souls on to the ground. We look at it solemnly, from the time it consists of two leaves peeping above the ground and a soft white root, till we have to raise our faces to look at it; but we find no reason for that upward starting.

We look into dead ducks aud lambs. In the evening we carry them home, spread newspapers on the floor, and lie working with them till midnight. With a startled feeling near akin to ecstasy we open the lump of flesh called a heart, and find little doors and strings inside. We feel them, and put the heart away, but every now and then return to look, and to feel them again. Why we like them so we can hardly tell.

A gander drowns itself in our dam. We take it out, and open it on the bank, and kneel, looking at it. Above are the organs divided by delicate tissues; below are the intestines artistically curved in a spiral form, and each tier covered by a delicate network of blood-vessels standing out red against the faint blue background. Each branch of the blood-vessels is comprised of a trunk, bifurcating and rebifurcating into the most delicate hair-like threads, symmetrically arranged. We are struck with its singular beauty. And, moreover — and here we drop from our kneeling into a sitting posture — this also we remark: Of that same exact shape and outline is our thorn-tree seen against the sky in mid-winter; of that shape also is delicate metallic tracery between our rocks; in that exact path does our water flow when without a furrow we lead it from the dam; so shaped are the antlers of the horned beetle. How are these things related that such deep union should exist between them all? Is it chance? Or are they not all the fine branches of one trunk, whose sap flows through us all? That would explain it. We nod over the gander's inside.

This thing we call existence, — is it not a something which has its roots far down below in the dark, and its branches stretching out into the immensity above, which we among the branches cannot see? Not a chance jumble; a living thing, a *One*. The thought gives us intense satisfaction, we cannot tell why.

We nod over the gander; then start up suddenly, look into the blue sky, throw the dead gander and the refuse into the dam, and go to work again.

And so it comes to pass in time that the earth ceases for us to be a weltering chaos. We walk in the great hall of life, looking up and round reverentially. Nothing is despicable, — all is meaning-full; nothing is small, — all is part of a whole, whose beginning and end we know not. The life that throbs in us is a pulsation from it, — too mighty for our comprehension, not too small.

And so it comes to pass at last that, whereas the sky was at first a small blue rag stretched out over us, and so low that our hands might touch it, pressing down on us, it raises itself into an immeasurable blue arch over our heads, and we begin to live again.

CHAPTER II.

WALDO lay on his stomach on the red sand. The small ostriches he herded wandered about him, pecking at the food he had cut, or at pebbles and dry sticks. On his right lay the graves, to his left the dam ; in his hand was a large wooden post covered with carvings, at which he worked. Doss lay before him, basking in the winter sunshine, and now and again casting an expectant glance at the corner of the nearest ostrich-camp. The scrubby thorn-trees under which they lay yielded no shade, but none was needed in that glorious June weather, when in the hottest part of the afternoon the sun was but pleasantly warm ; and the boy carved on, not looking up, yet conscious of the brown serene earth about him and the intensely blue sky above.

Presently, at the corner of the camp, Em appeared, bearing a covered saucer in one hand, and in the other a jug with a cup in the top. She was grown into a premature little old woman of sixteen, ridiculously fat. The jug and saucer she put down on the ground before the dog and his master, and dropped down beside them herself, panting and out of breath.

" Waldo, as I came up the camps I met some one on horseback, and I do believe it must be the new man that is coming."

The new man was an Englishman, to whom the Boer-woman had hired half the farm.

"Hum!" said Waldo.

"He is quite young," said Em, holding her side, "and he has brown hair, and beard curling close to his face, and such dark blue eyes. And, Waldo, I was so ashamed! I was just looking back to see, you know, and he happened just to be looking back too, and we looked right into each other's faces; and he got red, and I got so red. I believe he is the new man."

"Yes," said Waldo.

"I must go now. Perhaps he has brought us letters from the post from Lyndall. You know she can't stay at school much longer; she must come back soon. And the new man will have to stay with us till his house is built. I must get his room ready. Good-by!"

She tripped off again, and Waldo carved on at his post. Doss lay with his nose close to the covered saucer, and smelt that some one had made nice little fat cakes that afternoon. Both were so intent on their occupation that not till a horse's hoofs beat beside them in the sand did they look up to see a rider drawing in his steed.

He was certainly not the stranger whom Em had described. A dark, somewhat French-looking little man of eight-and-twenty, rather stout, with heavy, cloudy eyes and pointed mustaches. His horse was a fiery creature, well-caparisoned; a highly-finished saddle-bag hung from the saddle; the man's hands were gloved, and he presented the appearance — an appearance rare on that farm — of a well-dressed gentleman.

12

In an uncommonly melodious voice he inquired whether he might be allowed to remain there for an hour. Waldo directed him to the farm-house, but the stranger declined. He would merely rest under the trees, and give his horse water. He removed the saddle, and Waldo led the animal away to the dam. When he returned, the stranger had settled himself under the trees, with his back against the saddle. The boy offered him of the cakes. He declined, but took a draught from the jug; and Waldo lay down not far off, and fell to work again. It mattered nothing if cold eyes saw it. It was not his sheep-shearing machine. With material loves, as with human, we go mad once, love out, and have done. We never get up the true enthusiasm a second time. This was but a thing he had made, labored over, loved, and liked, — nothing more, — not his machine.

The stranger forced himself lower down in the saddle, and yawned. It was a drowsy afternoon, and he objected to travel in these out-of-the-world parts. He liked better civilized life, where at every hour of the day a man may look for his glass of wine, and his easy-chair, and paper ; where at night he may lock himself into his room with his books, and a bottle of brandy, and taste joys mental and physical. The world said of him — the all-knowing, omnipotent world, whom no locks can bar, who has the cat-like propensity of seeing best in the dark — the world said, that better than the books he loved the brandy, and better than books or brandy, that which it had been better had he loved less. But for the world he cared nothing ; he smiled blandly in its teeth. All life is a dream ; if wine, and philosophy, and women keep the dream from becoming a nightmare, so much the better. It is all they are fit for, all they can be used for. There was another side to his life and thought; but of that the world knew nothing, and said nothing, as the way of the wise world is.

The stranger looked from beneath his sleepy eye-lids at the brown earth that stretched away, beautiful in spite of itself, in that June sunshine; looked at the graves, the gables of the farm-house showing over the stone walls of the camps, at the clownish fellow at his feet, and yawned. But he had drunk of the hind's tea, and must say something.

"Your father's place, I presume?" he inquired sleepily.

"No; I am only a servant."

"Dutch people?"

"Yes."

"And you like the life?"

The boy hesitated. "On days like these."

"And why on these?"

The boy waited. "They are very beautiful."

The stranger looked at him. It seemed that as the fellow's dark eyes looked across the brown earth they kindled with an intense satisfaction; then they looked back at the carving.

What had that creature, so coarse-clad and clown-ish, to do with the subtle joys of the weather? Him-self, white-handed and delicate, *he* might hear the music which shimmering sunshine and solitude play on the finely-strung chords of Nature; but that fel-low! Was not the ear in that great body too gross for such delicate mutterings?

Presently he said, "May I see what you work at?"

The fellow handed his wooden post. It was by no means lovely. The men and birds were almost gro tesque in their labored resemblance to nature, and bore signs of patient thought. The stranger turned the thing over on his knee.

"Where did you learn this work?"

"I taught myself."

"And these zigzag lines represent —"

"A mountain."

The stranger looked. "It has some meaning, has it not?"

The boy muttered confusedly, "Only things."

The questioner looked down at him — the huge, unwieldy figure, in size a man's, in right of its child-like features and curling hair a child's; and it hurt him — it attracted him, and it hurt him. It was something between pity and sympathy.

"How long have you worked at this?"

"Nine months."

From his pocket the stranger drew his pocket-book, and took something from it. He could fasten the post to his horse in some way, and throw it away in the sand when at a safe distance.

"Will you take this for your carving?"

The boy glanced at the five-pound note, and shook his head. "No; I cannot."

"You think it is worth more?" asked the stranger, with a little sneer.

He pointed with his thumb to a grave. "No; it is for him."

"And who is there?" asked the stranger.

"My father."

The man silently returned the note to his pocket-book, and gave the carving to the boy; and, drawing his hat over his eyes, composed himself to sleep. Not being able to do so, after a while he glanced over the fellow's shoulder to watch him work. The boy carved letters into the back.

"If," said the stranger, with his melodious voice, rich with a sweetness that never showed itself in the clouded eyes — for sweetness will linger on in the voice long after it has died out in the eyes — "if for such a purpose, why write that upon it?"

The boy glanced round at him, but made no answer. He had almost forgotten his presence.

"You surely believe," said the stranger, "that some day, sooner or later, these graves will open, and those Boer-uncles with their wives walk about here in the red sand, with the very fleshly legs with which they went to sleep? Then why say, 'He sleeps forever?' You believe he will stand up again?"

"Do you?" asked the boy, lifting for an instant his heavy eyes to the stranger's face.

Half taken aback, the stranger laughed. It was as though a curious little tadpole which he held under his glass should suddenly lift its tail and begin to question him.

"I? — no." He laughed his short thick laugh. "I am a man who believes nothing, hopes nothing, fears nothing, feels nothing. I am beyond the pale of humanity; no criterion of what you should be who live here among your ostriches and bushes."

The next moment the stranger was surprised by a sudden movement on the part of the fellow, which brought him close to the stranger's feet. Soon after he raised his carving, and laid it across the man's knee.

"Yes, I will tell you," he muttered; "I will tell you all about it."

He put his finger on the grotesque little manikin

at the bottom (ah! that man who believed nothing, hoped nothing, felt nothing; *how he loved him!*), and with eager finger the fellow moved upwards, explaining over fantastic figures and mountains, to the crowning bird from whose wing dropped a feather. At the end he spoke with broken breath — short words, like one who utters things of mighty import.

The stranger watched more the face than the carving; and there was now and then a show of white teeth beneath the mustaches as he listened.

"I think," he said blandly, when the boy had done, "that I partly understand you. It is something after this fashion, is it not?" He smiled. "In certain valleys there was a hunter." He touched the grotesque little figure at the bottom. "Day by day he went to hunt for wild-fowl in the woods; and it chanced that once he stood on the shores of a large lake. While he stood waiting in the rushes, for the coming of the birds, a great shadow fell on him, and in the water he saw a reflection. He looked up to the sky; but the thing was gone. Then a burning desire came over him to see once again that reflection in the water, and all day he watched and waited; but night came, and it had not returned. Then he went home with his empty bag, moody and silent. His comrades came questioning about him to know the reason, but he answered them nothing; he sat alone and brooded. Then his friend came to him, and to him he spoke.

"'I have seen to-day,' he said, 'that which I never saw before — a vast white bird, with silver wings outstretched, sailing in the everlasting blue. And now it is as though a great fire burned within my breast. It was but a sheen, a shimmer, a reflection in the water;

but now I desire nothing more on earth than to hold
her.' "

" His friend laughed.

" ' It was but a beam playing on the water, or the
shadow of your own head. To-morrow you will forget
her,' he said.

"But to-morrow, and to-morrow, and to-morrow the
hunter walked alone. He sought in the forest and in
the woods, by the lakes and among the rushes, but he
could not find her. He shot no more wild-fowl; what
were they to him ?

" ' What ails him ? ' said his comrades.

" ' He is mad,' said one.

" ' No; but he is worse,' said another; 'he would
see that which none of us have seen, and make himself a wonder.'

" ' Come, let us forswear his company,' said all.

" So the hunter walked alone.

" One night, as he wandered in the shade, very heart-
sore and weeping, an old man stood before him,
grander and taller than the sons of men.

" ' Who are you ?' asked the hunter.

" ' I am Wisdom,' answered the old man; 'but some
men called me Knowledge. All my life I have grown
in these valleys; but no man sees me till he has
sorrowed much. The eyes must be washed with tears
that are to behold me; and, according as a man has
suffered, I speak.'

" And the hunter cried, 'Oh, you who have lived
here so long, tell me, what is that great wild bird I
have seen sailing in the blue ? They would have
me believe she is a dream; the shadow of my own
head.'

" The old man smiled.

"'Her name is Truth. He who has once seen her never rests again. Till death he desires her.'

"And the hunter cried, 'Oh, tell me where I may find her.'

"But the man said, 'You have not suffered enough,' and went.

"Then the hunter took from his breast the Shuttle of Imagination, and wound on it the thread of his Wishes; and all night he sat and wove a net.

"In the morning he spread the golden net open on the ground, and into it he threw a few grains of Credulity, which his father had left him, and which he kept in his breast-pocket. They were like white puff-balls, and when you trod on them a brown dust flew out. Then he sat by to see what would happen. The first that came into the net was a snow-white bird, with dove's eyes, and he sang a beautiful song, 'A human-God! a human-God! a human-God!' it sang. The second that came was black and mystical, with dark, lovely eyes, that looked into the depths of your soul, and he sang only this, 'Immortality!'

"And the hunter took them both in his arms, for he said, 'They are surely of the beautiful Family of Truth.'

"Then came another, green and gold, who sang in a shrill voice, like one crying in the market-place, 'Reward after Death! Reward after Death!'

"And he said, 'You are not so fair; but you are fair too,' and he took it.

"And others came, brightly colored, singing pleasant songs, till all the grains were finished. And the hunter gathered all his birds together, and built a strong iron cage called a new creed, and put all his birds in it.

"Then the people came about, dancing and singing.

"'Oh, happy hunter!' they cried. 'Oh, wonderful man! Oh, delightful birds! Oh, lovely songs!'

"No one asked where the birds had come from, nor how they had been caught; but they danced and sang before them, and the hunter too was glad, for he said, 'Surely Truth is among them. In time she will moult her feathers, and I shall see her snow-white form.'

"But the time passed, and the people sang and danced; but the hunter's heart grew heavy. He crept alone, as of old, to weep; the terrible desire had awakened again in his breast. One day, as he sat alone weeping, it chanced that Wisdom met him. He told the old man what he had done.

"And Wisdom smiled sadly.

"'Many men,' he said, 'have spread that net for Truth; but they have never found her. On the grains of Credulity she will not feed; in the net of Wishes her feet cannot be held; in the air of these valleys she will not breathe. The birds you have caught are of the brood of Lies. Lovely and beautiful, but still lies; Truth knows them not.'

"And the hunter cried out in bitterness, —

"'And must I then sit still, to be devoured of this great burning?'

"And the old man said: 'Listen, and in that you have suffered much and wept much, I will tell you what I know. He who sets out to search for Truth must leave these valleys of Superstition forever, taking with him not one shred that has belonged to them. Alone he must wander down into the land of Absolute Negation and Denial; he must abide there; he must resist temptation; when the light breaks he must arise and follow it into the country of Dry Sunshine. The mountains of Stern Reality will rise before him; he must climb them; *beyond* them lies Truth.'

"'And he will hold her fast! He will hold her in his hands!' the hunter cried.

"Wisdom shook his head.

"'He will never see her, never hold her. The time is not yet.'

"'Then there is no hope?' cried the hunter.

"'There is this,' said Wisdom. 'Some men have climbed on those mountains; circle above circle of bare rock they have scaled; and wandering there in those high regions some have chanced to pick up on the ground, one white, silver feather dropped from the wing of Truth. And it shall come to pass,' said the old man, raising himself prophetically and pointing with his finger to the sky, 'it shall come to pass, that, when enough of those silver feathers shall have been gathered by the hands of men, and shall have been woven into a cord, and the cord into a net, that in *that* net Truth may be captured. *Nothing but Truth can hold Truth.*'

"The hunter arose. 'I will go,' he said.

"But Wisdom detained him.

"'Mark you well — who leaves these valleys *never* returns to them. Though he should weep tears of blood seven days and nights upon the confines, he can never put his foot across them. Left, — they, are left forever. Upon the road which you would travel, there is no reward offered. Who goes, goes freely, for the great love that is in him. The work is his reward.'

" 'I go,' said the hunter; 'but upon the mountains, tell me, which path shall I take?'

" 'I am the child of The-Accumulated-Knowledge-of-Ages,' said the man; 'I can walk only where many men have trodden. On those mountains few feet have passed; each man strikes out a path for himself. He goes at his own peril; my voice he hears no more. I may follow after him, but I cannot go before him.'

" Then Knowledge vanished.

" And the hunter turned. He went to his cage, and with his hands broke down the bars, and the jagged iron tore his flesh. It is sometimes easier to build than to break.

" One by one he took his plumed birds, and let them fly. But, when he came to his dark-plumed bird, he held it, and looked into its beautiful eyes, and the bird uttered its low deep cry, — 'Immortality!'

" And he said quickly, 'I cannot part with it. It is not heavy; it eats no food. I will hide it in my breast; I will take it with me.' And he buried it there, and covered it over with his cloak.

" But the thing he had hidden grew heavier, heavier, heavier, — till it lay on his breast like lead. He could not move with it. He could not leave those valleys with it. Then again he took it out, and looked at it.

" 'Oh, my beautiful, my heart's own!' he cried, 'may I not keep you?'

" He opened his hands sadly.

" 'Go,' he said. 'It may happen that in Truth's song one note is like to yours; but *I* shall never hear it.'

"Sadly he opened his hand, and the bird flew from him forever.

"Then from the Shuttle of Imagination he took the thread of his Wishes and threw it on the ground, and the empty shuttle he put into his breast; for the thread was made in those valleys, but the shuttle came from an unknown country. He turned to go; but now the people came about him, howling.

"'Fool, hound, demented lunatic!' they cried. 'How dared you break your cage and let the birds fly?'

"The hunter spoke; but they would not hear him.

"'Truth! who is she? Can you eat her? Can you drink her? Who has ever seen her? Your birds were real; all could hear them sing. Oh, fool, vile reptile, atheist!' they cried, 'you pollute the air.'

"'Come, let us take up stones and stone him!' cried some.

"'What affair is it of ours?' said others. 'Let the idiot go!' and went away. But the rest gathered up stones and mud, and threw at him. At last, when he was bruised and cut, the hunter crept away into the woods. And it was evening about him."

At every word the stranger spoke the fellow's eyes flashed back on him, — yes, and yes, and yes! The stranger smiled. It was almost worth the trouble of exerting oneself, even on a lazy afternoon, to win those passionate flashes, more thirsty and desiring than the love-glances of a woman.

"He wandered on and on," said the stranger, "and the shade grew deeper. He was on the borders now of the land where it is always night. Then he stepped into it, and there was no light there. With his hands he groped; but each branch, as he touched it, broke off, and the earth was covered with cinders. At every step his foot sank in, and a fine cloud of impalpable ashes flew up into his face; and it was dark. So he sat down upon a stone, and buried his face in his hands, to wait in that land of Negation and Denial till the light came.

"And it was night in his heart also.

"Then from the marshes to his right and left cold mists arose, and closed about him. A fine imperceptible rain fell in the dark, and great drops gathered on his hair and clothes. His heart beat slowly, and a numbness crept through all his limbs. Then, looking up, two merry whisp lights came dancing. He lifted his head to look at them. Nearer, nearer they came. So warm, so bright, they danced like stars of fire. They stood before him at last. From the centre of the radiating flame in one looked out a woman's face, laughing, dimpled, with streaming yellow hair. In the centre of the other were merry laughing ripples, like the bubbles on a glass of wine. They danced before him.

"'Who are you,' asked the hunter, 'who alone come to me in my solitude and darkness?'

"'We are the twins Sensuality!' they cried. 'Our father's name is Human-Nature, and our mother's name is Excess. We are as old as the hills and rivers, — as old as the first man; but we never die,' they laughed.

"'Oh, let me wrap my arms about you!' cried the first; 'they are soft and warm. Your heart is frozen now, but I will make it beat. Oh, come to me!'

"'I will pour my hot life into you,' said the second; 'your brain is numb, and your limbs are dead now, but they shall live with a fierce free life. Oh, let me pour it in!'

"'Oh, follow us!' they cried, 'and live with us. Nobler hearts than yours have sat here in this darkness to wait; and they have come to us and we to them, and they have never left us, — never. All else is a delusion; but *we* are real, we are real. Truth is a shadow; the valleys of Superstition are a farce; the earth is of ashes, the trees all rotten; but we — feel us — we live! You cannot doubt us. Feel us, how warm we are! Oh, come to us! come with us!'

"Nearer and nearer round his head they hovered, and the cold drops melted on his forehead. The bright light shot into his eyes, dazzling him, and the frozen blood began to run. And he said, —

"'Yes; why should I die here in this awful darkness? They are warm, they melt my frozen blood!' and he stretched out his hands to take them.

"Then in a moment there arose before him the image of the thing he had loved, and his hand dropped to his side.

"'Oh, come to us!' they cried.

"But he buried his face.

"'You dazzle my eyes,' he cried, 'you make my heart warm; but you cannot give me what I desire. I will wait here, — wait till I die. Go!'

"He covered his face with his hands, and would not listen; and when he looked up again they were two twinkling stars, that vanished in the distance.

"And the long, long night rolled on.

"All who leave the valley of Superstition pass through that dark land; but some go through it in a few days, some linger there for months, some for years, and some die there."

The boy had crept closer; his hot breath almost touched the stranger's hand; a mystic wonder filled his eyes.

"At last for the hunter a faint light played along the horizon, and he rose to follow it; and he reached that light at last, and stepped into the broad sunshine. Then before him rose the almighty mountains of Dry-facts and Realities. The clear sunshine played on them, and the tops were lost in the clouds. At the foot many paths ran up. An exultant cry burst from the hunter. He chose the straightest, and began to climb; and the rocks and ridges resounded with his song. They had exaggerated; after all, it was not so high, nor was the road so steep! A few days, a few weeks, a few months at most, and then the top! Not one feather only would he pick up; he would gather all that other men had found, — weave the net, — capture Truth,— hold her fast,— touch her with his hands, — clasp her!

"He laughed in the merry sunshine, and sang loud. Victory was very near. Nevertheless after a while the path grew steeper. He needed all his breath for climbing, and the singing died away. On the right and left rose huge rocks, devoid of lichen or moss, and in the lava-like earth chasms yawned. Here and there he saw a sheen of white bones. Now too the path began to grow less and less marked; then it became a mere trace, with a foot-mark here and there; then it ceased altogether. He sang no more, but struck forth a path for himself, until he reached a mighty wall of rock, smooth and without break, stretching as far as the eye could see. 'I will rear a stair against it; and, once this wall climbed, I shall be almost there,' he said bravely; and worked. With his Shuttle of Imagination he dug out stones; but half of them would not fit, and half a month's work would roll down because those below were ill-chosen. But the hunter worked on, saying always to himself, 'Once this wall climbed, I shall be almost there. This great work ended!'

"At last he came out upon the top, and he looked about him. Far below rolled the white mist over the valleys of Superstition, and above him towered the mountains. They had seemed low before; they were of an immeasurable height now, from crown to foundation surrounded by walls of rock, that rose tier above tier in mighty circles. Upon them played the eternal sunshine. He uttered a wild cry. He bowed himself on to the earth, and when he rose his face was white. In absolute silence he walked on. He was very silent now. In those high regions the rarefied air is hard to breathe by those born in the valleys; every breath he drew hurt him, and the blood oozed out from the tips of his fingers. Before the next wall of rock he began to work. The height of this seemed infinite, and he said nothing. The sound of his tool rang night and day upon the iron rocks into which he cut steps. Years passed over him, yet he worked on; but the wall towered up always above him to heaven. Sometimes he prayed that a little moss or lichen might spring up on those bare walls to be a companion to him; but it never came." The stranger watched the boy's face.

"And the years rolled on; he counted them by the steps he had cut — a few for a year — only a few. He sang no more; he said no more, 'I will do this or that' — he only worked. And at night when the twilight settled down, there looked out at him from the holes and crevices in the rocks strange wild faces.

"'Stop your work, you lonely man, and speak to us,' they cried.

"'My salvation is in work. If I should stop but for one moment, you would creep down upon me,' he replied. And they put out their long necks farther.

"'Look down into the crevice at your feet,' they said. 'See what lie there, — white bones! As brave and strong a man as you climbed to these rocks. And he looked up. He saw there was no use in striving; he would never hold Truth, never see her, never find her. So he lay down here, for he was very tired. He went to sleep forever. He put himself to sleep. Sleep is very tranquil. You are not lonely when you are asleep, neither do your hands ache, nor your heart.' And the hunter laughed between his teeth.

"'Have I torn from my heart all that was dearest; have I wandered alone in the land of night; have I resisted temptation; have I dwelt where the voice of my kind is never heard, and labored alone, to lie down and be food for you, ye harpies?'

"He laughed fiercely; and the echoes of Despair slunk away, for the laugh of a brave, strong heart is as a death-blow to them.

"Nevertheless they crept out again, and looked at him.

"'Do you know that your hair is white?' they said, 'that your hands begin to tremble like a child's. Do you see that the point of your Shuttle is gone? It is cracked already. If you should ever climb this stair,' they said, 'it will be your last. You will never climb another.'

13

" And he answered, ' *I know it !* ' and worked on.

" The old, thin hands cut the stones ill and jaggedly, for the fingers were stiff and bent. The beauty and the strength of the man was gone.

" At last an old, wizened, shrunken face looked out above the rocks. It saw the eternal mountains rise with walls to the white clouds; but its work was done.

" The old hunter folded his tired hands, and lay down by the precipice where he had worked away his life. It was the sleeping time at last. Below him over the valleys rolled the thick white mist. Once it broke; and through the gap the dying eyes looked down on the trees and fields of their childhood. From afar seemed borne to him the cry of his own wild birds, and he heard the noise of people singing as they danced. And he thought he heard among them the voices of his old comrades; and he saw far off the sunlight shine on his early home. And great tears gathered in the hunter's eyes.

" ' Ah! they who die there do not die alone,' he cried.

" Then the mists rolled together again, and he turned his eyes away.

" ' I have sought,' he said, ' for long years I have labored; but I have not found her. I have not rested, I have not repined, and I have not seen her; now my strength is gone. Where I lie down worn out, other men will stand, young and fresh. By the steps that I have cut they will climb; by the stairs that I have built they will mount. They will never know the name of the man who made them. At the clumsy work they will laugh; when the stones roll they will curse me. But they will mount, and on *my* work; they will climb, and by *my* stair. They

will find her, and through me. And no man liveth
to himself, and no man dieth to himself.'

"The tears rolled from beneath the shrivelled eyelids. If Truth had appeared above him in the clouds
now, he could not have seen her; the mist of death
was in his eyes.

"'My soul hears their glad step coming,' he said;
'and they shall mount! they shall mount!' He
raised his shrivelled hand to his eyes.

"Then slowly from the white sky above, through
the still air, came something falling, falling, falling.
Softly it fluttered down, and dropped on to the breast
of the dying man. He felt it with his hands. It
was a feather. He died holding it."

The boy had shaded his eyes with his hand. On
the wood of the carving great drops fell. The
stranger must have laughed at him, or remained
silent. He did so.

"How did you know it?" the boy whispered at
last. "It is not written there — not on that wood.
How did you know it?"

"Certainly," said his stranger, "the whole of the
story is not written here, but it is suggested. And the
attribute of all true art, the highest and the lowest, is
this, — that it says more than it says, and takes you
away from itself. It is a little door that opens into
an infinite hall, where you may find what you please.
Men, thinking to detract, say, 'People read more in
this or that work of genius than was ever written in
it,' not perceiving that they pay the highest compli-
ment. If we pick up the finger and nail of a real
man, we can decipher a whole story, — could almost
reconstruct the creature again, from head to foot.
But half the body of a Mumboo-jumbow idol leaves

us utterly in the dark as to what the rest was like. We see what we see, but nothing more. There is nothing so universally intelligible as truth. It has a thousand meanings, and suggests a thousand more." He turned over the wooden thing. "Though a man should carve it into matter with the least possible manipulative skill, it will yet find interpreters. It is the soul that looks out with burning eyes through the most gross fleshly filament. Whosoever should portray truly the life and death of a little flower — its birth, sucking in of nourishment, reproduction of its kind, withering and vanishing — would have shaped a symbol of all existence. All true facts of Nature or the mind are related. Your little carving represents some mental facts as they really are, therefore fifty different true stories might be read from it. What your work wants is not truth, but beauty of external form, the other half of art." He leaned almost gently towards the boy. "Skill may come in time, but you will have to work hard. The love of beauty and the desire for it must be born in a man; the skill to reproduce it he must make. He must work hard."

"All my life I have longed to see you," the boy said.

The stranger broke off the end of his cigar, and lit it. The boy lifted the heavy wood from the stranger's knee, and drew yet nearer him. In the dog-like manner of his drawing near, there was something superbly ridiculous, unless one chanced to view it in another light. Presently the stranger said, whiffing, "Do something for me."

The boy started up.

"No, stay where you are. I don't want you to go

anywhere; I want you to talk to me. Tell me what you have been doing all your life."

The boy slunk down again. Would that the man had asked him to root up bushes with his hands, for his horse to feed on, or to run to the far end of the plain for the fossils that lay there, or to gather the flowers that grew on the hills at the edge of the plain; he would have run and been back quickly — but now!

"I have never done anything," he said.

"Then tell me of that nothing. I like to know what other folks have been doing whose word I can believe. It is interesting. What was the first thing you ever wanted very much?"

The boy waited to remember, then began hesitatingly; but soon the words flowed. In the smallest past we find an inexhaustible mine when once we begin to dig at it.

A confused, disordered story — the little made large, and the large small, and nothing showing its inward meaning. It is not till the past has receded many steps, that before the clearest eyes it falls into co-ordinate pictures. It is not till the "I" we tell of has ceased to exist, that it takes its place among other objective realities, and finds its true niche in the picture. The present and the near past is a confusion, whose meaning flashes on us as it slinks away into the distance.

The stranger lit one cigar from the end of another, and puffed and listened with half-closed eyes.

"I will remember more to tell you if you like," said the fellow.

He spoke with that extreme gravity common to all very young things who feel deeply. It is not till twenty that we learn to be in deadly earnest and to laugh. The stranger nodded, while the fellow sought for something more to relate. He would tell all to this man of his, — all that he knew, all that he had felt, his most inmost sorest thought. Suddenly the stranger turned upon him.

"Boy," he said, "you are happy to be here."

Waldo looked at him. Was his delightful one ridiculing him? Here, with this brown earth and these low hills, while the rare, wonderful world lay all beyond. Fortunate to be here.

The stranger read his glance.

"Yes," he said; "here with the karroo-bushes and red sand. Do you wonder what I mean? To all who have been born in the old faith there comes a time of danger, when the old slips from us, and we have not yet planted our feet on the new. We hear the voice from Sinai thundering no more, and the still small voice of reason is not yet heard. We have proved the religion our mothers fed us on to be a delusion; in our bewilderment we see no rule by which to guide our steps day by day; and yet every day we must step somewhere." The stranger leaned forward and spoke more quickly. "We have never once been taught by word or act to distinguish between religion and the moral laws on which it has artfully fastened itself, and from which it has sucked its vitality. When we have dragged down the weeds and creepers that covered the solid wall and have found them to be rotten wood, we imagine the wall itself to be rotten wood too. We find it is solid and standing only when we fall headlong against it. We have been taught that all right and wrong originate in the will of an irresponsible being. It is some time before we see how the inexorable 'Thou shalt and shalt not,' are carved into the nature of things. This is the time of danger."

His dark, misty eyes looked into the boy's.

"In the end Experience will inevitably teach us that the laws for a wise and noble life have a foundation infinitely deeper than the fiat of any being, God or man, — even in the groundwork of human nature. She will teach us that whoso sheddeth man's blood, though by man his blood be not shed, though no man avenge and no hell await, yet every drop shall blister on his soul and eat in the name of the dead. She will teach that whoso takes a love not lawfully his own gathers a flower with a poison on its petals; that whoso revenges, strikes with a sword that has two edges, — one for his adversary, one for himself; that who lives to himself is dead, though the ground is not yet on him; that who wrongs another clouds his own sun; and that who sins in secret stands accused and condemned before the one Judge who deals eternal justice, — his own all-knowing self.

"Experience *will* teach us this, and reason will show us why it *must* be so; but at first the world swings before our eyes, and no voice cries out, 'This is the way, walk ye in it!' You are happy to be here, boy! When the suspense fills you with pain, you build stone walls, and dig earth for relief. Others have stood where you stand to-day, and have felt as you feel; and another relief has been offered them, and they have taken it.

"When the day has come when they have seen the path in which they might walk, they have not the strength to follow it. Habits have fastened on them from which nothing but death can free them;

which cling closer than his sacerdotal sanctimony
to a priest; which feed on the intellect like a
worm, sapping energy, hope, creative power, all that
makes a man higher than a beast, — leaving only
the power to yearn, to regret, and to sink lower in
the abyss.

"Boy," he said, and the listener was not more un-
smiling now than the speaker, "you are happy to be
here. Stay where you are. If you ever pray, let
it be only the one old prayer — 'Lead us not into
temptation.' Live on here quietly. The time may
yet come when you will be that which other men
have hoped to be and never will be now."

The stranger rose, shook the dust from his sleeve,
and, ashamed at his own earnestness, looked across
the bushes for his horse.

"We should have been on our way already," he
said. "We shall have a long ride in the dark to-
night."

Waldo hastened to fetch the animal; but he returned leading it slowly. The sooner it came the
sooner would its rider be gone.

The stranger was opening his saddle-bag, in which
were a bright French novel and an old brown volume.
He took the latter, and held it out to the boy.

"It may be of some help to you," he said carelessly. "It was a gospel to me when I first fell on
it. You must not expect too much; but it may give
you a centre round which to hang your ideas, instead
of letting them lie about in a confusion that makes
the head ache. We of this generation are not des-
tined to eat and be satisfied as our fathers were; we
must be content to go hungry."

He smiled his automaton smile, and rebuttoned the

bag. Waldo thrust the book into his breast, and while he saddled the horse the stranger made inquiries as to the nature of the road and the distance to the next farm.

When the bags were fixed Waldo took up his wooden post, and began to fasten it on to the saddle, tying it with the little blue cotton handkerchief from his neck. The stranger looked on in silence. When it was done, the boy held the stirrup for him to mount.

"What is your name?" he inquired, ungloving his right hand when he was in the saddle.

The boy replied.

"Well, I trust we shall meet again some day, sooner or later."

He shook hands with the ungloved hand; then drew on the glove, and touched his horse, and rode slowly away. The boy stood to watch him.

Once when the stranger had gone half across the plain he looked back.

"Poor devil!" he said, smiling and stroking his mustache. Then he looked to see if the little blue handkerchief were still safely knotted. "Poor devil!"

He smiled, and then he sighed wearily, very wearily.

And Waldo waited till the moving speck had disappeared on the horizon; then he stooped and kissed passionately a hoof-mark in the sand. Then he called his young birds together, and put his book under his arm, and walked home along the stone-wall. There was a rare beauty to him in the sunshine that evening.

CHAPTER III.

GREGORY ROSE FINDS HIS AFFINITY.

THE new man, Gregory Rose, sat at the door of his dwelling, his arms folded, his legs crossed, and a profound melancholy seeming to rest over his soul. His house was a little square daub-and-wattle building, far out in the karroo, two miles from the homestead. It was covered outside with a sombre coating of brown mud, two little panes being let into the walls for windows. Behind it were the sheep kraals, and to the right a large dam, now principally containing baked mud. Far off the little "kopje" concealed the homestead, and was not itself an object conspicuous enough to relieve the dreary monotony of the landscape.

Before the door sat Gregory Rose in his shirt-sleeves, on a camp-stool, and ever and anon he sighed deeply. There was that in his countenance for which even his depressing circumstances failed to account. Again and again he looked at the little "kopje," at the milk-pail at his side, and at the brown pony who a short way off cropped the dry bushes, — and sighed.

Presently he rose and went into his house. It was one tiny room, the whitewashed walls profusely covered with prints cut from the "Illustrated London News," and in which there was a noticeable preponderance of female faces and figures. A stretcher filled one end of the hut, and a rack for a gun, and

a little hanging looking-glass diversified the gable
opposite, while in the centre stood a chair and table.
All was scrupulously neat and clean, for Gregory kept
a little duster folded in the corner of his table-drawer,
just as he had seen his mother do, and every morning
before he went out he said his prayers, and made his
bed, and dusted the table and the legs of the chairs,
and even the pictures on the wall and the gun-
rack.

On this hot afternoon he took from beneath his
pillow a watch-bag made by his sister Jemima, and
took out the watch. Only half-past four ! With a
suppressed groan he dropped it back, and sat down
beside the table. Half-past four ! Presently he
roused himself. He would write to his sister Jemima.
He always wrote to her when he was miserable. She
was his safety-valve. He forgot her when he was
happy ; but he used her when he was wretched.

He took out ink and paper. There was a family
crest and motto on the latter, for the Roses since
coming to the colony had discovered that they were
of distinguished lineage. Old Rose himself, an honest
English farmer, knew nothing of his noble descent ;
but his wife and daughter knew, — especially his
daughter. There were Roses in England who kept
a park and dated from the Conquest. So the colonial
" Rose Farm " became " Rose Manor " in remembrance of the ancestral domain, and the claim of the
Roses to noble blood was established, — in their own
minds at least.

Gregory took up one of the white, crested sheets ;
but on deeper reflection he determined to take a pink
one, as more suitable to the state of his feelings. He
began : —

"Kopje Alone, Monday Afternoon.

"My dear Jemima, — "

Then he looked up into the little glass opposite. It was a youthful face reflected there, with curling brown beard and hair; but in the dark blue eyes there was a look of languid longing that touched him. He re-dipped his pen and wrote, —

"When I look up into the little glass that hangs opposite me, I wonder if that changed and sad face — "

Here he sat still and reflected. It sounded almost as if he might be conceited or unmanly to be looking at his own face in the glass. No, that would not do. So he looked for another pink sheet, and began again.

Kopje Alone, Monday Afternoon.

Dear Sister, — It is hardly six months since I left you to come to this spot, yet could you now see me I know what you would say, — I know what mother would say, — "Can that be our Greg, — that thing with the strange look in his eyes?"

Yes, Jemima, it is your Greg, and the change has been coming over me ever since I came here; but it is greatest since yesterday. You know what sorrows I have passed through, Jemima; how unjustly I was always treated at school, — the masters keeping me back and calling me a blockhead, though, as they themselves allowed, I had the best memory of any boy in the school, and could repeat whole books from beginning to end. You know how cruelly father always used me, calling me a noodle and a milk-sop, just because he could n't understand my fine nature. You know how he has made a farmer of me instead of a minister, as I ought to have been. You know it all, Jemima; and how I have borne it all, not as a woman who whines for every touch, but as a man should, — in silence.

But there are things, — there is *a* thing, — which the soul longs to pour forth into a kindred ear.

Dear sister, have you ever known what it is to keep wanting and wanting and wanting to kiss some one's mouth, and you may not, — to touch some one's hand, and you cannot ? I am in love, Jemima.

The old Dutch-woman, from whom I hire this place, has a little step-daughter, and her name begins with *E*.

She is English. I do not know how her father came to marry a Boer-woman. It makes me feel so strange to put down that letter that I can hardly go on writing, — *E*. I've loved her ever since I came here. For weeks I have not been able to eat or drink ; my very tobacco, when I smoke, has no taste ; and I can remain for no more than five minutes in one place, and sometimes feel as though I were really going mad.

Every evening I go there to fetch my milk. Yesterday she gave me some coffee. The spoon fell on the ground. She picked it up; when she gave it me her finger touched mine. Jemima, I do not know if I fancied it; I shivered hot, and she shivered too. I thought, "It is all right; she will be mine; she loves me !" Just then, Jemima, in came a fellow, — a great, coarse fellow, a German, — a ridiculous fellow, with curls right down to his shoulders; it makes one *sick* to look at him. He's only a servant of the Boer-woman's, and a low, vulgar, uneducated thing, that's never been to boarding-school in his life. He

had been to the next farm seeking sheep. When
he came in she said, "Good evening, Waldo. Have
some coffee!" *and she kissed him.*

All last night I heard nothing else but "Have some
coffee! have some coffee!" If I went to sleep for a
moment I dreamed that her finger was pressing mine;
but when I woke with a start I heard her say, "Good
evening, Waldo. Have some coffee!"

Is this madness?

I have not eaten a mouthful to-day. This evening
I go and propose to her. If she refuses me, I shall go
and kill myself to-morrow. There is a dam of water
close by. The sheep have drunk most of it up, but
there is still enough if I tie a stone to my neck.

It is a choice between death and madness. I can
endure no more. If this should be the last letter you
ever get from me, think of me tenderly, and forgive
me. Without her life would be a howling wilderness,
— a long tribulation. She is my affinity; the one love
of my life, of my youth, of my manhood; my sunshine; my God-given blossom.

" They never loved who dreamed that they loved once,
    And who saith, 'I loved once'? —
Not angels, whose deep eyes look down through realms of light!"

Your disconsolate brother, on what is, in all proba-
bility, the last and distracted night of his life,

GREGORY NAZIANZEN ROSE.

P. S. — Tell mother to take care of my pearl studs.
I left them in the wash-hand-stand drawer. Don't let
the children get hold of them.

P. P. S. — I shall take this letter with me to the
farm. If I turn down one corner you may know I

have been accepted; if not, you may know it is all up with your heart-broken brother.   G. N. R.

Gregory having finished this letter read it over with much approval, put it in an envelope, addressed it, and sat contemplating the ink-pot, somewhat relieved in mind.

The evening turned out chilly and very windy after the day's heat. From afar off, as Gregory neared the homestead on the brown pony, he could distinguish a little figure in a little red cloak at the door of the cow-kraal. Em leaned over the poles that barred the gate, and watched the frothing milk run through the black fingers of the herdsman, while the unwilling cows stood with tethered heads by the milking-poles. She had thrown the red cloak over her own head, and held it under her chin with a little hand, to keep her ears from the wind, that playfully shook it, and tossed the little fringe of yellow hair into her eyes.

"Is it not too cold for you to be standing here?" said Gregory, coming softly close to her.

"Oh, no; it is so nice. I always come to watch the milking. That red cow with the short horns is bringing up the calf of the white cow that died. She loves it so, — just as if it were her own! It is so nice to see her lick its little ears, — just look!"

"The clouds are black. I think it is going to rain to-night," said Gregory.

"Yes," answered Em, looking up as well as she could for the little yellow fringe.

"But I'm sure you must be cold," said Gregory, and put his hand under the cloak, and found there a small fist doubled up, soft, and very warm. He held it fast in his hand.

"Oh, Em, I love you better than all the world besides! Tell me, *do* you love me a little?"

"Yes, I do," said Em, hesitating, and trying softly to free her hand.

"Better than everything, — better than all the world, darling?" he asked, bending down so low that the yellow hair was blown into his eyes.

"I don't know," said Em, gravely. "I do love you very much; but I love my cousin who is at school, and Waldo, very much. You see, I have known them so long!"

"Oh, Em, do not talk to me so coldly," Gregory cried, seizing the little arm that rested on the gate, and pressing it till she was half afraid. The herdsman had moved away to the other end of the kraal now, and the cows, busy with their calves, took no notice of the little human farce. "Em, if you talk so to me, I will go mad! You must love me, — love me better than all! You must give yourself to me. I have loved you since that first moment when I saw you walking by the stone-wall with a jug in your hands. You were made for me, created for me! I will love you till I die! Oh, Em, do not be so cold, so cruel to me!"

He held her arm so tightly that her fingers relaxed their hold, and the cloak fluttered down on to the ground, and the wind played more roughly than ever with the little yellow head.

"I do love you very much," she said; "but I do not know if I want to marry you. I love you better than Waldo, but I can't tell if I love you better than Lyndall. If you would let me wait for a week, I think perhaps I could tell you."

Gregory picked up the cloak, and wrapped it round her.

"If you could but love me as I love you," he said; "but no woman *can* love as a man can. I will wait till next Saturday; I will not once come near you till then. Good-by! Oh, Em," he said, turning again, and twining his arm about her, and kissing her surprised little mouth, "if you are not my wife I cannot live. I have never loved another woman, and I never shall, — never, never!"

"You make me afraid," said Em. "Come let us go, and I will fill your pail."

"I want no milk. Good-by! You will not see me again till Saturday."

Late that night, when every one else had gone to bed, the yellow-haired little woman stood alone in the kitchen. She had come to fill the kettle for the next morning's coffee, and now stood before the fire. The warm reflection lit the grave old-womanish little face, that was so unusually thoughtful this evening.

"Better than all the world, better than everything, — he loves me better than everything!" She said the words aloud, as if they were more easy to believe if she spoke them so. She had given out so much love in her little life, and had got none of it back with interest. Now one said, "I love you better than all the world." One loved her better than she loved him. How suddenly rich she was! She kept clasping and unclasping her hands. So a beggar feels who falls asleep on the pavement wet and hungry, and who wakes in a palace-hall with servants and lights, and a feast before him. Of course the beggar's is only a dream, and he wakes from it; and this was real.

Gregory had said to her, "I will love you as long as I live." She said the words over and over to herself like a song.

14

"I will send for him to-morrow, and I will tell him how I love him back," she said.

But Em needed not to send for him. Gregory discovered on reaching home that Jemima's letter was still in his pocket. And, therefore, much as he disliked the appearance of vacillation and weakness, he was obliged to be at the farm-house before sunrise to post it.

"If I see her," Gregory said, "I shall only bow to her. She shall see that I am a man, one who keeps his word."

As to Jemima's letter, he had turned down one corner of the page, and then turned it back, leaving a deep crease. That would show that he was neither accepted nor rejected, but that matters were in an intermediate condition. It was a more poetical way than putting it in plain words.

Gregory was barely in time with his letter, for Waldo was starting when he reached the homestead, and Em was on the doorstep to see him off. When he had given the letter, and Waldo had gone, Gregory bowed stiffly and prepared to remount his own pony, but somewhat slowly. It was still early; none of the servants were about. Em came up close to him, and put her little hand softly on his arm as he stood by his horse.

"I do love you best of all," she said. She was not frightened now, however much he kissed her. "I wish I was beautiful and nice," she added, looking up into his eyes as he held her against his breast.

"My darling, to me you are more beautiful than all the women in the world; dearer to me than everything it holds. If you were in hell, I would go after you to find you there! If you were dead, though my body moved, my soul would be under the ground with you. All life as I pass it with you in my arms will be perfect to me. It will pass, — pass like a ray of sunshine."

Em thought how beautiful and grand his face was as she looked up into it. She raised her hand gently, and put it on his forehead.

"You are so silent, so cold, my Em," he cried. "Have you nothing to say to me?"

A little shade of wonder filled her eyes.

"I will do everything you tell me," she said.

What else could she say? Her idea of love was only service.

"Then, my own precious one, promise never to kiss that fellow again. I cannot bear that you should love any one but me. You must not! I will not have it! If every relation I had in the world were to die to-morrow, I would be quite happy if I still only had you! My darling, my love, why are you so cold? Promise me not to love him any more. If you asked *me* to do anything for *you*, I would do it, though it cost my life."

Em put her hand very gravely round his neck.

"I will never kiss him," she said, "and I will try not to love any one else. But I do not know if I will be able."

"Oh, my darling, I think of *you* all night, all day. I think of nothing else, love, nothing else," he said, folding his arms about her.

Em was a little conscience-stricken; even that morning she had found time to remember that in six months her cousin would come back from school, and she had thought to remind Waldo of the lozenges for his cough, even when she saw Gregory coming.

"I do not know how it is," she said humbly, nestling to him, "but I cannot love you so much as you love me. Perhaps it is because I am only a woman; but I *do* love you as much as I can."

Now the Kaffir maids were coming from the huts. He kissed her again, eyes and mouth and hands, and left her.

Tant' Sannie was well satisfied when told of the betrothment. She herself contemplated marriage within the year with one or other of her numerous "vrijers," and she suggested that the weddings might take place together.

Em set to work busily to prepare her own household linen and wedding garments. Gregory was with her daily, almost hourly, and the six months which elapsed before Lyndall's return passed, as he felicitously phrased it, "like a summer night, when you are dreaming of some one you love."

Late one evening, Gregory sat by his little love, turning the handle of her machine as she drew her work through it, and they talked of the changes they would make when the Boer-woman was gone, and the farm belonged to them alone. There should be a new room here, and a kraal there. So they chatted on. Suddenly Gregory dropped the handle, and impressed a fervent kiss on the fat hand that guided the linen.

"You are so beautiful, Em," said the lover. "It comes over me in a flood suddenly, how I love you."

Em smiled.

"Tant' Sannie says when I am her age no one will look at me; and it is true. My hands are as short and broad as a duck's foot, and my forehead is so low, and I have n't any nose. I *can't* be pretty."

She laughed softly. It was so nice to think he should be so blind.

"When my cousin comes to-morrow, you will see a beautiful woman, Gregory," she added presently. "She is like a little queen; her shoulders are so up-right, and her head looks as though it ought to have a little crown upon it. You must come to see her to-morrow as soon as she comes. I am sure you will love her."

"Of course I shall come to see her, since she is your cousin; but do you think I could *ever* think any woman as lovely as I think you?"

He fixed his seething eyes upon her.

"You could not help seeing that she is prettier," said Em, slipping her right hand into his; "but you will never be able to like any one so much as you like me."

Afterwards, when she wished her lover good-night, she stood upon the doorstep to call a greeting after him; and she waited, as she always did, till the brown pony's hoofs became inaudible behind the "kopje."

Then she passed through the room where Tant' Sannie lay snoring, and, through the little room that was all draped in white, waiting for her cousin's return, on to her own room.

She went to the chest of drawers to put away the work she had finished, and sat down on the floor before the lowest drawer. In it were the things she was preparing for her marriage. Piles of white linen, and some aprons and quilts; and in the little box in the corner, a spray of orange-blossoms which she had brought from a "smouse." There too was a ring Gregory had given her, and a veil his sister had sent, and there was a little roll of fine embroidered work which

Trana had given her. It was too fine and good even for Gregory's wife, — just right for something very small and soft. She would keep it. And she touched it gently with her forefinger, smiling; and then she blushed, and hid it far behind the other things. She knew so well all that was in that drawer, and yet she turned them all over as though she saw them for the first time, packed them all out, and packed them all in, without one fold or crumple; and then sat down and looked at them.

To-morrow evening when Lyndall came she would bring her here, and show it all to her. Lyndall would so like to see it — the little wreath, and the ring, and the white veil! It would be so nice! Then Em fell to seeing pictures. Lyndall should live with them till she herself got married some day.

Every day when Gregory came home, tired from his work, he would look about and say, "Where is my wife? Has no one seen my wife? Wife, some coffee!" and she would give him some.

Em's little face grew very grave at last, and she knelt up and extended her hands over the drawer of linen.

"Oh, God!" she said, "I am so glad! I do not know what I have done that I should be so glad. Thank you!"

CHAPTER IV.

LYNDALL.

SHE was more like a princess, yes, far more like a princess, than the lady who still hung on the wall in Tant' Sannie's bedroom. So Em thought. She leaned back in the little armchair; she wore a gray dressing-gown, and her long hair was combed out and hung to the ground. Em, sitting before her, looked up with mingled respect and admiration.

Lyndall was tired after her long journey, and had come to her room early. Her eyes ran over the familiar objects. Strange to go away for four years, and come back, and find that the candle standing on the dressing-table still cast the shadow of an old crone's head in the corner beyond the clothes-horse. Strange that even a shadow should last longer than man! She looked about among the old familiar objects; all was there, but the old self was gone.

"What are you noticing?" asked Em.

"Nothing, and everything. I thought the windows were higher. If I were you, when I get this place I should raise the walls. There is not room to breathe here; one suffocates."

"Gregory is going to make many alterations," said Em; and drawing nearer to the gray dressing-gown, respectfully, "Do you like him, Lyndall? Is he not handsome?"

"He must have been a fine baby," said Lyndall, looking at the white dimity curtain that hung above the window.

Em was puzzled.

"There are some men," said Lyndall, "whom you never can believe were babies at all; and others you never see without thinking how very nice they must have looked when they wore socks and pink sashes."

Em remained silent; then she said with a little dignity, "When you know him you will love him as I do. When I compare other people with him, they seem so weak and little. *Our* hearts are so cold, our loves are mixed up with so many other things. But he — no one is worthy of his love. I am not. It is so great and pure."

"You need not make yourself unhappy on that point, — your poor return for his love, my dear," said Lyndall. "A man's love is a fire of olive-wood. It leaps higher every moment; it roars, it blazes, it shoots out red flames; it threatens to wrap you round and devour you, — you who stand by like an icicle in the glow of its fierce warmth. You are self-reproached at your own chilliness and want of reciprocity. The next day, when you go to warm your hands a little, you find a few ashes. 'T is a long love and cool against a short love and hot; men, at all events, have nothing to complain of."

"You speak so because you do not know men," said Em, instantly assuming the dignity of superior knowledge so universally affected by affianced and married women in discussing man's nature with their uncontracted sisters. "You will know them too some day, and then you will think differently," she said, with the condescending magnanimity which superior knowledge can always afford to show to ignorance.

Lyndall's little lip quivered in a manner indicative of intense amusement. She twirled a massive ring upon her forefinger — a ring more suitable for the hand of a man, and noticeable in design — a diamond cross let into gold, with the initials "R. R." below it.

"Ah, Lyndall," Em cried, "perhaps you are engaged yourself — that is why you smile. Yes; I am sure you are. Look at this ring!"

Lyndall drew the hand quickly from her.

"I am not in so great a hurry to put my neck beneath any man's foot; and I do not so greatly admire the crying of babies," she said, as she closed her eyes half wearily and leaned back in the chair. "There are other women glad of such work."

Em felt rebuked and ashamed. How could she take Lyndall, and show her the white linen and the wreath and the embroidery? She was quiet for a little while, and then began to talk about Trana and the old farm-servants, till she saw her companion was weary; then she rose and left her for the night. But after Em was gone Lyndall sat on, watching the old crone's face in the corner, and with a weary look, as though the whole world's weight rested on these frail young shoulders.

The next morning, Waldo, starting off before breakfast with a bag of mealies slung over his shoulder to feed the ostriches, heard a light step behind him.

"Wait for me; I am coming with you," said Lyndall, adding as she came up to him, "if I had not gone to look for you yesterday you would not have come to greet me till now. Do you not like me any longer, Waldo?"

"Yes — but — you are changed."

It was the old clumsy, hesitating mode of speech.

"You liked the pinafores better?" she said quickly. She wore a dress of a simple cotton fabric, but very fashionably made, and on her head was a broad white hat. To Waldo she seemed superbly attired. She saw it. "My dress has changed a little," she said, "and I also; but not to you. Hang the bag over your other shoulder, that I may see your face. You say so little that if one does not look at you, you are an uncomprehended cipher." Waldo changed the bag, and they walked on side by side. "You have improved," she said. "Do you know that I have sometimes wished to see you while I was away; not often, but still sometimes."

They were at the gate of the first camp now. Waldo partly emptied his bag of mealies, and they walked on over the dewy ground.

"Have you learned much?" he asked her simply, remembering how she had once said, "When I come back again I shall know everything that a human being can."

She laughed, —

"Are you thinking of my old boast? Yes; I have learned something, though hardly what I expected, and not *quite* so much. In the first place, I have learned that one of my ancestors must have been a very great fool; for they say nothing comes out in a man but one of his forefathers possessed it before him. In the second place, I have discovered that of all cursed places under the sun, where the hungriest soul can hardly pick up a few grains of knowledge, a girls' boarding-school is the worst. They are called finishing-schools, and the name tells accurately what they are. They finish everything but imbecility and weakness, and that they cultivate. They are nicely adapted machines for experimenting on the question, ' Into how little space can a human soul be crushed ? ' I have seen some souls so compressed that they would have fitted into a small thimble, and found room to move there, — wide room. A woman who has been for many years at one of those places carries the mark of the beast on her till she dies, though she may expand a little afterwards, when she breathes in the free world."

"Were you miserable ?" he asked, looking at her with quick anxiety.

"I ? — No. I am never miserable, and never happy. I wish I were. But I should have run away from the place on the fourth day, and hired myself to the first Boer-woman whose farm I came to, to make fire under her soap-pot, if I had had to live as the rest of the drove did. Can you form an idea, Waldo, of what it must be to be shut up with cackling old women, who are without knowledge of life, without love of the beautiful, without strength, to have your soul cultured by them ? It is suffocation only to breathe the air they breathe; but I made them give me room. I told them I should leave, and they knew I came there on my own account; so they gave me a bedroom without the companionship of one of those things that were having their brains slowly diluted and squeezed out of them. I did not learn music, because I had no talent; and when the drove made cushions, and hideous flowers that the roses laugh at, and a footstool in six weeks that a machine would have made better in five minutes, I went to my room. With the money saved from such work I bought books and newspapers, and at night I

sat up. I read and epitomized what I read; and I
found time to write some plays, and find out how
hard it is to make your thoughts look anything but
imbecile fools when you paint them with ink on paper.
In the holidays I learned a great deal more. I made
acquaintances, saw a few places and many people, and
some different ways of living, which is more than any
books can show one. On the whole I am not dissatisfied with my four years. I have not learned what I
expected; but I have learned something else. What
have you been doing?"

"Nothing."

"That is not possible. I shall find out by-and-by."

They still stepped on side by side over the dewy
bushes. Then suddenly she turned on him.

"Don't you wish you were a woman, Waldo?"

"No," he answered readily.

She laughed.

"I thought not. Even you are too worldly-wise for
that. I never met a man who did. This is a pretty
ring," she said, holding out her little hand, that the
morning sun might make the diamonds sparkle.
"Worth fifty pounds at least. I will give it to the
first man who tells me he would like to be a woman.
There might be one on Robben Island [1] who would win
it perhaps, but I doubt it even there. It is delightful
to be a woman; but every man thanks the Lord de-
voutly that he is n't one."

She drew her hat to one side to keep the sun out of
her eyes as she walked. Waldo looked at her so intently that he stumbled over the bushes. Yes, this
was his little Lyndall who had worn the check pina-

[1] Lunatics at the Cape are sent to Robben Island.

fores; he saw it now, and he walked closer beside her. They reached the next camp.

"Let us wait at this camp and watch the birds," she said, as an ostrich hen came bounding towards them, with velvety wings outstretched, while far away over the bushes the head of the cock was visible as he sat brooding on the eggs.

Lyndall folded her arms on the gate bar, and Waldo threw his empty bag on the wall, and leaned beside her.

"I like these birds," she said; "they share each other's work, and are companions. Do you take an interest in the position of women, Waldo?"

"No."

"I thought not. No one does, unless they are in need of a subject upon which to show their wit. And as for you, from of old you can see nothing that is not separated from you by a few millions of miles, and strewed over with mystery. If women were the inhabitants of Jupiter, of whom you had happened to hear something, you would pore over us and our condition night and day; but because we are before your eyes you never look at us. You care nothing that *this* is ragged and ugly," she said, putting her little finger on his sleeve; "but you strive mightily to make an imaginary leaf on an old stick beautiful. I 'm sorry you don't care for the position of women; I should have liked us to be friends; and it is the only thing about which I think much, or feel much, — if, indeed, I have any feeling about anything," she added flippantly, re-adjusting her dainty little arms. "When I was a baby, I fancy my parents left me out in the frost one night, and I got nipped internally; it feels so!"

"I have only a few old thoughts," he said, "and I

think them over and over again, always beginning
where I left off. I never get any further; I am weary
of them."

"Like an old hen that sits on its eggs month after
month, and they never come out?" she said quickly.
"I am so pressed in upon by new things that, lest
they should trip one another up, I have to keep forcing them back. My head swings sometimes. But this
one thought stands, never goes, — if I might but be
one of those born in the future; then, perhaps, to be
born a woman will not be to be born branded."

Waldo looked at her. It was hard to say whether
she were in earnest or mocking.

"I know it is foolish. Wisdom never kicks at the
iron walls it can't bring down," she said. "But we
are cursed, Waldo; born cursed from the time our
mothers bring us into the world till the shrouds are
put on us. Do not look at me as though I were talking
nonsense. Everything has two sides, — the outside
that is ridiculous, and the inside that is solemn."

"I am not laughing," said the boy, sedately enough;
"but what curses you?"

He thought she would not reply to him she waited
so long.

"It is not what is done to us, but what is made of
us," she said at last, "that wrongs us. No man can
be really injured but by what modifies himself. We
all enter the world little plastic beings, with so much
natural force, perhaps, but for the rest — blank; and
the world tells us what we are to be, and shapes us
by the ends it sets before us. To you it says, *Work!*
and to us it says, *Seem!* To you it says, As you
approximate to man's highest ideal of God, as your
arm is strong and your knowledge great, and the

power to labor is with you, so you shall gain all that human heart desires. To us it says, Strength shall not help you, nor knowledge, nor labor. You shall gain what men gain, but by other means. And so the world makes men and women.

"Look at this little chin of mine, Waldo, with the dimple in it. It is but a small part of my person; but though I had a knowledge of all things under the sun, and the wisdom to use it, and the deep loving heart of an angel, it would not stead me through life like this little chin. I can win money with it, I can win love; I can win power with it, I can win fame. What would knowledge help me? The less a woman has in her head the lighter she is for climbing. I once heard an old man say that he never saw intellect help a woman so much as a pretty ankle; and it was the truth. They begin to shape us to our cursed end," she said, with her lips drawn in to look as though they smiled, "when we are tiny things in shoes and socks. We sit with our little feet drawn up under us in the window, and look out at the boys in their happy play. We want to go. Then a loving hand is laid on us. 'Little one, you cannot go,' they say; 'your little face will burn, and your nice white dress be spoiled.' We feel it must be for our good, it is so lovingly said; but we cannot understand, and we kneel still with one little cheek wistfully pressed against the pane. Afterwards we go and thread blue beads, and make a string for our neck; and we go and stand before the glass. We see the complexion we were not to spoil, and the white frock, and we look into our own great eyes. Then the curse begins to act on us. It finishes its work when we are grown women, who no more look out wistfully at a more healthy life; we are contented.

We fit our sphere as a Chinese woman's foot fits her shoe, exactly as though God had made both; and yet he knows nothing of either. In some of us the shaping to our end has been quite completed. The parts we are not to use have been quite atrophied, and have even dropped off; but in others — and we are not less to be pitied — they have been weakened and left. We wear the bandages, but our limbs have not grown to them; we know that we are compressed, and chafe against them.

"But what does it help? A little bitterness, a little longing when we are young, a little futile searching for work, a little passionate striving for room for the exercise of our powers, — and then we go with the drove. A woman must march with her regiment. In the end she must be trodden down or go with it; and if she is wise she goes.

"I see in your great eyes what you are thinking," she said, glancing at him; "I always know what the person I am talking to is thinking of. How is this woman who makes such a fuss worse off than I? I will show you by a very little example. We stand here at this gate this morning, both poor, both young, both friendless; there is not much to choose between us. Let us turn away just as we are, to make our way in life. This evening you will come to a farmer's house. The farmer, albeit you come alone and on foot, will give you a pipe of tobacco and a cup of coffee and a bed. If he has no dam to build and no child to teach, to-morrow you can go on your way with a friendly greeting of the hand. I, if I come to the same place to-night, will have strange questions asked me, strange glances cast on me. The Boer-wife will shake her head and give me food to eat with the Kaffirs, and a right to sleep with the dogs. That would be the first step in our progress, — a very little one, but every step to the end would repeat it. We were equals once when we lay new-born babes on our nurse's knees. We shall be equals again when they tie up our jaws for the last sleep."

Waldo looked in wonder at the little quivering face; it was a glimpse into a world of passion and feeling wholly new to him.

"Mark you," she said, "we have always this advantage over you, — we can at any time step into ease and competence, where you must labor patiently for it. A little weeping, a little wheedling, a little self-degradation, a little careful use of our advantages, and then some man will say, 'Come, be my wife!' With good looks and youth marriage is easy to attain. There are men enough; but a woman who has sold herself, even for a ring and a new name, need hold her skirt aside for no creature in the street. They both earn their bread in one way. Marriage for love is the beautifulest external symbol of the union of souls; marriage without it is the uncleanliest traffic that defiles the world." She ran her little finger savagely along the topmost bar, shaking off the dozen little dew-drops that still hung there. "And they tell us we have men's chivalrous attention!" she cried. "When we ask to be doctors, lawyers, law-makers, anything but ill-paid drudges, they say, 'No; but you have men's chivalrous attention; now think of that and be satisfied! What would you do without it?'"

The bitter little silvery laugh, so seldom heard, rang out across the bushes. She bit her little teeth together.

15

"I was coming up in Cobb and Co.'s the other day. At a little wayside hotel we had to change the large coach for a small one. We were ten passengers, eight men and two women. As I sat in the house the gentlemen came and whispered to me, 'There is not room for all in the new coach, take your seat quickly.' We hurried out, and they gave me the best seat, and covered me with rugs, because it was drizzling. Then the last passenger came running up to the coach, — an old woman with a wonderful bonnet, and a black shawl pinned with a yellow pin.

"'There is no room,' they said; 'you must wait till next week's coach takes you up;' but she climbed on to the step, and held on at the window with both hands.

"'My son-in-law is ill, and I must go and see him,' she said.

"'My good woman,' said one, 'I am really exceedingly sorry that your son-in-law is ill; but there is absolutely no room for you here.'

"'You had better get down,' said another, 'or the wheel will catch you.'

"I got up to give her my place.

"'Oh, no, no!' they cried, 'we will not allow that.'

"'I will rather kneel,' said one, and he crouched down at my feet; so the woman came in.

"There were nine of us in that coach, and only one showed chivalrous attention, — and that was a woman to a woman.

"I shall be old and ugly too one day, and I shall look for men's chivalrous help, but I shall not find it.

"The bees are very attentive to the flowers till their honey is done, and then they fly over them. I don't know if the flowers feel grateful to the bees; they are great fools if they do."

"But some women," said Waldo, speaking as though the words forced themselves from him at that moment, "some women have power."

She lifted her beautiful eyes to his face.

"Power! Did you ever hear of men being asked whether other souls should have power or not? It is born in them. You may dam up the fountain of water, and make it a stagnant marsh, or you may let it run free and do its work; but *you* cannot say whether it shall be there; *it is there*. And it will act, if not openly for good, then covertly for evil; but it will act. If Goethe had been stolen away a child, and reared in a robber horde in the depths of a German forest, do you think the world would have had Faust and Iphigenie? But he would have been Goethe still — stronger, wiser than his fellows. At night, round their watch-fire, he would have chanted wild songs of rapine and murder, till the dark faces about him were moved and trembled. His songs would have echoed on from father to son, and nerved the heart and arm, — for evil. Do you think if Napoleon had been born a woman that he would have been contented to give small tea-parties and talk small scandal? He would have risen; but the world would not have heard of him as it hears of him now, — a man great and kingly, with all his sins; he would have left one of those names that stain the leaf of every history, — the names of women, who, having power, but being denied the right to exercise it openly, rule in the dark, covertly, and by stealth, through the men whose passions they feed on and by whom they climb.

"Power!" she said suddenly, smiting her little hand upon the rail. "Yes, we have power; and since we are not to expend it in tunnelling mountains, nor healing diseases, nor making laws, nor money, nor on any extraneous object, we expend it on *you*. You are our goods, our merchandise, our material for operating on; we buy you, we sell you, we make fools of you, we act the wily old Jew with you, we keep six of you crawling to our little feet, and praying only for a touch of our little hand; and they say truly, there was never an ache or pain or a broken heart but a woman was at the bottom of it. We are not to study law, nor science, nor art, so we study you. There is never a nerve or fibre in your man's nature but we know it. We keep six of you dancing in the palm of one little hand," she said, balancing her outstretched arm gracefully, as though tiny beings disported themselves in its palm. "There — we throw you away, and you sink to the devil," she said, folding her arms composedly. "There was never a man who said one word for woman but he said two for man, and three for the whole human race."

She watched the bird pecking up the last yellow grains; but Waldo looked only at her.

When she spoke again it was very measuredly.

"They bring weighty arguments against us when we ask for the perfect freedom of women," she said; "but, when you come to the objections, they are like pumpkin devils with candles inside, — hollow, and can't bite. They say that women do not wish for the sphere and freedom we ask for them, and would not use it.

"If the bird *does* like its cage, and *does* like its sugar, and will not leave it, why keep the door so very carefully shut? Why not open it, only a little? Do they know, there is many a bird will not break its wings against the bars, but would fly if the doors were open." She knit her forehead, and leaned farther over the bars.

"Then they say, 'If the women have the liberty you ask for, they will be found in positions for which they are not fitted!' If two men climb one ladder, did you ever see the weakest anywhere but at the foot? The surest sign of fitness is success. The weakness never wins but where there is handicapping. Nature left to herself will as beautifully apportion a man's work to his capacities as long ages ago she graduated the colors on the bird's breast. If we are not fit, you give us to no purpose the right to labor; the work will fall out of our hands into those that are wiser."

She talked more rapidly as she went on, as one talks of that over which they have brooded long, and which lies near their hearts.

Waldo watched her intently.

"They say women have one great and noble work left them, and they do it ill. That is true; they do it execrably. It is the work that demands the broadest culture, and they have not even the narrowest. The lawyer may see no deeper than his law-books, and the chemist see no further than the windows of his laboratory, and they may do their work well. But the woman who does woman's work needs a many-sided, multiform culture; the heights and depths of human life must not be beyond the reach of her vision; she must have knowledge of men and things in many states, a wide catholicity of sympathy, the strength that springs from knowledge, and the magnanimity which springs from strength. *We* bear the world, and *we* make it. The souls of little children are marvellously delicate and tender things, and keep forever the shadow that first falls on them, and that is the mother's, or at best a woman's. There was never a great man who had not a great mother — it is hardly an exaggeration. The first six years of our life make us; all that is added later is veneer; and yet some say, if a woman can cook a dinner or dress herself well she has culture enough.

"The mightiest and noblest of human work is given to us, and we do it ill. Send a navvy into an artist's studio to work, and see what you will find there! And yet, thank God, we have this work," she added quickly; "it is the one window through which we see into the great world of earnest labor. The meanest girl who dances and dresses becomes something higher when her children look up into her face, and ask her questions. It is the only education we have, and this they cannot take from us."

She smiled slightly; "They say that we complain of woman's being compelled to look upon marriage as a profession; but that she is free to enter upon it or leave it as she pleases.

"Yes, and a cat set afloat in a pond is free to sit in the tub till it dies there, it is under no obligation to wet its feet; and a drowning man may catch at a straw or not, just as he likes; it is a glorious liberty! Let any man think for five minutes of what old maidenhood means to a woman, and then let him be silent. Is it easy to bear through life a name that in itself signifies defeat; to dwell, as nine out of

ten unmarried women must, under the finger of another woman ? Is it easy to look forward to an old
age without honor, without the reward of useful
labor, without love ? I wonder how many men there
are who would give up everything that is dear in life
for the sake of maintaining a high ideal purity."

She laughed a little laugh that was clear without
being pleasant. " And then, when they have no other
argument against us, they say, 'Go on; but when
you have made women what you wish, and her children inherit her culture, you will defeat yourself.
Man will gradually become extinct from excess of
intellect, the passions which replenish the race will
die.' Fools !" she said, curling her pretty lip. " A
Hottentot sits at the roadside, and feeds on a rotten
bone he has found there, and takes out his bottle of
Cape-smoke, and swills at it, and grunts with satisfaction ; and the cultured child of the nineteenth century
sits in his armchair, and sips choice wines with the
lip of a connoisseur, and tastes delicate dishes with
a delicate palate, and with a satisfaction of which
the Hottentot knows nothing. Heavy jaw and sloping forehead — all have gone with increasing intellect ; but the animal appetites are there still, — refined,
discriminative, but immeasurably intensified. Fools !
Before men forgave or worshipped, while they still
were weak on their hind legs, did they not eat and
drink, and fight for wives ? When all the later ad-
ditions to humanity have vanished, will not the foundation on which they are built remain ? "

She was silent then for a while, and said somewhat
dreamily, more as though speaking to herself than to
him, —

"They ask, 'What will you gain, even if man does

not become extinct ? You will have brought justice and equality on to the earth, and sent love from it. When men and women are equals they will love no more. Your highly-cultured women will not be lovable, will not love.'

"Do they see nothing, understand nothing ? It is Tant' Sannie who buries husbands one after another, and folds her hands resignedly, — 'The Lord gave, and the Lord hath taken away, and blessed be the name of the Lord,' — and she looks for another. It is the hard-headed, deep thinker who, when the wife who has thought and worked with him goes, can find no rest, and lingers near her till he finds sleep beside her.

"A great soul draws and is drawn with a more fierce intensity than any small one. By every inch we grow in intellectual height our love strikes down its roots deeper, and spreads out its arms wider. It is for love's sake yet more than for any other that we look for that new time." She had leaned her head against the stones, and watched with her sad, soft eyes the retreating bird. "Then when that time comes," she said lowly, "when love is no more bought or sold, when it is not a means of making bread, when each woman's life is filled with earnest, independent labor, — then love will come to her, a strange sudden sweetness breaking in upon her earnest work ; not sought for, but found. Then, but not now — "

Waldo waited for her to finish the sentence, but she seemed to have forgotten him.

"Lyndall," he said, putting his hand upon her — she started — "if you think that that new time will be so great, so good, you who speak so easily — "

She interrupted him.

"Speak! speak!" she said; "the difficulty is not to speak; the difficulty is to keep silence."

"But why do you not try to bring that time?" he said with pitiful simplicity. "When you speak I believe all you say; other people would listen to you also."

"I am not so sure of that," she said with a smile.

Then over the small face came the weary look it had worn last night as it watched the shadow in the corner. Ah, so weary!

"I, Waldo, I?" she said. "I can do nothing good for myself, nothing for the world, till some one wakes me. I am asleep, swathed, shut up in self; till I have been delivered I can deliver no one."

He looked at her wondering, but she was not looking at him.

"To see the good and the beautiful," she said, "and to have no strength to live it, is only to be Moses on the mountain of Nebo, with the land at your feet and no power to enter. It would be better not to see it. Come," she said, looking up into his face, and seeing its uncomprehending expression, "let us go, it is getting late. Doss is anxious for his breakfast also," she added, wheeling round and calling to the dog, who was endeavoring to unearth a mole, an occupation to which he had been zealously addicted from the third month, but in which he had never on any single occasion proved successful.

Waldo shouldered his bag, and Lyndall walked on before in silence, with the dog close to her side. Perhaps she thought of the narrowness of the limits within which a human soul may speak and be understood by its nearest of mental kin, of how soon it reaches that solitary land of the individual experience, in which no fellow footfall is ever heard. Whatever her thoughts may have been, she was soon interrupted. Waldo came close to her, and standing still, produced with awkwardness from his breast-pocket a small carved box.

"I made it for you," he said, holding it out.

"I like it," she said, examining it carefully.

The workmanship was better than that of the grave-post. The flowers that covered it were delicate, and here and there small conical protuberances were let in among them. She turned it round critically. Waldo bent over it lovingly.

"There is one strange thing about it," he said earnestly, putting a finger on one little pyramid. "I made it without these, and I felt something was wrong; I tried many changes, and at last I let these in, and then it was right. But why was it? They are not beautiful in themselves."

"They relieve the monotony of the smooth leaves, I suppose."

He shook his head as over a weighty matter.

"The sky is monotonous," he said, "when it is blue, and yet it is beautiful. I have thought of that often; but it is not monotony and it is not variety makes beauty. What is it? The sky, and your face, and this box, — the same thing is in them all, only more in the sky and in your face. But what is it?"

She smiled, —

"So you are at your old work still. Why, why, why? What is the reason? It is enough for me," she said, "if I find out what is beautiful and what is ugly, what is real and what is not. Why it is there, and over the final cause of things in general, I don't trouble myself; there must be one, but what is it to me ? If I howl to all eternity, I shall never get hold of it; and if I did, I might be no better off. But you Germans are born with an aptitude for burrowing; you can't help yourselves. You must sniff after reasons, just as that dog must after a mole. He knows perfectly well he will never catch it, but he's under the imperative necessity of digging for it."

"But he *might* find it."

"*Might ;* but he never has and never will. Life is too short to run after 'mights'; we must have certainties."

She tucked the box under her arm and was about to walk on, when Gregory Rose, with shining spurs, an ostrich feather in his hat, and a silver-headed whip, careered past. He bowed gallantly as he went by. They waited till the dust of the horse's hoofs had laid itself.

"There," said Lyndall, "goes a true woman — one born for the sphere that some women have to fill without being born for it. How happy he would be sewing frills into his little girl's frocks, and how pretty he would look sitting in a parlor, with a rough man making love to him! Don't you think so ? "

"I shall not stay here when he is master," Waldo answered, not able to connect any kind of beauty with Gregory Rose.

"I should imagine not. The rule of a woman is tyranny; but the rule of a man-woman grinds fine. Where are you going ? "

" Anywhere."

" What to do ? "

" See, — see everything."

" You will be disappointed."

" And were you ? "

"Yes; and you will be more so. I want some things that men and the world give; you do not. If you have a few yards of earth to stand on, and a bit of blue over you, and something that you cannot see to dream about, you have all that you need, all that you know how to use. But I like to see real men. Let them be as disagreeable as they please, they are more interesting to me than flowers, or trees, or stars, or any other thing under the sun. Sometimes," she added, walking on, and shaking the dust daintily from her skirts, "when I am not too busy trying to find a new way of doing my hair that will show my little neck to better advantage, or over other work of that kind, sometimes it amuses me intensely to trace out the resemblance between one man and another; to see how Tant' Sannie and I, you and Bonaparte, Saint Simon on his pillar and the Emperor dining off larks' tongues, are one and the same compound, merely mixed in different proportions. What is microscopic in one is largely developed in another; what is a rudimentary in one man is an active organ in another; but all things are in all men, and one soul is the model of all. We shall find nothing new in human nature after we have once carefully dissected and analyzed the one being we ever shall truly know, — ourself. The Kaffir girl threw some coffee on my arm in bed this morning; I felt displeased, but said nothing. Tant' Sannie would have thrown the saucer at her and sworn for an hour; but the feeling would be the same irritated displeasure. If a huge animated stomach like Bonaparte were put under a glass by a skilful mental microscopist, even he would be found to have an embryonic doubling somewhere indicative of a heart, and rudimentary buddings that might have become conscience and sincerity.— Let me take your arm, Waldo. How full you are of mealie dust. No, never mind; it will brush off. — And sometimes what is more amusing still than tracing the likeness between man and man is to trace the analogy there always is between the progress and development of one individual and of a whole nation; or again, between a single nation and the entire human race. It is pleasant when it dawns on you that the one is just the other written out in large letters; and very odd to find all the little follies and virtues, and developments and retrogressions, written out in the big world's book that you find in your little internal self. It is the most amusing thing I know of; but of course being a woman, I have not often time for such amusements. Professional duties always first, you know. It takes a great deal of time and thought always to look perfectly exquisite, even for a pretty woman. Is the old buggy still in existence, Waldo?"

"Yes; but the harness is broken."

"Well, I wish you would mend it. You must teach me to drive. I must learn something while I am here. I got the Hottentot girl to show me how to make 'sarsarties' this morning; and Tant' Sannie is going to teach me to make kappjes. I will come and sit with you this afternoon while you mend the harness."

"Thank you."

"No, don't thank me; I come for my own pleasure. I never find any one I can talk to. Women bore me, and men, I talk so to, 'Going to the ball this evening? Nice little dog that of yours. Pretty little ears. So fond of pointer pups!' And they think me fascinating, charming! Men are like the earth and we are the moon; we turn always one side to them, and they think there is no other, because they don't see it; — but there is."

They had reached the house now.

"Tell me when you set to work," she said, and walked towards the door.

Waldo stood to look after her, and Doss stood at his side, a look of painful uncertainty depicted on his small countenance, and one little foot poised in the air. Should he stay with his master or go? He looked at the figure with the wide straw hat moving towards the house, and he looked up at his master; then he put down the little paw and went. Waldo watched them both in at the door, and then walked away alone. He was satisfied that at least his dog was with her.

CHAPTER V.

It was just after sunset, and Lyndall had not yet
returned from her first driving-lesson, when the lean
colored woman standing at the corner of the house to
enjoy the evening breeze, saw coming along the road
a strange horseman. Very narrowly she surveyed him
as slowly he approached. He was attired in the deep-
est mourning, the black crape round his tall hat totally
concealing the black felt, and nothing but a dazzling
shirt-front relieving the funereal tone of his attire.
He rode much forward in his saddle, with his chin
resting on the uppermost of his shirt-studs, and there
was an air of meek subjection to the will of Heaven,
and to what might be in store for him, that bespoke
itself even in the way in which he gently urged his
steed. He was evidently in no hurry to reach his des-
tination, for the nearer he approached to it the slacker
did his bridle hang. The colored woman having duly
inspected him dashed into the dwelling.

"Here is another one," she cried; " a widower, — I
see it by his hat."

"Good Lord!" said Tant' Sannie; "it's the seventh
I 've had this month; but the men know where sheep
and good looks, and money in the bank are to be
found," she added, winking knowingly. "How does
he look?"

"Nineteen, weak eyes, white hair, little round nose," said the maid.

"Then it's he! then it's he!" said Tant' Sannie, triumphantly; "Little Piet Vander Walt, whose wife died last month; two farms, twelve thousand sheep. I've not seen him; but my sister-in-law told me about him, and I dreamed about him last night."

Here Piet's black hat appeared in the doorway, and the Boer-woman drew herself up in dignified silence, extended the tips of her fingers, and motioned solemnly to a chair. The young man seated himself, sticking his feet as far under it as they would go, and said mildly, —

"I am Little Piet Vander Walt, and my father is Big Piet Vander Walt."

Tant' Sannie said solemnly, "Yes."

"Aunt," said the young man, starting up spasmodically, "can I 'off-saddle?'"

"Yes."

He seized his hat, and disappeared with a rush through the door.

"I told you so! I knew it!" said Tant' Sannie. "The dear Lord doesn't send dreams for nothing. Didn't I tell you this morning that I dreamed of a great beast like a sheep, with red eyes, and that I killed it? Wasn't the white wool his hair, and the red eyes his weak eyes, and my killing him meant marriage? Get supper ready quickly; the sheep's inside and roaster-cakes. We shall sit up to-night."

To young Piet Vander Walt that supper was a period of intense torture. There was something over-awing in that assembly of English people, with their incomprehensible speech; and, moreover, it was his first courtship. His first wife had courted him, and ten months of severe domestic rule had not raised his spirit nor courage. He ate little, and when he raised a morsel to his lips, glanced guiltily round to see if he were not observed. He had put three rings on his little finger, with the intention of sticking it out stiffly when he raised a coffee-cup; now the little finger was curled miserably among its fellows. It was small relief when the meal was over, and Tant' Sannie and he repaired to the front room. Once seated there, he set his knees close together, stood his black hat upon them, and wretchedly turned the brim up and down. But supper had cheered Tant' Sannie, who found it impossible longer to maintain that decorous silence, and whose heart yearned over the youth.

"I was related to your Aunt Selena who died," said Tant' Sannie. "My mother's step-brother's child was married to her father's brother's step-nephew's niece."

"Yes, Aunt," said the young man, "I knew we were related."

"It was her cousin," said Tant' Sannie, now fairly on the flow, "who had the cancer cut out of her breast by the other doctor, who was not the right doctor they sent for, but who did it quite as well."

"Yes, Aunt," said the young man.

"I've heard about it often," said Tant' Sannie. "And he was the son of the old doctor that they say died on Christmas Day; but I don't know if that's true. People do tell such awful lies. Why should he die on Christmas Day more than any other day?"

"Yes, Aunt, why?" said the young man, meekly.

"Did you ever have the toothache?" asked Tant' Sannie.

"No, Aunt."

16

"Well, they say that doctor, — not the son of the old doctor that died on Christmas Day; the other that didn't come when he was sent for, — he gave such good stuff for the toothache that if you opened the bottle in the room where any one was bad they got better directly. You could see it was good stuff," said Tant' Sannie; "it tasted horrid. *That* was a real doctor! He used to give a bottle so high," said the Boer-woman, raising her hand a foot from the table, "you could drink at it for a month and it wouldn't get done, and the same medicine was good for all sorts of sicknesses, — croup, measles, jaundice, dropsy. *Now* you have to buy a new kind for each sickness. The doctors aren't so good as they used to be."

"No, Aunt," said the young man, who was trying to gain courage to stick out his legs and clink his spurs together. He did so at last.

Tant' Sannie had noticed the spurs before; but she thought it showed a nice manly spirit, and her heart warmed yet more to the youth.

"Did you ever have convulsions when you were a baby?" asked Tant' Sannie.

"Yes," said the young man.

"Strange!" said Tant' Sannie; "I had convulsions too. Wonderful that we should be so much alike!"

"Aunt," said the young man, explosively, "can we sit up to-night?"

Tant' Sannie hung her head and half-closed her eyes; but finding that her little wiles were thrown away, the young man staring fixedly at his hat, she simpered "Yes," and went away to fetch candles.

In the dining-room Em worked at her machine, and Gregory sat close beside her, his great blue eyes turned

to the window where Lyndall leaned out talking to
Waldo.

Tant' Sannie took two candles out of the cupboard,
and held them up triumphantly, winking all round the
room.

"He's asked for them," she said.

"Does he want them for his horse's rubbed back?"
asked Gregory, new to up-country life.

"No," said Tant' Sannie, indignantly; "we're going to sit up!" and she walked off in triumph with the
candles.

Nevertheless, when all the rest of the house had retired, when the long candle was lighted, when the
coffee-kettle was filled, when she sat in the elbow-
chair, with her lover on a chair close beside her, and
when the vigil of the night was fairly begun, she began to find it wearisome. The young man looked
chilly, and said nothing.

"Won't you put your feet on my stove?" said
Tant' Sannie.

"No, thank you, Aunt," said the young man; and
both lapsed into silence.

At last Tant' Sannie, afraid of going to sleep, tapped
a strong cup of coffee for herself, and handed another
to her lover. This visibly revived both.

"How long were you married, Cousin?"

"Ten months, Aunt."

"How old was your baby?"

"Three days when it died."

"It's very hard when we must give our husbands
and wives to the Lord," said Tant' Sannie.

"Very," said the young man; "but it's the Lord's
will."

"Yes," said Tant' Sannie, and sighed.

"She was such a good wife, Aunt: I 've known her break a churn-stick over a maid's head for only letting dust come on a milk-cloth."

Tant' Sannie felt a twinge of jealousy. She had never broken a churn-stick on a maid's head.

"I hope your wife made a good end," she said.

"Oh, beautiful, Aunt: she said up a psalm and two hymns and a half before she died."

"Did she leave any messages?" asked Tant' Sannie.

"No," said the young man; "but the night before she died I was lying at the foot of her bed; I felt her foot kick me.

" 'Piet,' she said.

" 'Annie, my heart,' said I.

" 'My little baby that died yesterday has been here, and it stood over the wagon-box,' she said.

" 'What did it say?' I asked.

" 'It said that if I died you must marry a fat woman.'

" 'I will,' I said, and I went to sleep again. Presently she woke me.

" 'The little baby has been here again, and it says you must marry a woman over thirty, and who 's had two husbands.'

"I did n't go to sleep after that for a long time, Aunt; but when I did she woke me.

" 'The baby has been here again,' she said, 'and it says you must n't marry a woman with a mole.' I told her I would n't; and the next day she died."

"That was a vision from the Redeemer," said Tant' Sannie.

The young man nodded his head mournfully. He thought of a younger sister of his wife's who was not fat, and who *had* a mole, and of whom his wife had always been jealous, and he wished the little baby had liked better staying in heaven than coming and standing over the wagon-chest.

"I suppose that's why you came to me," said Tant' Sannie.

"Yes, Aunt. And pa said I ought to get married before shearing-time. It is bad if there's no one to see after things then; and the maids waste such a lot of fat."

"When do you want to get married?"

"Next month, Aunt," said the young man, in a tone of hopeless resignation. "May I kiss you, Aunt?"

"Fie! fie!" said Tant' Sannie, and then gave him a resounding kiss. "Come, draw your chair a little closer," she said; and their elbows now touching they sat on through the night.

The next morning at dawn, as Em passed through Tant' Sannie's bedroom, she found the Boer-woman pulling off her boots preparatory to climbing into bed.

"Where is Piet Vander Walt?"

"Just gone," said Tant' Sannie; "and I am going to marry him this day four weeks. I am dead sleepy," she added; "the stupid thing does n't know how to talk love-talk at all," and she climbed into the four-poster, clothes and all, and drew the quilt up to her chin.

On the day preceding Tant' Sannie's wedding, Gregory Rose sat in the blazing sun on the stone-wall behind his daub-and-wattle house. It was warm, but he was intently watching a small buggy that was being recklessly driven over the bushes in the direction of the farm-house. Gregory never stirred till it had vanished; then finding the stones hot he slipped down and walked into the house. He kicked the little pail that lay in the docrway, and sent it into one corner; that did him good. Then he sat down on the box, and began cutting letters out of a piece of newspaper. Finding that the snippings littered the floor, he picked them up, and began scribbling on his blotting-paper. He tried the effect of different initials before the name Rose, — G. Rose, E. Rose, L. Rose, L. Rose, L. L. L. L. Rose. When he had covered the sheet, he looked at it discontentedly a little while, then suddenly began to write a letter.

BELOVED SISTER, — It is a long while since I last wrote to you, but I have had no time. This is the first morning I have been at home since I don't know when. Em always expects me to go down to the farm-house in the morning; but I did n't feel as though I could stand the ride to-day.

I have much news for you.

Tant' Sannie, Em's Boer step-mother, is to be married to-morrow. She is gone to town to-day, and the wedding feast is to be at her brother's farm. Em and I are going to ride over on horseback, but her cousin is going to ride in the buggy with that German. I don't think I've written to you since she came back from school. I don't think you would like her at all, Jemima; there's something so proud about her. She thinks just because she's handsome there's nobody good enough to talk to her, and just as if there had nobody else but her been to boarding-school before.

They are going to have a grand affair to-morrow: all the Boers about are coming, and they are going to dance all night; but I don't think I shall dance at all; for, as Em's cousin says, these Boer dances are low things. I am sure I only danced at the last to please Em. I don't know why she is fond of dancing.

Em talked of our being married on the same day as Tant' Sannie; but I said it would be nicer for her if she waited till the shearing was over, and I took her down to see you. I suppose she will have to live with us (Em's cousin, I mean), as she has not anything in the world but a poor fifty pounds. I don't like her *at all*, Jemima, and I don't think you would. She's got such queer ways; she's always driving about in a gig with that low German, and I don't think it's at all the thing for a woman to be going about with a man she's not engaged to. Do you? If it was me now, who am a kind of connection, of course it would be different. The way she treats me, considering that I am so soon to be her cousin, is not at all nice. I took down my album the other day with your likenesses in it, and I told her she could look at it, and put it down close to her; but she just said, Thank you, and never even touched it, as much as to say, What are your relations to me?

She gets the wildest horses in that buggy, and a horrid snappish little cur, belonging to the German, sitting in front, and then she drives out alone. I don't think it's at all proper for a woman to drive out alone; I would n't allow it if she was *my* sister. The other morning, I don't know how it happened, I was going in the way from which she was coming, and that little beast, they call him Doss, began to bark when he saw me, — he always does, the little wretch, — and the horses began to spring, and kicked the splash-board all to pieces. It was a sight to see, Jemima. She has got the littlest hands I ever saw, — I could hold them both in one of mine, and not know that I'd got anything except that they were so soft; but she held those horses in as though they were made of iron. When I wanted to help her she said, "No, thank you; I can manage them myself. I've got a pair of bits that would break their jaws if I used them well," and she laughed and drove away. It's so unwomanly.

Tell father my hire of the ground will not be out for six months, and before that Em and I will be married. My pair of birds is breeding now, but I haven't been down to see them for three days. I don't seem to care about anything any more. I don't know what it is; I'm not well. If I go into town on Saturday, I will let the doctor examine me; but perhaps she'll go in herself. It's a very strange thing, Jemima, but she never will send her letters to post by me. If I ask her she has none, and the very next day she goes in and posts them herself. You mustn't say anything about it, Jemima, but *twice* I've brought her letters from the post in a gentleman's hand, and I'm sure they were both from the same person, because I noticed every little mark, even the dotting of the *i*'s. Of course it's nothing to *me;* but for Em's sake I can't help feeling an interest in her, however much I may dislike her myself; and I hope she's up to nothing. I pity the man who marries *her;* I wouldn't be him for *anything*. If I had a wife with pride, I'd make her give it up, *sharp*. I don't believe in a man who can't make a woman obey him. Now, Em — I'm very fond of her, as you know, but if I tell her to put on a certain dress, that dress she puts on; and if I tell her to sit on a certain seat, on that seat she sits; and if I tell her not to speak to a certain individual, she does not speak to him. If a man lets a woman do what he doesn't like, *he's a muff.*

Give my love to mother and the children. The "veld" here is looking pretty good, and the sheep are better since we washed them. Tell father the dip he recommended is very good.

Em sends her love to you. She is making me some woollen shirts; but they don't fit me so nicely as those mother made me.

Write soon to

Your loving brother,

GREGORY.

P. S. She drove past just now. I was sitting on the kraal wall right before her eyes, and she never even bowed.   G. N. R.

CHAPTER VI.

A BOER-WEDDING.

" I did n't know before you were so fond of riding hard," said Gregory, to his little betrothed.

They were cantering slowly on the road to Oom Muller's, on the morning of the wedding.

"Do you call this riding hard?" asked Em, in some astonishment.

"Of course I do! It's enough to break the horses' necks, and knock one up for the whole day besides," he added testily; then twisted his head to look at the buggy that came on behind. "I thought Waldo was such a mad driver. They are taking it easily enough to-day," said Gregory. "One would think the black stallions were lame."

"I suppose they want to keep out of our dust," said Em. "See, they stand still as soon as we do."

Perceiving this to be the case, Gregory rode on.

"It's all that horse of yours; she kicks up such a confounded dust I can't stand it myself," he said.

Meanwhile the cart came on slowly enough.

"Take the reins," said Lyndall, "and make them walk. I want to rest and watch their hoofs to-day, not to be exhilarated, — I am so tired."

She leaned back in her corner, and Waldo drove on slowly in the gray dawn light along the level road. They passed the very milk-bush behind which, so many years before, the old German had found the

Kaffir woman. But their thoughts were not with him that morning; they were the thoughts of the young, that run out to meet the future, and labor in the present. At last he touched her arm.

"What is it?"

"I feared you had gone to sleep, and might be jolted out," he said, "you sat so quietly."

"No; do not talk to me. I am not asleep;" but after a time she said suddenly, "it must be a terrible thing to bring a human being into the world."

Waldo looked round; she sat drawn into the corner, her blue cloud wound tightly about her, and she still watched the horses' feet. Having no comment to offer on her somewhat unexpected remark, he merely touched up his horses.

"I have no conscience, — none," she added; "but I would not like to bring a soul into this world. When it sinned, and when it suffered, something like a dead hand would fall on me, — 'You did it, — you; for your own pleasure you created this thing! See your work!' If it lived to be eighty it would always hang like a millstone round my neck, — have the right to demand good from me, and curse me for its sorrow. A parent is only like to God; if his work turns out bad, so much the worse for him; he *dare* not wash his hands of it. Time and years can never bring the day when you can say to your child, 'Soul, what have I to do with you?'"

Waldo said dreamily, —

"It is a marvellous thing that one soul should have power to cause another."

She heard the words as she heard the beating of the horses' hoofs; her thoughts ran on in their own line.

"They say, 'God sends the little babies.' Of all the
dastardly revolting lies men tell to suit themselves, I
hate that most. I suppose my father said so when he
knew he was dying of consumption, and my mother
when she knew she had nothing to support me on;
and they created me to feed like a dog from stranger
hands. Men do not say God sends the books, or the
newspaper articles, or the machines they make, and
then sigh and shrug their shoulders, and say they
can't help it. Why do they say so about other things?
Liars! 'God sends the little babies!'" She struck
her foot fretfully against the splash-board. "The
small children say so earnestly. *They* touch the little
stranger reverently who has just come from God's far
country, and they peep about the room to see if not
one white feather has dropped from the wing of the
angel that brought him. On their lips the phrase
means much; on all others it is a *deliberate lie!*
Noticeable, too," she said, dropping in an instant
from the passionate into a low mocking tone, "when
people are married, though they should have sixty
children, they throw the whole *onus* on God. When
they are not, we hear nothing about God's having
sent them. When there has been no legal contract
between the parents, who sends the little children
then? The devil, perhaps!" she laughed her little
silvery mocking laugh. "Odd that some men should
come from hell and some from heaven, and yet all
look so much alike when they get here."

Waldo wondered at her. He had not the key to
her thoughts, and did not see the string on which
they were strung. She drew her cloud tighter about
her.

"It must be very nice to believe in the devil," she

said. "I wish I did. If it would be of any use I would pray three hours, night and morning, on my bare knees, 'God, let me believe in Satan.' He is so useful to those people who do. They may be as selfish and as sensual as they please, and, between God's will and the devil's action, always have some one to throw their sin on. But we, wretched unbelievers, we bear our own burdens; we must say, 'I, myself, did it, *I*. Not God, not Satan; I, myself!' That is the sting that strikes deep. Waldo," she said gently, with a sudden and complete change of manner, "I like you so much I love you." She rested her cheek softly against his shoulder. "When I am with you, I never know that I am a woman and you are a man; I only know that we are both things that think. Other men, when I am with them, whether I love them or not, they are mere bodies to me; but you are a spirit. I like you. Look," she said, quickly, sinking back into her corner, "what a pretty pinkness there is on all the hill-tops! The sun will rise in a moment."

Waldo lifted his eyes to look round over the circle of golden hills; and the horses, as the first sunbeams touched them, shook their heads and champed their bright bits, till the brass settings in their harness glittered again.

It was eight o'clock when they neared the farmhouse: a red-brick building, with kraals to the right and a small orchard to the left. Already there were signs of unusual life and bustle; one cart, a wagon, and a couple of saddles against the wall betokened the arrival of a few early guests, whose numbers would soon be largely increased. To a Dutch countrywedding guests start up in numbers astonishing to one who has merely ridden through the plains of sparsely inhabited karroo.

As the morning advances, riders on many shades of steeds appear from all directions, and add their saddles to the long rows against the walls, shake hands, drink coffee, and stand about outside in groups to watch the arriving carts and ox-wagons, as they are unburdened of their heavy freight of massive Tantes and comely daughters, followed by swarms of children of all sizes, dressed in all manner of print and moleskin, who are taken care of by Hottentot, Kaffir, and half-caste nurses, whose many-shaded complexions, ranging from light yellow up to ebony black, add variety to the animated scene. Everywhere is excitement and bustle, which gradually increases as the time for the return of the wedding party approaches. Preparations for the feast are actively advancing in the kitchen; coffee is liberally handed round, and amid a profound sensation, and the firing of guns, the horse-wagon draws up, and the wedding party alight. Bride and bridegroom, with their attendants, march solemnly to the marriage-chamber, where bed and box are decked out in white, with ends of ribbon and artificial flowers, and where on a row of chairs the party solemnly seat themselves. After a time bridesmaid and best man rise, and conduct in with ceremony each individual guest, to wish success and to kiss bride and bridegroom. Then the feast is set on the table, and it is almost sunset before the dishes are cleared away, and the pleasure of the day begins. Everything is removed from the great front room, and the mud floor well rubbed with bullock's blood, glistens like polished mahogany. The female portion of the assembly flock into the side-rooms to

attire themselves for the evening, and reissue clad
in white muslin, and gay with bright ribbons and
brass jewelry, The dancing begins as the first tallow candles are stuck up about the walls, the music
coming from a couple of fiddlers in a corner of the
room. Bride and bridegroom open the ball, and the
floor is soon covered with whirling couples, and every
one's spirits rise. The bridal pair mingle freely in
the throng, and here and there a musical man sings
vigorously as he drags his partner through the "Blue
Water" or "John Speriwig;" boys shout and applaud,
and the enjoyment and confusion are intense, till
eleven o'clock comes. By this time the children who
swarm in the side-rooms are not to be kept quiet
longer, even by hunches of bread and cake; there is
a general howl and wail, that rises yet higher than
the scraping of fiddles, and mothers rush from their
partners to knock small heads together, and cuff
little nursemaids, and force the wailers down into unoccupied corners of beds, under tables, and behind
boxes. In half an hour every variety of childish
snore is heard on all sides, and it has become perilous
to raise or set down a foot in any of the side-rooms
lest a small head or hand should be crushed. Now
too the busy feet have broken the solid coating of the
floor, and a cloud of fine dust arises, that makes a
yellow halo round the candles, and sets asthmatic
people coughing, and grows denser, till to recognize
any one on the opposite side of the room becomes impossible, and a partner's face is seen through a yellow mist.

At twelve o'clock the bride is led to the marriage-
chamber and undressed; the lights are blown out,
and the bridegroom is brought to the door by the best

man, who gives him the key; then the door is shut and locked, and the revels rise higher than ever. There is no thought of sleep till morning, and no unoccupied spot where sleep may be found.

It was at this stage of the proceedings, on the night of Tant' Sannie's wedding, that Lyndall sat near the doorway in one of the side-rooms, to watch the dancers as they appeared and disappeared in the yellow cloud of dust. Gregory sat moodily in a corner of the large dancing-room. His little betrothed touched his arm.

"I wish you would go and ask Lyndall to dance with you," she said; "she must be so tired; she has sat still the whole evening."

"I have asked her three times," replied her lover, shortly. "I'm not going to be *her* dog, and creep to *her* feet, just to give her the pleasure of kicking me, — not for you, Em, nor for anybody else."

"Oh, I did n't know you had asked her, Greg," said his little betrothed, humbly; and she went away to pour out coffee.

Nevertheless, some time after, Gregory found he had shifted so far round the room as to be close to the door where Lyndall sat. After standing for some time he inquired whether he might not bring her a cup of coffee. She declined; but still he stood on (why should he not stand there as well as anywhere else?), and then he stepped into the bedroom.

"May I not bring you a stove, Miss Lyndall, to put your feet on?"

"Thank you."

He sought for one, and put it under her feet.

"There is a draught from that broken window; shall I stuff something in the pane?"

"No; we want air."

Gregory looked round, but nothing else suggesting itself he sat down on a box on the opposite side of the door. Lyndall sat before him, her chin resting in her hand; her eyes, steel-gray by day, but black by night, looked through the doorway into the next room. After a time he thought she had entirely forgotten his proximity, and he dared to inspect the little hands and neck, as he never dared when he was in momentary dread of the eyes being turned upon him. She was dressed in black, which seemed to take her yet further from the white-clad, gewgawed women about her; and the little hands were white, and the diamond ring glittered. Where had she got that ring? He bent forward a little and tried to decipher the letters, but the candle-light was too faint. When he looked up, her eyes were fixed on him. She was looking at him, — not, Gregory felt, as she had ever looked at him before; not as though he were a stump or a stone, that chance had thrown in her way. To-night, whether it were critically, or kindly, or unkindly he could not tell, but she looked at him, — at the man, Gregory Rose, — with attention. A vague elation filled him. He clinched his fist tight to think of some good idea he might express to her; but of all those profound things he had pictured himself as saying to her, when he sat alone in the daub-and-wattle house, not one came. He said at last, —

"These Boer dances are very low things;" and then, as soon as it had gone from him, he thought it was not a clever remark, and wished it back.

Before Lyndall replied, Em looked in at the door.

"Oh, come!" she said; "they are going to have the cushion-dance. I do not want to kiss any of these fellows. Take me quickly!"

17

She slipped her hand into Gregory's arm.

"It is so dusty, Em; do you care to dance any more?" he asked, without rising.

"Oh, I do not mind the dust, and the dancing rests me."

But he did not move.

"I feel tired; I do not think I shall dance again," he said.

Em withdrew her hand, and a young farmer came to the door and bore her off.

"I have often imagined," remarked Gregory — but Lyndall had risen.

"I am tired," she said. "I wonder where Waldo is; he must take me home. These people will not leave off till morning, I suppose; it is three already."

She made her way past the fiddlers, and a bench full of tired dancers, and passed out at the front door. On the "stoep" a group of men and boys were smoking, peeping in at the windows, and cracking coarse jokes. Waldo was certainly not among them, and she made her way to the carts and wagons drawn up at some distance from the homestead.

"Waldo," she said, peering into a large cart, "is that you? I am so dazed with the tallow candles, I see nothing."

He had made himself a place between the two seats. She climbed up, and sat on the sloping floor in front.

"I thought I should find you here," she said, drawing her skirt up about her shoulders. "You must take me home presently, but not now."

She leaned her head on the seat near to his, and they listened in silence to the fitful twanging of the fiddles as the night-wind bore it from the farm-house, and to the ceaseless thud of the dancers, and the peals

of gross laughter. She stretched out her little hand
to feel for his.

"It is so nice to lie here and hear that noise," she
said. "I like to feel that strange life beating up
against me. I like to realize forms of life utterly unlike mine." She drew a long breath. "When my own
life feels small, and I am oppressed with it, I like to
crush together, and see in a picture, in an instant, a
multitude of disconnected unlike phases of human life,
— a mediæval monk with his string of beads pacing the
quiet orchard, and looking up from the grass at his
feet to the heavy fruit-trees; little Malay boys playing
naked on a shining sea-beach; a Hindoo philosopher
alone under his banyan tree, thinking, thinking, thinking, so that in the thought of God he may lose himself; a troop of Bacchanalians dressed in white, with
crowns of vine-leaves, dancing along the Roman
streets; a martyr on the night of his death looking
through the narrow window to the sky, and feeling
that already he has the wings that shall bear him up"
(she moved her hand dreamily over her face); "an
Epicurean discoursing at a Roman bath to a knot of
his disciples on the nature of happiness; a Kaffir
witch-doctor seeking for herbs by moonlight, while
from the huts on the hill-side come the sound of dogs
barking, and the voices of women and children; a
mother giving bread and milk to her children in little
wooden basins and singing the evening song. I like
to see it all; I feel it run through me, — that life be-
longs to me; it makes my little life larger, it breaks
down the narrow walls that shut me in."

She sighed, and drew a long breath.

"Have you made any plan?" she asked him,
presently.

"Yes," he said, the words coming in jets, with pauses between; "I will take the gray mare, — I will travel first, — I will see the world, — then I will find work."

"What work?"

"I do not know."

She made a little impatient movement.

"That is no plan; travel — see the world — find work! If you go into the world aimless, without a definite object, dreaming, dreaming, — you will be definitely defeated, bamboozled, knocked this way and that. In the end you will stand with your beautiful life all spent, and nothing to show. They talk of genius, — it is nothing but this, that a man knows what he can do best, and does it, and nothing else. Waldo," she said, knitting her little fingers closer among his, "I wish I could help you; I wish I could make you see that you must decide what you will be and do. It does not matter what you choose, — be a farmer, business-man, artist, what you will, — but know your aim, and live for that one thing. We have only one life. The secret of success is concentration; wherever there has been a great life, or a great work, that has gone before. Taste everything a little, look at everything a little; but live for one thing. Anything is possible to a man who knows his end, and moves straight for it, and for it alone. I will show you what I mean," she said, concisely; "words are gas till you condense them into pictures.

"Suppose a woman, young, friendless as I am, the weakest thing on God's earth. But she must make her way through life. What she would be she cannot be because she is a woman; so she looks carefully at herself and the world about her, to see where her path

must be made. There is no one to help her; she
must help herself. She looks. These things she has,
— a sweet voice, rich in subtle intonations; a fair,
very fair face, with a power of concentrating in itself,
and giving expression to, feelings that otherwise must
have been dissipated in words ; a rare power of entering into other lives unlike her own, and intuitively
reading them aright. These qualities she has. How
shall she use them ? A poet, a writer, needs only the
mental; what use has he for a beautiful body that
registers clearly mental emotions ? And the painter
wants an eye for form and color, and the musician an
ear for time and tune, and the mere drudge has no
need for mental gifts. But there is one art in which
all she has would be used, for which they are all
necessary, — the delicate, expressive body, the rich
voice, the power of mental transposition. The actor,
who absorbs and then reflects from himself other human lives, needs them all, but needs not much more.
This is her end; but how to reach it ? Before her
are endless difficulties ; seas must be crossed, poverty
must be endured, loneliness, want. She must be content to wait long before she can even get her feet
upon the path. If she has made blunders in the past,
if she has weighted herself with a burden which she
must bear to the end, she must but bear the burden
bravely, and labor on. There is no use in wailing
and repentance here; the next world is the place for
that; this life is too short. By our errors we see
deeper into life. They help us." She waited for a
while. "If she does all this, — if she waits patiently, if she is never cast down, never despairs, never
forgets her end, moves straight towards it, bending men and things most unlikely to her purpose,

— she must succeed at last. Men and things are plastic; they part to the right and left when one comes among them moving in a straight line to one end. I know it by my own little experience," she said. "Long years ago I resolved to be sent to school. It seemed a thing utterly out of my power; but I waited, I watched, I collected clothes, I wrote, took my place at the school; when all was ready I bore with my full force on the Boer-woman, and she sent me at last. It was a small thing; but life is made up of small things, as a body is built up of cells. What has been done in small things can be done in large. Shall be," she said softly.

Waldo listened. To him the words were no confession, no glimpse into the strong, proud, restless heart of the woman. They were general words with a general application. He looked up into the sparkling sky with dull eyes.

"Yes," he said; "but when we lie and think, and think, we see that there is nothing worth doing. The universe is so large, and man is so small —"

She shook her head quickly.

"But we must not think so far; it is madness; it is a disease. We know that no man's work is great, and stands forever. Moses is dead, and the prophets; and the books that our grandmothers fed on the mould is eating. Your poet and painter and actor, — before the shouts that applaud them have died their names grow strange; they are milestones that the world has passed. Men have set their mark on mankind forever, as they thought; but time has washed it out as it has washed out mountains and continents." She raised herself on her elbow. "And what, if we *could* help mankind, and leave the traces of our work upon

it to the end? Mankind is only an ephemeral blossom on the tree of time; there were others before it
opened; there will be others after it has fallen.
Where was man in the time of the dicynodont, and
when hoary monsters wallowed in the mud? Will he
be found in the eons that are to come? We are
sparks, we are shadows, we are pollen, which the next
wind will carry away. We are dying already; it is
all a dream.

"I know that thought. When the fever of living
is on us, when the desire to become, to know, to do, is
driving us mad, we can use it as an anodyne to still
the fever and cool our beating pulses. But it is a
poison, not a food. If we live on it, it will turn our
blood to ice; we might as well be dead. We must
not, Waldo; I want your life to be beautiful, to end
in something. You are nobler and stronger than I,"
she said; "and as much better as one of God's great
angels is better than a sinning man. Your life must
go for something."

"Yes, we will work," he said.

She moved closer to him, and lay still, his black
curls touching her smooth little head.

Doss, who had lain at his master's side, climbed
over the bench, and curled himself up in her lap.
She drew her skirt up over him, and the three sat
motionless for a long time.

"Waldo," she said, suddenly, "they are laughing
at us."

"Who?" he asked, starting up.

"They, — the stars!" she said softly. "Do you
not see? — there is a little, white, mocking finger
pointing down at us from each one of them! We are
talking of to-morrow, and to-morrow; and our hearts

are so strong; we are not thinking of something that can touch us softly in the dark, and make us still forever. They are laughing at us, Waldo."

Both sat looking upwards.

"Do you ever pray?" he asked her, in a low voice.

"No."

"I never do; but I might when I look up there. I will tell you," he added, in a still lower voice, "where I could pray. If there were a wall of rock on the edge of a world, and one rock stretched out far, far into space, and I stood alone upon it, — alone, with stars above me, and stars below me, — I would not say anything; but the feeling would be prayer."

There was an end to their conversation after that, and Doss fell asleep on her knee. At last the nightwind grew very chilly.

"Ah," she said, shivering, and drawing the skirt about her shoulders, "I am cold. 'Span-in' the horses, and call me when you are ready."

She slipped down and walked towards the house, Doss stiffly following her, not pleased at being roused. At the door she met Gregory.

"I have been looking for you everywhere; may I not drive you home?" he said.

"Waldo drives me," she replied, passing on; and it appeared to Gregory that she looked at him in the old way, without seeing him. But before she had reached the door an idea had occurred to her, for she turned.

"If you wish to drive me, you may."

Gregory went to look for Em, whom he found pouring out coffee in the back room. He put his hand quickly on her shoulder.

" You must ride with Waldo; I am going to drive your cousin home."

"But I can't come just now, Greg; I promised Tant' Annie Muller to look after the things while she went to rest a little."

" Well, you can come presently, can't you? I did n't say you were to come now. I'm sick of this thing," said Gregory, turning sharply on his heel. " Why must I sit up the whole night because your step-mother chooses to get married?"

"Oh, it's all right, Greg; I only meant—"

But he did not hear her, and a man had come up to have his cup filled.

An hour after Waldo came in to look for her, and found her still busy at the table.

" The horses are ready," he said; " but if you would like to have one dance more, I will wait."

She shook her head wearily.

"No; I am quite ready. I want to go."

And soon they were on the sandy road the buggy had travelled an hour before. Their horses, with heads close together, nodding sleepily as they walked in the starlight, you might have counted the rise and fall of their feet in the sand; and Waldo in his saddle nodded drowsily also. Only Em was awake, and watched the starlit road with wide-open eyes. At last she spoke.

"I wonder if all people feel so old, so very old, when they get to be seventeen?"

"Not older than before," said Waldo, sleepily, pulling at his bridle.

Presently she said again, "I wish I could have been a little child always. You are good then. You are never selfish; you like every one to have everything;

but when you are grown-up there are some things you like to have all to yourself; you don't like any one else to have any of them."

"Yes," said Waldo, sleepily, and she did not speak again.

When they reached the farm-house all was dark, for Lyndall had retired as soon as they got home.

Waldo lifted Em from her saddle, and for a moment she leaned her head on his shoulder, and clung to him.

"You are very tired," he said, as he walked with her to the door; "let me go in and light a candle for you."

"No, thank you; it is all right," she said. "Good-night, Waldo, dear."

But when she went in she sat long alone in the dark.

CHAPTER VII.

WALDO GOES OUT TO TASTE LIFE, AND EM STAYS AT HOME AND TASTES IT.

At nine o'clock in the evening, packing his bundles for the next morning's start, Waldo looked up, and was surprised to see Em's yellow head peeping in at his door. It was many a month since she had been there. She said she had made him sandwiches for his journey, and she stayed a while to help him put his goods into the saddle-bags.

"You can leave the old things lying about," she said; "I will lock the room, and keep it waiting for you to come back some day."

To come back some day! Would the bird ever return to its cage? But he thanked her. When she went away, he stood on the doorstep, holding the candle till she had almost reached the house. But Em was that evening in no hurry to enter, and instead of going in at the back door walked with lagging footsteps round the low brick wall that ran before the house. Opposite the open window of the parlor she stopped. The little room, kept carefully closed in Tant' Sannie's time, was well lighted by a paraffine lamp; books and work lay strewn about it, and it wore a bright, habitable aspect. Beside the lamp, at the table in the corner sat Lyndall, the open letters and papers of the day's post lying scattered before her, while she perused the columns of a newspaper. At the centre table, with his arms folded on an open paper, which there was not light enough to read, sat Gregory. He was looking at her. The light from the open window fell on Em's little face, under its white kappje as she looked in, but no one glanced that way.

"Go and fetch me a glass of water," Lyndall said at last.

Gregory went out to find it; when he put it down at her side, she merely moved her head in recognition, and he went back to his seat and his old occupation. Then Em moved slowly away from the window, and through it came in spotted, hard-winged insects, to play round the lamp, till, one by one, they stuck to its glass, and fell to the foot dead.

Ten o'clock struck. Then Lyndall rose, gathered up her papers and letters, and wished Gregory goodnight. Some time after Em entered; she had been sitting all the while on the loft ladder, and had drawn her kappje down very much over her face.

Gregory was piecing together the bits of an envelope when she came in.

"I thought you were never coming," he said, turning round quickly, and throwing the fragments on to the floor. "You know I have been shearing all day, and it is ten o'clock already."

"I'm sorry. I did not think you would be going so soon," she said in a low voice.

"I can't hear what you say. What makes you mumble so? Well, good-night, Em."

He stooped down hastily to kiss her.

"I want to talk to you, Gregory."

"Well, make haste," he said pettishly. "I'm

awfully tired. I've been sitting here all the evening. Why couldn't you come and talk before?"

"I will not keep you long," she answered, very steadily now. "I think, Gregory, it would be better if you and I were never to be married."

"Good heavens! Em, what do you mean? I thought you were so fond of me? You always *professed* to be. What on earth have you taken into your head now?"

"I think it would be better," she said, folding her hands over each other, very much as though she were praying.

"Better, Em! What do you mean? Even a woman can't take a freak all about nothing! You must have *some* reason for it, and I'm sure I've done nothing to offend you. I wrote only to-day to my sister, to tell her to come up next month to our wedding, and I've been as affectionate and happy as possible. Come — what's the matter?"

He put his arm half round her shoulder, very loosely.

"I think it would be better," she answered slowly.

"Oh, well," he said, drawing himself up, "if you won't enter into explanations, you won't; and I'm not the man to beg and pray — not to any woman, and you know that! If you don't want to marry me, I can't oblige you to, of course."

She stood quite still before him.

"You women never *do* know your own minds for two days together; and of course you know the state of your own feelings best; but it's very strange. Have you really made up your mind, Em?"

"Yes."

"Well, I'm very sorry. I'm sure I've not been in

anything to blame. A man can't always be billing and cooing; but, as you say, if your feeling for me has changed, it's much better you should n't marry me. There's nothing so foolish as to marry some one you don't love; and I only wish for your happiness, I'm sure. I dare say you'll find some one can make you much happier than *I* could; the first person we love is seldom the right one. You are very young; it's quite natural you should change."

She said nothing.

"Things often seem hard at the time, but Providence makes them turn out for the best in the end," said Gregory. "You'll let me kiss you, Em, just for old friendship's sake." He stooped down. "You must look upon me as a dear brother, as a cousin, at least; as long as I am on the farm I shall always be glad to help you, Em."

Soon after the brown pony was cantering along the footpath to the daub-and-wattle house, and his master as he rode whistled " John Speriwig " and the "Thorn Kloof Schottische."

The sun had not yet touched the outstretched arms of the prickly pear upon the " kopje," and the early cocks and hens still strutted about stiffly after the night's roost, when Waldo stood before the wagon-house saddling the gray mare. Every now and then he glanced up at the old familiar objects; they had a new aspect that morning. Even the cocks, seen in the light of parting, had a peculiar interest, and he listened with conscious attention while one crowed clear and loud as it stood on the pigsty wall. He wished good-morning softly to the Kaffir woman who was coming up from the huts to light the fire. He was leaving them all to that old life, and from his height he looked down on them pityingly. So they would keep on crowing, and coming to light fires, when for him that old colorless existence was but a dream.

He went into the house to say good-by to Em, and then he walked to the door of Lyndall's room to wake her; but she was up, and standing in the door-way.

"So you are ready," she said.

Waldo looked at her with sudden heaviness; the exhilaration died out of his heart. Her gray dressing-gown hung close about her, and below its edge the little bare feet were resting on the threshold.

"I wonder when we shall meet again, Waldo? What you will be, and what I?"

"Will you write to me?" he asked of her.

"Yes; and if I should not, you can still remember, wherever you are, that you are not alone."

"I have left Doss for you," he said.

"Will you not miss him?"

"No; I want you to have him. He loves you better than he loves me."

"Thank you." They stood quiet.

"Good-by!" she said, putting her little hand in his, and he turned away; but when he reached the door she called to him, "Come back, I want to kiss you." She drew his face down to hers, and held it with both hands, and kissed it on the forehead and mouth. "Good-by, dear!"

When he looked back, the little figure with its beautiful eyes was standing in the doorway still.

CHAPTER VIII.

THE KOPJE.

"Good-morning !"

Em, who was in the store-room measuring the Kaffirs' rations, looked up, and saw her former lover standing betwixt her and the sunshine. For some days after that evening on which he had ridden home whistling, he had shunned her. She might wish to enter into explanations, and he, Gregory Rose, was not the man for that kind of thing. If a woman had once thrown him overboard, she must take the consequences, and stand by them. When, however, she showed no inclination to revert to the past, and shunned him more than he shunned her, Gregory softened.

"You must let me call you Em still, and be like a brother to you till I go," he said; and Em thanked him so humbly that he wished she had n't. It was n't so easy after that to think himself an injured man.

On that morning he stood some time in the doorway, switching his whip, and moving rather restlessly from one leg to the other.

"I think I 'll just take a walk up to the camps and see how your birds are getting on. Now Waldo 's gone you 've no one to see after things. Nice morning, is n't it ?" Then he added suddenly, "I 'll just go round to the house and get a drink of water first;" and somewhat awkwardly walked off. He might have found water in the kitchen, but he never glanced towards the buckets. In the front room a monkey and two tumblers stood on the centre table; but he merely looked round, peeped into the parlor, looked round again, and then walked out at the front door, and found himself again at the store-room without having satisfied his thirst. "Awfully nice morning this," he said, trying to pose himself in a graceful and indifferent attitude against the door. "It is n't hot and it is n't cold. It 's awfully nice."

"Yes," said Em.

"Your cousin, now," said Gregory, in an aimless sort of way, — "I suppose she 's shut up in her room writing letters."

"No," said Em.

"Gone for a drive, I expect? Nice morning for a drive."

"No."

"Gone to see the ostriches, I suppose?"

"No." After a little silence Em added, "I saw her go by the kraals to the 'kopje.'"

Gregory crossed and uncrossed his legs.

"Well, I think I 'll just go and have a look about," he said, "and see how things are getting on before I go to the camps. Good-by; so long."

Em left for a while the bags she was folding and went to the window, the same through which, years before, Bonaparte had watched the slouching figure cross the yard. Gregory walked to the pigsty first, and contemplated the pigs for a few seconds; then turned round, and stood looking fixedly at the wall of the fuel-house as though he thought it wanted repairing; then he started off suddenly with the evident intention of going to the ostrich-camps; then

18

paused, hesitated, and finally walked off in the direction of the "kopje."

Then Em went back to the corner, and folded more sacks.

On the other side of the "kopje" Gregory caught sight of a white tail waving among the stones, and a succession of short, frantic barks told where Doss was engaged in howling imploringly to a lizard who had crept between two stones, and who had not the slightest intention of resunning himself at that particular moment.

The dog's mistress sat higher up, under the shelving rock, her face bent over a volume of plays upon her knee. As Gregory mounted the stones she started violently, and looked up; then resumed her book.

"I hope I am not troubling you," said Gregory, as he reached her side. "If I am, I will go away. I just—"

"No; you may stay."

"I fear I startled you."

"Yes; your step was firmer than it generally is, I thought it was that of some one else."

"Who could it be but me?" asked Gregory, seating himself on a stone at her feet.

"Do you suppose you are the only man who would find anything to attract him to this 'kopje'?"

"Oh, no," said Gregory.

He was not going to argue that point with her, nor any other; but no old Boer was likely to take the trouble of climbing the "kopje," and who else was there?

She continued the study of her book.

"Miss Lyndall," he said at last, "I don't know why it is you never talk to me."

"We had a long conversation yesterday," she said, without looking up.

"Yes; but you ask me questions about sheep and oxen. I don't call that talking. You used to talk to Waldo, now," he said, in an aggrieved tone of voice. "I've heard you when I came in, and then you've just left off. You treated me like that from the first day; and you couldn't tell from just looking at me that I couldn't talk about the things you like. I'm sure I know as much about such things as Waldo does," said Gregory, in exceeding bitterness of spirit.

"I do not know what things you refer to. If you will enlighten me, I am quite prepared to speak of them," she said, reading as she spoke.

"Oh, you never used to ask Waldo like that," said Gregory, in a more sorely aggrieved tone than ever. "You used just to begin."

"Well, let me see," she said, closing her book and folding her hands on it. "There at the foot of the 'kopje' goes a Kaffir; he has nothing on but a blanket; he is a splendid fellow — six feet high, with a magnificent pair of legs. In his leather bag he is going to fetch his rations, and I suppose to kick his wife with his beautiful legs when he gets home. He has a right to; he bought her for two oxen. There is a lean dog going after him, to whom I suppose he never gives more than a bone from which he has sucked the marrow; but his dog loves him, as his wife does. There is something of the master about him in spite of his blackness and wool. See how he brandishes his stick, and holds up his head!"

"Oh, but aren't you making fun?" said Gregory, looking doubtfully from her to the Kaffir herd, who rounded the "kopje."

"No; I am very serious. He is the most interesting and intelligent thing I can see just now, except
perhaps Doss. He is profoundly suggestive. Will
his race melt away in the heat of a collision with a
higher? Are the men of the future to see his bones
only in museums, — a vestige of one link that spanned
between the dog and the white man? He wakes
thoughts that run far out into the future and back
into the past."

Gregory was not quite sure how to take these re-
marks. Being about a Kaffir, they appeared to be of
the nature of a joke; but, being seriously spoken,
they appeared earnest; so he half laughed and half
not, to be on the safe side.

"I've often thought so myself. It's funny we
should both think the same; I knew we should if
once we talked. But there are other things, — love,
now," he added. "I wonder if we should think alike
about that. I wrote an essay on love once; the master said it was the best I ever wrote, and I can remember the first sentence still, — 'Love is something
that you feel in your heart.'"

"That was a trenchant remark. Can't you remember any more?"

"No," said Gregory, regretfully; "I've forgotten
the rest. But tell me what do you think about
love?"

A look, half of abstraction, half of amusement, played
on her lips.

"I don't know much about love," she said, "and I
do not like to talk of things I do not understand;
but I have heard two opinions. Some say the devil
carried the seed from hell, and planted it on the earth
to plague men and make them sin; and some say, that

when all the plants in the garden of Eden were pulled up by the roots, one bush that the angels had planted was left growing, and it spread its seed over the whole earth, and its name is love. I do not know which is right — perhaps both. There are different species that go under the same name. There is a love that begins in the head, and goes down to the heart, and grows slowly ; but it lasts till death, and asks less than it gives. There is another love, that blots out wisdom, that is sweet with the sweetness of life and bitter with the bitterness of death, lasting for an hour ; but it is worth having lived a whole life for that hour. I cannot tell, perhaps the old monks were right when they tried to root love out ; perhaps the poets are right when they try to water it. It is a blood-red flower, with the color of sin ; but there is always the scent of a god about it."

Gregory would have made a remark ; but she said, without noticing, —

"There are as many kinds of loves as there are flowers : everlastings that never wither ; speedwells that wait for the wind to fan them out of life ; blood-red mountain-lilies that pour their voluptuous sweetness out for one day, and lie in the dust at night. There is no flower has the charm of all — the speedwell's purity, the everlasting's strength, the mountain-lily's warmth ; but who knows whether there is not a love that holds all — friendship, passion, worship ?

" Such a love," she said in her sweetest voice, " will fall on the surface of strong, cold, selfish life as the sunlight falls on a torpid winter world ; there, where the trees are bare, and the ground frozen, till it rings to the step like iron, and the water is solid, and the air is sharp as a two-edged knife, that cuts the unwary. But when its sun shines on it, through its whole dead crust a throbbing yearning wakes; the trees feel him, and every knot and bud swell, aching to open to him. The brown seeds, who have slept deep under the ground, feel him, and he gives them strength, till they break through the frozen earth, and lift two tiny, trembling green hands in love to him. And he touches the water, till down to its depths it feels him and melts, and it flows, and the things, strange sweet things that were locked up in it, it sings as it runs, for love of him. Each plant tries to bear at least one fragrant little flower for him, and the world that was dead lives, and the heart that was dead and self-centred throbs, with an upward, out-ward yearning, and it has become that which it seemed impossible ever to become. There, does that satisfy you ? " she asked, looking down at Gregory. " Is that how you like me to talk ? "

" Oh, yes," said Gregory, " that is what I have already thought. We have the same thoughts about everything. How strange ! "

" Very," said Lyndall, working with her little toe, at a stone in the ground before her.

Gregory felt he must sustain the conversation. The only thing he could think of was to recite a piece of poetry. He knew he had learned many poems about love ; but the only thing that would come into his mind now was the " Battle of Hohenlinden," and " Not a drum was heard," neither of which seemed to bear directly on the subject in hand.

But unexpected relief came to him from Doss, who, too deeply lost in contemplation of his crevice, was surprised by the sudden descent of the stone Lyndall's foot had loosened, which, rolling against his little fore paw, carried away a piece of white skin. Doss stood on three legs, holding up the paw with an expression of extreme self-commiseration; he then proceeded to hop slowly upwards in search of sympathy.

"You have hurt that dog," said Gregory.

"Have I?" she replied indifferently, and reopened the book, as though to resume her study of the play.

"He's a nasty, snappish little cur!" said Gregory, calculating from her manner that the remark would be indorsed. "He snapped at my horse's tail yesterday, and nearly made it throw me. I wonder his master did n't take him, instead of leaving him here to be a nuisance to all of us!"

Lyndall seemed absorbed in her play; but he ventured another remark.

"Do you think now, Miss Lyndall, that he 'll ever have anything in the world, — that German, I mean, — money enough to support a wife on, and all that sort of thing? *I* don't. He's what *I* call a soft."

She was spreading her skirt out softly with her left hand for the dog to lie down on it.

"I think I *should* be rather astonished if he ever became a respectable member of society," she said. "I don't expect to see him the possessor of bank-shares, the chairman of a divisional council, and the father of a large family, wearing a black hat, and going to church twice on a Sunday. He would rather astonish me if he came to such an end."

"Yes; I don't expect *anything* of him either," said Gregory, zealously.

"Well, I don't know," said Lyndall; "there are some small things I rather look to him for. If he were to invent wings, or carve a statue that one might look at for half an hour without wanting to look at something else, I should not be surprised. He may do some little thing of that kind, perhaps, when he has done fermenting, and the sediment has all gone to the bottom."

Gregory felt that what she said was not wholly intended as blame.

"Well, I don't know," he said sulkily; "to me he looks like a fool. To walk about always in that dead-and-alive sort of way, muttering to himself like an old Kaffir witch-doctor! He works hard enough, but it's always as though he didn't know what he was doing. You don't know how he looks to a person who sees him for the first time."

Lyndall was softly touching the little sore foot as she read, and Doss, to show he liked it, licked her hand.

"But, Miss Lyndall," persisted Gregory, "what do you really think of him?"

"I think," said Lyndall, "that he is like a thorn-tree which grows up very quietly, without any one's caring for it, and one day suddenly breaks out into yellow blossoms."

"And what do you think I am like?" asked Gregory, hopefully.

Lyndall looked up from her book.

"Like a little tin duck floating on a dish of water, that comes after a piece of bread stuck on a needle, and the more the needle pricks it the more it comes on."

"Oh, you *are* making fun of me now, — you really are!" said Gregory, feeling wretched. "You *are* making fun, aren't you, now?"

"Partly. It is always diverting to make comparisons."

"Yes; but you don't compare me to anything nice, and you do other people. What is Em like, now?"

"The accompaniment of a song. She fills up the gaps in other people's lives, and is always number two; but I think she is like many accompaniments, — a great deal better than the song she is to accompany."

"She is not half so good as you are!" said Gregory, with a burst of uncontrollable ardor.

"She is so much better than I that her little finger has more goodness in it than my whole body. I hope you may not live to find out the truth of that fact."

"You are like an angel," he said, the blood rushing to his head and face.

"Yes, probably; angels are of many orders."

"You are the one being that I love!" said Gregory, quivering. "I thought I loved before, but I know now! Do not be angry with me. I know you could never like me; but if I might but always be near you to serve you I would be utterly, utterly happy. I would ask nothing in return! If you could only take everything I have and use it. I want nothing but to be of use to you."

She looked at him for a few moments.

"How do you know," she said slowly, "that you could not do something to serve me? You could serve me by giving me your name."

He started, and turned his burning face to her.

"You are very cruel; you are ridiculing me," he said.

"No, I am not, Gregory. What I am saying is plain, matter-of-fact business. If you are willing to give me your name within three weeks' time, I am willing to marry you; if not, well. I want nothing more than your name. That is a clear proposal, is it not?"

He looked up. Was it contempt, loathing, pity, that moved in the eyes above? He could not tell; but he stooped over the little foot, and kissed it.

She smiled.

" Do you really mean it?" he whispered.

" Yes. You wish to serve me, and to have nothing in return! — you shall have what you wish." She held out her fingers for Doss to lick. " Do you see this dog? He licks my hand because I love him; and I allow him to. Where I do not love I do not allow it. I believe you love me; I too could love so, that to lie under the foot of the thing I loved would be more heaven than to lie in the breast of another.— Come! let us go. Carry the dog," she added; "he will not bite you if I put him in your arms. So — do not let his foot hang down."

They descended the "kopje." At the bottom he whispered, "Would you not take my arm, the path is very rough?"

She rested her fingers lightly on it.

" I may yet change my mind about marrying you, before the time comes. It is very likely. Mark you!" she said, turning round on him; "I remember your words, — *You will give everything, and expect nothing.* The knowledge that you are serving me is to be your reward; and you will have that. You will serve me, and greatly. The reasons I have for marrying you I need not inform you of now; you will probably discover some of them before long."

" I only want to be of some use to you," he said.

It seemed to Gregory that there were pulses in the

soles of his feet, and the ground shimmered as on a summer's day. They walked round the foot of the "kopje," and past the Kaffir huts. An old Kaffir maid knelt at the door of one, grinding mealies. That she should see him walking so, made his heart beat so fast that the hand on his arm felt its pulsation. It seemed that she must envy him.

Just then Em looked out again at the back window, and saw them coming. She cried bitterly all the while she sorted the skins.

But that night when Lyndall had blown her candle out, and half turned round to sleep, the door of Em's bedroom opened.

"I want to say good-night to you, Lyndall," she said, coming to the bedside and kneeling down.

"I thought you were asleep," Lyndall replied.

"Yes, I have been asleep; but I had such a vivid dream," she said, holding the other's hands, "and that awoke me. I never had so vivid a dream before. It seemed I was a little girl again, and I came somewhere into a large room. On a bed in the corner there was something lying dressed in white, and its little eyes were shut, and its little face was like wax. I thought it was a doll, and I ran forward to take it; but some one held up her finger and said, 'Hush! it is a little dead baby.' And I said, 'Oh, I must go and call Lyndall, that she may look at it also.' And they put their faces close down to my ear and whispered, 'It is Lyndall's baby.' And I said, 'She cannot be grown up yet; she is only a little girl! Where is she?' And I went to look for you, but I could not find you. And when I came to some people who were dressed in black, I asked them where you were, and they looked down at their black clothes, and shook their heads, and said nothing; and I could not find you anywhere. And then I awoke.

"Lyndall," she said, putting her face down upon the hands she held, "it made me think about that time when we were little girls and used to play together, when I loved you better than anything else in the world. It is n't any one's fault that they love you; they can't help it. And it is n't your fault; you don't make them love you. I know it."

"Thank you, dear," Lyndall said. "It is nice to be loved, but it would be better to be good."

Then they wished good-night, and Em went back to her room. Long after Lyndall lay in the dark, thinking, thinking, thinking; and as she turned round wearily to sleep, she muttered, "There are some wiser in their sleeping than in their waking."

CHAPTER IX.

LYNDALL'S STRÁNGER.

A FIRE is burning in the unused hearth of the cabin. The fuel blazes up, and lights the black rafters, and warms the faded red lions on the quilt, and fills the little room with a glow of warmth and light made brighter by contrast, for outside the night is chill and misty.

Before the open fireplace sits a stranger, his tall, slight figure reposing in the broken armchair, his keen blue eyes studying the fire from beneath delicately pencilled, drooping eyelids. One white hand plays thoughtfully with a heavy flaxen mustache; yet once he starts, and for an instant the languid lids raise themselves; there is a keen, intent look upon the face as he listens for something. Then he leans back in his chair, fills his glass from the silver flask in his bag, and resumes his old posture.

Presently the door opens noiselessly. It is Lyndall, followed by Doss. Quietly as she enters, he hears her, and turns.

"I thought you were not coming."

"I waited till all had gone to bed. I could not come before."

She removed the shawl that enveloped her, and the stranger rose to offer her his chair; but she took her seat on a low pile of sacks before the window.

"I hardly see why I should be outlawed after this fashion," he said, reseating himself, and drawing his chair a little nearer to her; "these are hardly the quarters one expects to find after travelling a hundred miles in answer to an invitation."

"I said, 'Come if you wish.'"

"And I did wish. Yet you give me a cold reception."

"I could not take you to the house. Questions would be asked which I could not answer without prevarication."

"Your conscience is growing to have a certain vir-gin tenderness," he said, in a low melodious voice.

"I have no conscience. I spoke one deliberate lie this evening. I said the man who had come looked rough, — we had best not have him in the house; therefore I brought him here. It was a deliberate lie, and I hate lies. I tell them if I must, but they hurt me."

"Well, you do not tell lies to yourself, at all events. You are candid, so far."

She interrupted him. "You got my short letter?"

"Yes; that is why I came. You sent a very fool-ish reply; you must take it back. Who is this fellow you talk of marrying?"

"A young farmer."

"Lives here?"

"Yes; he has gone to town to get things for our wedding."

"What kind of a fellow is he?"

"A fool."

"And you would rather marry him than me?"

"Yes; because you are not one."

"That is a novel reason for refusing to marry a

man," he said, leaning his elbow on the table, and watching her keenly.

"It is a wise one," she said shortly. "If I marry him, I shall shake him off my hand when it suits me. If I remained with him for twelve months, he would never have dared to kiss my hand. As far as I wish he should come, he comes, and no farther. Would you ask me what you might, and what you might not do?"

Her companion raised the mustache with a caressing movement from his lip, and smiled. It was not a question that stood in need of any answer.

"Why do you wish to enter on this semblance of marriage?"

"Because there is only one point on which I have a conscience. I have told you so."

"Then why not marry me?"

"Because if once you have me, you would hold me fast. I shall never be free again." She drew a long, low breath.

"What have you done with the ring I gave you?" he said.

"Sometimes I wear it; then I take it off and wish to throw it into the fire; the next day I put it on again, and sometimes I kiss it."

"So you do love me a little?"

"If you were not something more to me than any other man in the world, do you think — " She paused. "I love you when I see you; but when you are away from me, I hate you."

"Then I fear I must be singularly invisible at the present moment," he said. "Possibly if you were to look less fixedly into the fire, you might perceive me."

He moved his chair slightly so as to come between her and the firelight.   She raised her eyes to his face.

"If you do love me," he asked her, "why will you not marry me ? "

"Because if I had been married to you for a year, I should have come to my senses, and seen that your hands and your voice are like the hands and the voice of any other man.   I cannot quite see that now.   But it is all madness.   You call into activity one part of my nature; there is a higher part that you know nothing of, that you never touch.   If I married you, afterwards it would arise and assert itself, and I should hate you always, as I do now sometimes."

"I like you when you grow metaphysical and ana-lytical," he said, leaning his face upon his hand.   "Go a little farther in your analysis ; say, ' I love you with the right ventricle of my heart, but not the left, and with the left auricle of my heart, but not the right ; and, this being the case, my affection for you is not of a duly elevated, intellectual, and spiritual nature.'   I like you when you get philosophical."

She looked quietly at him ; he was trying to turn her own weapons against her.

"You are acting foolishly, Lyndall," he said, sud-denly changing his manner, and speaking earnestly, "most foolishly ; you are acting like a little child.   I am surprised at you.   It is all very well to have ideals and theories ; but you know as well as any one can that they must not be carried into the practical world.   I love you.   I do not pretend that it is in any high, superhuman sense; I do not say that I should like you as well if you were ugly and deformed, or that I should continue to prize you whatever your treatment of me might be, or to love you though you were a

spirit without any body at all. That is sentimentality
for beardless boys. Every one not a mere child (and
you are not a child, except in years) knows what love
between a man and a woman means. I love you with
that love. I would not have believed it possible that
I could have brought myself twice to ask any woman
to be my wife, more especially one without wealth,
without position, and who — "

"Yes, go on. Do not grow sorry for me. Say
what you were going to, — 'who has put herself into
my power, and who has lost the right of meeting me
on equal terms.' Say what you think; at least we
two may speak the truth to each other."

Then she added after a pause, —

"I believe you do love me as much as you possibly
could love anything, and I believe that when you ask
me to marry you, you are performing the most gener-
ous act you ever have performed in the course of your
life, or ever will. But at the same time if I had re-
quired your generosity, it would not have been shown
me. If when I got your letter a month ago hinting
at your willingness to marry me I had at once written
imploring you to come, you would have read the letter,
'Poor little devil!' you would have said, and torn it
up. The next week you would have sailed for Europe,
and have sent me a check for a hundred and fifty
pounds (which I would have thrown in the fire), and
I would have heard no more of you." The stranger
smiled. "But because I declined your proposal, and
wrote that in three weeks I should be married to another, then what you call love woke up. Your man's
love is a child's love for butterflies. You follow till
you have the thing, and break it. If you have broken
one wing, and the thing flies still, then you love it

19

more than ever, and follow till you break both; then
you are satisfied when it lies still on the ground."

" You are profoundly wise in the ways of the world;
you have seen far into life," he said.

He might as well have sneered at the firelight.

"I have seen enough to tell me that you love me
because you cannot bear to be resisted, and want to
master me. You liked me at first because I treated
you and all men with indifference. You resolved to
have me because I seemed unattainable. That is all
your love means."

He felt a strong inclination to stoop down and kiss
the little lips that defied him; but he restrained himself. He said quietly, " And you loved me — ? "

" Because you are strong. You are the first man I
ever was afraid of. And " — a dreamy look came into
her face — " because I like to experience, I like to try.
You don't understand that."

He smiled.

" Well, since you will not marry me, may I inquire
what your intentions are, — the plan you wrote of.
You asked me to come and hear it, and I have come."

" I said : ' Come if you wish.' If you agree to it,
well ; if not, I marry on Monday."

" Well ? "

She was still looking beyond him at the fire.

" I cannot marry you," she said slowly, " because I
cannot be tied ; but if you wish, you may take me
away with you, and take care of me; then when we
do not love any more we can say good-by. I will not
go down country," she added; "I will not go to
Europe. You must take me to the Transvaal. That
is out of the world. People we meet there we need
not see again in our future lives."

"Oh, my darling," he said, bending tenderly, and holding his hand out to her, "why will you not give yourself entirely to me? One day you will desert me and go to another."

She shook her head, without looking at him.

"No; life is too long. But I will go with you."

"When?"

"To-morrow. I have told them that before daylight I go to the next farm. I will write from the town, and tell them the facts. I do not want them to trouble me; I want to shake myself free of these old surroundings; I want them to lose sight of me. You can understand that this is necessary for me."

He seemed lost in consideration; then he said, —

"It is better to have you on those conditions than not at all. If you *will* have it, let it be so."

He sat looking at her. On her face was the weary look that rested there so often now when she sat alone. Two months had not passed since they parted; but the time had set its mark on her. He looked at her carefully, from the brown, smooth head to the little crossed feet on the floor. A worn look had grown over the little face, and it made its charm for him stronger. For pain and time, which trace deep lines and write a story on a human face, have a strangely different effect on one face and another. The face that is only fair, even very fair, they mar and flaw; but to the face whose beauty is the harmony between that which speaks from within and the form through which it speaks, power is added by all that causes the outer man to bear more deeply the impress of the inner. The pretty woman fades with the roses on her cheeks, and the girlhood that lasts an hour; the beautiful woman finds her fulness of

bloom only when a past has written itself on her, and
her power is then most irresistible when it seems
going.

From under their half-closed lids the keen eyes
looked down at her. Her shoulders were bent; for a
moment the little figure had forgotten its queenly
bearing, and drooped wearily; the wide, dark eyes
watched the fire very softly.

It certainly was not in her power to resist him, nor
any strength in her that made his own at that moment
grow soft as he looked at her.

He touched one little hand that rested on her knee.

"Poor little thing!" he said; "you are only a
child."

She did not draw her hand away from his, and
looked up at him.

"You are very tired?"

"Yes."

She looked into his eyes as a little child might
whom a long day's play had saddened.

He lifted her gently up, and set her on his knee.

"Poor little thing!" he said.

She turned her face to his shoulder, and buried it
against his neck; he wound his strong arm about her,
and held her close to him. When she had sat for a
long while, he drew with his hand the face down, and
held it against his arm. He kissed it, and then put
it back in its old resting-place.

"Don't you want to talk to me?"

"No."

"Have you forgotten the night in the avenue?"

He could feel that she shook her head.

"Do you want to be quiet now?"

"Yes."

They sat quite still, excepting that only sometimes he raised her fingers softly to his mouth.

Doss, who had been asleep in the corner, waking suddenly, planted himself before them, his wiry legs moving nervously, his yellow eyes filled with anxiety. He was not at all sure that she was not being retained in her present position against her will, and was not a little relieved when she sat up and held out her hand for the shawl.

"I must go," she said.

The stranger wrapped the shawl very carefully about her.

"Keep it close around your face, Lyndall; it is very damp outside. Shall I walk with you to the house?"

"No. Lie down and rest; I will come and wake you at three o'clock."

She lifted her face that he might kiss it, and, when he had kissed it once, she still held it that he might kiss it again. Then he let her out. He had seated himself at the fireplace, when she reopened the door.

"Have you forgotten anything?"

"No."

She gave one long, lingering look at the old room. When she was gone, and the door shut, the stranger filled his glass, and sat at the table sipping it thoughtfully.

The night outside was misty and damp; the faint moonlight, trying to force its way through the thick air, made darkly visible the outlines of the buildings. The stones and walls were moist, and now and then a drop, slowly collecting, fell from the eaves to the ground. Doss, not liking the change from the cabin's warmth, ran quickly to the kitchen doorstep; but his

mistress walked slowly past him, and took her way
up the winding footpath that ran beside the stone-
wall of the camps. When she came to the end of the
last camp, she threaded her way among the stones and
bushes till she reached the German's grave. Why
she had come there she hardly knew; she stood looking down. Suddenly she bent and put one hand on
the face of a wet stone.

"I shall never come to you again," she said.

Then she knelt on the ground, and leaned her face
upon the stones.

"Dear old man, good old man, I am so tired!"
she said (for we come to the dead to tell secrets we
would never have told to the living). "I am so tired.
There is light, there is warmth," she wailed; "why
am I alone, so hard, so cold? I am so weary of myself! It is eating my soul to its core, — self, self,
self! I cannot bear this life! I cannot breathe, I
cannot live! Will nothing free me from myself?"
She pressed her cheek against the wooden post. "I
want to love! I want something great and pure to
lift me to itself! Dear old man, I cannot bear it any
more! I am so cold, so hard, so hard; will no one
help me?"

The water gathered slowly on her shawl, and fell
on the wet stones; but she lay there crying bitterly.
For so the living soul will cry to the dead, and the
creature to its God; and of all this crying there comes
nothing. The lifting up of the hands brings no salvation; redemption is from within, and neither from
God nor man: it is wrought out by the soul itself,
with suffering and through time.

Doss, on the kitchen doorstep, shivered, and wondered where his mistress stayed so long; and once,

sitting sadly there in the damp, he had dropped asleep, and dreamed that old Otto gave him a piece of bread, and patted him on the head, and when he woke his teeth chattered, and he moved to another stone to see if it was drier. At last he heard his mistress's step, and they went into the house together. She lit a candle, and walked to the Boer-woman's bedroom. On a nail under the lady in pink hung the key of the wardrobe. She took it down, and opened the great press. From a little drawer she took fifty pounds, all she had in the world, relocked the door, and turned to hang up the key. Then she paused, hesitated. The marks of tears were still on her face, but she smiled.

"Fifty pounds for a lover! A noble reward!" she said, and opened the wardrobe, and returned the notes to the drawer, where Em might find them.

Once in her own room, she arranged the few articles she intended to take to-morrow, burned her old letters, and then went back to the front room to look at the time. There were two hours yet before she must call him, She sat down at the dressing-table to wait, and leaned her elbows on it, and buried her face in her hands. The glass reflected the little brown head with its even parting, and the tiny hands on which it rested. "One day I shall love something utterly, and then I shall be better," she said once. Presently she looked up. The large dark eyes from the glass looked back at her. She looked deep into them.

"We are all alone, you and I," she whispered; "no one helps us, no one understands us; but we will help ourselves." The eyes looked back at her. There was a world of assurance in their still depths. So they had looked at her ever since she could remember, when it was but a small child's face above a blue pinafore. "We shall never be quite alone, you and I," she said; "we shall always be together, as we were when we were little."

The beautiful eyes looked into the depths of her soul.

"We are not afraid; we will help ourselves!" she said. She stretched out her hand, and pressed it over them on the glass. "Dear eyes! we will never be quite alone till they part us;—till then!"

CHAPTER X.

GREGORY ROSE HAS AN IDEA.

GREGORY ROSE was in the loft putting it neat. Outside the rain poured; a six months' drought had broken, and the thirsty plain was drenched with water. What it could not swallow ran off in mad rivulets to the great sloot, that now foamed like an angry river across the flat. Even the little furrow between the farm-house and the kraal was now a stream, knee-deep, which almost bore away the Kaffir women who crossed it. It had rained for twenty-four hours, and still the rain poured on. The fowls had collected — a melancholy crowd — in and about the wagon-house, and the solitary gander, who alone had survived the six months' want of water, walked hither and thither printing his webbed foot-marks on the mud, to have them washed out the next instant by the pelting rain, which at eleven o'clock still beat on the walls and roofs with unabated ardor.

Gregory, as he worked in the loft, took no notice of it beyond stuffing a sack into the broken pane to keep it out; and, in spite of the pelt and patter, Em's clear voice might be heard through the open trap-door from the dining-room, where she sat at work, singing the "Blue Water," —

> " And take me away,
> And take me away,
> And take me away,
> To the Blue Water," —

that quaint, childish song of the people, that has a world of sweetness, and sad, vague yearning when sung over and over dreamily by a woman's voice as she sits alone at her work. But Gregory heard neither that nor yet the loud laughter of the Kaffir maids, that every now and again broke through from the kitchen, where they joked and worked. Of late Gregory had grown strangely impervious to the sounds and sights about him. His lease had run out, but Em had said, "Do not renew it; I need one to help me; just stay on." And she had added, "You must not remain in your own little house; live with me; you can look after my ostriches better so."

And Gregory did not thank her. What difference did it make to him, paying rent or not, living there or not; it was all one. But yet he came. Em wished that he would still sometimes talk of the strength and master-right of man; but Gregory was as one smitten on the cheek-bone. She might do what she pleased, he would find no fault, had no word to say. He had forgotten that it is man's right to rule. On that rainy morning he had lighted his pipe at the kitchen fire, and when breakfast was over, stood in the front door watching the water rush down the road, till the pipe died out in his mouth. Em saw she must do something for him, and found him a large calico duster. He had sometimes talked of putting the loft neat, and to-day she could find nothing else for him to do. So she had the ladder put to the trap-door, that he need not go out in the wet, and Gregory with the broom and duster mounted to the loft. Once at work he worked hard. He dusted down the very rafters, and cleaned the broken candle-moulds and bent forks that had stuck in the thatch for twenty years. He placed the black bottles neatly in rows, on an old box in the corner, and piled the skins on one another, and sorted the rubbish in all the boxes; and at eleven o'clock his work was almost done. He seated himself on the packing-case which had once held Waldo's books, and proceeded to examine the contents of another, which he had not yet looked at. It was carelessly nailed down. He loosened one plank, and began to lift out various articles of female attire, — old-fashioned caps, aprons, dresses with long pointed bodies, such as he remembered to have seen his mother wear when he was a little child. He shook them out carefully to see there were no moths, and then sat down to fold them up again one by one. They had belonged to Em's mother, and the box, as packed at her death, had stood untouched and forgotten these long years. She must have been a tall woman, that mother of Em's, for when he stood up to shake out a dress, the neck was on a level with his, and the skirt touched the ground. Gregory laid a nightcap out on his knee, and began rolling up the strings; but presently his fingers moved slower and slower, then his chin rested on his breast, and finally the imploring blue eyes were fixed on the frill abstractedly. When Em's voice called to him from the foot of the ladder, he started, and threw the nightcap behind him.

She was only come to tell him that his cup of soup was ready; and when he could hear that she was gone, he picked up the nightcap again, and a great brown sun-kappje, — just such a kappje and such a dress as one of those he remembered to have seen a Sister of Mercy wear. Gregory's mind was very full of thought. He took down a fragment of an old look-ing-glass from behind a beam, and put the kappje on. His beard looked somewhat grotesque under it; he put up his hand to hide it — that was better. The blue eyes looked out with the mild gentleness that became eyes looking out from under a kappje. Next he took the brown dress, and, looking round furtively, slipped it over his head. He had just got his arms in the sleeves, and was trying to hook up the back, when an increase in the patter of the rain at the window, made him drag it off hastily. When he perceived there was no one coming, he tumbled the things back into the box, and covering it carefully, went down the ladder.

Em was still at her work, trying to adjust a new needle in the machine. Gregory drank his soup, and then sat before her, an awful and mysterious look in his eyes.

"I am going to town to-morrow," he said.

"I'm almost afraid you won't be able to go," said Em, who was intent on her needle; "I don't think it is going to leave off to-day."

"I am going," said Gregory.

Em looked up.

"But the sloots are as full as rivers — you cannot go. We can wait for the post," she said.

"I am not going for the post," said Gregory, impressively.

Em looked for explanation; none came.

"When will you be back?"

"I am not coming back."

"Are you going to your friends?"

Gregory waited, then caught her by the wrist.

"Look here, Em," he said between his teeth, "I can't stand it any more. I am going to her."

Since that day, when he had come home and found

Lyndall gone, he had never talked of her; but Em knew who it was who needed to be spoken of by no name.

She said, when he had released her hand, "But you do not know where she is?"

"Yes, I do. She was in Bloemfontein when I heard last. I will go there, and I will find out where she went then, and then, and then! I will have her."

Em turned the wheel quickly, and the ill-adjusted needle broke into twenty fragments.

"Gregory," she said, "she does not want us; she told us so clearly in the letter she wrote." A flush rose on her face as she spoke. "It will only be pain to you, Gregory. Will she like to have you near her?"

There was an answer he might have made, but it was his secret, and he did not choose to share it. He said only, —

"I am going."

"Will you be gone long, Gregory?"

"I do not know; perhaps I shall never come back. Do what you please with my things. I cannot stay here!"

He rose from his seat.

"People say, forget, forget!" he cried, pacing the room. "They are mad! They are fools! Do they say so to men who are dying of thirst — forget, forget? Why is it only to us they say so? It is a lie to say that time makes it easy; it is afterwards, afterwards, that it eats in at your heart!

"All these months," he cried bitterly, "I have lived here quietly, day after day, as if I cared for what I ate, and what I drank, and what I did! I care for nothing! I cannot bear it! I will not. Forget, forget!" ejaculated Gregory. "You can forget all the world, but you cannot forget yourself. When one thing is more to you than yourself, how are you to forget it?

"I read," he said — "yes; and then I come to a word she used, and it is all back with me again! I go to count my sheep, and I see her face before me, and I stand and let the sheep run by. I look at you, and in your smile, a something at the corner of your lips, I see her. How can I forget her when, whenever I turn, she is there, and not there? I cannot, I will not, live where I do not see her.

"I know what you think," he said, turning upon Em. "You think I am mad; you think I am going to see whether she will not like me! I am not so foolish. I should have known at first she never could suffer me. Who am I, what am I, that she should look at me? It was right that she left me; right that she should not look at me. If any one says it is not, it is a lie! I am not going to speak to her," he added, "only to see her; only to stand sometimes in a place where she has stood before."

CHAPTER XI.

AN UNFINISHED LETTER.

GREGORY ROSE had been gone seven months. Em sat alone on a white sheepskin before the fire.

The August night-wind, weird and shrill, howled round the chimneys and through the crannies, and in walls and doors, and uttered a long low cry as it forced its way among the clefts of the stones on the "kopje." It was a wild night. The prickly-pear tree, stiff and upright as it held its arms, felt the wind's might, and knocked its flat leaves heavily together, till great branches broke off. The Kaffirs, as they slept in their straw huts, whispered one to another that before morning there would not be an armful of thatch left on the roofs; and the beams of the wagon-house creaked and groaned as if it were heavy work to resist the importunity of the wind.

Em had not gone to bed. Who could sleep on a night like this? So in the dining-room she had lighted a fire, and sat on the ground before it, turning the roaster-cakes that lay on the coals to bake. It would save work in the morning; and she blew out the light because the wind through the window-chinks made it flicker and run; and she sat singing to herself as she watched the cakes. They lay at one end of the wide hearth on a bed of coals, and at the other end a fire burned up steadily, casting its amber glow over Em's light hair and black dress, with the ruffle

of crape about the neck, and over the white curls of
the sheepskin on which she sat.

Louder and more fiercely yet howled the storm;
but Em sang on, and heard nothing but the words of
her song, and heard them only faintly, as something
restful. It was an old, childish song she had often
heard her mother sing long ago, —

> " Where the reeds dance by the river,
> Where the willow's song is said,
> On the face of the morning water,
> Is reflected a white flower's head."

She folded her hands and sang the next verse
dreamily —

> " Where the reeds shake by the river,
> Where the moonlight's sheen is shed
> On the face of the sleeping water,
> Two leaves of a white flower float dead.
>   Dead, dead, dead!"

She echoed the refrain softly till it died away, and
then repeated it. It was as if, unknown to herself, it
harmonized with the pictures and thoughts that sat
with her there alone in the firelight. She turned
the cakes over, while the wind hurled down a row of
bricks from the gable, and made the walls tremble.

Presently she paused and listened; there was a
sound as of something knocking at the back doorway.
But the wind had raised its level higher, and she
went on with her work. At last the sound was repeated. Then she rose, lit the candle at the fire, and
went to see. Only to satisfy herself, she said, that
nothing could be out on such a night.

She opened the door a little way, and held the light
behind her to defend it from the wind. The figure

of a tall man stood there, and before she could speak he had pushed his way in, and was forcing the door to close behind him.

"Waldo!" she cried in astonishment.

He had been gone more than a year and a half.

"You did not expect to see me," he answered, as he turned towards her; "I should have slept in the out-house, and not troubled you to-night; but through the shutter I saw glimmerings of a light."

"Come in to the fire," she said; "it is a terrific night for any creature to be out. Shall we not go and fetch your things in first?" she added.

"I have nothing but this," he said, motioning to the little bundle in his hand.

"Your horse?"

"Is dead."

He sat down on the bench before the fire.

"The cakes are almost ready," she said. "I will get you something to eat. Where have you been wandering all this while?"

"Up and down, up and down," he answered wearily; "and now the whim has seized me to come back here. Em," he said, putting his hand on her arm as she passed him, "have you heard from Lyndall lately?"

"Yes," said Em, turning quickly from him.

"Where is she? I had one letter from her, but that is almost a year ago now, — just when she left. Where is she?"

"In the Transvaal. I will go and get you some supper; we can talk afterwards."

"Can you give me her exact address? I want to write to her."

But Em had gone into the next room.

20

When food was on the table, she knelt down before the fire, turning the cakes, babbling restlessly, eagerly, now of this, now of that. She was glad to see him; Tant' Sannie was coming soon to show her her new baby; he must stay on the farm now and help her. And Waldo himself was well content to eat his meal in silence, asking no more questions.

"Gregory is coming back next week," she said. "He will have been gone just a hundred and three days to-morrow. I had a letter from him yesterday."

"Where has he been?"

But his companion stooped to lift a cake from the fire.

"How the wind blows! One can hardly hear one's own voice," she said. "Take this warm cake; no one's cakes are like mine. Why, you have eaten nothing!"

"I am a little weary," he said; "the wind was mad to-night."

He folded his arms, and rested his head against the fireplace, whilst she removed the dishes from the table. On the mantelpiece stood an ink-pot and some sheets of paper. Presently he took them down, and turned up the corner of the tablecloth.

"I will write a few lines," he said, "till you are ready to sit down and talk."

Em, as she shook out the tablecloth, watched him bending intently over his paper. He had changed much. His face had grown thinner; his cheeks were almost hollow, though they were covered by a dark growth of beard.

She sat down on the skin beside him, and felt the little bundle on the bench; it was painfully small and soft. Perhaps it held a shirt and a book, but nothing more. The old black hat had a piece of unhemmed muslin twisted round it, and on his elbow was a large patch so fixed on with yellow thread that her heart ached. Only his hair was not changed, and hung in silky beautiful waves almost to his shoulders. To-morrow she would take the ragged edge off his collar, and put a new band round his hat. She did not interrupt him, but she wondered how it was that he sat to write so intently after his long weary walk. He was not tired now; his pen hurried quickly and restlessly over the paper, and his eye was bright. Presently Em raised her hand to her breast, where lay the letter yesterday had brought her. Soon she had forgotten him as entirely as he had forgotten her; each was in his own world with his own. He was writing to Lyndall. He would tell her all he had seen, all he had done, though it were nothing worth relating. He seemed to have come back to her, and to be talking to her now he sat there in the old house.

" — and then I got to the next town, and my horse was tired, so I could go no farther, and looked for work. A shopkeeper agreed to hire me as salesman. He made me sign a promise to remain six months, and he gave me a little empty room at the back of the store to sleep in. I had still three pounds of my own, and when you have just come from the country three pounds seems a great deal.

" When I had been in the shop three days, I wanted to go away again. A clerk in a shop has the lowest work to do of all people. It is much better to break stones; you have the blue sky above you, and only the stones to bend to. I asked my master to let me go, and I offered to give him my two pounds, and the bag of mealies I had bought with the other pound; but he would not.

"I found out afterwards he was giving me only half as much as he gave to the others — that was why. I had fear when I looked at the other clerks, that I would at last become like them. All day they were bowing and smirking to the women who came in; smiling, when all they wanted was, to get their money from them. They used to run and fetch the dresses and ribbons to show them, and they seemed to me like worms with oil on. There was one respectable thing in that store; it was the Kaffir storeman. His work was to load and unload, and he never needed to smile except when he liked, and he never told lies.

"The other clerks gave me the name of 'Old Salvation;' but there was one person I liked very much. He was clerk in another store. He often went past the door. He seemed to me not like others; his face was bright and fresh like a little child's. When he came to the shop I felt I liked him. One day I saw a book in his pocket, and that made me feel near him. I asked him if he was fond of reading, and he said Yes, when there was nothing else to do. The next day he came to me, and asked me if I did not feel lonely; he never saw me going out with the other fellows; he would come and see me that evening, he said.

"I was glad, and bought some meat and flour, because the gray mare and I always ate mealies; it is the cheapest thing; when you boil it hard you can't eat much of it. I made some cakes, and I folded my great coat on the box to make it soft for him; and at last he came.

" 'You 've got a rummy place here,' he said.

"You see there was nothing in it but packing-cases for furniture, and it was rather empty. While I was putting the food on the box he looked at my books; he read their names out aloud. 'Elementary Physiology,' 'First Principles.'

" ' Golly !' he said, ' I 've got a lot of dry stuff like that at home, I got for Sunday-school prizes; but I only keep them to light my pipe with now; they come in handy for that.' Then he asked me if I had ever read a book called the 'Black-eyed Creole.' 'That is the style for me,' he said; 'there where the fellow takes the nigger-girl by the arm, and the other fellow cuts off. That 's what I like.'

"But what he said after that I don't remember, only it made me feel as if I were having a bad dream, and I wanted to be far away.

"When he had finished eating he did not stay long; he had to go and see some girls home from a prayer-meeting; and he asked how it was he never saw me walking out with any on Sunday afternoons. He said he had lots of sweethearts, and he was going to see one the next Wednesday on a farm, and he asked me to lend my mare. I told him she was very old. But he said it did n't matter; he would come the next day to fetch her.

"After he was gone my little room got back to its old look. I loved it so; I was so glad to get into it at night, and it seemed to be reproaching me for bringing him there. The next day he took the gray mare. On Thursday he did not bring her back, and on Friday I found the saddle and bridle standing at my door.

"In the afternoon he looked into the shop, and

called out, 'Hope you got your saddle, Farber? Your bag-of-bones kicked out six miles from this. I'll send you a couple of shillings to-morrow, though the old hide wasn't worth it. Good-morning.'

"But I sprang over the counter, and got him by his throat. My father was so gentle with her; he never would ride her up hill, and now this fellow had murdered her! I asked him where he had killed her, and I shook him till he slipped out of my hand. He stood in the door grinning.

"'It didn't take much to kill *that* bag-of-bones, whose master sleeps in a packing-case, and waits till his company's finished to eat on the plate. Shouldn't wonder if you fed her on sugar-bags,' he said; 'and if you think I've jumped her, you'd better go and look yourself. You'll find her along the road by the "aas-vogels" that are eating her.'

"I caught him by his collar, and I lifted him from the ground, and I threw him out into the street, half-way across it. I heard the book-keeper say to the clerk that there was always the devil in those mum fellows; but they never called me Salvation after that.

"I am writing to you of very small things, but there is nothing else to tell; it has been all small, and you will like it. Whenever anything has happened, I have always thought I would tell it to you. The back thought in my mind is always you. After that only one old man came to visit me. I had seen him in the streets often; he always wore very dirty black clothes and a hat with crape round it, and he had one eye, — so I noticed him. One day he came to my room with a subscription-list for a minister's salary. When I said I had nothing to give, he looked at me with his one eye.

"'Young man,' he said, 'how is it I never see you in the house of the Lord?' I thought he was trying to do good, so I felt sorry for him, and I told him I never went to chapel. 'Young man,' he said, 'it grieves me to hear such godless words from the lips of one so young, — so far gone in the paths of destruction. Young man, if you forget God, God will forget you. There is a seat on the right-hand side as you go at the bottom door that you may get. If you are given over to the enjoyment and frivolities of this world, what will become of your never-dying soul?'

"He would not go till I gave him half a crown for the minister's salary. Afterwards I heard he was the man who collected the pew-rents, and got a percentage. I didn't get to know any one else.

"When my time in that shop was done I hired myself to drive one of a transport-rider's wagons.

"That first morning, when I sat in the front and called to my oxen, and saw nothing about me but the hills with the blue coming down to them, and the karroo bushes, I was drunk; I laughed; my heart was beating till it hurt me. I shut my eyes tight, that when I opened them I might see there were no shelves about me. There must be a beauty in buying and selling, if there is beauty in everything; but it is very ugly to me. My life as transport-rider would have been the best life in the world if I had had only one wagon to drive. My master told me he would drive one, I the other, and he would hire another person to drive the third. But the first day I drove two to help him, and after that he let me drive all three. Whenever we came to a hotel he stopped behind to get a drink, and when he rode up to the wagons he

could never stand; the Hottentot and I used to lift
him up. We always travelled all night, and used to
out-span for five or six hours in the heat of the day
to rest. I planned that I would lie under the wagon,
and read for an hour or two every day before I went
to sleep, and I did for the first two or three; but after
that I only wanted to sleep like the rest, and I packed
my books away. When you have three wagons to
look after all night, you are sometimes so tired you
can hardly stand. At first when I walked along driving my wagons in the night it was glorious; the stars
had never looked so beautiful to me; and on the dark
nights when we rode through the bush there were
will-o'-the-wisps dancing on each side of the road. I
found out that even the damp and dark are beautiful.
But I soon changed, and saw nothing but the road
and my oxen. I only wished for a smooth piece of
road, so that I might sit at the front and doze. At
the places where we out-spanned there were sometimes rare plants and flowers, the festoons hanging
from the bush-trees, and nuts and insects, such as we
never see here; but after a little while I never looked
at them; I was too tired. I ate as much as I could,
and then lay down on my face under the wagon till
the boy came to wake me to 'in-span,' and then we
drove on again all night; so it went, so it went. I
think sometimes when we walked by my oxen I called
to them in my sleep, for I know I thought of nothing;
I was like an animal. My body was strong and well
to work; but my brain was dead. If you have not
felt it, Lyndall, you cannot understand it. You may
work, and work, and work, till you are only a body, not
a soul. Now, when I see one of those evil-looking men
that come from Europe, — navvies, with the beast-like

sunken face, different from any Kaffir's, — I know
what brought that look into their eyes; and if I have
only one inch of tobacco I give them half. It is work,
grinding mechanical work, that they or their ancestors have done that has made them into beasts. You
may work a man's body so that his soul dies. Work
is good. I have worked at the old farm from the sun's
rising till its setting, but I have had time to think and
time to feel. You may work a man so that all but
the animal in him is gone; and that grows stronger
with physical labor. You may work a man till he is
a devil. I know it, because I have felt it. You will
never understand the change that came over me. No
one but I will ever know how great it was. But I
was never miserable; when I could keep my oxen
from sticking fast, and when I could find a place to
lie down in, I had all I wanted. After I had driven
eight months a rainy season came. For eighteen
hours out of the twenty-four we worked in the wet.
The mud went up to the axles sometimes, and we had
to dig the wheels out, and we never went far in a day.
My master swore at me more than ever, but when he
had done he always offered me his brandy-flask. When
I first came he had offered it me, and I had always
refused; but now I drank as my oxen did when I gave
them water, — without thinking. At last I bought
brandy for myself whenever we passed a hotel.

"One Sunday we out-spanned on the banks of a
swollen river to wait for its going down. It was
drizzling still, so I lay under the wagon on the mud.
There was no dry place anywhere; and all the dung
was wet, so there was no fire to cook food. My little
flask was filled with brandy, and I drank some and
went to sleep. When I woke it was drizzling still,

so I drank some more. I was stiff and cold; and my
master, who lay by me, offered me his flask, because
mine was empty. I drank some, and then I thought
I would go and see if the river was going down. I
remember that I walked to the road, and it seemed to
be going away from me. When I woke up, I was
lying by a little bush on the bank of the river. It
was afternoon; all the clouds had gone, and the sky
was deep blue. The Bushman boy was grilling ribs
at the fire. He looked at me, and grinned from ear
to ear. 'Master was a little nice,' he said, 'and lay
down in the road. Something might ride over master,
so I carried him there.' He grinned at me again. It
was as though he said, 'You and I are comrades. I
have lain in a road too. I know all about it.' When
I turned my head from him I saw the earth, so pure
after the rain, so green, so fresh, so blue;— and I
was a drunken carrier, whom his leader had picked
up in the mud, and laid at the roadside to sleep out
his drink. I remembered my old life, and I remembered you. I saw how, one day, you would read
in the papers,— 'A German carrier, named Waldo
Farber, was killed through falling from his wagon,
being instantly crushed under the wheel. Deceased
was supposed to have been drunk at the time of the
accident.' There are those notices in the paper every
month. I sat up, and I took the brandy-flask out of
my pocket, and I flung it as far as I could into the
dark water. The Hottentot boy ran down to see if
he could catch it; it had sunk to the bottom. I never
drank again. But, Lyndall, sin looks much more terrible to those who look at it than to those who do it.
A convict, or a man who drinks, seems something so
far off and horrible when we see him; but to himself

he seems quite near to us, and like us. We wonder what kind of a creature he is; but he is just we ourselves. We are only the wood, the knife that carves on us is the circumstance.

"I do not know why I kept on working so hard for that master. I think it was as the oxen come every day and stand by the yokes; they do not know why. Perhaps I would have been with him still; but one day we started with loads for the Diamond Fields. The oxen were very thin then, and they had been standing about in the yoke all day without food while the wagons were being loaded. Not far from the town was a hill. When we came to the foot the first wagon stuck fast. I tried for a little while to urge the oxen, but I soon saw the one span could never pull it up. I went to the other wagon to loosen that span to join them on in front, but the transport-rider, who was lying at the back of the wagon, jumped out.

"'They shall bring it up the hill; and if half of them die for it, they shall do it alone,' he said.

"He was not drunk, but in a bad temper, for he had been drunk the night before. He swore at me, and told me to take the whip and help him. We tried for a little time, then I told him it was no use, they could never do it. He swore louder, and called to the leaders to come on with their whips, and together they lashed. There was one ox, a black ox, so thin that the ridge of his backbone almost cut through his flesh.

"'It is you, devil, is it, that will not pull?' the transport-rider said. 'I will show you something.' He looked like a devil.

"He told the boys to leave off flogging, and he held

the ox by the horn, and took up a round stone, and knocked its nose with it till the blood came. When he had done, they called to the oxen, and took up their whips again, and the oxen strained with their backs bent, but the wagon did not move an inch.

"'So you won't, won't you?' he said. 'I'll help you.'

"He took out his clasp-knife, and ran it into the leg of the trembling ox three times, up to the hilt. Then he put the knife in his pocket, and they took their whips. The oxen's flanks quivered, and they foamed at the mouth. Straining, they moved the wagon a few feet forward, then stood with bent backs to keep it from sliding back. From the black ox's nostril foam and blood were streaming on to the ground. It turned its head in its anguish, and looked at me, with its great starting eyes. It was praying for help in its agony and weakness, and they took their whips again. The creature bellowed out aloud. If there is a God, it was calling to its Maker for help. Then a stream of clear blood burst from both nostrils; it fell on the ground, and the wagon slipped back. The man walked up to it.

"'You are going to lie down, devil, are you? We'll see you don't take it too easy.'

"The thing was just dying. He opened his clasp-knife and stooped down over it. I do not know what I did then. But afterwards I know I had him on the stones, and I was kneeling on him. The boys dragged me off. I wish they had not. I left him standing in the sand in the road, shaking himself, and I walked back to the town. I took nothing from that accursed wagon, so I had only two shillings. But it did not matter. The next day I got work at a wholesale store. My work was to pack and unpack goods, and to carry boxes, and I had only to work from six in the morning till six in the evening; so I had plenty of time. I hired a little room, and subscribed to a library, so I had everything I needed; and in the week of Christmas holidays I went to see the sea. I walked all night, Lyndall, to escape the heat, and a little after sunrise I got to the top of a high hill. Before me was a long, low, blue, monotonous mountain. I walked looking at it, but I was thinking of the sea I wanted to see. At last I wondered what that curious blue thing might be; then it struck me it was the sea. I would have turned back again, only I was too tired. I wonder if all the things we long to see — the churches, the pictures, the men in Europe — will disappoint us so! You see I had dreamed of it so long. When I was a little boy, minding sheep behind the 'kopje,' I used to see the waves stretching out as far as the eye could reach in the sunlight. My sea! Is the ideal always more beautiful than the real?

"I got to the beach that afternoon, and I saw the water run up and down on the sand, and I saw the white foam breakers; they were pretty, but I thought I would go back the next day. It was not my sea.

"But I began to like it when I sat by it that night in the moonlight; and the next day I liked it better; and before I left I loved it. It was not like the sky and stars, that talk of what has no beginning and no end; but it is so human. Of all the things I have ever seen, only the sea is like a human being; the sky is not, nor the earth. But the sea is always moving, always something deep in itself is stirring it. It never rests; it is always wanting, wanting, wanting.

It hurries on; and then it creeps back slowly, without
having reached, moaning. It is always asking a question, and it never gets the answer. I can hear it in
the day and in the night; the white foam breakers
are saying that which I think. I walk alone with
them when there is no one to see me, and I sing
with them. I lie down on the sand and watch them
with my eyes half shut. The sky is better, but it is
so high above our heads. I love the sea. Sometimes
we must look down too. After five days I went back
to Grahamstown.

"I had glorious books, and in the night I could sit
in my little room and read them; but I was lonely.
Books are not the same things when you are living
among people. I cannot tell why, but they are dead.
On the farm they would have been living beings to
me; but here, where there were so many people about
me, I wanted some one to belong to me. I was lonely.
I wanted something that was flesh and blood. Once
on this farm there came a stranger; I did not ask his
name, but he sat among the karroo and talked with
me. Now, wherever I have travelled I have looked
for him — in hotels, in streets, in passenger-wagons
as they rushed in, through the open windows of
houses I have looked for him, but I have not found
him, — never heard a voice like his. One day I went
to the Botanic Gardens. It was a half holiday, and
the band was to play. I stood in the long raised
avenue and looked down. There were many flowers,
and ladies and children were walking about, beautifully dressed. At last the music began. I had not
heard such music before. At first it was slow and
even, like the every-day life, when we walk through
it without thought or feeling; then it grew faster,

then it paused, hesitated, then it was quite still for an instant, and then it burst out. Lyndall, they made heaven right when they made it all music. It takes you up and carries you away, away, till you have the things you longed for; you are up close to them. You have got out into a large, free, open place. I could not see anything while it was playing; I stood with my head against my tree; but, when it was done, I saw that there were ladies sitting close to me on a wooden bench, and the stranger who had talked to me that day in the karroo was sitting between them. The ladies were very pretty, and their dresses beautiful. I do not think they had been listening to the music, for they were talking and laughing very softly. I heard all they said, and could even smell the rose on the breast of one. I was afraid he would see me; so I went to the other side of the tree, and soon they got up and began to pace up and down in the avenue. All the time the music played they chatted, and he carried on his arm the scarf of the prettiest lady. I did not hear the music; I tried to catch the sound of his voice each time he went by. When I was listening to the music I did not know I was badly dressed; now I felt so ashamed of myself. I never knew before what a low, horrible thing I was, dressed in tancord. That day on the farm, when we sat on the ground under the thorn-trees, I thought he quite belonged to me; now, I saw he was not mine. But he was still as beautiful. His brown eyes are more beautiful than any one's eyes, except yours.

"At last they turned to go, and I walked after them. When they got out of the gate he helped the ladies into a phaeton, and stood for a moment with his foot on the step talking to them. He had a little

cane in his hand, and an Italian greyhound ran after
him. Just when they drove away one of the ladies
dropped her whip.

"'Pick it up, fellow,' she said; and when I brought
it her she threw sixpence on the ground. I might
have gone back to the garden then; but I did not
want music : I wanted clothes, and to be fashionable
and fine. I felt that my hands were coarse, and that
I was vulgar. I never tried to see him again.

"I stayed in my situation four months after that,
but I was not happy. I had no rest. The people
about me pressed on me, and made me dissatisfied. I
could not forget them. Even when I did not see
them they pressed on me, and made me miserable.
I did not love books; I wanted people. When I
walked home under the shady trees in the street I
could not be happy, for when I passed the houses
I heard music, and saw faces between the curtains.
I did not want any of them, but I wanted some one
for mine, for me. I could not help it. I wanted a
finer life.

"Only one day something made me happy. A nurse
came to the store with a little girl belonging to one of
our clerks. While the maid went into the office to
give a message to its father, the little child stood
looking at me. Presently she came close to me and
peeped up into my face.

"'Nice curls, pretty curls,' she said; 'I like curls.'

"She felt my hair all over with her little hands.
When I put out my arm she let me take her and set
her on my knee. She kissed me with her soft mouth.
We were happy till the nurse-girl came and shook
her, and asked her if she was not ashamed to sit on
the knee of that strange man. But I do not think my

little one minded. She laughed at me as she went out.

"If the world were all children, I could like it; but men and women draw me so strangely, and then press me away, till I am in agony. I was not meant to live among people. Perhaps some day, when I am grown older, I will be able to go and live among them and look at them as I look at the rocks and bushes, without letting them disturb me, and take myself from me; but not now. So I grew miserable; a kind of fever seemed to eat me; I could not rest, or read, or think; so I came back here. I knew you were not here, but it seemed as though I should be nearer you; and it is you I want, — you that the other people suggest to me, but cannot give."

He had filled all the sheets he had taken, and now lifted down the last from the mantelpiece. Em had dropped asleep, and lay slumbering peacefully on the skin before the fire. Out of doors the storm still raged, but in a fitful manner, as though growing half weary of itself. He bent over his paper again, with eager flushed cheek, and wrote on.

"It has been a delightful journey, this journey home. I have walked on foot. The evening before last, when it was just sunset, I was a little footsore and thirsty, and went out of the road to look for water. I went down into a deep little 'kloof.' Some trees ran along the bottom, and I thought I should find water there. The sun had quite set when I got to the bottom of it. It was very still, — not a leaf was stirring anywhere. In the bed of the mountain torrent I thought I might find water. I came to the bank, and leaped down into the dry bed. The floor on which I

21

stood was of fine white sand, and the banks rose on every side like the walls of a room. Above there was a precipice of rocks, and a tiny stream of water oozed from them and fell slowly on to the flat stone below. Each drop you could hear fall like a little silver bell. There was one among the trees on the bank that stood cut out against the white sky. All the other trees were silent; but this one shook and trembled against the sky. Everything else was still; but those leaves were quivering, quivering. I stood on the sand; I could not go away. When it was quite dark, and the stars had come, I crept out. Does it seem strange to you that it should have made me so happy? It is because I cannot tell you how near I felt to things that we cannot see but we always feel. To-night has been a wild, stormy night. I have been walking across the plain for hours in the dark. I have liked the wind, because I have seemed forcing my way through to you. I knew you were not here, but I would hear of you. When I used to sit on the transport wagon half-sleeping, I used to start awake because your hands were on me. In my lodgings, many nights I have blown the light out, and sat in the dark, that I might see your face start out more distinctly. Sometimes it was the little girl's face who used to come to me behind the 'kopje' when I minded sheep, and sit by me in her blue pinafore; sometimes it was older. I love both. I am very helpless, I shall never do anything; but you will work, and I will take your work for mine. Sometimes such a sudden gladness seizes me when I remember that somewhere in the world you are living and working. You are my very own; nothing else is my own so. When I have finished I am going to look at your room door — "

He wrote; and the wind, which had spent its fury, moaned round and round the house, most like a tired child weary with crying.

Em woke up, and sat before the fire, rubbing her eyes, and listening, as it sobbed about the gables, and wandered away over the long stone walls.

"How quiet it has grown now," she said, and sighed herself, partly from weariness and partly from sympathy with the tired wind. He did not answer her; he was lost in his letter.

She rose slowly after a time, and rested her hand on his shoulder.

"You have many letters to write," she said.

"No," he answered; "it is only one to Lyndall."

She turned away, and stood long before the fire looking into it. If you have a deadly fruit to give, it will not grow sweeter by keeping.

"Waldo, dear," she said, putting her hand on his, "leave off writing."

He threw back the dark hair from his forehead, and looked at her.

"It is no use writing any more," she said.

"Why not?" he asked.

She put her hand over the papers he had written.

"Waldo," she said, "Lyndall is dead."

CHAPTER XII.

GREGORY'S WOMANHOOD.

SLOWLY over the flat came a cart. On the back seat sat Gregory, his arms folded, his hat drawn over his eyes. A Kaffir boy sat on the front seat driving, and at his feet sat Doss, who, now and again, lifted his nose and eyes above the level of the splash-board, to look at the surrounding country; and then, with an exceedingly knowing wink of his left eye, turned to his companions, thereby intimating that he clearly perceived his whereabouts. No one noticed the cart coming. Waldo, who was at work at his carpenter's table in the wagon-house, saw nothing, till chancing to look down he perceived Doss standing before him, the legs trembling, the little nose wrinkled, and a series of short suffocating barks giving utterance to his joy at reunion.

Em, whose eyes had ached with looking out across the plain, was now at work in a back room, and knew nothing till, looking up, she saw Gregory, with his straw hat and blue eyes, standing in the doorway. He greeted her quietly, hung his hat up in its old place behind the door, and for any change in his manner or appearance he might have been gone only the day before to fetch letters from the town. Only his beard was gone, and his face was grown thinner. He took off his leather gaiters, said the afternoon was hot and the roads dusty, and asked for some tea.

They talked of wool, and the cattle, and the sheep, and Em gave him the pile of letters that had come for him during the months of absence, but of the thing that lay at their hearts neither said anything. Then he went out to look at the kraals, and at supper Em gave him hot cakes and coffee. They talked about the servants, and then eat their meal in quiet. She asked no questions, When it was ended Gregory went into the front room, and lay in the dark on the sofa.

"Do you not want a light?" Em asked, venturing to look in.

"No," he answered; then presently called to her, "Come and sit here; I want to talk to you."

She came, and sat on a footstool near him.

"Do you wish to hear anything?" he asked.

She whispered, "Yes, if it does not hurt you."

"What difference does it make to me?" he said. "If I talk or am silent, is there any change?"

Yet he lay quiet for a long time. The light through the open door showed him to her, where he lay, with his arm thrown across his eyes. At last he spoke. Perhaps it was a relief to him to speak.

To Bloemfontein in the Free State, to which through an agent he had traced them, Gregory had gone. At the hotel where Lyndall and her stranger had stayed he put up; he was shown the very room in which they had slept. The colored boy who had driven them to the next town, told him in which house they had boarded, and Gregory went on. In that town he found they had left the cart, and bought a spider and four grays, and Gregory's heart rejoiced. Now, indeed, it would be easy to trace their course. And he turned his steps northwards.

At the farm-houses where he stopped, the ooms and tantes remembered clearly the spider with its four gray horses. At one place the Boer-wife told how the tall, blue-eyed Englishman had bought milk, and asked the way to the next farm. At the next farm the Englishman had bought a bunch of flowers, and given half a crown for them to the little girl. It was quite true; the Boer-mother made her get it out of the box, and show it. At the next place they had slept. Here they told him that the great bull-dog, who hated all strangers, had walked in in the evening, and laid its head on the lady's lap. So at every place he heard something, and traced them step by step.

At one desolate farm the Boer had a good deal to tell. The lady had said she liked a wagon that stood before the door. Without asking the price, the Englishman had offered a hundred and fifty pounds for the old thing, and bought oxen worth ten pounds for sixteen. The Dutchman chuckled, for he had the " Salt-reim's" money in the box under his bed. Gregory laughed too, in silence; he could not lose sight of them now, so slowly they would have to move with that cumbrous ox-wagon. Yet, when that evening came, and he reached a little wayside inn, no one could tell him anything of the travellers.

The master, a surly creature, half-stupid with Boer-brandy, sat on the bench before the door, smoking. Gregory sat beside him, questioning, but he smoked on. He remembered nothing of such strangers. How should he know who had been there months and months before ? He smoked on. Gregory, very weary, tried to awake his memory, said that the lady he was seeking for was very beautiful, had a little mouth, and tiny, very tiny, feet. The man only smoked on as sullenly as at first. What were little, very little mouths and feet to him. But his daughter leaned out in the window above. She was dirty and lazy, and liked to loll there when travellers came, to hear the men talk, but she had a soft heart. Presently a hand came out of the window, and a pair of velvet slippers touched his shoulder, tiny slippers with black flowers. He pulled them out of her hand. Only one woman's feet had worn them, he knew that.

"Left here last summer by a lady," said the girl; "might be the one you are looking for. Never saw any feet so small."

Gregory rose and questioned her.

They might have come in a wagon and spider, she could not tell. But the gentleman was very handsome, tall, lovely figure, blue eyes, wore gloves always when he went out. An English officer, perhaps; no Africander, certainly.

Gregory stopped her.

The lady? Well, she was pretty, rather, the girl said; very cold, dull air, silent. They stayed for, it might be, five days; slept in the wing over against the stoep; quarrelled sometimes, she thought — the lady. She had seen everything when she went in to wait. One day the gentleman touched her hair; she drew back from him as though his fingers poisoned her. Went to the other end of the room if he came to sit near her. Walked out alone. Cold wife for such a handsome husband, the girl thought; she evidently pitied him, he was such a beautiful man. They went away early one morning, how, or in which way, the girl could not tell.

Gregory inquired of the servants, but nothing more was to be learned; so the next morning he saddled his horse and went on. At the farms he came to the good old ooms and tantes asked him to have coffee, and the little shoeless children peeped out at the stranger from behind ovens and gables; but no one had seen what he asked for. This way and that he rode to pick up the thread he had dropped; but the spider and the wagon, the little lady and the handsome gentleman, no one had seen. In the towns he fared yet worse.

Once, indeed, hope came to him. On the stoep of a hotel, at which he stayed the night in a certain little village, there walked a gentleman, grave and kindly-looking. It was not hard to open conversation with him about the weather; and then — Had he ever seen such and such people, a gentleman and lady, a spider and wagon, arrive at that place? The kindly gentleman shook his head. What was the lady like, he inquired.

Gregory painted. Hair like silken floss, small mouth, under lip very full and pink, upper lip pink, but very thin and curled; there were four white spots on the nail of her right hand forefinger, and her eyebrows were very delicately curved.

The gentleman looked thoughtful, as trying to remember.

"Yes; and a rose-bud tinge in the cheeks; hands like lilies, and perfectly seraphic smile."

"That is she! that is she!" cried Gregory.

Who else could it be? He asked where she had gone to. The gentleman most thoughtfully stroked his beard. He would try to remember. Were not her ears — Here such a violent fit of coughing seized him that he ran away into the house. An ill-fed clerk and a dirty barman standing in the doorway laughed aloud. Gregory wondered if they could be laughing at the gentleman's cough; and then he heard some one laughing in the room into which the gentleman had gone. He must follow him and try to learn more; but he soon found that there was nothing more to be learned there. Poor Gregory!

Backwards and forwards, backwards and forwards, from the dirty little hotel where he had dropped the thread, to this farm and to that, rode Gregory, till his heart was sick and tired. That from that spot the wagon might have gone its own way and the spider another was an idea that did not occur to him. At last he saw it was no use lingering in that neighborhood, and pressed on.

One day, coming to a little town, his horses knocked up, and he resolved to rest them there. The little hotel of the town was a bright and sunny place, like the jovial face of the clean little woman who kept it, and who trotted about talking always, — talking to the customers in the tap-room, and to the maids in the kitchen, and to the passers-by when she could hail them from the windows, — talking, as good-natured women with large mouths and small noses always do, in season and out.

There was a little front parlor in the hotel kept for strangers who wanted to be alone. Gregory sat there to eat his breakfast, and the landlady dusted the room, and talked of the great finds at the Diamond Fields, and the badness of maid-servants, and the shameful conduct of the Dutch parson in that town to the English inhabitants. Gregory ate his breakfast, and listened to nothing. He had asked his one question, had had his answer; now she might talk on.

Presently a door in the corner opened, and a woman

came out, — a Mozambiquer, with a red handkerchief
twisted round her head. She carried in her hand a
tray, with a slice of toast crumbled fine, and a half-
filled cup of coffee, and an egg broken open, but not
eaten. Her ebony face grinned complacently as she
shut the door softly, and said, "Good-morning."

The landlady began to talk to her.

"You are not going to leave her really, Ayah, are
you?" she said. "The maids say so; but I'm sure
you would n't do such a thing."

The Mozambiquer grinned.

"Husband says I must go home."

"But she has n't got any one else, and won't have
any one else. Come now," said the landlady, "I've
no time to be sitting always in a sick room, not if I
was paid anything for it."

The Mozambiquer only showed her white teeth good-
naturedly for answer, and went out, and the landlady followed her.

Gregory, glad to be alone, watched the sunshine as
it came over the fuchsias in the window, and ran up
and down on the panelled door in the corner. The
Mozambiquer had closed it loosely behind her, and
presently something touched it inside. It moved a
little, then it was still, then moved again; then
through the gap a small nose appeared, and a yellow
ear over-lapping one eye; then the whole head ob-
truded, placed itself critically on one side, wrinkled
its nose disapprovingly at Gregory, and withdrew.
Through the half-open door came a faint scent of vine-
gar, and the room was dark and still.

Presently the landlady came back.

"Left the door open," she said, bustling to shut it;
"but a darky will be a darky, and never carries a

head on its shoulders like other folks. Not ill, I hope,
sir?" she said, looking at Gregory when she had
shut the bedroom door.

"No," said Gregory, "no."

The landlady began putting the things together.

"Who," asked Gregory, "is in that room?"

Glad to have a little innocent piece of gossip to
relate, and some one willing to hear it, the landlady
made the most of a little story as she cleared the
table. Six months before a lady had come alone to
the hotel in a wagon, with only a colored leader and
driver. Eight days after a little baby had been born.
If Gregory stood up and looked out at the window, he
would see a blue gum-tree in the graveyard; close by
it was a little grave. The baby was buried there. A
tiny thing, only lived two hours, and the mother
herself almost went with it. After a while she was
better; but one day she got up out of bed, dressed
herself without saying a word to any one, and went
out. It was a drizzly day; a little time after some
one saw her sitting on the wet ground under the blue
gum-tree, with the rain dripping from her hat and
shawl. They went to fetch her, but she would not
come until she chose. When she did she had gone
to bed, and had not risen again from it; never would,
the doctor said.

She was very patient, poor thing. When you went
in to ask her how she was she said always "Better,"
or "Nearly well!" and lay still in the darkened
room, and never troubled any one. The Mozambiquer
took care of her, and she would not allow any one
else to touch her; would not so much as allow any
one else to see her foot uncovered. She was strange
in many ways, but she paid well, poor thing; and

now the Mozambiquer was going, and she would have to take up with some one else.

The landlady prattled on pleasantly, and now carried away the tray with the breakfast-things. When she was gone, Gregory leaned his head on his hands, but he did not think long.

Before dinner he had ridden out of the town to where on a rise a number of transport-wagons were out-spanned. The Dutchman driver of one wondered at the stranger's eagerness to free himself of his horses. Stolen perhaps; but it was worth his while to buy them at so low a price. So the horses changed masters, and Gregory walked off with his saddle-bags slung across his arm. Once out of sight of the wagons he struck out of the road and walked across the "veld," the dry, flowering grasses waving everywhere about him; half way across the plain he came to a deep gully which the rain torrents had washed out, but which was now dry. Gregory sprang down into its red bed. It was a safe place, and quiet. When he had looked about him he sat down under the shade of an overhanging bank and fanned himself with his hat, for the afternoon was hot, and he had walked fast. At his feet the dusty ants ran about, and the high red bank before him was covered by a network of roots and fibres washed bare by the rains. Above his head rose the clear blue African sky; at his side were the saddle-bags full of women's clothing. Gregory looked up half plaintively into the blue sky.

"Am I, am I Gregory Nazianzen Rose?" he said.

It was all so strange, he sitting there in that sloot in that up-country plain!—strange as the fantastic, changing shapes in a summer cloud. At last, tired out, he fell asleep, with his head against the bank.

When he woke the shadow had stretched across the sloot, and the sun was on the edge of the plain. Now he must be up and doing. He drew from his breast-pocket a little sixpenny looking-glass, and hung it on one of the roots that stuck out from the bank. Then he dressed himself in one of the old-fashioned gowns and a great pinked-out collar. Then he took out a razor. Tuft by tuft the soft brown beard fell down into the sand, and the little ants took it to line their nests with. Then the glass showed a face surrounded by a frilled cap, white as a woman's, with a little mouth, a very short upper lip, and a receding chin.

Presently a rather tall woman's figure was making its way across the veld. As it passed a hollowed-out ant-heap it knelt down, and stuffed in the saddle-bags with the man's clothing, closing up the ant-hill with bits of ground to look as natural as possible. Like a sinner hiding his deed of sin, the hider started once and looked round, but yet there was no one near save a "meerkat," who had lifted herself out of her hole and sat on her hind legs watching. He did not like that even she should see, and when he rose she dived away into her hole. Then he walked on leisurely, that the dusk might have reached the village streets before he walked there. The first house was the smith's, and before the open door two idle urchins lolled. As he hurried up the street in the gathering gloom he heard them laugh long and loudly behind him. He glanced round fearingly, and would almost have fled, but that the strange skirts clung about his legs. And after all it was only a spark that had alighted on the head of one, and not the strange figure they laughed at.

The door of the hotel stood wide open, and the light fell out into the street. He knocked, and the land-

lady came. She peered out to look for the cart that
had brought the traveller; but Gregory's heart was
brave now he was so near the quiet room. He told
her he had come with the transport wagons that stood
outside the town.

He had walked in, and wanted lodgings for the
night.

It was a deliberate lie, glibly told; he would have
told fifty, though the recording angel had stood in the
next room with his pen dipped in the ink. What
was it to him? He remembered that she lay there
saying always, "I am better."

The landlady put his supper in the little parlor
where he had sat in the morning. When it was on
the table she sat down in the rocking-chair, as her
fashion was, to knit and talk, that she might gather
news for her customers in the tap-room. In the white
face under the queer, deep-fringed cap she saw nothing of the morning's traveller. The new-comer was
communicative. She was a nurse by profession, she
said; had come to the Transvaal, hearing that good
nurses were needed there. She had not yet found
work. The landlady did not perhaps know whether
there would be any for her in that town?

The landlady put down her knitting, and smote her
fat hands together.

If it was n't the very finger of God's Providence, as
though you saw it hanging out of the sky, she said.
Here was a lady ill and needing a new nurse that very
day, and not able to get one to her mind, and now—
well, if it was n't enough to convert all the atheists
and freethinkers in the Transvaal she did n't know!

Then the landlady proceeded to detail facts.

"I 'm sure you will suit her," she added; "you 're

just the kind. She has heaps of money to pay you with; has everything that money can buy. And I got a letter with a check in it for fifty pounds the other day from some one, who says I'm to spend it for her, and not to let her know. She is asleep now, but I'll take you in to look at her."

The landlady opened the door of the next room, and Gregory followed her. A table stood near the bed, and a lamp burning low stood on it; the bed was a great four-poster with white curtains, and the quilt was of rich crimson satin. But Gregory stood just inside the door with his head bent low, and saw no farther.

"Come nearer; I'll turn the lamp up a bit, that you can have a look at her. A pretty thing, isn't she?" said the landlady.

Near the foot of the bed was a dent in the crimson quilt, and out of it Doss's small head and bright eyes looked knowingly.

"See how the lips move; she is in pain," said the landlady.

Then Gregory looked up at what lay on the cushion. A little white, white face, transparent as an angel's, with a cloth bound round the forehead, and with soft short hair, tossed about on the pillow.

"We had to cut it off," said the woman, touching it with her forefinger. "Soft as silk, like a wax doll's."

But Gregory's heart was bleeding.

"Never get up again, the doctor says," said the landlady.

Gregory uttered one word. In an instant the beautiful eyes opened widely, looked round the room and into the dark corners.

"Who is here? Whom did I hear speak?"

Gregory had sunk back behind the curtain; the landlady drew it aside, and pulled him forward.

"Only this lady, ma'am, — a nurse by profession. She is willing to stay and take care of you, if you can come to terms with her."

Lyndall raised herself on her elbow, and cast one keen scrutinizing glance over him.

"Have I never seen you before?" she asked.

"No."

She fell back wearily.

"Perhaps you would like to arrange the terms between yourselves," said the landlady. "Here is a chair. I will be back presently."

Gregory sat down, with bent head and quick breath. She did not speak, and lay with half-closed eyes, seeming to have forgotten him.

"Will you turn the lamp down a little?" she said at last; "I cannot bear the light."

Then his heart grew braver in the shadow, and he spoke. Nursing was to him, he said, his chosen life's work. He wanted no money; if— She stopped him.

"I take no service for which I do not pay," she said. "What I gave to my last nurse I will give to you; if you do not like it, you may go."

And Gregory muttered humbly, he would take it.

Afterwards she tried to turn herself. He lifted her. Ah! a shrunken little body, he could feel its weakness as he touched it. His hands were to him glorified for what they had done.

"Thank you; that is so nice. Other people hurt me when they touch me," she said. "Thank you." Then after a little while she repeated humbly, "Thank you; they hurt me so."

Gregory sat down trembling. His little ewe-lamb, could they hurt her?

The doctor said of Gregory four days after, "She is the most experienced nurse I ever came in contact with."

Gregory, standing in the passage, heard it, and laughed in his heart. What need had he of experience? Experience teaches us in a millennium what passion teaches us in an hour. A Kaffir studies all his life the discerning of distant sounds; but he will never hear my step, when my love hears it, coming to her window in the dark over the short grass.

At first Gregory's heart was sore when day by day the body grew lighter, and the mouth he fed took less; but afterwards he grew accustomed to it, and was happy. For passion has *one* cry, one only, — "Oh, to touch thee, beloved!"

In that quiet room Lyndall lay on the bed with the dog at her feet, and Gregory sat in his dark corner, watching.

She seldom slept, and through those long, long days she would lie watching the round streak of sunlight that came through the knot in the shutter, or the massive lion's paw on which the wardrobe rested. What thoughts were in those eyes? Gregory wondered; he dared not ask.

Sometimes Doss, where he lay on her feet, would dream that they two were in the cart, tearing over the veld, with the black horses snorting, and the wind in their faces; and he would start up in his sleep and bark aloud. Then awaking, he would lick his mistress's hand almost remorsefully, and slink quietly down into his place.

Gregory thought she had no pain, she never

22.

groaned; only sometimes, when the light was near her, he thought he could see slight contractions about her lips and eyebrows.

He slept on the sofa outside her door.

One night he thought he heard a sound, and, opening it softly, he looked in. She was crying out aloud, as if she and her pain were alone in the world. The light fell on the red quilt, and the little hands that were clasped over the head. The wide-open eyes were looking up, and the heavy drops fell slowly from them.

"I cannot bear any more, not any more," she said in a deep voice. "O, God, God! Have I not borne in silence? Have I not endured these long, long months? But now, now, O God, I cannot!"

Gregory knelt in the doorway, listening.

"I do not ask for wisdom, not human love, not work, not knowledge, not for all things I have longed for," she cried; "only a little freedom from pain! only one little hour without pain! Then I will suffer again."

She sat up, and bit the little hand Gregory loved.

He crept away to the front door, and stood looking out at the quiet starlight. When he came back, she was lying in her usual posture, the quiet eyes looking at the lion's claw. He came close to the bed.

"You have much pain to-night?" he asked her.

"No, not much."

"Can I do anything for you?"

"No, nothing."

She still drew her lips together, and motioned with her fingers towards the dog who lay sleeping at her feet. Gregory lifted him and laid him at her side. She made Gregory turn open the bosom of her nightdress that the dog might put his black muzzle between her breasts. She crossed her arms over him. Gregory left them lying there together.

The next day, when they asked her how she was, she answered, "Better."

"Some one ought to tell her," said the landlady; "we can't let her soul go out into eternity not knowing, especially when I don't think it was all right about the child. You ought to go and tell her, Doctor."

So the little doctor, edged on and on, went in at last. When he came out of the room he shook his fist in the landlady's face.

"Next time you have any devil's work to do, do it yourself," he said, and shook his fist in her face again, and went away swearing.

When Gregory went into the bedroom he only found her moved, her body curled up, and drawn close to the wall. He dared not disturb her. At last, after a long time, she turned.

"Bring me food," she said, "I want to eat. Two eggs, and toast, and meat, — two large slices of toast, please."

Wondering, Gregory brought a tray with all that she had asked for.

"Sit me up, and put it close to me," she said; "I am going to eat it all." She tried to draw the things near her with her fingers, and rearranged the plates. She cut the toast into long strips, broke open both eggs, put a tiny morsel of bread into her own mouth, and fed the dog with pieces of meat put into his jaws with her fingers.

"Is it twelve o'clock yet?" she said; "I think I do not generally eat so early. Put it away, please.

carefully — no, do not take it away — only on the table. When the clock strikes twelve I will eat it."

She lay down trembling. After a little while she said, —

"Give me my clothes."

He looked at her.

"Yes; I am going to dress to-morrow. I should get up now, but it is rather late. Put them on that chair. My collars are in the little box, my boots behind the door."

Her eyes followed him intently as he collected the articles one by one and placed them on the chair as she directed.

"Put it nearer," she said. "I cannot see it;" and she lay watching the clothes, with her hand under her cheek.

"Now open the shutter wide," she said. "I am going to read."

The old, old tone was again in the sweet voice. He obeyed her, and opened the shutter, and raised her up among the pillows.

"Now bring my books to me," she said, motioning eagerly with her fingers; "the large book, and the reviews, and the plays. I want them all."

He piled them round her on the bed; she drew them greedily closer, her eyes very bright, but her face as white as a mountain-lily.

"Now the big one off the drawers. No, you need not help me to hold my book," she said. "I can hold it for myself."

Gregory went back to his corner, and for a little time the restless turning over of leaves was to be heard.

"Will you open the window," she said, almost

querulously, "and throw this book out? It is so utterly foolish! I thought it was a valuable book; but the words are merely strung together. They make no sense. Yes, — so!" she said with approval, seeing him fling it out into the street. "I must have been very foolish when I thought that book good."

Then she turned to read, and leaned her little elbows resolutely on the great volume, and knit her brows. This was Shakspeare; it must mean something.

"I wish you would take a handkerchief and tie it tight round my head, it aches so."

He had not been long in his seat when he saw drops fall from beneath the hands that shaded the eyes on to the page.

"I am not accustomed to so much light; it makes my head swim a little," she said. "Go out and close the shutter."

When he came back, she lay shrivelled up among the pillows.

He heard no sound of weeping, but the shoulders shook. He darkened the room completely.

When Gregory went to his sofa that night she told him to wake her early; she would be dressed before breakfast. Nevertheless, when morning came, she said it was a little cold, and lay all day watching her clothes upon the chair. Still she sent for her oxen in the country; they would start on Monday and go down to the Colony.

In the afternoon she told him to open the window wide, and draw the bed near it.

It was a leaden afternoon, the dull rain-clouds rested close to the roofs of the houses, and the little street was silent and deserted. Now and then a gust of wind eddying round caught up the dried leaves, whirled them hither and thither under the trees, and dropped them again into the gutter. Then all was quiet. She lay looking out. Presently the bell of the church began to toll, and up the village street came a long procession. They were carrying an old man to his last resting-place. She followed them with her eyes till they turned in among the trees at the gate.

" Who was that ? " she asked.

" An old man," he answered; " a very old man They say he was ninety-four; but his name I do not know."

She mused a while, looking out with fixed eyes.

" That is why the bell rang so cheerfully," she said. " When the old die it is well; they have had their time. It is when the young die that the bells weep drops of blood."

" But the old love life," he said, for it was sweet to hear her speak.

She raised herself on her elbow.

" They love life, they do not want to die," she answered; " but what of that ? They have had their time. They knew that a man's life is three-score years and ten; they should have made their plans accordingly. But the young," she said, " the young, cut down cruelly when they have not seen, when they have not known, when they have not found, — it is for them that the bells weep blood. I heard in the ringing it was an old man. When the old die, — Listen to the bell ! it is laughing, — ' It is right, it is right; he has had his time.' They cannot ring so for the young."

She fell back exhausted; the hot light died from her eyes, and she lay looking out into the street. By and by stragglers from the funeral began to come back and disappear here and there among the houses; then all was quiet, and the night began to settle down upon the village street. Afterwards, when the room was almost dark, so that they could not see each other's faces, she said, "It will rain to-night," and moved restlessly on the pillows. "How terrible when the rain falls down on you!"

He wondered what she meant, and they sat on in the still darkening room. She moved again.

"Will you presently take my cloak, — the new gray cloak from behind the door, — and go out with it. You will find a little grave at the foot of the tall blue gum-tree; the water drips off the long, pointed leaves; you must cover it up with that."

She moved restlessly, as though in pain.

Gregory assented, and there was silence again. It was the first time she had ever spoken of her child.

"It was so small," she said; "it lived such a little while, — only three hours. They laid it close by me, but I never saw it; I could feel it by me." She waited. "Its feet were so cold, I took them in my hand to make them warm, and my hand closed right over them, they were so little." There was an uneven trembling in the voice. "It crept close to me; it wanted to drink; it wanted to be warm." She hardened herself, — "I did not love it; its father was not my prince; *I* did not care for it; but it was so little." She moved her hand. "They might have kissed it, one of them, before they put it in. It never did any one any harm in all its little life. They might have kissed it, one of them."

Gregory felt that some one was sobbing in the room.

Late on in the evening, when the shutter was closed and the lamp lighted, and the rain-drops beat on the roof, he took the cloak from behind the door and went away with it. On his way back he called at the village post-office, and brought back a letter. In the hall he stood reading the address. How could he fail to know whose hand had written it? Had he not long ago studied those characters on the torn fragments of paper in the old parlor? A burning pain was at Gregory's heart. If now, now at the last, one should come, should step in between! He carried the letter into the bedroom, and gave it her. "Bring me the lamp nearer," she said. When she had read it, she asked for her desk.

Then Gregory sat down in the lamp-light on the other side of the curtain, and heard the pencil move on the paper. When he looked round the curtain, she was lying on the pillow, musing. The open letter lay at her side; she glanced at it with soft eyes. The man with the languid eyelids must have been strangely moved before his hand set down those words: "Let me come back to you! My darling, let me put my hand round you, and guard you from all the world. As my wife they shall never touch you. I have learned to love you more wisely, more tenderly than of old; you shall have perfect freedom. Lyndall, grand little woman, for your own sake be my wife!

"Why did you send that money back to me? You are cruel to me. It is not rightly done."

She rolled the little red pencil softly between her fingers, and her face grew very soft. Yet —

"It cannot be," she wrote; "I thank you much for

the love you have shown me; but I cannot listen.
You will call me mad, foolish, — the world would do
so; but I know what I need, and the kind of path I
must walk in. I cannot marry you. I shall always
love you for the sake of what lay by me those three
hours; but there it ends. I must know and see; I
cannot be bound to one whom I love as I love you. I
am not afraid of the world; I will fight the world.
One day — perhaps it may be far off — I shall find
what I have wanted all my life, — something nobler,
stronger, than I, before which I can kneel down. You
lose nothing by not having me now; I am a weak, selfish, erring woman. One day I shall find something
to worship, and then I shall be — "

"Nurse," she said, "take my desk away; I am
suddenly so sleepy; I will write more to-morrow."
She turned her face to the pillow; it was the sudden
drowsiness of great weakness. She had dropped
asleep in a moment, and Gregory moved the desk
softly, and then sat in the chair watching. Hour
after hour passed, but he had no wish for rest, and
sat on, hearing the rain cease, and the still night
settle down everywhere. At a quarter-past twelve he
rose, and took a last look at the bed where she lay
sleeping so peacefully; then he turned to go to his
couch. Before he had reached the door she had
started up, and was calling him back.

"You are sure you have put it up?" she said
with a look of blank terror at the window. "It
will not fall open in the night, the shutter — you are
sure?"

He comforted her. Yes, it was tightly fastened.

"Even if it is shut," she said in a whisper, "you

cannot keep it out! You feel it coming in at four
o'clock, creeping, creeping, up, up; deadly cold!"
She shuddered.

He thought she was wandering, and laid her little
trembling body down among the blankets.

"I dreamed just now that it was not put up," she
said, looking into his eyes; "and it crept right in,
and I was alone with it."

"What do you fear?" he asked tenderly.

"The gray dawn," she said, glancing round at the
window. "I was never afraid of anything, never
when I was a little child, but I have always been
afraid of that. You will not let it come in to me?"

"No, no; I will stay with you," he continued.

But she was growing calmer. "No; you must go
to bed. I only awoke with a start; you must be
tired. I am childish, that is all;" but she shivered
again.

He sat down beside her. After some time she said,
"Will you not rub my feet?"

He knelt down at the foot of the bed, and took the
tiny foot in his hand; it was swollen and unsightly
now, but as he touched it, he bent down and covered
it with kisses.

"It makes it better when you kiss it; thank you.
What makes you all love me so?" Then dreamily
she muttered to herself, "Not utterly bad, not quite
bad — what makes them all love me so?"

Kneeling there, rubbing softly, with his cheek
pressed against the little foot, Gregory dropped to
sleep at last. How long he knelt there he could not
tell, but when he started up awake she was not looking at him. The eyes were fixed on the far corner,
gazing wide and intent, with an unearthly light.

He looked round fearfully. What did she see there? God's angels come to call her? Something fearful? *He* saw only the purple curtain, with the shadows that fell from it. Softly he whispered, asking what she saw there.

And she said, in a voice strangely unlike her own, " I see the vision of a poor weak soul striving after good. It was not cut short; and in the end it learned, through tears and much pain, that holiness is an infinite compassion for others; that greatness is to take the common things of life, and walk truly among them; that" — she moved her white hand and laid it on her forehead — " happiness is a great love and much serving. It was not cut short; and it loved what it had learned — it loved — and — "

Was that all she saw in the corner?

Gregory told the landlady the next morning that she had been wandering all night. Yet when he came in to give her her breakfast, she was sitting up against the pillows, looking as he had not seen her look before.

" Put it close to me," she said, " and when I have had breakfast I am going to dress."

She finished all he had brought her, eagerly.

" I am sitting up quite by myself," she said. " Give me his meat; " and she fed the dog herself, cutting his food small for him. She moved to the side of the bed.

" Now bring the chair near and dress me. It is being in this room so long, and looking at that miserable little bit of sunshine that comes in through the shutter, that is making me so ill. Always that lion's paw ! " she said with a look of disgust at it. " Come and dress me." Gregory knelt on the floor before her, and tried to draw on one stocking, but the little swollen foot refused to be covered.

"It is very funny that I should have grown so fat since I have been so ill," she said, peering down curiously. "Perhaps it is want of exercise." She looked troubled, and said again, "Perhaps it is want of exercise." She wanted Gregory to say so too. But he only found a larger pair; and then tried to force the shoes — oh, so tenderly! — on to her little feet.

"There," she said, looking down at them when they were on, with the delight of a small child over its first shoes, "I could walk far now. How nice it looks!"

"No," she said, seeing the soft gown he had prepared for her, "I will not put that on. Get one of my white dresses, — the one with the pink bows. I do not even want to think I have been ill. It is thinking and thinking of things that makes them real," she said. "When you draw your mind together, and resolve that a thing shall not be, it gives way before you; it is not. Everything is possible if one is resolved," she said. She drew in her little lips together, and Gregory obeyed her; she was so small and slight now, it was like dressing a small doll. He would have lifted her down from the bed when he had finished, but she pushed him from her, laughing very softly. It was the first time she had laughed in those long dreary months.

"No, no; I can get down myself," she said, slipping cautiously on to the floor. "You see!" She cast a defiant glance of triumph when she stood there. "Hold the curtain up high, I want to look at myself."

He raised it, and stood holding it. She looked into

the glass on the opposite wall. Such a queenly little figure in its pink and white. Such a transparent little face, refined by suffering into an almost angel-like beauty! The face looked at her; she looked back, laughing softly. Doss, quivering with excitement, ran round her, barking. She took one step towards the door, balancing herself with outstretched hands.

"I am nearly there," she said.

Then she groped blindly.

"Oh, I cannot see! I cannot see! Where am I?" she cried.

When Gregory reached her, she had fallen with her face against the sharp foot of the wardrobe, and cut her forehead. Very tenderly he raised the little crushed heap of muslin and ribbons, and laid it on the bed. Doss climbed up, and sat looking down at it. Very softly Gregory's hands disrobed her.

"You will be stronger to-morrow, and then we shall try again," he said; but she neither looked at him nor stirred.

When he had undressed her, and laid her in bed, Doss stretched himself across her feet and lay whining softly.

So she lay all that morning, and all that afternoon.

Again and again Gregory crept close to the bedside and looked at her; but she did not speak to him. Was it stupor or was it sleep that shone under those half-closed eyelids? Gregory could not tell.

At last in the evening he bent over her.

"The oxen have come," he said; "we can start to-morrow if you like. Shall I get the wagon ready to-night?"

Twice he repeated his question. Then she looked

up at him, and Gregory saw that all hope had died out of the beautiful eyes. It was not stupor that shone there, it was despair.

"Yes, let us go," she said.

"It makes no difference," said the doctor; "staying or going, it is close now."

So the next day Gregory carried her out in his arms to the wagon which stood in-spanned before the door. As he laid her down on the "kartel" she looked far out across the plain. For the first time she spoke that day.

"That blue mountain, far away; let us stop when we get to it, not before." She closed her eyes again. He drew the sails down before and behind, and the wagon rolled away slowly. The landlady and the negroes stood to watch it from the stoep.

Very silently the great wagon rolled along the grass-covered plain. The driver on the front box did not clap his whip or call to his oxen, and Gregory sat beside him with folded arms. Behind them, in the closed wagon, she lay with the dog at her feet, very quiet, with folded hands. He, Gregory, dared not be in there. Like Hagar, when she laid her treasure down in the wilderness, he sat afar off, — "For she said, Let me not see the death of the child."

Evening came, and yet the blue mountain was not reached, and all the next day they rode on slowly, but still it was far off. Only at evening they reached it; not blue now, but low and brown, covered with long waving grasses and rough stones. They drew the wagon up close to its foot for the night. It was a sheltered, warm spot.

When the dark night had come, when the tired oxen were tied to the wheels, and the driver and leader had rolled themselves in their blankets before the fire, and gone to sleep, then Gregory fastened down the sails of the wagon securely. He fixed a long candle near the head of the bed, and lay down himself on the floor of the wagon near the back. He leaned his head against the kartel, and listened to the chewing of the tired oxen, and to the crackling of the fire, till, overpowered by weariness, he fell into a heavy sleep. Then all was very still in the wagon. The dog slept on his mistress's feet, and only two mosquitoes, creeping in through a gap in the front sail, buzzed drearily round.

The night was grown very old when from a long, peaceful sleep Lyndall awoke. The candle burned at her head, the dog lay on her feet; but he shivered; it seemed as though a coldness struck up to him from his resting-place. She lay with folded hands, looking upwards; and she heard the oxen chewing, and she saw the two mosquitoes buzzing drearily round and round, and her thoughts, — her thoughts ran far back into the past.

Through these months of anguish a mist had rested on her mind; it was rolled together now, and the old clear intellect awoke from its long torpor. It looked back into the past; it saw the present; there was no future now. The old strong soul gathered itself together for the last time; it knew where it stood.

Slowly raising herself on her elbow, she took from the sail a glass that hung pinned there. Her fingers were stiff and cold. She put the pillow on her breast, and stood the glass against it. Then the white face on the pillow looked into the white face in the glass. They had looked at each other often so before. It had been a child's face once, looking out above its blue pinafore; it had been a woman's face, with a dim shadow in the eyes, and a something which had said, "We are not afraid, you and I; we are together; we will fight, you and I." Now to-night it had come to this. The dying eyes on the pillow looked into the dying eyes in the glass; they knew that their hour had come. She raised one hand and pressed the stiff fingers against the glass. They were growing very stiff. She tried to speak to it, but she would never speak again. Only, the wonderful, yearning light was in the eyes still. The body was dead now, but the soul, clear and uncloudy, looked forth.

Then slowly, without a sound, the beautiful eyes closed. The dead face that the glass reflected was a thing of marvellous beauty and tranquillity. The gray dawn crept in over it, and saw it lying there.

Had she found what she sought for — something to worship? Had she ceased from being? Who shall tell us? There is a veil of terrible mist over the face of the hereafter.

CHAPTER XIII.

DREAMS.

"TELL me what a soul desires, and I will tell you what it is." So runs the phrase.

"Tell me what a man dreams, and I will tell you what he loves." That also has its truth.

For, ever from the earliest childhood to the latest age, day by day, and step by step, the busy waking life is followed and reflected by the life of dreams, — waking dreams, sleeping dreams. Weird, misty, and distorted as the inverted image of a mirage, or a figure seen through the mountain mist, they are still the reflections of a reality.

On the night when Gregory told his story, Waldo sat alone before the fire, his untasted supper before him. He was weary after his day's work, — too weary to eat. He put the plate down on the floor for Doss, who licked it clean, and then went back to his corner. After a time the master threw himself across the foot of the bed without undressing, and fell asleep there. He slept so long that the candle burned itself out, and the room was in darkness. But he dreamed a lovely dream as he lay there.

In his dream, to his right rose high mountains, their tops crowned with snow, their sides clothed with bush, and bathed in the sunshine. At their feet was the sea, blue and breezy, — bluer than any earthly sea, —

like the sea he had dreamed of in his boyhood. In
the narrow forest that ran between the mountains
and the sea, the air was rich with the scent of the
honey-creeper that hung from dark green bushes, and
through the velvety grass little streams ran purling
down into the sea. He sat on a high square rock
among the bushes, and Lyndall sat by him and sang
to him. She was only a small child, with a blue pinafore, and a grave, grave little face. He was looking
up at the mountains, — then suddenly, when he looked
round, she was gone. He slipped down from his rock
and went to look for her, but he found only her little
footmarks ; he found them on the bright green grass,
and in the moist sand, and there where the little
streams ran purling down into the sea. In and out,
in and out, and among the bushes where the honey-
creeper hung, he went looking for her. At last, far
off in the sunshine, he saw her gathering shells upon
the sand. She was not a child now, but a woman ;
and the sun shone on her soft brown hair, and in her
white dress she put the shells she gathered. She
was stooping, but when she heard his step she stood
up, holding her skirt close about her, and waited for
his coming. One hand she put in his, and together
they walked on over the glittering sand and pink sea-
shells ; and they heard the leaves talking, and they
heard the waters babbling on their way to the sea,
and they heard the sea singing to itself, — singing,
singing.

At last they came to a place where was a long reach
of pure white sand ; there she stood still, and dropped
on to the sand one by one the shells that she had
gathered. Then she looked up into his face with her
beautiful eyes. She said nothing, but she lifted one

hand and laid it softly on his forehead; the other she laid on his heart.

With a cry of suppressed agony Waldo sprang from the bed, flung open the upper half of the door, and leaned out, breathing heavily.

Great God! it might be only a dream, but the pain was very real, as though a knife ran through his heart, — as though some treacherous murderer crept on him in the dark! The strong man drew his breath like a frightened woman.

"Only a dream! but the pain was very real," he muttered, as he pressed his right hand upon his breast. Then he folded his arms on the door, and stood looking out into the starlight.

The dream was with him still; the woman who was his friend was not separated from him by years, — only that very night he had seen her. He looked up into the night sky that all his life long had mingled itself with his existence. There were a thousand faces that he loved looking down at him, a thousand stars in their glory, in crowns, and circles, and solitary grandeur. To the man they were not less dear than to the boy, — they had been not less mysterious; yet he looked up at them and shuddered; at last turned away from them with horror. Such countless multitudes, stretching out far into space, and yet not in one of them all was she! Though he searched through them all, to the farthest, faintest point of light, nowhere should he ever say, "She is here!" To-morrow's sun would rise and gild the world's mountains, and shine into its thousand valleys; it would set and the stars creep out again. Year after year, century after century, the old changes of Nature would go on, day and night, summer and winter, seed-time and harvest; but in none of them all would she have part.

He shut the door to keep out their hideous shining, and because the dark was intolerable lit a candle, and paced the little room, faster and faster yet. He saw before him the long ages of eternity that would roll on, on, on, and never bring her. She would exist no more. A dark mist filled the little room.

"Oh, little hand! oh, little voice! oh, little form!" he cried; "oh, little soul that walked with mine! oh, little soul, that looked so fearlessly down into the depths, do you exist no more forever—for all time?" He cried more bitterly, "It is for this hour — this — that men blind reason, and crush out thought! For this hour — this, this — they barter truth and knowledge, take any lie, any creed, so it does not whisper to them of the dead that they are dead! O God! God! for a hereafter!"

Pain made his soul weak; it cried for the old faith. They are the tears that fall into the new-made grave that cement the power of the priest. For the cry of the soul that loves and loses is this, only this: "Bridge over death; blend the here with the hereafter; cause the mortal to robe itself in immortality; let me not say of my dead that it is dead! I will believe all else, bear all else, endure all else!"

Muttering to himself, Waldo walked with bent head, the mist in his eyes.

To the soul's wild cry for its own there are many answers. He began to think of them. Was not there one of them all from which he might suck one drop of comfort?

"You shall see her again," says the Christian, the

true Bible Christian. " Yes; you shall see her again.
' And I saw the dead, great and small, stand before
God. And the books were opened, and the dead were
judged from those things which were written in the
books. And whosoever was not found written in the
book of life was cast into the lake of fire, which is
the second death.' Yes; you shall see her again.
She died so, — with her knee unbent, with her hand
unraised, with a prayer unuttered, in the pride of her
intellect and the strength of her youth. She loved
and she was loved; but she said no prayer to God;
she cried for no mercy; she repented of no sin! Yes;
you *shall* see her again."

In his bitterness Waldo laughed low.

Ah, he had long ceased to hearken to the hellish
voice.

But yet another speaks.

"You shall see her again," says the nineteenth-
century Christian, deep into whose soul modern un-
belief and thought have crept, though he knows it
not. He it is who uses his Bible as the pearl-fishers
use their shells, sorting out gems from refuse; he sets
his pearls after his own fashion, and he sets them
well. " Do not fear," he says; "hell and judgment
are not. God is love. I know that beyond this blue
sky above us is a love as widespreading over all. The
All-Father will show her to you again; not spirit only,
— the little hands, the little feet you loved, you shall
lie down and kiss them if you will. Christ arose, and
did eat and drink; so shall she arise. The dead, all
the dead, raised incorruptible! God is love. You
shall see her again."

It is a heavenly song, this of the nineteenth-cen-
tury Christian. A man might dry his tears to listen

to it, but for this one thing — Waldo muttered to himself confusedly, —

"The thing I loved was a woman, proud and young; it had a mother once, who, dying, kissed her little baby, and prayed God that she might see it again. If it had lived, the loved thing would itself have had a son, who, when he closed the weary eyes and smoothed the wrinkled forehead of his mother, would have prayed God to see that old face smile again in the hereafter. To the son heaven will be no heaven, if the sweet worn face is not in one of the choirs; he will look for it through the phalanx of God's glorified angels; and the youth will look for the maid, and the mother for the baby. 'And whose then shall she be at the resurrection of the dead?'"

"Ah, God! ah, God! a beautiful dream!" he cried; "but can any one dream it, not sleeping?"

Waldo paced on, moaning in agony and longing.

He heard the transcendentalist's high answer, —

"What have you to do with flesh, — the gross and miserable garment in which spirit hides itself? You shall see her again. But the hand, the foot, the forehead you loved, you shall see no more. The loves, the fears, the frailties that are born with the flesh, with the flesh they shall die. Let them die! There is that in man that cannot die, — a seed, a germ, an embryo, a spiritual essence. Higher than she was on earth, as the tree is higher than the seed, the man than the embryo, so shall you behold her, — changed, glorified!"

High words, ringing well, they are the offering of jewels to the hungry, of gold to the man who dies for bread. Bread is corruptible, gold is incorruptible;

bread is light, gold is heavy; bread is common, gold
is rare; but the hungry man will barter all your mines
for one morsel of bread. Around God's throne there
may be choirs and companies of angels, cherubim and
seraphim rising tier above tier, but not for one of them
all does the soul cry aloud. Only perhaps for a little
human woman full of sin, that it once loved.

"Change is death, change is death;" he cried. "I
want no angel, only she, — no holier and no better,
with all her sins upon her; so give me her or give me
nothing!"

And, truly, does not the heart love its own
with the strongest passion for their very frailties?
Heaven might keep its angels if men were but left
to men.

"Change is death!" he cried; "change is death!
Who dares to say the body never dies, because it
turns again to grass and flowers? And yet they
dare to say the spirit never dies, because in space
some strange unearthly being may have sprung up
upon its ruins. Leave me! leave me!" he cried in
frantic bitterness. "Give me back what I have lost,
or give me nothing!"

For the soul's fierce cry for immortality is this, —
only this: Return to me after death the thing as it
was before. Leave me in the hereafter the being
that I am to-day. Rob me of the thoughts, the feelings, the desires that are my life, and you have left
nothing to take; your immortality is annihilation,
your hereafter is a lie.

Waldo flung open the door, and walked out into the
starlight, his pain-stricken thoughts ever driving him
on as he paced there.

"There must be a hereafter because man longs for

it," he whispered. "Is not all life from the cradle to the grave one long yearning for that which we never touch? There must be a hereafter because we cannot think of any end to life. Can we think of a beginning? Is it easier to say, 'I was not' than to say 'I shall not be'? And yet, where were we ninety years ago? Dreams, dreams! Ah, all dreams and lies! No ground anywhere."

He went back into the cabin, and walked there. Hour after hour passed, and he was dreaming.

For, mark you, men *will* dream. The most that can be asked of them is but that the dream be not in too glaring discord with the thing they know. He walked with bent head.

All dies, all dies! The roses are red with the matter that once reddened the cheek of the child; the flowers bloom the fairest on the last-year's battle-ground; the work of death's finger cunningly wreathed over, is at the heart of all things, even of the living. Death's finger is everywhere. The rocks are built up of a life that was. Bodies, thoughts, and loves die: from where springs that whisper to the tiny soul of man, "You shall not die"? Ah! is there no truth of which this dream is shadow?

He fell into perfect silence. And at last, as he walked there with his bent head, his soul passed down the steps of contemplation into that vast land where there is always peace, — that land where the soul, gazing long, loses all consciousness of its little self, and almost feels its hand on the old mystery of Universal Unity that surrounds it.

"No death, no death," he muttered; "there is that which never dies, — which abides. It is but the individual that perishes, the whole remains. It is the

organism that vanishes, the atoms are there. It is
but the man that dies, the Universal Whole of which
he is part reworks him into its inmost self. Ah, what
matter that man's day be short, — that the sunrise
sees him, and the sunset sees his grave; that of which
he is but the breath has breathed him forth and drawn
him back again! That abides, — we abide."

For the little soul that cries aloud for continued
personal existence for itself and its beloved, there is
no help. For the soul which knows itself no more as
a unit, but as a part of the Universal Unity of which
the beloved also is a part, which feels within itself
the throb of the Universal Life, — for that soul there
is no death.

"Let us die, beloved, you and I, that we may pass
on forever through the Universal Life!" In that
deep world of contemplation all fierce desires die out,
and peace comes down. He, Waldo, as he walked
there, saw no more the world that was about him;
cried out no more for the thing that he had lost. His
soul rested. Was it only John, think you, who saw
the heavens open? The dreamers see it every day.

Long years before the father had walked in the
little cabin, and seen choirs of angels, and a prince
like unto men, but clothed in immortality. The son's
knowledge was not as the father's, therefore the dream
was new-tinted; but the sweetness was all there, the
infinite peace that men find not in the little cankered
kingdom of the tangible. The bars of the real are set
close about us; we cannot open our wings but they
strike against them, and drop bleeding. But when
we glide between the bars into the great unknown beyond, we may sail forever in the glorious blue, seeing
nothing but our own shadows.

So age succeeds age, and dream succeeds dream, and of the joy of the dreamer no man knoweth but he who dreameth.

Our fathers had their dream; we have ours; the generation that follows will have its own. Without dreams and phantoms man cannot exist.

CHAPTER XIV.

WALDO GOES OUT TO SIT IN THE SUNSHINE.

IT had been a princely day. The long morning had melted slowly into a rich afternoon. Rains had covered the karroo with a heavy coat of green, that hid the red earth everywhere. In the very chinks of the stone-walls dark green leaves hung out, and beauty and growth had crept even into the beds of the sandy furrows, and lined them with weeds. On the broken sod-walls of the old pigsty chickweeds flourished, and ice-plants lifted their transparent leaves. Waldo was at work in the wagon-house again. He was making a kitchen-table for Em. As the long curls gathered in heaps before his plane, he paused for an instant, now and again, to throw one down to a small naked negro, who had crept from its mother, who stood churning in the sunshine, and had crawled into the wagon-house. From time to time the little animal lifted its fat hand as it expected a fresh shower of curls, till Doss, jealous of his master's noticing any other small creature but himself, would catch the curl in his mouth, and roll the little Kaffir over in the sawdust, much to that small animal's contentment. It was too lazy an afternoon to be really ill-natured, so Doss satisfied himself with snapping at the little negro's fingers, and sitting on him till he laughed. Waldo, as he worked, glanced down at them now and then, and smiled; but he never looked out across the plain. He was conscious without looking of that broad green earth; it made his work pleasant to him. Near the shadow at the gable the mother of the little negro stood churning. Slowly she raised and let fall the stick in her hands, murmuring to herself a sleepy chant, such as her people love; it sounded like the humming of far-off bees.

A different life showed itself in the front of the house, where Tant' Sannie's cart stood ready inspanned, and the Boer-woman herself sat in the front room drinking coffee. She had come to visit her stepdaughter, probably for the last time, as she now weighed two hundred and sixty pounds, and was not easily able to move. On a chair sat her mild young husband, nursing the baby, — a pudding-faced, weak-eyed child.

"You take it and get into the cart with it," said Tant' Sannie. "What do you want here, listening to our woman's talk?"

The young man arose, and meekly went out with the baby.

"I'm very glad you are going to be married, my child," said Tant' Sannie, as she drained the last drop from her coffee-cup. "I wouldn't say so while that boy was here, it would make him too conceited; but marriage is the finest thing in the world. I've been at it three times, and if it pleased God to take this husband from me, I should have another. There's nothing like it, my child, — nothing."

"Perhaps it might not suit all people, at all times, as well as it suits you, Tant' Sannie," said Em. There was a little shade of weariness in the voice.

"Not suit every one!" said Tant' Sannie. "If the beloved Redeemer didn't mean men to have wives what did He make women for? That's what I say. If a woman's old enough to marry, and doesn't, she's sinning against the Lord, — it's a wanting to know better than Him. What, does she think the Lord took all that trouble in making her for nothing? It's evident He wants babies, otherwise why does He send them? Not that I've done much in that way myself," said Tant' Sannie, sorrowfully; "but I've done my best."

She rose with some difficulty from her chair, and began moving slowly towards the door.

"It's a strange thing," she said, "but you can't love a man till you've had a baby by him. Now there's that boy there, — when we were first married, if he only sneezed in the night I boxed his ears; now if he lets his pipe-ash come on my milk-cloths, I don't think of laying a finger on him. There's nothing like being married," said Tant' Sannie, as she puffed towards the door. "If a woman's got a baby and a husband, she's got the best things the Lord can give her, — if only the baby does n't have convulsions. As for a husband, it's very much the same who one has. Some men are fat, and some men are thin; some men drink brandy, and some men drink gin; but it all comes to the same thing in the end; it's all one. A man's a man, you know."

Here they came upon Gregory, who was sitting in the shade before the house. Tant' Sannie shook hands with him.

"I'm glad you're going to get married," she said. "I hope you'll have as many children in five years as a cow has calves, and more too. I think I'll just go and have a look at your soap-pot before I start," she said, turning to Em. "Not that I believe in this new plan of putting soda in the pot. If the dear Father had meant soda to be put into soap, what would He have made milk-bushes for, and stuck them all over the veld as thick as lambs in the lambing season?"

She waddled off after Em in the direction of the built-in soap-pot, leaving Gregory as they found him, with his dead pipe lying on the bench beside him, and his blue eyes gazing out far across the flat, like one who sits on the sea-shore, watching that which is fading, fading from him. Against his breast was a letter found in a desk, addressed to himself, but never posted. It held only four words: "You must marry Em." He wore it in a black bag round his neck. It was the only letter she had ever written to him.

"You see if the sheep don't have the scab this year!" said Tant' Sannie, as she waddled after Em. "It's with all these new inventions that the wrath of God *must* fall on us. What were the children of Israel punished for, if it wasn't for making a golden calf? I may have my sins, but I do remember the tenth commandment: 'Honor thy father and thy mother that it may be well with thee, and that thou mayst live long in the land which the Lord thy God giveth thee!' It's all very well to say we honor them, and then to be finding out things that they never knew, and doing things in a way that they never did them! *My* mother boiled soap with bushes, and I will boil soap with bushes. If the wrath of God is to fall upon this land," said Tant' Sannie, with the serenity of conscious virtue, "it shall not be through me. Let them make their steam-wagons and their fire-carriages; let them go on as though the dear Lord didn't know what He was about when He gave horses and oxen legs, — the destruction of the Lord will follow them. I don't know how such people read their Bibles. When do we hear of Moses or Noah riding on a railway ? The Lord sent fire-carriages out of heaven in those days : there's no chance of His sending them for us if we go on in this way," said Tant' Sannie, sorrowfully, thinking of the splendid chance which this generation had lost.

Arrived at the soap-pot she looked over into it thoughtfully.

"Depend upon it you'll get the itch, or some other disease; the blessing of the Lord 'll never rest upon it," said the Boer-woman. Then suddenly she broke forth. "And she eighty-two, and goats, and rams, and eight thousand morgen, and the rams real angora, and two thousand sheep, and a short-horn bull," said Tant' Sannie, standing upright and planting a hand on each hip.

Em looked at her in silent wonder. Had connubial bliss and the joys of motherhood really turned the old Boer-woman's head ?

"Yes," said Tant' Sannie ; "I had almost forgotten to tell you. By the Lord if I had him here ! We were walking to church last Sacrament Sunday, Piet and I. Close in front of us was old Tant' Trana, with dropsy and cancer, and can't live eight months. Walking by her was something with its hands under its coat-tails, flap, flap, flap ; and its chin in the air, and a stick-up collar, and the black hat on the very back of the head. I knew him ! 'Who's that ?' I asked. 'The rich Englishman that Tant' Trana married last week.' 'Rich Englishman ! I'll rich Englishman him,' I said ; 'I'll tell Tant' Trana a thing

or two.' My fingers were just in his little white
curls. If it had n't been the blessed sacrament, he
would n't have walked so 'sourka, sourka, courka,'
any more. But I thought, Wait till I 've had it, and
then — But he, sly fox, son of Satan, seed of the
Amalekite, he saw me looking at him in the church.
The blessed sacrament was n't half over when he
takes Tant' Trana by the arm, and out they go. I
clap my baby down to its father, and I go after them.
But," said Tant' Sannie, regretfully, "I could n't get
up to them ; I am too fat. When I got to the corner,
he was pulling Tant' Trana up into the cart. 'Tant'
Trana,' I said, 'you 've married a Kaffir's dog, a Hottentot's "brakje."' I had n't any more breath. He
winked at me ; he winked at *me*," said Tant' Sannie,
her sides shaking with indignation, "first with one
eye, and then with the other, and then drove away.
Child of the Amalekite !" said Tant' Sannie, "if it
had n't been the blessed sacrament. Lord, Lord,
Lord ! "

Here the little Bush-girl came running to say that
the horses would stand no longer, and still breathing
out vengeance against her old adversary she labored
towards the cart. Shaking hands and affectionately
kissing Em, she was with some difficulty drawn up
Then slowly the cart rolled away, the good Boer-
woman putting her head out between the sails to
smile and nod. Em stood watching it for a time,
then as the sun dazzled her eyes she turned away.
There was no use in going to sit with Gregory ; he
liked best sitting there alone, staring across the green
karroo ; and till the maid had done churning there
was nothing to do ; so Em walked away to the wagon-
house, and climbed on to the end of Waldo's table, and

sat there, swinging one little foot slowly to and fro, while the wooden curls from the plane heaped themselves up against her black print dress.

"Waldo," she said at last, "Gregory has given me the money he got for the wagon and oxen, and I have fifty pounds besides, that once belonged to some one. I know what she would have liked to have done with it. You must take it and go to some place and study for a year or two."

"No, little one, I will not take it," he said, as he planed slowly away; "the time was when I would have been very grateful to any one who would have given me a little money, a little help, a little power of gaining knowledge. But now, I have gone so far alone I may go on to the end. I don't want it, little one."

She did not seem pained at his refusal, but swung her foot to and fro, the little old wrinkled forehead more wrinkled up than ever.

"Why is it always so, Waldo, — always so?" she said; "we long for things, and long for them, and pray for them; we would give all we have to come near to them, but we never reach them. Then at last, too late, just when we don't want them any more, when all the sweetness is taken out of them, then they come. We don't want them then," she said, folding her hands resignedly on her little apron. After a while she added, "I remember once, very long ago, when I was a very little girl, my mother had a work-box full of colored reels. I always wanted to play with them, but she would never let me. At last one day she said I might take the box. I was so glad I hardly knew what to do. I ran round the house, and sat down with it on the back steps. But when I opened the box all the cottons were taken out."

She sat for a while longer, till the Kaffir maid had finished churning, and was carrying the butter towards the house. Then Em prepared to slip off the table, but first she laid her little hand on Waldo's. He stopped his planing and looked up.

"Gregory is going to the town to-morrow. He is going to give in our banns to the minister; we are going to be married in three weeks."

Waldo lifted her very gently from the table. He did not congratulate her; perhaps he thought of the empty box, but he kissed her forehead gravely.

She walked away towards the house, but stopped when she had got half way. "I will bring you a glass of buttermilk when it is cool," she called out; and soon her clear voice came ringing out through the back windows as she sang the "Blue Water" to herself, and washed the butter.

Waldo did not wait till she returned. Perhaps he had at last really grown weary of work; perhaps he felt the wagon-house chilly (for he had shuddered two or three times), though that was hardly likely in that warm summer weather; or, perhaps, and most probably, one of his old dreaming fits had come upon him suddenly. He put his tools carefully together, ready for to-morrow, and walked slowly out. At the side of the wagon-house there was a world of bright sunshine, and a hen with her chickens was scratching among the gravel. Waldo seated himself near them with his back against the red-brick wall. The long afternoon was half spent, and the "kopje" was just beginning to cast its shadow over the round-headed yellow flowers that grew between it and the farm-house. Among the flowers the white butterflies hovered, and on the old kraal mounds three white kids gambolled, and at the door of one of the huts an old gray-headed Kaffir woman sat on the ground mending her mats. A balmy, restful peacefulness seemed to reign everywhere. Even the old hen seemed well satisfied. She scratched among the stones and called to her chickens when she found a treasure; and all the while clucked to herself with intense inward satisfaction. Waldo, as he sat with his knees drawn up to his chin and his arms folded on them, looked at it all and smiled. An evil world, a deceitful, treacherous, mirage-like world, it might be; but a lovely world for all that, and to sit there, gloating in the sunlight, was perfect. It was worth having been a little child, and having cried and prayed, so one might sit there. He moved his hands as though he were washing them in the sunshine. There will always be something worth living for while there are shimmery afternoons. Waldo chuckled with intense inward satisfaction as the old hen had done; she, over the insects and the warmth; he, over the old brickwalls, and the haze, and the little bushes. Beauty is God's wine, with which He recompenses the souls that love Him; he makes them drunk.

The fellow looked, and at last stretched out one hand to a little ice-plant that grew on the sod-wall of the sty; not as though he would have picked it, but as it were in a friendly greeting. He loved it. One little leaf of the ice-plant stood upright, and the sun shone through it. He could see every little crystal cell like a drop of ice in the transparent green, and it thrilled him.

There are only rare times when a man's soul can

see Nature. So long as any passion holds its revel there, the eyes are holden that they should not see her.

Go out if you will, and walk alone on the hillside in the evening, but if your favorite child lies ill at home, or your lover comes to-morrow, or at your heart there lies a scheme for the holding of wealth, then you will return as you went out; you will have seen nothing. For Nature, ever, like the old Hebrew God, cries out, "Thou shalt have no other gods before me." Only then, when there comes a pause, a blank in your life, when the old idol is broken, when the old hope is dead, when the old desire is crushed, then the Divine compensation of Nature is made manifest. She shows herself to you. So near she draws you, that the blood seems to flow from her to you through a still uncut cord; you feel the throb of her life.

When that day comes that you sit down broken, without one human creature to whom you cling, with your loves the dead and the living-dead; when the very thirst for knowledge through long-continued thwarting has grown dull; when in the present there is no craving, and in the future no hope, — then, oh, with a beneficent tenderness, Nature enfolds you.

Then the large white snowflakes as they flutter down, softly, one by one, whisper soothingly, "Rest, poor heart, rest!" It is as though our mother smoothed our hair, and we are comforted.

And yellow-legged bees as they hum make a dreamy lyric; and the light on the brown stone-wall is a great work of art; and the glitter through the leaves makes the pulses beat.

Well to die then; for if you live, so surely as the years come, so surely as the spring succeeds the winter, so surely will passions arise. They will creep back, one by one, into the bosom that has cast them forth, and fasten there again, and peace will go. Desire, ambition, and the fierce agonizing flood of love for the living — they will spring again. Then Nature will draw down her veil; with all your longing you shall not be able to raise one corner; you cannot bring back those peaceful days. Well to die then!

Sitting there with his arms folded on his knees, and his hat slouched down over his face, Waldo looked out into the yellow sunshine that tinted even the very air with the color of ripe corn, and was happy.

He was an uncouth creature, with small learning, and no prospect in the future but that of making endless tables and stone walls, yet it seemed to him as he sat there that life was a rare and very rich thing. He rubbed his hands in the sunshine. Ah, to live on so, year after year, how well! Always in the present, letting each day glide, bringing its own labor, and its own beauty, — the gradual lighting up of the hills, night and the stars, firelight and the coals! To live on so, calmly, far from the paths of men; and to look at the lives of clouds and insects; to look deep into the heart of flowers, and see how lovingly the pistil and the stamens nestle there together; and to see in the thorn-pods how the little seeds suck their life through the delicate curled-up string, and how the little embryo sleeps inside! Well, how well, to sit so on one side, taking no part in the world's life; but when great men blossom into books, looking into those flowers also, to see how the world of men too opens beautifully, leaf after leaf. Ah! life is delicious; well to live long, and see the darkness breaking, and

the day coming, — the day when soul shall not thrust
back soul that would come to it; when men shall not
be driven to seek solitude, because of the crying out
of their hearts for love and sympathy. Well to live
long and see the new time breaking! Well to live
long; life is sweet, sweet, sweet! In his breast
pocket, where of old the broken slate used to be, there
was now a little dancing shoe of his friend who was
sleeping. He could feel it when he folded his arm
tight against his breast; and that was well also. He
drew his hat lower over his eyes, and sat so motionless that the chickens thought he was asleep, and
gathered closer around him. One even ventured to
peck at his boot, but he ran away quickly. Tiny,
yellow fellow that he was, he knew that men were
dangerous; even sleeping they might awake. But
Waldo did not sleep, and coming back from his sunshiny dream, stretched out his hand for the tiny
thing to mount. But the chicken eyed the hand
askance, and then ran off to hide under its mother's
wing, and from beneath it it sometimes put out its
round head to peep at the great figure sitting there.
Presently its brothers ran off after a little white moth,
and it ran out to join them; and when the moth fluttered away over their heads, they stood looking up
disappointed, and then ran back to their mother.

Waldo through his half-closed eyes looked at them.
Thinking, fearing, craving, those tiny sparks of
brother life, what were they, so real there in that old
yard on that sunshiny afternoon? A few years —
where would they be? Strange little brother spirits!
He stretched his hand towards them, for his heart
went out to them; but not one of the little creatures
came nearer him, and he watched them gravely for a

time; then he smiled, and began muttering to himself after his old fashion. Afterwards he folded his arms upon his knees, and rested his forehead on them. And so he sat there in the yellow sunshine, muttering, muttering, muttering to himself.

It was not very long after when Em came out at the back door with a towel thrown across her head, and in her hand a cup of milk.

"Ah," she said, coming close to him, "he is sleeping now. He will find it when he wakes, and be glad of it."

She put it down upon the ground beside him. The mother-hen was at work still among the stones, but the chickens had climbed about him, and were perching on him. One stood upon his shoulder, and rubbed its little head softly against his black curls; another tried to balance itself on the very edge of the old felt hat. One tiny fellow stood upon his hand, and tried to crow; another had nestled itself down comfortably on the old coat-sleeve, and gone to sleep there.

Em did not drive them away; but she covered the glass softly at his side. "He will wake soon," she said, "and be glad of it."

But the chickens were wiser.